W9-BTB-424

Praise for Nancy Atherton and Her Aunt Dimity Series

Aunt Dimity Slays the Dragon

"One of the most charming entries in an enduringly popular series."

—*Booklist*

Aunt Dimity: Vampire Hunter

"One of Aunt Dimity's most suspenseful mysteries. Loyal fans will be thrilled by every new revelation." —*Kirkus Reviews*

Aunt Dimity Goes West

"Just the ticket to ease out of a stressful day." —*Deadly Pleasures*

Aunt Dimity and the Deep Blue Sea

"The eleventh Aunt Dimity mystery is testament to the staying power of Atherton's cozier-than-cozy premise....Rainy Sunday afternoon reading." —*Booklist*

Aunt Dimity and the Next of Kin

"This is a book entirely without edge, cynicism or even rudeness—this is the way life really ought to be if only we were all better behaved. Put on the teakettle and enjoy." —*Rocky Mountain News*

"This is Atherton at her coziest....Fans of the series will not be disappointed." —*Over My Dead Body!* (The Mystery Magazine)

"Cozy mystery lovers wouldn't dream of missing an entry in this series." —*Kingston Observer*

Aunt Dimity: Snowbound

"Witty, engaging and filled with interesting detail that will make the cottage-in-the-English-countryside fanciers among us sigh.... Just the thing to veg out on when life gets too much."

—*The Lincoln Journal Star*

"The perfect tale for a cold winter's night." —*Publishers Weekly*

"Fans of this series will be delirious with joy....What a treat!"

—*Kingston Observer*

A PENGUIN MYSTERY

Introducing Aunt Dimity, Paranormal Detective

Nancy Atherton is the author of fourteen Aunt Dimity mysteries, many of them bestsellers. The first book in the series, *Aunt Dimity's Death,* was voted "One of the Century's 100 Favorite Mysteries" by the Independent Mystery Booksellers Association. She lives in Colorado Springs, Colorado.

Introducing Aunt Dimity, Paranormal Detective

THE FIRST TWO BOOKS IN THE BELOVED SERIES

Aunt Dimity's Death

AND

Aunt Dimity and the Duke

NANCY ATHERTON

PENGUIN BOOKS

PENGUIN BOOKS

Published by the Penguin Group Penguin Group (USA) Inc., 375 Hudson Street, New York, New York 10014, USA • Penguin Group (Canada), 90 Eglinton Avenue East, Suite 700, Toronto, Ontario, Canada M4P 2Y3 (a division of Pearson Penguin Canada Inc.) • Penguin Books Ltd, 80 Strand, London WC2R 0RL, England • Penguin Ireland, 25 St Stephen's Green, Dublin 2, Ireland (a division of Penguin Books Ltd) • Penguin Group (Australia), 250 Camberwell Road, Camberwell, Victoria 3124, Australia (a division of Pearson Australia Group Pty Ltd) • Penguin Books India Pvt Ltd, 11 Community Centre, Panchsheel Park, New Delhi – 110 017, India •Penguin Group (NZ), 67 Apollo Drive, Rosedale, North Shore 0632, New Zealand (a division of Pearson New Zealand Ltd) • Penguin Books (South Africa) (Pty) Ltd, 24 Sturdee Avenue, Rosebank, Johannesburg 2196, South Africa

Penguin Books Ltd, Registered Offices:
80 Strand, London WC2R 0RL, England

This volume first published in Penguin Books 2009

1   3   5   7   9   10   8   6   4   2

Aunt Dimity's Death first published in the United States of America by Viking Penguin,
a division of Penguin Books USA Inc. 1992
Published in Penguin Books 1993
Copyright © Nancy T. Atherton, 1992
All rights reserved

Aunt Dimity and the Duke first published in the United States of America by Viking Penguin,
a division of Penguin Books USA Inc. 1994
Published in Penguin Books 1995
Copyright © Nancy T. Atherton, 1994
All rights reserved

PUBLISHER'S NOTE

LIBRARY OF CONGRESS CATALOGING IN PUBLICATION DATA
Atherton, Nancy.
[Aunt Dimity's death]
Introducing Aunt Dimity, paranormal detective : the first two books in the beloved series /
Nancy Atherton.
p. cm.—(A Penguin mystery)
ISBN 978-0-14-311606-6
1. Dimity, Aunt (Fictitious character)—Fiction. 2. Women detectives—England—Cornwall (County)—
Fiction. 3. Cornwall (England : County)—Fiction. 4. Inheritance and succession—Fiction. 5.
Americans—England—Fiction. I. Atherton, Nancy. Aunt Dimity and the duke. II. Title.
PS3551.T426A94 2009
813'.54—dc22   2009016069

Printed in the United States of America
Set in Perpetua with Phyllis Display

Aunt Dimity's Death

For the Handsome Prince

One

When I learned of Aunt Dimity's death, I was stunned. Not because she was dead, but because I had never known she'd been alive.

Maybe I should explain.

When I was a little girl, my mother used to tell me stories. She would tuck me in, sit Reginald in her lap, and spin tale after tale until my eyelids drooped and I nodded off to sleep. She would then tuck Reginald in beside me, so that his would be the first face I saw when I opened my eyes again come morning.

Reginald was my stuffed rabbit. He had once had two button eyes and a powder-pink flannel hide, but he had gone blind and gray in my service, with a touch of purple near his hand-stitched whiskers, a souvenir of the time I'd had him try my grape juice. (He spit it out.) He stood nine inches tall and as far as I knew, he had appeared on earth the same day I had, because he had been at my side forever. Reginald was my confidant and my companion in adventure—he was the main reason I never felt like an only child.

My mother found Reginald useful, too. She taught third and fourth grade at an elementary school on the northwest side of Chicago, where we lived, and she knew the value of props. When the world's greatest trampoline expert—me—refused to settle down at bedtime, she would turn Reginald around on her lap and address him directly. "Well, if Lori doesn't want to listen, I'll tell the story to you, Reginald." It worked like a charm every time.

My mother was well aware that there was nothing I loved more than stories. She read the usual ones aloud: *How the Elephant Got Its Trunk, Green Eggs and Ham, The Bluebird of Happiness,* and all the others that came from books. But my favorite stories (and Reginald's, too) were the ones she didn't read, the ones that came from her own voice and hands and eyes.

These were the Aunt Dimity stories. They were the best, my

mom's special treat, reserved for nights when even back-scratching failed to soothe me into slumber. I must have been an impossibly rest-less child, because the Aunt Dimity stories were endless: *Aunt Dimity's Cottage, Aunt Dimity in the Garden, Aunt Dimity Buys a Torch,* and on and on. My eyes widened with excitement at that last title—I was thrilled by the thought of Aunt Dimity preparing to set out for darkest Africa—until my mom reduced my excitement (and the size of my eyes) by explaining that, in Aunt Dimity's world, a "torch" was a flashlight.

I should have guessed. Aunt Dimity's adventures were never grand or exotic, though they took place in some unnamed, magical land, where a flashlight was a torch, a truck was a lorry (which made Regi-nald laugh, since that was my name, too), and tea was the sovereign remedy for all ills. The adventures themselves, however, were strictly down-to-earth. Aunt Dimity was the most mundane heroine I had ever encountered, and her adventures were extraordinarily ordinary. Nonetheless, I could never get enough of them.

One of my great favorites, told over and over again, until I could have told it myself had I wanted to (which I didn't, of course, because my mother's telling was part of the tale), was *Aunt Dimity Goes to the Zoo.* It began on "a beautiful spring day when Aunt Dimity decided to go to the zoo. The daffodils bobbed in the breeze, the sun danced on every windowpane, and the sky was as blue as cornflowers. And when Aunt Dimity got to the zoo, she found out why: All the rain in the world was waiting for her there, gathered in one enormous black cloud which hovered over the zoo and dared her to set foot inside the gate."

But did that stop Aunt Dimity? Never! She opened her trusty brolly ("umbrella," explained my mother), charged into the most drenching downpour in the history of downpours—and had a mar-velous time. She had the whole zoo to herself and she got to see how all the animals behaved in the rain, how some of them hid in their shelters while others bathed and splashed and shook showers of drop-lets from their fur. "When she'd seen all she wanted to see," my mother concluded, "Aunt Dimity went home to warm herself before the fire and feast on buttered brown bread and a pot of tea, smiling quietly as she remembered her lovely day at the zoo."

I suppose what captivated me about Aunt Dimity was her ability to spit in life's eye. Take *Aunt Dimity Buys a Torch:* Aunt Dimity goes to "Harrod's, of all places" to buy a flashlight. She makes the mistake of going on the weekend before Christmas, when the store is jam-packed with shoppers and the clerks are all seasonal help who couldn't tell her where the flashlights were even if they had the time, which they don't because of the mad crush, and she winds up never buying the flashlight. For anyone else it would have been a tiresome mistake. For Aunt Dimity, it was just another adventure, one which became more hilarious floor by floor. And in the end she goes home to warm herself before the fire, feast on buttered brown bread and a pot of tea, and chuckle to herself as she remembers her day at Harrod's. Of all places.

Aunt Dimity was indomitable, in a thoroughly ordinary way. Nothing stopped her from enjoying what there was to enjoy. Nothing kept her from pursuing what she came to pursue. Nothing dampened her spirits because it was *all* an adventure. I was entranced.

It wasn't until I was in my early teens that I noticed a resemblance between Aunt Dimity and my mother. Like Aunt Dimity, my mother took great delight in the small things in life. Like her, too, she was blessed with an uncommon amount of common sense. Such gifts would be useful to anyone, but to my mother, they must have proved invaluable. My father had died shortly after I was born, and a lapsed insurance policy had left her in fairly straitened circumstances.

My mother was forced to sell our house and most of its contents, and to return to teaching much sooner than she'd planned. It must have been a wrench to move into a modest apartment, even more of a wrench to leave me with the downstairs neighbor while she went off to work, but she never let it show. She was a single mother before single mothers hit the headlines, and she managed the job very well, if I do say so myself. I never wanted for anything, and when I decided to leave Chicago for college in Boston, she somehow managed to send me, without a moment's hesitation. Around me, she was always cheerful, energetic, and competent. Just like Aunt Dimity.

My mother was a wise woman, and Aunt Dimity was one of her greatest gifts to me. I can't count the number of times Aunt Dimity rescued me from potential aggravation. Years later, when nearsighted old ladies ran their grocery carts over my toes, I would recall the very large man who had stepped on Aunt Dimity's foot at Harrod's. She guessed his weight to within five pounds. She knew because she subsequently asked him his exact weight, a scene which left me convulsed with giggles every time my mother recounted it. Remembering that, I found myself guessing the eyeglass prescriptions of my grocery-cart-wielding little old ladies. Though I never had the nerve to confirm my estimates, the thought made me laugh instead of growl.

By all accounts, I had a naturally buoyant spirit as a child and the Aunt Dimity stories certainly helped it along. But even naturally buoyant spirits sink at times. Mine took a nosedive when I found myself living the bits that never appeared in the Aunt Dimity stories: the bits when there was no wood for the fire and no butter for the brown bread, when all the lovely days turned dreary. It was nothing unusual, nothing extraordinary or exotic or grand, nothing that hasn't happened a million times to a million people. But this time it happened to me and it all happened at once, with no space for a breath in between. I was on one of those downward spirals that come along every once in a while and suddenly nothing was funny anymore.

It started when my marriage dissolved, not messily, but painfully nonetheless. By the time we sat down to draw up papers, all I wanted was a quick, clean break—and that was all I got. I could have stuck around to fight for property settlements or alimony, but by then I was tired of fighting, tired of sticking around, and, above all, I despised the thought of living *off* a man I no longer lived *with*.

I faced the Newly Divorced Woman's Semiobligatory *Wanderjahr* with no sense of adventure at all. About to turn thirty, I had little money, less energy, and absolutely no idea of what I wanted to do next. Before moving to Los Angeles, where my former husband's job with an accounting firm had taken me, I had worked in the rare book department of my university's library. I moved back to Boston, but by the time I arrived, my old position was gone—literally. The humidity control device, installed at great expense to protect the rare book collection from the ravages of time, had gone haywire, causing an electrical fire that no amount of humidity could extinguish. The books had gone up in smoke and so, too, had my prospects for employment.

Getting a new job in the same field was out of the question. I had no formal library degree, and the curator, at whose knee I had learned more about old books than any six library school graduates combined, was an opinionated maverick. A personal recommendation from Dr. Stanford J. Finderman tended to close doors rather than open them, and I soon discovered that the job market for informally trained rare book specialists was as soft as my head must have been when I'd first decided I could make a living as one. Had I known what the future held in store for me, I would have gone to motorcycle mechanics' school.

My mother wanted me to come home to the safe haven of our yellow-brick apartment building in Chicago, but I would have none of that. The only motherly assistance I would accept was a steady supply of home-baked cookies, mailed Federal Express and packed to withstand a nuclear blast. I never mentioned how often those cookies were all that stood between me and an empty stomach.

I stayed with a friend from college days, Meg Thomson, until the divorce was final. She introduced me to the wonderful world of temping and as soon as I'd registered with a reputable Boston agency, I struck out on my own. With high hopes, I joined the ranks of the urban pioneers—mainly because the only apartment I could afford was located in what real estate agents like to call a "fringe" neighborhood.

I can confirm the rumor about the poor preying upon the poor. Two weeks after I'd moved in, my place was ransacked. The intruder had apparently had a temper tantrum when he discovered that I was just as impoverished as the rest of my neighbors. I came home to an unrecognizable heap of torn clothing, splintered furniture, and a veritable rainbow of foodstuffs smeared decoratively across my walls.

That was pretty disheartening, but the worst part was finding Reginald. The boon companion of my childhood had been slit from cottontail to whiskers, his stuffing yanked out and strewn about the room. It took me three days to find what remained of his left ear. I interred him in a shoebox, too sickened to attempt his repair, knowing that my clumsy needlework could never match the beautiful stitches that had helped him survive an adventuresome bunnyhood. On the fourth day, shoebox in hand, I moved out, beginning what was to become a long sequence of moves in and out of apartments which, if not exactly squalid, were still a far cry from my predivorce standards of domestic comfort. In April of that year, an ad in the Cambridge *Tab* led me to share an apartment with two other women in a three-decker on a quiet street in West Somerville. I'd just settled in when my mother died.

There was no warning. The doctor told me that she had died peacefully in her sleep, which helped a little, but not enough. I felt that I should have been there, that I might have been able to do something, anything, to help her. Up to that point I had been able to bounce back from every blow more or less intact, but this one almost flattened me.

I flew back to Chicago at once. There was no need for me to arrange the funeral—my mother and Father Zherzshinski had taken care of that. The memorial mass at St. Boniface's was attended by scores of her former pupils, each of whom had a story to tell, a fond memory to share. In among the flood of flowers was an anonymous bouquet of white lilacs that had come all the way from England. I gazed at it and marveled at the many lives my mother had shaped, all unknown to me.

My mother had also arranged for the Salvation Army to pick up her furniture and clothing, knowing full well that her brilliant daughter had no place to put them and no means of paying for their storage. I spent a week at the old apartment, packing the rest of her possessions—mementos, photograph albums, books—and settling her accounts. She had left just enough savings to cover the funeral expenses, to ship her things to Boston, and to get me back there, with very little left over. I was neither surprised nor disappointed. Elementary school teachers are paid in love, not money, and I had never expected an inheritance.

I took on an overload of temp jobs when I got back, and not purely for financial reasons. Exhaustion is a great analgesic—it numbs emotion, silences thought—and I craved the release. The months passed in a blur. I stopped seeing my friends, stopped writing letters, stopped chatting with my roommates and coworkers. By the time April rolled around again, the only person I talked to was Meg Thomson, but that was because she kept in touch with me, not the other way round. And not even Meg could get me to open up about my mother's death. Did I mention a downward spiral? This is the point where I was about ready to auger in.

That's when I got the letter saying that Aunt Dimity was dead.

Two

It was the perfect capper to a perfect day. April had roared in like an ill-tempered lion and I had just survived yet another week in yet another unfamiliar office, coping with yet another phone system (picture the control room at the Kennedy Space Center) and managerial style ("Are we up, up, up for another tee-rific day?"). I had been on the run since six that morning and had skipped lunch to get ahead on the filing, only to learn that I wouldn't be needed for the full day after all, since the office was closing at three in honor of the boss's birthday. Shrunken paycheck in hand, and dreading the empty hours to come, I dragged myself home through a bone-chilling drizzle, more sleet than rain, wondering how many more tee-rific days I could stand.

The apartment was deserted when I got there, pretty much the way it always was. One of my roommates was an intern, the other a premed student, and their Byzantine hours meant that I had the place to myself most of the time, which suited me just fine.

It was the best living arrangement I had found so far, but it wasn't exactly the Ritz. Not even the Holiday Inn. My furniture consisted of a mattress on the floor, a borrowed card table, a chair rescued from a life on the streets, and a wooden crate on which rested my one and only lamp. Reginald's shoebox lived in the closet, and I kept my clothes in the same cardboard boxes I had used throughout my many moves. It saved a lot of time packing. My mother's things, sealed in boxes, had stood along one wall since they'd arrived from Chicago.

I flicked on the hall light, slipped out of my wet sneakers and jacket, and grabbed my mail from the basket on the hall table. Changing into jeans and an oversized flannel shirt, I sorted through the mail, braced for the usual barrage of threats from various credit card companies who were unimpressed with my increasingly erratic payment schedule. Legalized hate mail is what I called it, and it was the only kind of mail I had received since my mother's death.

That and junk mail. The plain envelope nestled in among the bills was probably another promotional scheme, and I regarded it sourly. Just what I needed: an invitation to time-share in Bermuda, when the closest I would ever get to Bermuda was the pair of shorts I'd come across in the Salvation Army store last weekend.

Instead, it contained a letter from a law firm, the name of which was plastered (tastefully) across the letterhead: *Willis &Willis*. This is it, I thought, feeling a little queasy. The credit card companies are taking me to court. What were they going to do, repossess my mattress? With a sinking heart, I read on.

In polite, formal phrases, Willis & Willis apologized for the delay in reaching me, admitting to some difficulty in finding my current address (no surprise to me, since I'd moved six times in the past year). Willis & Willis went on to say that they were sorry to inform me of the death of Miss Dimity Westwood, whom I would recognize as Aunt Dimity. At which point, all thoughts of credit card companies and promotional campaigns vanished and I sat down, rather suddenly.

Aunt Dimity? Dead?

I was stunned, all right. In fact, I was downright spooked. As far as I could remember, I had never told anyone about Aunt Dimity. She belonged to my mom and to me and was far too special to share, except, of course, with Reginald. But he was in no position to be talking to law firms. Hurriedly, I skimmed through the rest of the letter.

Willis & Willis would be most grateful if I would stop by their offices at my earliest possible convenience to discuss some matters of interest. An appointment would not be necessary, as they would see me whenever I chose to appear on their doorstep. With sincere sympathy, they remained my most humble servants, William Willis, etc.

I spread the letter on the folding table and stared at it. The stationery was real enough. The words were real enough. The only thing that wasn't remotely real was their message. "Well, Reginald?" I said, glancing at the closet door. "What do you make of this? Pretty weird, huh?"

I didn't really expect an answer. I had decided long ago that the day Reginald started speaking to me was the day I checked myself into the nearest funny farm. Then again, a fictional character had just walked out of my earliest childhood and tapped me on the shoulder. Maybe, if I listened harder, I'd begin to hear Reginald after all.

I read the letter through once more, slowly this time, then examined it with a professional eye. The stationery was cream colored, stiff, and heavy. When held up to the light, the watermark and laid lines confirmed its quality. It hadn't been run off on a computer printer, either, but typed on a real typewriter and signed with a real fountain pen. I had the distinct impression that Willis & Willis wanted me to see this, wanted me to feel that I was worth more effort than computerized efficiency would allow. I wondered if the very best law firms employed scribes to handwrite correspondence in order to demonstrate their painstaking concern for the affairs of special clients.

Certain phrases seemed to stand out, as though in boldface. Miss Dimity Westwood. No appointment necessary. William Willis. And, most interesting, those "matters of interest" to discuss. Curiouser and curiouser. I glanced at my watch, glanced back at the letter, then looked once more at the closet door.

"What the hell, Reginald," I said. "It's not as though I had plans for the afternoon. As Aunt Dimity would say, it's an adventure."

As with many adventures, this one didn't get off to the start I had in mind. The law office was located a few blocks south of Post Office Square and I worked out a combination of bus routes to get there. It didn't seem like a bad trip: two buses and a short walk, no more than an hour, tops. Of course, I hadn't looked out the window yet.

I don't know what's worse about a blizzard in April: the fact that it's so wet and slushy, or the fact that it's in April. No wonder they call it the cruelest month. The two buses and the short walk turned into two hours of howling wind, driving sleet, and ankle-deep slush. Plus the heat didn't work on the second bus. I might have been able to shrug it off if I'd had proper winter clothing, but I had lived in LA just long enough to get rid of my nice warm woolen sweaters, down parka, and snow boots and I hadn't found the money to replace them yet. Most of the time it didn't matter, since I made it a point to be outside as little as possible.

This time, it mattered. My windbreaker and sneakers were no

match for the storm, and by the time I found Willis & Willis, I was soaked to the skin, red faced from the wind, and shivering uncontrollably. If I hadn't been afraid of dying from exposure, I would have been too embarrassed to approach their door. What a mess.

And what a door. Not that I saw it right away. I had to get past the gate first. The gate in the wall. The wall that rose up from the edge of the sidewalk and bore a brass plate engraved with the address mentioned in the letter. I checked and rechecked the numbers as carefully as I could, considering the velocity of the wind. It was the right place. I buzzed a buzzer, was scanned by a camera, and for God alone knows what reason, the gate unlocked and I let myself in. It wasn't until I was halfway down the path that I saw the door.

It was the exact door-equivalent of the elegant stationery: polished to a satin sheen and massive, with a lion-head knocker gleaming dully through the swirling snow. The storm seemed to abate for a moment so that I could admire the gleaming lion, and the building over which it kept watch.

Three

Clearly, the law firm of Willis & Willis had no more use for glass and steel than they had for laser printers. They didn't have an office, they had a mansion, a gracious old mansion, surrounded and dwarfed, though not in the least intimidated, by office towers on every side. Don't ask me how it got there or, more incredible still, how it stayed there, but there it was, an oasis of charm and dignity in a concrete desert.

Great, I thought, Willis & Willis Meets the Little Match Girl. I staggered up the stairs and placed my hand on the lion's burnished head, knowing full well that I looked like something any self-respecting cat would refuse to drag in.

Two thumps brought a slightly rumpled looking man to the door. He was in his midthirties, had a short, neatly trimmed beard, and was wearing a well-worn dark tweed jacket and corduroy pants. If I'd had any sense of drama I would have chosen that moment to collapse into his arms—he was a big guy and looked sturdy enough to take it. He stood staring at me, while the snowflakes made little wet splashes on his glasses and the ice water dripped from the end of my nose. Then he smiled, so suddenly and with such radiance that I glanced furtively over my shoulder to see what he was smiling at.

"Hello," he said, with a warmth and intensity that seemed all out of proportion to the moment.

"Hello," I replied, a bit uncertainly.

"You must be Lori," he said, still beaming. My only response was another uncontrollable bout of shivering. It seemed to be enough. He threw the door wide and gestured for me to come in.

"I'm so sorry, standing around while you're freezing to death. Please, come in, come in and get warm." He took my elbow and guided me into the foyer. "Here, let me have your jacket. I'll see that it's dried. Please, have a seat. Can I get you anything? A cup of coffee? Tea?"

"Tea would be fine," I said. "But how did you know who I—"

"I'll be right back," he said abruptly, and hurried away.

Wondering which of the Willises he was, if indeed he was a Willis (did Willis & / or Willis answer their own door?), and baffled as to why *any* Willis would seem so happy to see me, I watched him disappear down the hall, then let my eyes wander around the room. I called it a foyer, but it was much grander, more like an entrance hall, with a high ceiling, oil paintings on the walls, and an enormous oriental rug that was more than capable of soaking up the sleet melting from my hair and shoes and jeans.

An ornate divided staircase curved up around the tapestry couch on which I sat, teeth chattering. There was a low table at my knees, and a tall vase filled with deep blue irises graced its flawless surface. I loved irises and the welcome reminder that, all evidence to the contrary, spring had to be just around the corner. An icy drop of water slithered down my neck, but I kept my eyes on the flowers, comforted by the thought that someday soon it would be warm again.

My host cleared his throat. I looked up and saw that he was carrying an armful of clothes—a hooded sweatshirt and some sweatpants, in crimson. Harvard, I thought.

"Here you are," he said, handing them over.

I looked at them blankly.

"I thought you might want to change into something dry," he offered. "I keep these on hand for the club, and trust me, they're clean." He patted his fairly ample midsection. "I don't use them as often as I should. I would've had proper clothes for you to change into, but I wasn't sure . . ." He looked me up and down in a way that wasn't remotely flirtatious. If it had been, at least I would have known what was going on. "Size eight?" he asked.

I nodded, not knowing what else to do.

His face lit up. "I'll remember that. But in the meantime, this is the best I can do. Will you take them for now, with my apologies? You can slip into them in the changing room. Right along here."

I hesitated. I didn't usually accept favors from strangers. Then I considered my blue-tinged fingertips and decided to force myself to make an exception this one time. I followed him down the hall, through a magnificent set of double doors and a sumptuous office, to what he had called the changing room. He set out a pile of towels and left, shutting the door behind him.

The changing room was to bathrooms what the Taj Mahal is to the Little Brown Church in the Vale. I would have gladly moved into it and lived there for the rest of my life. It was as elegantly appointed as the entrance hall and spacious enough to hold everything I owned, with room to spare. I had never seen anything like it: shower stall and whirlpool bath in gray marble, closet space galore, sleek reclining leather chair, massage table, full-length mirrors, telephone, stereo system, television, VCR, the works. But the best part of all was a carpet so thick and soft that my toes almost got lost in it. I took my time getting changed, savoring the sensation of being in a place designed to please the eye as well as the body. When I had finished, I tiptoed back into the office.

My host was sitting on the edge of the desk. He sprang to his feet when he saw me.

"Socks," he said.

"Excuse me?"

"Socks—I forgot dry socks. Here, take these, and give me those wet clothes. I'll be right back." We made our exchange and then he was gone again. The man was like a magic trick: now you see him, now you don't.

I pulled on the socks and popped back into the changing room to take a look at my new ensemble. It was about what I had expected, considering the fact that the donor was at least eight inches taller than I and a good deal heavier. The sweatpants were baggy enough for two of me, the sweatshirt, complete with its Harvard insignia, came down past my butt, and the heels of the socks reached well above my ankles. My hair was beginning to dry, and my short, dark curls completed the effect. It wasn't bad, if you go for the waif look.

"Comfy?" asked a now-familiar voice. I nearly jumped out of his socks. My host was looking in from the changing room doorway.

"Yes, thank you," I answered, "and I appreciate the dry clothes, but . . . do you think you could tell me who you are?"

"Whoops. Sorry about that," he apologized, "but you looked so

damned wet and miserable that I thought introductions could wait."
He began to chuckle. "I'll bet you thought I was the butler. . . ." He
changed his chuckle into a cough when he saw the look on my face,
which told him plainly that I didn't know *what* to think.

"I'm Bill Willis," he said hastily. "Not William. That's my father.
We're partners in the firm. Do you mind if I call you Lori?"

"No," I said.

"That's great," he said. "Terrific, in fact. I can't tell you how
happy . . . But please, come in here, sit down, and have your tea. I've
let Father know you've arrived and he'll be here shortly. He's thrilled
that you've come. We've both been looking forward to meeting you.
You have no idea." His unexpected burst of enthusiasm hit me like a
wave. I must have swayed on my feet because he was immediately at
my side.

"Are you all right?" he asked.

"I'm fine," I said as I waited for the room to stop spinning. This had
happened once or twice before on days when I skipped meals, but I
was mortified to have it happen now, in front of this rich, Harvard-
educated lawyer. Holding myself very erect, I walked past him into
the adjoining office and sat in one of the two high-backed leather
chairs that faced the massive desk. "I'm perfectly . . . fine."

"If you say so," he said doubtfully, crossing from the doorway to
the desk. A silver tea service had been placed there. He poured a cup
and brought it to me. "Maybe I should call for some food to go along
with this." He reached for the phone, but I held out a restraining
hand.

"Please don't," I said, in an effort to salvage what was left of my
dignity. "There's no need. I said I was perfectly fine, and I meant it."

He stroked his beard thoughtfully, then nodded, once. "Okay. If
that's what you want. But at least get some of the tea inside you. I
don't want Father to think I've been inhospitable, and he'll be here
any minute."

The sovereign remedy worked, as always, and by the time William
Willis, Sr., entered the room, I was able to view him with something
approaching equanimity. It was hard to believe he was related to Bill.

A slight, clean-shaven man in his early sixties, with a high forehead and a patrician nose, he was impeccably attired in a black three-piece suit. Not only did Willis, Sr., dress better than his son, but while Bill had been almost too friendly from the moment I'd staggered through the front door, his father was as formal as an etiquette book, as though he knew the exact amount of pressure—in pounds per square inch— his handshake should exert, under these and any other circumstances. He was scrupulously polite, but he gave no indication of being thrilled about anything. What could Bill have been talking about? Sprawled comfortably in the leather chair beside my own, he had fallen silent at his father's entrance, and was watching him with an inexplicable gleam of excitement in his eyes.

After the punctilious handshake, Willis, Sr., seated himself behind the desk, unlocked the center drawer, and removed a file folder, which he placed carefully on the desk before him. He opened the folder and studied its contents intently for a moment, then cleared his throat and raised his eyes to mine. "Before continuing, young lady, I must ask you a few questions. Please answer them truthfully. Be advised that the penalties for misrepresentation are grave."

I felt a sudden urge to look to Bill for support, but I quelled it. Bill, for his part, remained silent.

"May I see your driver's license?"

I pulled my wallet from the sweatshirt pocket and handed it to him.

"I see," said Willis, Sr. "Now, will you please state your full name and place of birth?"

Thus began what I came to think of as the Great Q and A, with Willis, Sr., intoning the Q's and me supplying the A's. What was my mother's family name? Where had I gone to school? Where had my father been born? Where had I worked? Who was my godfather? On and on, with an almost sacramental regularity, for what seemed like a very long time, question after question after question. I could see Bill out of the corner of my eye the entire time and the look on his face continued to perplex me. He began with barely the ghost of a smile tugging at the corners of his mouth. As the questions went on, the smile settled and gradually became more pronounced, until he was grinning like a fool. Willis, Sr., seemed to share my puzzlement: the only time he faltered was when he happened to look up from his papers and caught sight of his son's goofy grin. Aside from that, Willis, Sr., showed no emotion whatsoever, never hurrying, never slowing down, pausing only to turn to the next page in the file.

My fatigue must have put me in a highly suggestible state of mind, because it never once occurred to me to fire any questions back at him. Like "What business is it of yours?" or "Who the hell are you to grill me like this?" The setting was so artificial that I felt like a character in a play. I even felt a touch of pride at knowing my lines so well. The hypnotic rhythm lulled me into a kind of semiconscious complacency, until Willis, Sr., asked what turned out to be the last question.

"Now, young lady, would you please tell my son and me the story entitled *Aunt Dimity Buys a Torch?*"

I sat bolt upright in the chair, sputtered a few incoherent syllables—and fainted. The shock of hearing those words on a stranger's lips did what a polar expedition on top of a hectic day without food had failed to do: awakened my sense of drama. I vaguely remember gaping in astonishment and then I found myself gazing blearily into Willis, Sr.'s face from a prone position on a couch.

"Miss Shepherd, can you hear me?" asked Willis, Sr., leaning over to peer closely at my face. "Ah, you are awake. Good, good."

I hardly recognized the man. The cool politeness in his eyes had given way to a look of warm concern, a lock of white hair had fallen over his forehead, and the hand that had shaken mine with such formality was now solicitously tucking an afghan around me. Suddenly I could see a clear resemblance between father and son.

"I am so very sorry about this," he said, with a worried frown. "I had no idea it would affect you so severely. But the terms of the will are quite clear and I had to be certain you were who you claimed to be. I was under strict orders, you see, but I never dreamt—"

"How did you know?" I murmured muzzily. "How did you know about Aunt Dimity?"

"I think we shall have a bite of supper first. You appear to be in need of sustenance," said Willis, Sr. "And then *I* will answer *your* questions for a change. A change for the better in my opinion, and in yours, too, no doubt." He beamed down at me. "I am so happy that you are here, my dear. I feel as though I have known you for years."

However much I disliked having my questions deflected yet again, I had to admit that food sounded like an idea whose time had come. I pulled myself into a sitting position as Bill entered the room pushing a supper-laden trolley.

"Feeling perfectly fine, are we?" he asked cheerfully, and I felt myself blush. He wheeled the trolley to within my reach and pulled up chairs for himself and his father. "If you'd felt any better, we might have had to call an ambulance."

"This is no time for levity, my boy," admonished Willis, Sr., gently. "If you had given Miss Shepherd a proper meal when she arrived, we might have avoided this unfortunate incident."

"You're quite right, Father. I stand corrected," said Bill, and I sank a bit lower on the couch.

"Please, Miss Shepherd, try some of the consommé," said Willis, Sr. "There's nothing like a good beef broth after an upset. And then, if you're up to it, a bit of the roast, I think . . ."

The two men fussed over me, filling my plate and keeping it filled, and between bites I told them the story of Aunt Dimity's quest for a torch. I felt awkward, hauling out a part of my childhood for these two strangers to examine, but Willis, Sr., assured me that it was a necessary part of the Great Q and A, so I went ahead and told it, word for word, exactly as my mother had told it to me. The only difference was that this time it put the teller to sleep instead of the listeners. Although it was barely eight o'clock, I dozed off with a dessert plate still in my lap.

Four

I awoke in the small hours of the morning. The room was pitch-dark, but I didn't need light to know that I wasn't in my own bed. The mattress was firm and the pillows were soft—instead of the other way round—and when I stretched, my hands bumped into something which felt suspiciously like a headboard. Reaching to one side, my groping fingers found a nightstand, then a lamp. I turned it on.

Definitely not my room. A large, tweedy armchair sat in one corner, a small, graceful desk in another, the kind that sits in the front window of a fancy antique store and costs half the gross national product. A crystal carafe and a tumbler sat on the nightstand; the carafe was filled with water. The bed had a footboard to go with the headboard, and both were made of the same lustrous wood as the desk. The sheets and blankets were navy blue—very masculine—and the pillowcases bore a silver monogram in looping Florentine script: *W.*

For *Willis.*

I sat up as the rest of yesterday's events came flooding back, erasing my confusion and anchoring me firmly in . . . what? Yesterday morning I had been a struggling, semiemployed, ordinary person who slept on a mattress on the floor. This morning I found myself comfortably ensconced in an elegant bedroom, the honored guest of a venerable attorney. "What next?" I murmured, gazing about the room. "A glass coach and a Handsome Prince?"

The thought made me start as another memory settled into place, a sleepy memory of being carried up a long flight of stairs by the venerable attorney's son, the same son who had loaned me . . . I peeked under the covers and was relieved to spot the Harvard insignia. It was bad enough to know that I had been toted up to bed like a helpless child, but it could have been worse.

I still had plenty of questions, but they'd have to wait until the rest of the house had awakened. In the meantime . . . I swung my legs over the side of the bed. If I was careful and quiet, I should be able to take a look around. After all, it wasn't every day that I woke up with a mansion to explore.

Easing open a door at random, I discovered a spacious dressing room with empty shelves, empty hangers, an empty dressing table. The towels in the adjoining bathroom held the scent of fresh laundering, and everything else in it seemed to be brand-new: an undented tube of toothpaste, a toothbrush still in its wrapper, a dry bar of sandalwood soap placed between the double sinks. The shampoo and liquid soap dispensers in the shower were full, and an enormous loofah sat on one marble ledge, looking as though it hadn't touched water since it had first been wrested from the seafloor.

A second door opened on to a well-appointed parlor dominated by a wide, glass-fronted cabinet. Padding over, I saw that it held an assortment of trophies, plaques, and medals for everything from debating to Greek. There were a few sports awards, for odd things like squash and fencing, but most were for scholarly achievements. Each was polished and gleaming, and each was engraved with the name *William Willis.* The dates indicated that they were Bill's, rather than his father's, and a young Bill's at that; the triumphs of childhood and young manhood memorialized quietly, in a very private room.

The cabinet reminded me of the steamer trunk I had found while sorting through my mother's things; a trunk carefully packed with the symbols of my own academic achievements, which had not been inconsiderable. It had been a crushing discovery, like encountering a trunkful of my mother's unfulfilled dreams for me. I looked at the trophies before me and envied Bill. He had lived up to the promise of his early years, while the schoolteacher's daughter was living out of cardboard boxes.

I turned away from the cabinet and was promptly distracted from my gloomy thoughts by the sight of my clothes from the day before. They had been placed neatly on the coffee table, cleaned, dried, and pressed. I was amused to see my well-worn clothing treated so respectfully, but I was also a little embarrassed. I doubted that Bill had ever seen such threadbare jeans before, or such shabby sneakers.

A piece of paper stuck out of one of the sneakers. I unfolded it and saw that the words on it had been printed in caps and underlined:

<u>CALL 7404 AS SOON AS YOU GET UP</u>
<u>THE SOONER, THE BETTER!</u>

I glanced at my watch, saw that it was coming up on four A.M., then looked back at the note and shrugged. Maybe I'd get those answers sooner than I'd thought. I picked up the phone on the end table and dialed the extension. Bill answered on the first ring.

"Lori? How are you feeling?"

"Fine," I said, "but—"

"Great. You're up? You're dressed?"

"Yes, but—"

"Terrific. I'll be right down."

"But what—" I began, but he had already hung up. I grabbed my sneakers and by the time my laces were tied, Bill was at the parlor door, rosy-cheeked and slightly out of breath, wearing a bulky parka with a fur-trimmed hood.

"I was hoping you'd be awake before dawn," he said. "Now, come with me, and hurry. I have something to show you."

"What is it?"

"You'll see." His eyes danced as he turned on his heel and took off down the hall. I scurried to catch up and we nearly collided at the first corner because I was so busy gawking at my surroundings. But how could I help it?

My suite opened on to a paneled corridor hung with hunting scenes, and the rug beneath my feet depicted a chase, the hounds bounding up the hall to bay at a smug-looking fox who perched out of reach at the farthest edge. A turn took us into another long passageway, this one devoted to still lifes, the rug woven with pears and peaches and pale green grapes glistening against a background of burnt umber. Another turn and we were racing up a staircase of golden oak, the newel posts carved with a pattern of grape leaves, the balustrade with the curling tendrils of trailing vines. The landings were as big as my bedroom. If Bill was trying to impress me, he was succeeding.

"Behold the House of Willis," I murmured.

Bill heard me. "Do you like it?" he asked. "It's what happens when you come from a long line of pack rats. We shipped all of our worldly goods over from England more than two hundred years ago and as far as I can tell, not one member of my family has ever thrown anything out. I wouldn't be surprised to learn that some of these pots were used in the ancestral caves." The "pot" he was referring to at that moment was a pale blue porcelain bowl spilling over with orchids. The flowers alone were probably worth more than my weekly paycheck.

He said nothing else until we reached the bottom of a narrow staircase with unadorned plaster walls and simple wrought-iron railings. There he turned and whispered, "Servants' quarters. People sleeping."

In silence, we climbed the stairs and made our way down a short passageway and into a small room. It was empty save for a rack hung with an assortment of jackets, and a table heaped with heavy sweaters. A spiral staircase in the center of the room led to a trapdoor in the ceiling. I rested against the wall while Bill rummaged through the pile of sweaters. He plucked up a tightly woven Icelandic pullover and handed it to me. "Size eight," he said. "Put it on." He stood with one foot on the bottom step of the staircase and looked at me closely. "Are you all right?"

"Yes," I said, wheezing. "It's just . . . all those stairs."

"We can stay here for a minute, if you need—"

"No, I'm okay."

"You're sure?"

"I'm *positive*," I said, with some exasperation. "Let's get going."

He climbed up the spiral staircase and through the trapdoor, then closed the trapdoor behind me as I emerged into the chilly predawn darkness of the mansion's roof. There was no moon, but the storm had spent itself, the clouds had flown, and the sky was ablaze with stars. I could vaguely make out the shadowy shapes of vents and chimneys and . . . something else. I knew what it looked like, but I couldn't imagine what it might be doing up there.

"Come." Bill led me directly to the strange shape that looked like, but could not possibly be, a dentist's chair. Except that it was. Piled next to it was what appeared to be a fitted waterproof cover.

"Had it since college," Bill said, giving the headrest an affectionate pat. "Saw it at an auction and snapped it up. Knew exactly where I'd put it. Have a seat."

I looked at Bill and I looked at the chair and for a brief moment it crossed my mind that there might be an army of servants hiding behind the chimney pots, waiting for Bill's command to leap out and shout, "April Fool!"

"Hurry," he said. "It's almost over."

His sense of urgency was infectious——I climbed into the chair. It was upholstered in sheepskin, like the bucket seat of an expensive sports car, a welcome bit of customizing in this brisk weather. Bill levered it back until I was looking straight up into the star-filled sky.

"What am I looking for?" I asked.

"You'll know it when you see it," he replied.

I continued to gaze heavenward. With tall buildings towering on either side and the vastness of space stretched in between, I felt like a very small bug in a very big bottle. I didn't mind in the least when Bill placed his hand on my shoulder and whispered, "Be patient."

Then I saw them. Shooting stars. Not just one or two, but a dozen of them, silvery streaks that dashed across the velvet darkness, then vanished, as though the heavens were winking out at the end of time. I clutched the arms of the chair, dizzied by the sudden sensation that Bill's hand on my shoulder was the only thing keeping me from falling upward, into the stars.

It ended as quickly as it had begun.

"There are very few things in this world that really can't wait," Bill said after a moment of silence, "and a meteor shower is one of them. I take it as a good omen that the clouds parted in time for you to see the end of this one."

The warmth in his voice brought me back down to earth, so to speak, reminding me that I was sitting in a dentist's chair on the roof of a mansion in the middle of Boston, with a complete stranger as my guide. And that the complete stranger was talking to me in a tone of voice usually reserved for very, very good friends. I eyed him warily as he levered the chair into an upright position.

"Do you do this with all of your clients?" I asked.

"No, I do not," he said, a hint of amusement in his voice. "This is my private domain. There's something else I'd like you to see as long as we're up here—if you feel up to it, that is."

"If I feel . . ." I ignored his outstretched hand and clambered out of the chair on my own. "Look, Bill, in spite of my performance last night, I am not an invalid."

"Of course not." He pulled the fitted cover over the dentist's chair. "You're twenty pounds underweight, and a run up a flight of stairs leaves you puffing like a steam engine, but you're certainly not an invalid. Come on."

I stared at him, nonplussed, until he had almost disappeared in the shadows, then set out after him, ready to give him a piece of my mind. I made my way around chimney stacks and ventilators to a small domed structure in the center of the roof, but before I could say a word, he ducked through a low door, then stood back to let me enter. He shut the door, lit an oil lamp—and the walls sprang to life around us.

The entire interior, from the floor to the top of the dome, was covered with paintings—the Gemini twins, Orion with his belt and sword, and the regal queen, Cassiopeia, to name only a few. The paintings were inset with tiny faceted crystals that sparkled like miniature constellations, and the centerpiece was an old brass telescope that had been polished to within an inch of its life. Bill held the lamp high, clearly enjoying my wide-eyed amazement.

"Oh, my," I gasped at last, "this is *incredible*. Did you build it yourself?"

"The only thing I did was install a telephone. The rest"—he let his gaze wander across the glittering dome—"was Great-great-uncle Arthur's idea."

"Great-great-uncle Arthur?"

"Yes, well, every family has one eventually, and we had Arthur." Bill handed me the lantern, rummaged in a cupboard, and came up with a chamois cloth. As he spoke, he ran it across the smooth surface of the telescope. "He'd be considered eccentric in England, but here he was thought to be just plain nuts. He gave the family fits spending all that hard-earned cash on stargazing, but I, for one, am grateful to the old loon. Granted, it's not much good as an observatory now. Too many buildings, too much light from the city. But when he built it, the mansion was the tallest building around and the lights were fewer and farther between. Like this." He nodded at the oil lamp. "A softer light for a softer time.

"This is my bolt-hole," he continued. "I discovered it when I was a boy, and I've come here ever since, whenever I've needed to be by myself. Just me and the stars. And now, you."

There it was again, the warmth in his voice, and again it made me uneasy. "Thanks for showing it to me," I said, then tried to fill the uncomfortable silence by adding, "It's more than I deserve, really, after getting you in trouble with your father."

"After what?"

"What he said last night, about giving me a meal when I showed up. You did try, and I should have told him so."

"Oh, that." He folded the chamois cloth and returned it to the cupboard. "Don't worry about it."

"No, I mean it—I'm sorry I didn't say anything."

"It's okay."

"But it's not okay. I should have—"

"I understand, but there's no need—"

"Bill!" Did he think he had a monopoly on good manners? Here he was, showing me all of these lovely things, and he wouldn't even let me do something as commonplace as apologize for rude behavior. "If I want to say I'm sorry, I'll say I'm sorry, okay? I don't see why you won't—"

"Accepted," he said.

"What?"

"I accept your apology."

"Well . . . all right, then," I muttered, the wind leaking slowly from my sails.

"Good." He rubbed his hands together. "Now that we've settled that, let's go back to your rooms. There's one more thing I'd like to show you." He took the lantern from me, extinguished it, and opened the door.

I had hoped to see more of the mansion on the way back, so I was disappointed when we returned to the guest suite via the same route. Bill must have sensed it, because as we approached my door he said, "I'll give you a tour later, if you like. It's a wonderful place. You've seen some of the older parts, but we have an entire wing that would put IBM to shame. One of the reasons we've been so successful is that we're willing to take the best of both worlds: the gentility of the old and the efficiency of the new. Ah, good, they've arrived."

This last remark came as he opened the parlor door and I saw right away what had prompted it. During our absence, a vase had been placed on the coffee table, a slender crystal vase filled with deep blue irises. I gave a gasp of pleasure when I saw them.

"You like them?" Bill asked. "I hoped you might. I saw you looking at the ones downstairs and I thought—"

"They're my favorites. But how do you manage to find irises at this time of year? Isn't it a little early?"

"Where there's a Willis—" he began, but my groan cut him off. "The hothouse," he continued. "It's in the back. I'll be sure to include it in the tour." He jutted his chin in the direction of the one door in the suite I had yet to open. "Been in there yet?" When I shook my head, he frowned. "But that's the whole reason I put you in here! Come on." He opened the door, turned on a light, and stood aside as I entered a library as small and perfect as Great-great-uncle Arthur's observatory, though executed in a rather more sedate style.

"The big library is downstairs," Bill said. "This is Father's private stash."

I scanned the shelves, speechless. The collection was everything a collection should be. My old boss, Stan Finderman, would have approved wholeheartedly, and so did I. It wasn't full of showpieces. It was full of love and careful thought. The books were all related to polar exploration—Franklin's *A Journey to the Shores of the Polar Sea,* Ross's *A Voyage of Discovery,* and many others—some worth a small fortune, all priceless to the person who read and cherished them.

"And now for the grand finale," Bill said. He put a finger to his lips and tiptoed stealthily to a wall space between two of the bookcases. Pushing his sleeves up with a flourish, like some mad magician, he applied pressure to two places on the wall and, presto-chango, it swung open to reveal a staircase leading down.

"A mansion wouldn't be a mansion without a few secret passages, now, would it?" he said with a grin. "This one leads down to the changing room in Father's office. For all intents and purposes, you have your own private connection to all the comforts therein. You can lock the changing room door from the inside and use it anytime you like. But please—don't forget to unlock it when you're done."

"Wait a minute," I said as he closed the door in the wall. An appalling thought had just occurred to me. "If this is your father's collection, and if that staircase leads down to his office, then . . . Oh, Bill, this isn't his suite, is it? He didn't clear out to make room for me, did he?"

"Not at all. Father would have been happy to make way for you, but as it happens, he didn't. This used to be his suite—he used to live above the shop, so to speak—but he's on the ground floor now. We simply haven't gotten around to moving the books yet." Bill's gaze swept over the shelves. "It's ironic. All these stories about conquering the wilderness, and he's not allowed to climb the stairs in his own home."

"Not allowed?"

He glanced at me, then looked back to the books. "His heart," he said shortly. "Started acting up last spring. Hasn't been anything serious so far, but . . . I can't help worrying. My mother died when I was twelve, and aside from some desiccated aunts, it's been just the two of us ever since." He reached out to touch one of the books. "It's strange, isn't it? No one ever tells you that one day you'll worry about your parents the way they always worried about you."

I averted my eyes as my heart twisted inside of me. The fact was that I had never worried about my mother. She'd never been sick a day in her life. The only time she had ever been in a hospital had been to give birth to me. But Bill's words reminded me that I should have shown more concern for her, that I had failed her in that as I had failed her in so many other ways.

"But enough doom and gloom." Bill turned his back on the books. "As I said, there's no need to worry, not really. There's no reason Father shouldn't live to be a hundred, as long as he takes care of himself."

"You make sure he does," I said. "Because once he's gone . . ." I fell silent, hoping Bill hadn't noticed the tremor in my voice.

"Lori," he said. He touched my arm and I pulled away from him. I didn't need or want his sympathy, and I was annoyed with myself for provoking it.

"Breakfast is at nine," he said, after a pause. "The small dining room, downstairs, left, left, third door on the right. And Father would like to see you at ten. In his office." He walked to the door of the library, then turned. "And by the way—you're not my client. You're his."

It took a moment for his words to register, a moment more for me to realize that I had let him go without getting any of the answers I'd been looking for. What's more, as I returned to the small library for a closer look at Willis, Sr.'s books, I realized there was something else I wanted to know.

Why was Bill being so nice to me?

Five

The small dining room made me wonder what the big dining room was like. The table at which Bill and I sat—Willis, Sr., having opted for breakfast in his rooms—was long enough to seat twelve, and anything above a sedate murmur caused muted echoes to reverberate from the domed ceiling. The food was set out in silver chafing dishes along a sideboard, except for a small mountain of strawberries that loomed over a stoneware pitcher filled with cream. Two servants, casually attired in khaki twills and crewneck sweaters, poured our orange juice, then sat down with us and engaged Bill in a heated debate over some obscure point of contract law.

"Law students," Bill explained when they had cleared the table. "Live-in staff."

"How convenient," I said. "Your own private supply of slave labor."

"Absolutely. That's why we have a waiting list as long as my arm." Bill looked at his watch. "My father, the capitalist tyrant, should be waiting for us now. Shall we?" He led the way to the office. "The students were his idea," he continued. "Room and board and a chance for hands-on experience in our clinics, not to mention the opportunity to learn from one of the finest legal minds in the country. I refer, of course, to my father's. In exchange for which they do everything but cook. Some things are best left to a professional, don't you agree? I'm sure they'd be much better off somewhere else, but what can we do? They're champing at the bit to be trodden underfoot." He opened the office doors. "Aren't they, Father?"

Willis, Sr., looked up from his desk. "Aren't who what, my boy?"

"Miss Shepherd was commenting on your unorthodox solution to the servant problem."

"Ah, the students. They have worked out marvelously well, Miss Shepherd. I don't know where we would be without them, and they seem to find the experience worthwhile. Bill, did you hear? Young Walters was made a judge last week."

"Sandy Walters? But he couldn't even wash dishes!"

"I doubt that he will be required to," Willis, Sr., observed dryly, then turned his attention to me. "Forgive our prattle, Miss Shepherd. How are you this morning?"

"She's perfectly fine," said Bill, and I sent a low-level glare in his direction. "I'll leave you to it, then, Father. And I'll see *you* later." He nodded pleasantly at me as he left the room.

"My son appears to be in a lighthearted mood this morning." Willis, Sr., stared thoughtfully at the door for a moment, then smiled at me. "But let us proceed, Miss Shepherd. I am sure you must be feeling very impatient by now. Please make yourself comfortable. This may take some time, I'm afraid." I took a seat in the tall leather wing chair facing him.

"Twenty-five years ago," Willis, Sr., began, "I was contacted by a colleague in England. A client of his, a mildly eccentric woman of comfortable means, wished to draw up her will. Further, she wished to have her will administered by an American law firm, since one of the legatees would be an American. She was quite concerned about finding the right people to handle the case and I am pleased to say that she found our firm satisfactory."

I smiled at this and Willis, Sr., raised his eyebrows in polite inquiry. "Don't take this the wrong way," I said, "but it's easy to see why Willis & Willis would appeal to an Englishwoman. I can't imagine a less 'American' law firm."

"You are quite right," said Willis, Sr. "She admitted as much when I traveled to England to meet her. She wanted a firm which hadn't 'succumbed to the rat race,' as she put it. We were anachronistic enough to suit her taste exactly."

His gaze returned to the doors through which Bill had exited. "I suspect that my son influenced her in our favor as well. I brought him with me, you see. My father, who was then head of the firm, disapproved of such unprofessional behavior, but my wife had just passed away, and to be so far away from the boy for any extended period of time was out of the question." He looked once more at me. "In the end, it proved fortunate. Bill's presence seemed to reassure my client that the firm wasn't completely ossified.

"At any rate, she told me that she had a friend, an American friend who had a daughter, and that the will concerned certain tasks that her friend's child was to undertake. The daughter, apparently, did not know of my client's existence, and my client wished to maintain her anonymity until the time came for the will to be administered. 'It's my last appearance in the story,' she told me, 'and I would like it to be a surprise.'

"As you have undoubtedly guessed by now, your mother, the late Elizabeth Irene Shepherd, was the friend and you are the daughter. What I am permitted to reveal to you now is that my client was Miss Dimity Westwood, founder of the Westwood Trust, which supported, indeed still supports, a great number of charitable institutions in the United Kingdom.

"During her lifetime, Miss Westwood was widely respected, but something of a mystery—an invisible philanthropist, one might say, whose good works were better known than herself. She was also, if I may add a personal note, the most remarkable woman I have ever had the honor to know." Willis, Sr., leaned back in his chair and folded his hands across his waistcoat.

"I have practiced law for a good many years," he mused, "and I have seen every kind of scandal and battle royale imaginable. The cliché is true, I'm afraid: wills do frequently bring out the worst in those involved—the greed, the pettiness." He sighed. "I should not complain, I suppose, for I owe my livelihood to such disagreements. But I must say that it is a singularly pleasurable change of pace when a client such as Miss Westwood comes along.

"She was a voluminous correspondent, but I only met her in person that one time. Yet she was so generous, so kind, so . . ." He groped for the right word. "So good-humored," he concluded helplessly. "We stayed with her, you see, at her invitation, and not an hour passed during our visit when she didn't find something to laugh about, some incidental detail or absurdity that I would have overlooked completely. I felt quite renewed by the end of our ten days."

Willis, Sr., stared into the distance, lost in visions of the past, and

I watched his face, entranced. One meeting, twenty-five years ago, and he was still under her spell. I could almost see Dimity Westwood welcoming him to her home. She had looked beyond the professional demeanor of the lawyer and seen a grieving widower who couldn't bear to be parted from his young son. This was the man she had chosen to look after my interests and it was clear that she had chosen with her heart as well as her head. Miss Westwood had to be Aunt Dimity. But why was this the first time I had heard that she was a real person?

Willis, Sr., returned to the present. "Forgive an old man his distractions, Miss Shepherd. Now, where was I? Ah, yes." Leaning forward, he continued, "My task was quite simple, really. I was to familiarize myself with certain of Miss Westwood's personal documents, draw up the will to her specifications, and keep myself apprised of your whereabouts. I was not permitted to contact you, however, until after Miss Westwood's passing. I regret to say that the sad event occurred eleven months ago."

"Just when I disappeared from the face of the earth," I said.

"Precisely," said Willis, Sr. "I had learned of your divorce, naturally, and managed to trace your first change of address, but after that?" He clucked his tongue. "Oh, my. I enlisted my son's help in the search, but it wasn't until last week that I believed I'd finally found you, here, living across town from us. You can imagine how surprised I was to learn that you were so nearby. It was an unexpected, though quite welcome, turn of events.

"I was very pleased when you appeared so promptly, even more pleased when you responded to Miss Westwood's questions with the appropriate answers. If you will permit me," he added, "I would like to apologize once more for the distressing climax of that particular interview. Had I not been constrained by the terms of the will to carry it out, I assure you—"

"That's okay," I said. "Really, I understand. You had to make sure you had the right person, so . . . To tell you the truth, I'm finding it hard to believe I'm me, too, if you know what I mean. I grew up thinking that Aunt Dimity was an invention, a fantasy. And now you're telling me that she was real." I shook my head. "It'll take a while for it to sink in. But what exactly are we talking about? What tasks am I supposed to undertake?"

"Ah, yes," continued Willis, Sr. "Having ascertained to my satisfaction that you are the Lori Elizabeth Shepherd so named in the will, I must now ask you to examine the contents of these envelopes." From a drawer in his desk, he withdrew two envelopes, one pale blue, the other buff-colored. He stood up and walked around his desk to bring them to me. "You will, perhaps, care to read them in the privacy of your rooms." He indicated the changing room door. "There is a staircase that leads—"

"I know," I said. "Bill showed me."

"Did he?" Willis, Sr., said. His eyebrows rose in surprise, but I had no time to wonder why. The entire room seemed to fade as I saw what was written on the buff-colored envelope. It was my name, and it had been written in my mother's hand.

I put my mother's letter aside to read last. Curled in an armchair in the parlor of the guest suite, a single lamp shedding a pool of light around me, I slipped a letter opener beneath the flap of the pale blue envelope, then paused to look at it once more. My name had been written on the front of this one as well, in neat, unfamiliar handwriting. I didn't need subtitles to tell me whose it was, though. With great care, I slit open the envelope, and Aunt Dimity's voice came through, soft and clear.

My Dearest Lori,

No, I am not your fairy godmother. Neither am I a witch. I may be dead now, but I assure you that, while I was alive, I was the most ordinary person imaginable. And before you get any more silly ideas, no, I do not plan to return from the grave! I'm looking forward to a nice, long rest and many pleasant chats with your mother.

Yes, I just got word of Beth's death and I am so very sorry. I know how hard it will be for you. But I also know that you will weather this along with everything else. It may not seem so for a time, but it will come out right in the end.

I am getting ahead of myself, however, and I must remember not to do that. You have been so much a part of my life that it is altogether too easy for me to forget that we have never met.

You must be very perplexed. I would apologize if I felt sorry, but I freely admit to feeling no remorse whatsoever. It's as though I'm watching someone open an oddly shaped birthday present. The intrigue is half the fun, especially when one knows how delighted the recipient will be when the contents are finally revealed. My wrapping paper is more elaborate than most, to be sure, but then, I've never wrapped something quite so oddly shaped before. How does one wrap the past? How does one wrap the future? I have done my best.

But enough riddles, Dimity, or Lori shall begin to tear at her hair with frustration. Get on with it! Are you comfortable, my dear? And have you a cup of tea? Very well, then, let us begin.

Your mother was the dearest friend I have ever had. We met late in the autumn of 1940, in London, when I was a humble clerk in the War Office and she was a humble clerk on the General's staff. I refer to General Eisenhower, of course, but lest you become overly impressed, let me reiterate the word "humble." We were very small cogs in that very large machine. What glamour there was was the glamour of being young and aware that we were living the great adventure of our lives. I consider myself blessed to have shared it with your mother. I could not have invented a more ideal companion. I suspect that the circumstances of our meeting will sound familiar to you.

I occasionally had a day free of duties and on one such day I decided to visit the zoological gardens. For some reason I had become intensely curious to know what the war had done to them, so intensely curious that I didn't mind the circuitous route I had to take to get there, nor the promise of rain that hung in the air, a promise that was fulfilled as soon as I'd entered the grounds.

In my mad dash for shelter, I ran straight into Beth. I mean that quite literally. I knocked her down. I was ready to sink into the ground with embarrassment when Beth did a most unusual thing. She blinked up at me for a moment—and then began to laugh. Suddenly the absurdity of the situation was brought home to me: how could a bit of rain and an accidental collision compare to the war raging on all around us? Laughter was the only reasonable response. When I had helped her to her feet, I invited her back to my flat to dry off. We chatted the evening away over what was to be the first of many shared pots of tea. We became very close very quickly, as one did in those days.

That was how our friendship began, with laughter. Beth knew where to look to find the humour in any situation and I learned how to find it myself after a short time in her company. As you can imagine, this was invaluable during the war, but it has stood me in good stead under "normal" circumstances as well. It was a great gift and I remain indebted to her for it to this day.

When the war was over, and your mother was posted home, I accompanied her to the ship. Somehow we knew it was the last time we would ever set eyes on each other. It wasn't easy to find the humour in that, but we managed. As we walked toward the gangplank, Beth threatened to start another war if I didn't write to her, and I vowed, for the sake of world peace, to be a faithful correspondent.

I was and so, too, was Beth. Long letters, short notes, postal cards—we became closer with an ocean between us than we had been while living in the same city. We often spoke of visiting one another, but we never did. It seems strange to me now, but it did not seem strange then. Looking back on it, I suspect that we were trying to keep the world of our letters apart from the world in which we lived. Perhaps we had become so accustomed to the magic of words on paper that we were afraid a face-to-face meeting might break the spell.

Our letters were our refuge. We looked to them for stability, for continuity, in a world of change. Beth regaled me with tales of married life while I spun the saga of spinsterhood and, through it all, our friendship became stronger, deeper than ever before. I believe that your mother needed these letters very much. Although she loved you and your father dearly, still, she needed one place that was hers and hers alone. To my knowledge, she never told another living soul of our correspondence, save your father, naturally.

Shortly after the joyous event of your birth, your mother faced a most difficult time. Your father's death was a terrible blow, as I am sure you know. Beth refused my offer of financial assistance, but it was clear that she needed something, some special way to remind herself that this difficult time would pass.

With that thought in mind, I began to include stories in my letters. I wrote them for you, but they were directed toward your mother as well. The stories featured a heroine who was, like Beth, blessed with the gift of easy laughter. They were tales of commonplace courage and optimism, for I knew from my own experience that everyday virtues endure best, and that quiet courage is worth more than the grandest derring-do. Thus "Aunt Dimity" was born, a heroine for the common woman.

By telling the tales to you, your mother told them to herself. They served as a steady reminder that she already possessed those qualities that would see her through whatever life held in store for her. It was a small thing, perhaps, but great changes begin with small things. Witness our friendship. Little by little the stories, and the healing power of time, helped restore Beth's tranquillity.

By anyone's measure, Aunt Dimity was a roaring success. You didn't outgrow the stories until you were nearly twelve, long after you had put away most other childish things. And during that time Aunt Dimity had given me a great deal of pleasure and Beth a great deal of comfort. By then, I felt that I knew you quite well. I had tried to tailor my stories to your tastes, you see, which meant learning as much about you as I could. And though you eventually tired of hearing about Aunt Dimity, I never tired of hearing about you.

I have followed the events of your life ever since and, though sorely tempted at times, I have never broken my promise to your mother to keep the identity of Aunt Dimity's creator a secret.

Even now, I am keeping my promise. Beth and I agreed many years ago that, without this chapter, the story would be incomplete—and nothing bothered us more than a story with gaps. We decided to fill those gaps by bequeathing to you our complete correspondence, from the first pair of letters to these, the last. With Beth's approval, I engaged the firm of Willis & Willis to carry out our wishes.

You will find the correspondence waiting for you in my cottage, near the village of Finch in England. I disposed of my other properties, but I could not bring myself to dispose of the cottage. I grew up there, you see, and returned to it occasionally even after the war. It has always held a special place in my heart.

*There is a small task I would like you to perform while you are
there. William Willis will explain it to you at the appropriate time. It
is a favor I can ask of no one but you, and I am confident that you will
find it agreeable.*

*Please give my best wishes to William and to young Bill. Your
mother and I approved of them without reservation, and you may trust
them to look after your affairs as though they were their own.*

*I hope you are not too put out with Beth and me for keeping this
from you for so long. I know that the idea of being watched over from
afar will pinch at your independent spirit, but I assure you that it was
done with great respect and even greater*
love,
Dimity Westwood

I looked up from the letter and stared blindly across the room as
the words, and the images they evoked, settled over me like drifting
snow. It was difficult to accept the fact that a woman I had never
known had known so much about me, but I no longer doubted her existence. She knew too much to be a figment of anyone's imagination.

My mother had been in London during the war and she had ended
up on Eisenhower's staff. While there, she had been an indefatigable
explorer of the wartime city: she had told me of seeing the Tate Gallery shrouded in blackout curtains, St. Paul's Cathedral alight with
incendiaries, the streets cratered by bombing. She had met my father
during that time and she had often spoken of their first meeting. But
she had never spoken of this other momentous meeting, nor of the
forty-year friendship that had grown from it. As I turned it over in
my mind, though, I remembered the family ritual known as Quiet
Time.

Quiet Time came just after supper, when my mother retired to
her room, leaving Reginald and me engrossed in a storybook or some
other peaceful activity. She emerged from her room looking so re-
freshed and invigorated that I had always assumed she used that time
for a nap. Since I had been a fairly active—not to say rambunctious—
child, it wasn't an unreasonable assumption.

Now it seemed obvious that a renewal of spirit had been taking place behind her closed door. I placed Dimity's letter beside me on the couch and took up the buff-colored one. Looking over the familiar scrawl, I pictured my mother at her writing desk, bending over these pages as she had bent over so many others, and after a few deep breaths, I opened the envelope.

Something fell into my lap. It was a photograph, a very old photograph, stained in places, the corners creased, one missing altogether; a photograph of . . . nothing much, as far as I could tell: a gnarled old tree in the foreground of a grassy clearing, a valley beyond, some distant hills. It was no place I'd ever been, no place I recognized, and there was nothing else in it: no people, no animals, no buildings of any sort. Baffled, I set it aside and unfolded the pages of my mother's letter.

Sweetie,

All right, Sarah Bernhardt, dry your eyes and blow your nose. Your big scene is over.

I know what you're thinking right now, just as surely as if I were sitting there looking at you. You've never been much good at hiding your feelings, not just from me, but from the world at large. It has always been one of your most endearing and exasperating traits. Your thoughts are on your face right now, and I can tell that they are U-N-H-A-P-P-Y.

You feel as though Dimity and I have played a pretty mean trick on you and I can't blame you, because in a sense we have. But look at it this way: if I'd told you about everything, you'd know it all already and I'd be dead and that would be that. As it is, I may be dead, but you still have a lot to learn about me——the story continues, so to speak. I like the idea. I think you will, too, after you finish moping and feeling sorry for yourself.

You're probably wondering about the photograph. I am, too. That's why I'm giving it to you. This is serious, so I need your full attention. This is not something I can tell to Reginald.

Dimity said that she would tell you how we first met, and I'm sure she has. I'm equally sure that she hasn't told you the state she was in, that day at the zoo. Not to put too fine a point on it, she was a wreck.

She looked as though she hadn't eaten a solid meal or slept a good night's sleep in a month. The reason she ran into me was because she was walking around in a daze, only half aware of her surroundings. I took her back to her flat, got some tea and dry toast into her, then stayed with her until she fell asleep. I talked myself hoarse that evening, and the next, and gradually, over the course of a few weeks, I managed to coax her out of her shell. She talked about a lot of things after that, but she never mentioned what it was that had knocked her for such a loop.

After I got to know her better, I asked her about it. It was as though I'd slapped her. The color drained from her face, she said there were some things she couldn't speak of, even to me, and she made me promise never to ask her about it again. You know how I am about promises. I never asked her again, but I never ceased to wonder.

Dimity took me down to her cottage once, to show me the place where she'd grown up. While we were there, two of her neighbors pulled me aside. They were elderly and not very coherent, but I got the impression that Dimity had suffered some kind of nervous collapse the last time she'd been home. Apparently, they'd found her in the cottage one day, with photo albums strewn about her on the floor, mumbling to herself and clutching—you guessed it—this photograph.

They were convinced it had something to do with her condition, so they took it from her, then didn't know what to do with it. They were afraid to give it back to her, but they didn't want to destroy it, either, so they decided to pass it on to me for safekeeping. They said I was "what Dimity needed" and seemed to think I'd know the right time to return the photograph to her. I tried to explain about my promise, but they wouldn't take no for an answer.

So here I am, all these years later, still pondering the question of how an innocent-looking photograph could cause a woman like Dimity to fall apart. And why someone who opened her arms to the world kept one part of her life in darkness.

I'd like you to find out for me. I don't know how. I don't know where the picture was taken or by whom. The neighbors who gave it to me are no doubt dead and gone by now, so they won't be able to help you. It may even be that the answers died with Dimity, but if not, I know that my unstoppable baby girl will find them.

Why is it so important to me? I'm not sure. It's certainly too late to fix whatever it was that went wrong. But I can't help feeling that, whatever it was, it needs to be brought into the light. It can't hurt my friend now, and I'll rest easier, knowing you're looking for answers to questions I was never allowed to ask. You can tell me all about it the next time I see you.

And that's about all for now, except to tell you to scratch Reginald behind the ears for me. And to tell you that I love you very much. You will always be my favorite only child.

Mom

She almost tripped me up with that last paragraph—I guarantee that nothing turns on the waterworks faster than a dead parent telling you she loves you—and her mention of poor old Reginald nearly sent me running to the nearest tissue factory. But the story of the photograph put a halt to that. I picked it up and looked at it again, then looked down at the letters nestled together on the couch. All those years of friendship, and not one word about . . . it.

What had happened in that clearing? I studied the tree, tried to imagine how it would look today, if it hadn't been struck by lightning or chopped down or knocked over by the wind or . . . I stopped myself. That sort of thinking would get me nowhere.

I would go to the cottage. I would take care of Dimity's task, then turn the place inside out, if need be, looking for clues. I'd ask around the village, show everyone the photograph, and if that didn't work, I'd . . . I'd think of something else.

I would find out what had happened to Dimity, if I had to conduct a personal interview with every tree in the British Isles. I would find the answers to my mother's questions.

It was my last chance to do something right.

Six

$\mathscr{I}$ used the phone on the end table to call Willis, Sr., and he asked me to meet him in his office in half an hour. Standing at the tall windows in the parlor, I watched the gardener repair the damage from last night's unseasonable blizzard, kept an eye on the time, and tried to absorb what the letters had told me.

I suppose, somewhere in the back of my mind, there was a certain sense of disappointment. Surrounded as I was by the luxurious House of Willis, it was only natural to hope that my mother's wealthy friend had left me some small part of her estate. I certainly could have used it. Not that I was looking for a handout—Meg Thomson had tried to loan me money once and I had bitten her head off—but a small bequest for the daughter of a beloved friend? I could have accepted that.

Such minor regrets were overshadowed, however, by thoughts of the correspondence. That was a treasure beyond price. Where I would find a safe place to store forty years' worth of "long letters, short notes, and postal cards" from two voluble correspondents was a problem I'd solve when I got to it. For now, it was enough to know that, whatever else might happen, my mother's words would belong to me.

Sarah Bernhardt, indeed. My even-tempered mother had often teased me about being oversensitive and I was the first to admit that I sometimes let my emotions run away with me. So far, though, under what I thought were very challenging circumstances, I had kept them under control. I hoped she was proud of me for that, wherever she was.

I couldn't for the life of me imagine what kind of favor Dimity Westwood had in mind. A philanthropist had to be rich, after all, and if she could afford the long-term services of a firm like Willis & Willis, Dimity was surely rich enough to hire people to do whatever else needed doing. I had no special skills. I knew about old books, but there were all sorts of people who knew more about them than I did, especially in England. What could it be, then? Only time, and Willis, Sr., would tell.

I also counted on him to tell me how I was going to get to the cottage. The last time I'd looked, there hadn't been a huge selection of transatlantic bus routes, and the cost of flying over was more than my temp's wages could handle. But Dimity wouldn't have left me something I couldn't get to.

I wasn't sure if I should tell Willis, Sr., about the photograph. He might object to anything that took time away from carrying out Dimity's task. Then again, he might know something useful. I decided to wait and see. In the meantime, I'd wash my face and brush my hair and get myself ready for our meeting. I glanced down at my jeans and sighed—I was no doubt unique among Willis, Sr.'s well-heeled clientele. It was kind of him not to make me feel out of place.

I headed for the bathroom, got as far as the dressing room, and stopped dead in my tracks. The low shelves, empty that morning, now held shoes, women's shoes, five or six pairs of tasteful pumps and fashionable flats, and there were purses on the high shelves, tiny embroidered clutches, and shoulder bags in buttery leather. The racks were hung with dresses in dainty floral prints, silk blouses, pleated gabardine slacks, tweed blazers and skirts—all size eight.

I stared at them, openmouthed, as my blood pressure began to rise. I could almost hear it, like the faint whistle of a teakettle just coming to boil. So *that* was Bill's game, was it? I understood it all now: the irises, the star show, his father's books—the whole nine yards. Prince Charming bestows gifts on the wide-eyed beggar girl, dazzles her with his castle, then sweeps her off her feet with . . . *Had he picked out new underwear, too?*

The pent-up emotions of the past twenty-four hours fueled my indignation. Who was he to tell me what to wear? Willis, Sr., might know a thing or two about tailoring, but Bill looked as though he slept in his clothes. I looked upon those lovely dresses and thought only of the audacity, the gall, the sheer, unmitigated . . . Did he expect me to be *grateful*? I had never been so embarrassed in my life, and I was seriously annoyed with him for causing my humiliation.

A muffled knock sounded at the parlor door and when I opened it I found the object of my wrath standing there with frayed cuffs and bagged-out trousers, compounding his sins by looking extremely pleased with himself.

"How *dare* you," I snapped.

The smug look vanished.

"Come in," I said, "and sit down. There are a few things we need to get straight."

Bill sat on the edge of the couch and watched as I paced the room. In a small voice, he ventured, "You don't like the clothes?"

"Oh, they're beautiful," I said. "Just beautiful. I'm all set for the Governor's Ball." I closed in on him. "*Bill.* I don't *go* to the Governor's Ball. Where am I supposed to *wear* that stuff? To the *grocery?*"

"Well, I—" but he never had a chance. My wounded pride was on a rampage.

"But *you* wouldn't know about places like that," I said. "*You* have servants. Well, let me fill you in. The grocery is the place where you go when you have enough money to buy maybe three cans of tomato soup, right? It's the place where the express register is always just closing when you get there, so you and your tomato soup wind up in the regular checkout line, where you're invariably stuck behind the illiterate lady with the coupons for things that are *almost* the same as the things she has in her cart. And you have to stand there juggling soup cans while she argues every ounce, pound, liter, and gram, and you don't want to be *rude,* because she has blue hair and she's proba-bly living on dog food, but you also want to *scream,* because you'd think that just once she could manage to bring a coupon for the *right brand* of dog food. Heaven knows it's important to wear the proper dress for moments like that. That blue silk number in the back should be just right." When I paused to catch my breath, Bill made a brave attempt to rally.

"Now, Lori, I just thought that, when you went out, you might—"

"Go *out?* Like on *dates?* What makes you think I have time to go out on dates?" I took another deep breath and added, very evenly, "Thank you very much for your thoughtful gifts, but I'm afraid they don't suit my lifestyle." I strode to the door, then turned. "I'm going down to speak with your father. When I've gone, I'd be most grateful if you'd return everything to the shops. If it's all the same to you, Mr. Willis, I'd prefer to select my own wardrobe."

Willis, Sr., smiled at me from behind his desk as I entered the office, but his smile faded when he saw the look on my face.

"My dear Miss Shepherd," he said in alarm, "whatever is the matter?"

I closed the doors and strode restlessly over to the billowing fern in the corner. I plucked a small brown frond and crumbled it absently between my fingers. Keeping my back to the desk, I asked, "Do I look awful, Mr. Willis?"

"I beg your pardon?"

"Do I look like . . . like a wreck?"

"Miss Shepherd, I would never presume to—"

"I know," I said, holding perfectly still. "That's why I'm asking you."

When he failed to respond, I snuck a peek over my shoulder, then looked quickly back at the fern. His pained expression made me want to sink through the floor, but his voice was gentle when he began to speak.

"I would not put it quite that way, Miss Shepherd," he said. "I would say rather that you appear to have lived under a great deal of stress, and to have known too little joy as of late."

"That bad, huh?" Tears stung my eyes and I blinked them away.

"You misunderstand me, Miss Shepherd," said Willis, Sr. "Please allow me to make myself clear. My dear, to my eyes, you are lovely. Fatigued, yes, and under some strain, certainly, but quite charming nonetheless." He rose from his chair. "Please, Miss Shepherd, come and sit down." He gestured for me to join him on the couch, where he leaned back, tented his fingers, and stared silently at me for a few moments before going on. I kept my gaze fixed on his immaculate gray waistcoat.

"Miss Shepherd, I realize how unusual this experience must be for you. You have had quite a lot thrown at you in a very short period of time. You are no doubt feeling slightly overwhelmed by it all."

"Slightly," I agreed.

"It is only natural that you should. I confess, I can do little to remedy this. I can, however, assure you that I will fulfill my role as your legal adviser to the best of my ability. And, if you will permit me, I can do one more thing. I can offer the hope that you will someday look upon me as your friend." He lowered his eyes and added, "A somewhat antiquated friend, to be sure, but a friend with your interests at heart nonetheless."

I bit my lip to keep my chin from trembling. It had been a long time since I had let anyone say that to me, and a much longer time since I had let myself believe it. It was weak, it was childish, and it went against my better judgment, but I thought I might risk believing it now. I needed a friend. I needed someone I could talk to, someone I could trust in this . . . unusual situation.

If Willis, Sr., noticed my distress, he had the decency to move smoothly on to other things. He gathered some papers from his desk and returned with them to the couch. "Here we are," he said. "I trust you are prepared to proceed to the next step?"

"I'm ready when you are," I said, grateful to him for the change of subject.

"Excellent. Please feel free to stop me at any point, Miss Shepherd. I greatly dislike haste in these matters. It so often leads to misunderstandings." He straightened his waistcoat, then folded his hands atop the papers. "Shortly before her death, Miss Westwood collected the Aunt Dimity stories into a single volume, which she intended to publish posthumously."

"She's going to publish the Aunt Dimity stories?"

"That was her intent, Miss Shepherd. Arrangements have been made with a reputable publisher, and the illustrations are nearing completion."

"You mean, other people have read them already?"

"A small number of people, yes. My dear, does this trouble you?"

The sound of my mother's voice drifted through my mind. "I guess it does. Until yesterday evening I thought I was the only one who knew those stories. I guess I've always thought of them as *mine*."

"That," said Willis, Sr., "is undoubtedly why Miss Westwood wanted you and no one else to write an introductory essay for the volume."

"She did?" I looked at him in surprise. "Is that the favor she mentions in her letter?"

"It is. She wished for you to write an introduction focusing on the origins of the stories, which, according to Miss Westwood, are to be found in the collection of private correspondence now housed in her residence in England, near the village of Finch. I believe she refers to the correspondence in her letter to you?"

I nodded.

"You are to read the letters written by your mother and Dimity Westwood, locate within them the situations or characters or events that inspired the Aunt Dimity stories, and write about what you find." Willis, Sr., paused, then added softly, "I think I can understand your reluctance to have these stories published, Miss Shepherd. They must have been a treasured part of your childhood. But, my dear, you shall not lose the stories by sharing them."

Willis, Sr., would have made a brilliant teacher. He had a way of showing you things you should have seen for yourself, without making you feel like a fool. I would lose nothing by the stories' publication, and many children would gain a great deal. Aunt Dimity would come to life for them, too, and that was as it should be.

"You're right, Mr. Willis," I said sheepishly. "It's a fine idea. And I suppose they couldn't really publish the thing without me in it somewhere. I must be the world's greatest authority on Aunt Dimity."

"You are indeed," said Willis, Sr., with a contented nod. He glanced down at the paper on top of the stack, then continued. "You shall have one month—that is, thirty days from the time of your arrival at the cottage—in which to do the necessary research and writing. I shall contact you periodically to confer with you and to ask certain questions Miss Westwood has prepared."

"Questions? About what?"

"The questions concern the contents of both the letters and the stories, Miss Shepherd."

"I should be able to answer questions about the stories right now."

"Undoubtedly, but we shall follow Miss Westwood's wishes nonetheless. At the end of the month, if you have answered those questions satisfactorily and completed the introduction in the manner described by Miss Westwood, you shall receive a commission of . . . let me see . . ." He ran his finger down the sheet. "Ah, here it is." He looked up and smiled pleasantly. "You shall receive a commission of ten thousand dollars."

"*Ten thousand . . .*" My voice cracked. "Isn't that a bit much?" I added faintly.

"It is the value Miss Westwood placed on the task. It was, I understand, very close to her heart."

"It must have been." My mind flew to the stack of bills that was threatening to engulf my apartment at that very moment. I had expected to be paying them off with my Social Security checks, but now . . . *ten thousand dollars.* For one month's work. I sank back on the couch and raised a hand to my forehead.

Willis, Sr., peered at me worriedly. "Great heavens, I've done it again. Please, allow me to pour you a glass of sherry. You've gone quite pale."

While Willis, Sr., poured the sherry, I tried to gather my wits. It wasn't easy, since visions of hundred-dollar bills kept them fairly well scattered. But by the time he returned with the sherry, I had at least calmed down enough to listen attentively.

"Here you are, my dear. Drink that down while I continue." He waited until I'd taken a sip, then referred once more to his notes. "You need not depart for England until you are fully prepared to do so. Miss Westwood felt that you might require some time to take leave of your friends, make the necessary arrangements with your employer, and so on." Folding his hands, he added, "Miss Westwood also hoped that you would accept our hospitality and reside here at the mansion until it is time for you to leave."

"Is that a condition of the will?"

"No, Miss Shepherd, but it coincides with my own wishes. I should be only too happy to welcome you as a guest in my home for as long as you wish to stay." He leaned toward me and added confidentially, "It brings me great pleasure to have a fresh face in the house, especially one belonging to someone who is neither studying nor practicing the law."

I laughed. "I can understand that, Mr. Willis. Thank you, I'll stay, as long as it's no trouble."

"None at all." He consulted the notes and continued, "Funds have, of course, been made available to pay for your travel and for any expenses incurred before or during your visit to the cottage. These expenses need not, I might add, relate directly to the writing of the introduction. Miss Westwood wanted you to be able to concentrate, you see, and felt that you would be able to do so only if your ancillary needs and desires were satisfactorily met. Anything, therefore, that ensures your comfort and well-being shall be considered a necessary expense."

A bottomless expense account. I could pay the bills, take care of the rent, buy some new clothes—of my *own* choosing—without even touching the commission. I was so dazzled that I almost missed Willis, Sr.'s next words.

". . . also for your convenience, Miss Westwood specified that the arrangements for your trip and the disbursement of funds be directed by my son."

A mouthful of sherry nearly ended up on Willis, Sr.'s immaculate waistcoat.

"*Bill?*" I gasped.

"Indeed. Miss Westwood did not wish to trouble you with the day-to-day details of travel and finance. My son, therefore, shall be responsible for looking after you from now until you have completed your task. He shall supply your transportation, oversee your expenses, and accompany you to England to act as your . . . facilitator, for want of a better term." The expression on my face must have alarmed Willis, Sr., for he added reassuringly, "His role shall in no way limit your access to the funds, Miss Shepherd. You have only to ask, and you shall be given whatever you require."

"By Bill."

"Miss Westwood is quite specific on that point, yes."

"You mean that, without Bill, I can't do anything else?"

"I fear not."

"But why *him?*" I asked. "I'd much rather work with you."

"That is very kind of you, Miss Shepherd. I should be only too happy to be of service to you, but . . ." Willis, Sr., sighed. "I fear, alas, that my health will not permit it. I have for the past year been beset by some minor difficulties with—"

"Your heart," I broke in. "Bill told me about it—"

"Did he?" said Willis, Sr.

"This morning. And, like an idiot, I forgot. Of course you can't go off globe-trotting. Please—forget that I mentioned it." I scowled at my shoes for a second, then asked, "How much does Bill know about all of this?"

"I enlisted his aid in locating you, but other than that, I have told him nothing. Indeed, I have not yet informed him of the part he is to play in Miss Westwood's plan. I felt it would be best to withhold that information until I was certain of your participation." Willis, Sr., hesitated. "I do not wish to pry, Miss Shepherd, but do I detect a note of dismay?"

"Oh, yes," I said, my chin in my hands. "I think you could put it that way."

"Might I ask why?"

I turned to face him. "Do you know what your son did?"

"I tremble to think."

"He bought *clothes* for me! A whole closetful!" It sounded so trivial, now that I'd said it aloud, that I was afraid Willis, Sr., would laugh, but he seemed to understand exactly what I was getting at.

"Without consulting you? How very presumptuous of him." After a thoughtful pause, he added, "And how unlike him. If you will permit a personal observation, Miss Shepherd, my son has always been most reserved with the young ladies of his acquaintance."

"Reserved?" I said. "Bill?"

"I would go so far as to say he displays a certain degree of shyness in their company. I cannot imagine him selecting apparel for them." Willis, Sr., leaned toward me. "Tell me, has he done anything else you deem noteworthy?"

"He took me up on the roof this morning to look at a meteor shower."

Willis, Sr.'s jaw dropped. "He took you to Arthur's dome? Oh, but that is extraordinary. Unprecedented, in fact. The students have access to it, of course, but I have never known him to *invite* anyone up there, aside from myself. I cannot think why . . ." He frowned for a moment, clearly at a loss.

I wasn't at a loss. It stood to reason that Bill couldn't play Handsome Prince games with the rich and polished "young ladies of his acquaintance." What he needed was a Cinderella, a grateful orphan girl to mold as he pleased. Just thinking about it made my blood pressure rise all over again, but it wasn't something I could explain to his loving father.

"My dear Miss Shepherd," said Willis, Sr., finally, "I can offer no explanation for my son's curious behavior. I can only hope that you will believe me when I tell you that he has a good heart. I am sure he meant well, however clumsily he may have expressed himself.

"Be that as it may," he went on, "I am compelled to inform you that his actions do not constitute grounds for circumventing Miss Westwood's wishes. I confess that it saddens me, however, to think that my boy's presence has become intolerable to you——"

"That's not what I meant," I said hastily. "Your son isn't *intolerable,* Mr. Willis. He's just a little . . ."

"Rash?" suggested Willis, Sr.

"But in a thoughtful way," I assured him. "I'm sure that it's all a matter of . . . getting used to him."

Willis, Sr.'s face brightened. "I am so pleased to hear you say that, Miss Shepherd. You will proceed as planned, then? You will go to England and write the introduction? It meant so much to Miss Westwood."

"Of course I'll go," I said. "It means a lot to me, too."

"And you will accept my invitation to remain here as my guest?" he asked.

What could I do? Throw the old man's kindness back in his face? I nodded and he looked well pleased. He placed the papers on the coffee table and we sat in companionable silence. I was still somewhat dazed by the prospects that lay before me. The biggest decision I'd had to make lately was the number of books I'd allow myself to check out of the public library at one time. Now here I was, with an overseas trip, an unlimited expense account, and a chance to earn ten thousand dollars doing something I knew I would enjoy. I didn't know where to start. What did people *do* with expense accounts? I had no past experience to go on, but as I looked at Willis, Sr.'s patient smile, an idea began to take shape.

"Are you feeling okay, Mr. Willis?" I asked, twisting my hands nervously in my lap.

"How thoughtful of you to inquire," he said. "Yes, thank you, Miss Shepherd, I feel quite fit."

"Then would you . . . would you like to have dinner with me tonight?" I asked, adding hurriedly, "If you're not too busy, and if you don't have other plans, and if you're sure you're feeling—"

"Miss Shepherd," Willis, Sr., broke in gently, "I would be honored to accept your kind invitation." He placed a wrinkled hand on my fidgeting fingers, and I didn't have the slightest inclination to pull them away.

Seven

Willis, Sr., arranged for our dinner to be served in the large library on the ground floor, a room that might have been lifted, lock, stock, and bookplate, from one of the great English manor houses. "My great-uncle, Arthur Willis, saw an engraving of the library at Chatsworth," Willis, Sr., explained, "and decided to pattern his after it." The room was long and relatively narrow, with tall windows on one side and bookshelves on the other. A ladder and a narrow catwalk, resplendent in gold leaf, gave access to the highest shelves, and the ceiling was a marvel of sculpted plasterwork and medallion paintings.

We sat at a round table at one end of the room, I in my freshly laundered jeans and flannel shirt, and Willis, Sr., in a flawless charcoal-gray suit. He acknowledged my casual attire by slightly loosening the knot in his silk tie, and entertained me with talk of books and travel while the law students served our meal from the trolley Bill had used the night before. Midway through the fish course it occurred to me that, before going down to the cottage, I might visit the places in London my mother had visited during the war, as a sort of preamble to reading the letters and writing about the stories. It wasn't until the second sorbet that I got up the nerve to present it for Willis, Sr.'s appraisal. It received his full support.

I decided against telling him about the photograph. As gracious as he was, Willis, Sr., obviously felt that his first duty was to Dimity Westwood, which meant seeing to it that the introduction was completed on schedule. The sobering truth—the truth I couldn't share with him—was that I might not finish the introduction at all. One month was all the time I would have at the cottage, and it might not be enough time to do everything. My first duty was to my mother, and I didn't want to put Willis, Sr., in the position of having to disapprove of something I was determined to do anyway.

For the same reason, I couldn't tell Bill, either. I would have to get rid of him once we got to Finch, of course, send him to stay at a hotel or a local guest house, but that would be easy enough to do without arousing suspicion. If anyone would be sympathetic to a plea of decorum, it would be Willis, Sr. And, partners or not, I thought I knew who called the shots in the family firm.

Bill's behavior took a new and even stranger turn during the week we spent preparing for the trip.

The dressing room was empty when I returned to the guest suite after my dinner with Willis, Sr., but I was awakened the following morning by a scuffling noise in the hall. When I investigated, I found Bill and four staff members walking off with sixteen pieces of the most beautiful hand-rubbed leather luggage I had ever seen.

"More gifts?" I asked.

"I meant to head them off downstairs," said Bill, "but I was too late." He told the students to go ahead, then held up a particularly attractive garment bag. "You don't happen to like it, by any chance?"

"It's gorgeous, but no thanks," I said. "Every thief between here and Bangkok would find it irresistible."

"Right," he said, setting the bag on the floor. "What do you usually use, then?"

"Canvas carryalls," I replied. "Durable, lightweight, ordinary-looking, and when you're done with them, you roll them up and shove them in a drawer."

"Wouldn't nylon bags be lighter?" he asked.

"Yes, but they're harder to patch when they tear."

"Very practical," he observed.

"I'm a practical sort of person," I said.

"So I'm discovering." He shoved his hands in his pockets and rocked back on his heels. "Father told me about Dimity's plans, by the way. From this moment on, I am at your service. When would you like to get started?"

"Is ten too early for you?"

"Ten is perfect. Milady's carriage will await her at the appointed hour. Until then." He clicked his heels and executed a formal half bow, then picked up his share of the luggage and left.

I sighed and closed the door, wishing that someone would pull Bill aside and tell him that one simple offer of friendship was worth twenty Prince Charming routines.

For the next five days, Bill did everything but walk ten paces behind me. He was meek, he was polite, he was the very model of docility, but I didn't buy it for a minute. There were too many times when I caught him smiling to himself—as though he found his own performance vastly entertaining.

My "carriage" turned out to be Willis, Sr.'s Silver Shadow. Bill insisted that he was following his father's orders in using it, but I was not amused. It wasn't the car I minded so much. It was the little driving cap Bill wore, and the short woolen jacket, and the formal manner with which he opened the car door for me, as though he'd been rehearsing his role as chauffeur.

Our first stop was a local camping store, where I bought a pair of lightweight hiking boots—suitable for hill climbing—a durable down jacket, and a decent pair of jeans. I steered clear of anything fussy or feminine in order to demonstrate to Bill my idea of *useful* clothing. He kept his mouth shut and watched me like a hawk while I shopped, as though he were memorizing my every move. The salespeople treated him like a deaf-mute, nodding politely in his direction, but speaking only to me. It was mortifying, especially when he paid.

The next morning, I dropped by the temp agency to let them know that I would be unavailable for a while. They must have wondered why I'd bothered to give notice, once they'd ogled the Rolls, but I was burning no bridges. Bill continued to be on his best behavior, though he came close to going over the edge when he swept his cap off in a low bow to the women in the office and kissed my supervisor's hand.

That afternoon, when he introduced himself to my roommates as "Miss Shepherd's driver," I'd had enough. I made him hand over the checkbook and go wait in the car. I thought it was a perfect solution—I'd fill out the checks and he could sign them somewhere far away from me. Then I caught sight of him smiling his little smile and suspected that I had been outmaneuvered. It occurred to me—

fleetingly—that he might be aware of how reluctant I was to have him see my humble digs.

I spent two hours at my apartment, writing checks with such gay abandon that I broke out in a cold sweat at one point and had to call Willis, Sr., to get his okay before I could go on. When I finished, I gave my roommates my share of the rent, outlined the situation for them, and asked them to forward any calls or personal mail to the mansion until I returned. Since I got about as many phone calls as a Trappist monk, it didn't seem a lot to ask.

It took me twenty minutes to pack. When I finished, I sat down on my mattress beside my beat-up old canvas bags. The late afternoon sun filtered through the blinds, bathing the room in a muted gray light. The apartment was very quiet and my room looked very bare.

I didn't want to come back here. I would never admit it to Bill or to anyone else, but I didn't want the fairy tale to end. I wanted that ten thousand dollars so badly I could taste it. It would give me a chance to escape from the grind, to look for a real job, maybe buy some decent furniture. But if it came to a choice between earning the money and fulfilling my mother's request, I knew what I would choose. Ah, well, I thought, with no conviction at all, I had gotten used to doing without. I could get used to it all over again.

My gaze wandered the blank walls and came to rest on the closet door. Instantly, I was on my feet. I rescued Reginald's shoebox from the floor of the closet and looked in fondly at the ragged bits of pinkish-gray flannel.

"Mom says hello," I said softly. I reached in to touch a hand-stitched whisker. "Yes, Reginald, you're right. Things could be worse. At least both of my ears are still attached."

I put the box in my carry-on bag and went down the stairs and out into the first golden rays of sunset.

I also made time for a visit to Stan Finderman, my old boss. He lived in a restored eighteenth-century town house near the Gardner Museum and I found him at home, where he'd been working ever since his university office had burned to a crisp.

"Lori!" he boomed, standing on the doorstep. "How the hell are you and how's that punk who kidnapped you?" Stan had not approved of my move out of state. "Who's this?" he added, catching sight of Bill. "You finally get rid of that lunkhead husband of yours?"

Dr. Stanford J. ("Call me Stan") Finderman wasn't what most people thought of when they pictured a curator of a rare book collection. He was smaller than Mount Everest, but not by much, and his white hair was cropped in a no-nonsense crew cut. Like Willis, Sr., he was in his early sixties, but he could have snapped Willis, Sr., in two with one thumb and a finger. Nothing tickled Stan more than the fear-glazed eyes of less robust scholars ("pasty-faced wimps") who were meeting him for the first time.

They soon found out that Stan's brain was as imposing as his brawn. He had served in the Navy during World War II, gone through college on the GI Bill, and left the rest of his class squinting in the glare of his brilliance. If people wondered why he had gone into the rare book field—instead of, say, weight lifting or alligator wrestling—they had only to see him cradle a book in his meaty paws, and they stopped wondering. Books were Stan's first, last, and only love.

He seemed in remarkably good spirits for a man who'd seen his life's work go up in smoke. As we followed him down the narrow hallway, I explained the change in my marital status—"Best damned decision you ever made!"—and introduced Bill, then asked him about the tragedy.

"Best damned thing that ever happened," he bellowed. "Sued the company that made the damned machine, the bastards settled out of court, and now I've got more damned money than you can shake a stick at! Look at this!" He waved us into his box-littered living room. "Been trawling all winter and hauled in some beauties. Should be able to move 'em onto the shelves by next spring—if the goddamned builders get off their goddamned asses."

He gave Bill a measuring look, then leaned in close to him. "What do you know about books?" he demanded.

"Not a thing," Bill replied cheerfully.

I held my breath, anticipating an explosion. My old boss had no use for nonbibliophiles, and no reservations about telling them so, emphatically. I tensed when Stan poked Bill in the shoulder, then watched dumbfounded as Stan's face broke into a wide grin.

"I like a man who knows his limitations," said Stan. "You want a beer?"

"Love one, Dr. Finderman."

"And you can cut that crap. Call me Stan."

"Whatever you say, Stan." To complete my amazement, Bill tapped Stan lightly on the shoulder, adding, "Within reason."

Stan's eyes narrowed, but all he said was, "I like this one, Lori." He put his arm around Bill's shoulders and walked him over to a partially opened box near the leather sofa. "Park yourself here and have a look at this while I grab the beers. Just got some goodies from Fitz in Japan. He's a helluva judge of rice paper, for a goddamned Scot."

It was an hour before I could get a word in edgewise.

I had wanted to speak with Stan privately, a difficult enough proposition if anyone was within shouting distance; an impossible one with a third party in the same room. When I finally got a chance to speak, I gave Bill a stern look and said, "What we're about to discuss is supposed to be a surprise. If your father gets wind of it, I'll—"

"Lay off the guy, Lori," Stan said. "He's a lawyer, for Christ's sake. He knows how to keep his mouth shut. What's the big secret, anyway?"

I explained what I wanted, and as I'd expected, Stan knew where to get it. He even phoned ahead to make sure it would be available before accompanying us to the front door.

"I think you picked a winner this time, Lori," he said.

"Stan, Bill isn't—" I began, but Stan was already clapping Bill on the shoulder.

"You look after her, Willis," he said, "or you'll have me to answer to."

Bill very wisely said nothing.

A short drive took us to a cramped and dimly lit shop owned by a Mr. Trevor Douglas, purveyor of antique maps. Stan's call had produced the usual results and Mr. Douglas had already unearthed a beauty for my inspection: a delicate and intriguingly incomplete depiction of the Arctic wilderness printed in 1876; the fruit of many daring gambles, broken dreams, and lost lives. Mr. Douglas agreed to have it framed and delivered to the mansion as soon as possible. The price was daunting, but I considered the map to be a very necessary expense. Nothing would ensure my peace of mind as effectively as the thought of Willis, Sr.'s pleasure when he opened this package.

We were breakfasting with Willis, Sr., in the small dining room the following day when Bill looked up from his toast and marmalade. "Lori, I've been thinking. You've been to your apartment and your agency and you've said good-bye to your old boss, but what about your friends?"

"My friends?"

"Don't you want to say good-bye to them, too? Or at least tell them what's going on?"

"Well, I . . ." I fiddled with my eggcup, not knowing what to say. I had lost track of most of my friends over the past year.

"Yes, Miss Shepherd," Willis, Sr., joined in, "you must not allow your natural diffidence to prevent you from visiting your friends before you leave. It is quite in keeping with Miss Westwood's wishes." Father and son stared at me, their heads tilted at identical angles, until I felt like an antisocial geek.

"There is one person I'd like to see," I admitted finally, "but she doesn't live in Boston."

"Doesn't matter," said Bill.

I looked to Willis, Sr., and he nodded.

"Okay, then," I agreed, "I'll give her a call."

Meg Thomson was a short, unrepentantly heavyset woman, with an abrupt manner and a mile-wide mothering streak. If Meg thought you needed to hear something for your own good, you would hear it, whether you wanted to or not. And she was fiercely loyal. She lived in Maine, in a small coastal town about a hundred miles north of Boston, where she and her partner, Doug Fleming, owned a strange and wonderful art gallery. Doug lived in an apartment above the shop, but Meg had a ramshackle old house overlooking the beach.

The gallery specialized in science fiction and fantasy art, and touring the maze of paintings and sculptures was like traveling through a world of dreams made real. The business was usually on the verge of bankruptcy, but that never seemed to bother Meg. She had found where she wanted to be in life and she regarded the occasional scramble for rent money as just another dash of the spice that kept her life from getting too bland.

"Meg?" I said when I heard her voice. "It's me, Lori. Think you could put up a couple of houseguests?"

"I'll drive down tomorrow and pick you up," she replied without missing a beat.

"No need. I have a car." I smiled to myself and added, "A Rolls-Royce."

That did slow her down, but only for a minute.

"Okay, Shepherd. But if this Rolls-Royce of yours crashes and I don't get to hear the rest of the story, I'll never speak to you again."

I told her I'd be up the next day, sent my best wishes to Doug, and packed my bag.

Eight

Between traffic jams, detours, and a scenic route designed by a civil engineer with homicidal tendencies, Bill and I didn't reach the gallery until late afternoon the next day. There was no answer when I rang Doug's bell and the gallery was locked up tight, so we headed out to Meg's beach house. Bill parked the Rolls in her driveway and unloaded our bags while I ran up the stairs and banged on the screen door. Meg opened it, and I pointed over my shoulder.

"Want to take a picture?" I asked.

"I never doubted you," she said. "But who's that carrying the luggage, your manservant? Does he do windows?"

"It's a long story, Meg," I murmured.

"I'll bet," she replied, elbowing me in the ribs. She turned and hollered over her shoulder. "Doug! They're here!"

Doug Fleming was slender, balding, bespectacled, and gay. He and Meg had been lovers in college, and when that hadn't worked out, they had become best friends and, eventually, business partners. Their partnership was a finely tuned balancing act: where Meg was blunt and bossy, Doug was tactful and diffident. When it came to compassion, however, they were evenly matched; I wasn't the only friend they had helped through tough times.

I gave Doug a hello hug when he appeared, introduced Bill, then followed Meg inside, pausing in the living room to say hello to Van Gogh, Meg's one-eared cat, who was perched in his usual place atop the bookcase. Bill put our bags beside the couch, reached up to give Van Gogh a scratch behind the ear, and we all ended up in Meg's kitchen.

Since Meg only did housework when she was in a grumpy mood, I was relieved to see dishes in the sink and art catalogs stacked helter-skelter on every horizontal surface. Bill cleared off a chair for me, then stood behind it while Doug and Meg filled me in on the latest gallery news.

"We closed up shop early today to celebrate your visit," Doug concluded.

"But not early enough to get any food in the house," said Meg. "You want to hit King's Café?"

"I've got a better idea," said Bill. All eyes turned to him. "Why don't you three talk while I make dinner?"

"Sounds good to me," said Doug, "but I'll lend a hand in the kitchen, if you don't mind. I think these two want to get down to some serious gossiping."

Bill scanned the kitchen, then fixed his gaze on Meg's portly form. "Linguini," he said. "Garlic bread. Caesar salad, heavy on the anchovies. Cheap red wine. A nice, light, chocolate soufflé for dessert. And . . . maybe some Amaretto with the coffee."

"Shepherd," said Meg, "you'd better marry this guy."

"Oh, she will," said Bill.

"What?" I squeaked. Meg grabbed my arm and Doug all but shoved Bill out the kitchen door.

"We'd better get to the grocery before it closes," Doug urged.

"The grocery?" Bill's voice came through the open window. "Is that where they have the tomato soup?"

If Meg had let go of my arm, I would have gone straight out the window after him.

"Deep breaths, Shepherd," she murmured. "Deep breaths. Come on out on the porch. I think you need some fresh air."

"So let me see if I've got this straight," said Meg.

It had taken her a while to get a complete sentence out of me, but when she did, the whole story had come tumbling out, everything that had happened since the letter from Willis & Willis had arrived. A sense of calm had settled over me once I'd off-loaded the story, and I sat in a chair on the covered porch, Van Gogh purring drowsily in my lap, listening to the surf crash against the rocks below, and watching the sky. Dark clouds were moving in, lit now and then by flashes of lightning. A storm was brewing out at sea.

"You're ready to throw away ten grand looking for a needle in a haystack," Meg summarized, "but it's a needle your mother wants found, so I can understand that. You two always were pretty tight. I like the stuff about the letters, too."

"They're in a cottage," I said, "near a place called Finch." A dreamy smile crept across my face. "A cottage in England. Isn't that a kick? I can't wait to see what it looks like."

"Maybe you already know what it looks like," said Meg.

"How could I? It's not in the photograph, if that's what you mean. I went over the thing with a magnifying glass and there are no houses in sight." Van Gogh yawned and began licking my hand, and Meg directed her next comment to him.

"She sure can be thick at times, eh, Van? In fact, if I didn't know better, I'd say she had the brains of a lungfish." She leaned toward me, her elbows on her knees. "Now, think, Shepherd. In all those Aunt Dimity stories, didn't maybe just one include a pretty little cottage? C'mon, now, think."

I didn't have to think. Meg was right. *Aunt Dimity's Cottage.* If I closed my eyes I could almost see the lilacs and the slate roof (which my child self had pictured as a blackboard tent) and the foul-tempered cat who had driven Aunt Dimity to distraction. Suddenly I knew exactly what the cottage looked like, right down to the cushions in the window seat.

"Lilacs," I murmured. "There were white lilacs at the funeral, just like the ones at the cottage."

"I thought so," said Meg, with a satisfied nod. "No surprise, really. Dimity Westwood wrote her life into the stories. It's been known to happen." Meg leaned back against her cushions and looked out over the ocean. The jagged bolts of lightning were almost constant now, and thunder competed with the booming surf. A freshening breeze ruffled the spiky hair on the top of Meg's head as she reached down beside her chair.

"It's cooling off—better cover up." She tossed one of her blankets to me.

Meg's "blankets" were her own personal works of art, hand-knitted afghans so soft and beautiful that I flinched whenever I saw them piled in haphazard heaps around the house. "I make them to be used," Meg growled at anyone who dared to comment. I just shook mine out and draped it over my legs and the drowsy lapcat.

Meg snugged her own blanket in place, then frowned. "What I *don't* get is why you're so ticked off at Bill. He'll do whatever you want him to do. He's well educated, polite, filthy rich, and not at all bad-looking." Meg curled her legs under her and rested her chin on her hand. "Gee, that's enough to ruin anyone's day. My heart goes out to you. I think you need your head examined, Shepherd."

"Thanks, Meg. I knew I could count on you."

"Sorry, Shepherd, but he just doesn't strike me as the Svengali type. I watched him back there in the kitchen. He never took his eyes off of you. Okay, so maybe he made a bad joke about the forbidden subject of marriage, but I'm sure that's all it was—a joke."

"I'm tired of being the butt of his jokes, Meg," I said heatedly. "I'm tired of having my leg pulled, and I am *sick* and tired of him playacting and goofing around and smirking behind my back and . . . What are you looking at?"

"You. I haven't seen you this riled up in a long time."

"So?"

Meg continued to stare at me intently. She opened her mouth as if to say something, then closed it again and shook her head. "Nope. Not this time, Shepherd. This time you figure it out for yourself."

Before I could respond, the porch door opened and Doug came out, accompanied by the delicious aroma of garlicky tomato sauce. "Sorry to interrupt," he said, "but I can't find the cheese grater."

"Have you checked the garage?" asked Meg. "Never mind—let me see if I can find it. I'll be right back, Shepherd."

Van Gogh decided the storm was too close for comfort and scooted in after them, leaving me alone on the porch. As soon as the door had closed, a few fat drops hit the roof overhead; then the rain came rushing down, enclosing the porch in flickering, translucent walls. I got up from my chair and stood with my hands on the railing, spellbound. I didn't hear the porch door open once more.

"I'm sorry," said Bill, and I came out of my reverie, startled to find him standing beside me.

"I'm sorry," he repeated. "What I said before—it was out of line. I embarrassed you in front of your friends and I should never have done that. I apologize."

For a moment—one short moment—it was as though I could see Bill, really see him, for the first time. He wasn't such a Handsome Prince, after all. He wasn't young and dashing. He had no jutting jaw, no aristocratic nose, no piercing blue eyes, and not even a hint of flaxen hair. His nose was far from aquiline, in fact, and although his beard disguised it, his chin seemed to be a bit on the receding side. His neatly trimmed hair was more gray than anything else and behind his glasses, his eyes were a warm brown. He wasn't handsome in a classic way; but then, I'd never trusted classic faces. In that brief moment, it struck me that his was a face I could trust. A Handsome Prince is in the eye of the beholder, I mused silently, and I'm having no difficulty picturing Bill in full armor. I gulped and chased the image from my mind at sword-point.

"That's okay," I said stiffly, tightening my grip on the railing.

His shoulders slumped. He gave a soft sigh and looked out over the rain-swept sea.

"Really, Bill. It's no big deal." I glanced up at him and gently bumped his arm with my elbow. "I know how hard it can be to pass up a good opening."

"Do you?" said Bill. He reached over and brushed his fingertips across the back of my left hand. "I promise you, it won't happen again."

Between the rush of the rain and the pounding of my heart, I scarcely heard Doug's voice from the doorway. "I've tossed the salad," he announced. "And Meg says that if we don't eat pronto, she's going to chew a leg off the kitchen table."

For the rest of the evening, Bill behaved like a normal human being. He bantered with Meg, discussed the art market with Doug, played cat games with Van Gogh, and stopped treating me like visiting royalty. He even went to bed early so that my friends and I could have some time to ourselves. When we left the next day, he went so far as to let me forget my bag. Meg came puffing out to the car with it at the last minute.

"Look, Shepherd," she said, "I know you don't want to sully your gorgeous vehicle with this crummy piece of canvas, but I don't want it cluttering up my immaculate domain, either." She dumped it in the backseat behind Bill as Doug ran down the stairs.

"You be sure to write to us from England," he said.

"Waste of time," said Meg.

Doug and I looked at her in surprise.

"With your expense account," she explained, "you can afford to call."

I hugged the two of them, climbed into the car, and began the drive home.

It wasn't until we were stuck in a long line of cars waiting for a truck-load of fertilizer to be cleared from the interstate—which Bill had taken to avoid the tortuous scenic route—that I began to consider what Meg had hinted at. Was I riled up over nothing? I could see that I had been a bit defensive with Bill, but defense mechanisms hadn't evolved because it had been a slow Thursday afternoon. Fear was essential to self-preservation. It had worked for our caveman ancestors, and who was I to argue with history?

Still, it was possible that Bill's intentions had been good all along, and it did seem odd to be afraid of kindness. It was definitely not a survival trait.

As we crawled past the aromatic accident scene, Bill touched a button on the dashboard and my window hummed shut. I glanced at him, then closed my eyes and leaned back, feigning sleep. I had some serious thinking to do and I wanted no distractions.

Willis, Sr.'s map was waiting for me in the guest suite when I got back. It had been well padded and securely wrapped in brown paper, and a note from Trevor Douglas had been placed beside it on the coffee table. I dropped my bag on the floor and picked up the note, expecting it to contain the usual polite business phrases. Instead, Mr. Douglas had written:

Please thank Bill for directing me to that woodcarver friend of his. The man is a genius. I'll be sure to send more work his way.

Woodcarver friend? I put the note back on the table. Worried, I propped the package on the couch, tore off the wrapping paper, removed the padding, and stood back to see what Bill had done now. I stood there for a long time.

Trevor Douglas had not spoken lightly. Whoever had done this work *was* a genius. In almost no time at all, he had created a frame that was as subtle and intricate as the map itself: a two-inch band of polished wood carved with a frieze of animals—beavers, squirrels, raccoons, and other small creatures of the North American woods—linked by oak leaves and acorns, pine cones and needles. When I ran my fingers over the surface I could feel the care that had gone into its creation.

The phone rang.

"Hello," said Bill. "Thought I'd call to let you know that Father has planned a farewell luncheon for us tomorrow at two, in the small dining room. 'Fortification,' he called it, 'against the trials of airline fare.' Can you make it?"

"Sure, I can make it," I said. "And, uh, Bill—the map has arrived."

"Has it?"

"I'm looking at it right now," I said. "The frame is . . . it's beautiful, Bill. It's perfect. I'm . . ."

"I've come up with a scheme for giving it to Father. I can put it on his desk in the office tomorrow while you're saying good-bye, so he'll find it after we've gone. I think he'd prefer it that way. He's not fond of public displays of affection, you know."

"Then that's what we'll do," I agreed. "And Bill, I . . . I just want to say that . . ." I took a deep breath, then chickened out completely. "Trevor Douglas asked me to thank you for telling him about the woodcarver."

There was a prolonged silence on the line.

"Thanks for the message, Lori," Bill said at last. "I'll see you at lunch." And he hung up.

Unsettled, I cleared up the wrapping paper, then carried my canvas bag into the bedroom to unpack. "Why couldn't you just thank him?" I muttered fretfully, then paused in surprise as I opened the bag. A sheet of sketching paper was lying where my sweater had been. A single sentence from Meg was scrawled across it: *Your clothes are in the mail.* I flashed back to her lugging the bag to the car before I left. Sneaky, sneaky, I thought, then caught my breath when I saw what lay beneath the sketching paper.

There, folded with uncharacteristic care, was one of Meg's blankets. It was one I'd never seen before, done in rich, muted shades of gold and green and lilac and deep purple, like the hills of Scotland in full heathery bloom. I pulled it out and held it to my face and it was as soft as a baby's kiss, scented with salt air and the whisper of rain. How she had achieved that last effect, I had no idea, but it sent me spinning back to that stormy evening on her porch.

Almost without thinking, I touched the back of my left hand. It seemed to be tingling.

Nine

I spent the next morning browsing through Willis, Sr.'s books and packing my few bags. There was no need to hurry. The only thing left on my agenda was our bon voyage luncheon. I reread the letters from Dimity and my mother, paused to examine the photograph once again, then put them all into my carry-on bag along with Reginald.

I wasn't sure what to do with Meg's blanket. It was too bulky to fit in my carry-on and too precious to pack with my clothes; I quailed at the thought of some overworked baggage handler sending it to London, Ontario. I didn't want to leave it behind, either, but I didn't know what else to do. I presented the problem to Willis, Sr., when we met in the small dining room that afternoon, and his solution was simplicity itself.

"Leave it upstairs for now," he suggested. "I'll have one of the staff fetch it later and we'll send it to London by courier. It will be at the cottage when you arrive.

"I'm sorry to say that my son will be unable to join us," he continued. "He is rather busy, I'm afraid, putting his work in order before his departure. Please, sit here, Miss Shepherd, and I shall ring for the first course. Do you care for asparagus?"

It was a leisurely meal and Willis, Sr., was a charming host, as always. I brought up the subject of the Northwest Passage and he took it from there, regaling me with stories of the bravery—and foolishness—of the men who had risked their lives in search of it. Two hours later, as we lingered over the raspberry tarts, he returned to more familiar terrain.

"You may be interested to know, Miss Shepherd, that I have contacted the cottage's caretakers, Emma and Derek Harris, to let them know you are coming. The Harrises are a most pleasant couple. They knew Miss Westwood, of course, and were quite helpful during the renovation of the cottage. A few minor improvements," he added, "undertaken by Miss Westwood some time ago, to bring the cottage into the twentieth century."

I pictured a white-haired couple keeping a watchful eye on the cottage and became suddenly alert. "Do they live nearby?" I asked.

"I believe so," said Willis, Sr. "If I recall correctly, theirs is the next house up the road."

That made them Dimity's neighbors. Could the Harrises be the kindly old couple who had come to Dimity's aid? It seemed unlikely. If they had been elderly forty years ago, they'd be tombworthy by now. I would have questioned Willis, Sr., further, but Bill chose that moment to burst into the room, looking harassed.

"Change of plans, Lori," he said. "We're going to have to leave sooner than I'd expected." He glanced at his watch. "Immediately, in fact. Our flight isn't until seven, but Tom Fletcher tells me that the new security procedures for overseas flights can eat up a lot of time. Father, I'm bringing Tom out to the airport with me so I can finish some memos on the Taylor case. Aside from that, my desk is clear."

"You'd best be off, then," said Willis, Sr. "I shall meet you at the front entrance in, let us say, ten minutes?"

"Fine," said Bill. "What a day. . . ." He ran a hand through his already disheveled hair as he left the room.

Willis, Sr., folded his napkin and placed it beside his plate, then withdrew a flat, rectangular package from the inside pocket of his suitcoat. It was wrapped in gold foil.

"It seems that I must give you this now, Miss Shepherd. I do hope you will find it useful."

"Oh, but you shouldn't have. . . ." Taking the package from him, I peeled away the gold foil. "Honestly, you've already gone out of your way to . . ." I faltered when I saw what he had given me. "A map," I said, a bit unsteadily.

"A topographic map," corrected Willis, Sr. "My son happened to mention your purchase of walking shoes, and I thought you might be considering a foray into the local countryside during your stay. If so, you will find this map most helpful. Have you ever used a topographic map?"

"No," I said, "I've always hiked along posted trails."

"You'll pick it up in no time. You see, it shows the natural features and the elevations of the land surrounding the cottage. Here, I'll show you where the cottage is. . . ." Willis, Sr., opened the map and gave me a crash course in how to read it. When he finished, I reached out and squeezed his hand.

"This is a lovely present," I said. "Thank you."

"Not at all. I am very pleased that you like it." He sighed contentedly. "I have a great fondness for maps."

I raced up to the guest suite, hoping to catch Bill before he descended the hidden staircase with Willis, Sr.'s map. I wanted to show him what his father had given me—the irony was too delicious to keep to myself—but he had already come and gone by the time I got there, taking my bags as well as the map. I put Meg's blanket on the coffee table in the parlor, then went back down to meet Willis, Sr., at the front door.

"Do you have everything you need, Miss Shepherd?" he asked.

"I do now," I said, brandishing his gift.

"I shall telephone you regularly with Miss Westwood's questions—though I confess I should probably do so in any case."

"We'll be happy to hear from you," said Bill, joining us in the doorway. "You take care of yourself while I'm gone, Father. No wild parties, no rowdiness, or I'll have to come home and give you a stern lecture." He gripped his father's hand, hesitated, then leaned over and hugged him. Willis, Sr., stiffened for a moment, then raised a tentative hand to pat his son's back. Before either one of them could say a word, Bill turned and made his way to the car.

"Extraordinary," Willis, Sr., murmured.

"Thank you for everything," I said. "I'm going to miss you, you know. I'll talk to you soon."

"Soon," he agreed. I started down the steps. "And Miss Shepherd," he added, "I shall miss you, too."

Bill dictated memos until the last boarding call and by the time I'd stowed my carry-on bag under the seat in front of me, fastened my seat belt, and declined the free champagne, he'd fallen asleep. I was more than a little disappointed. I had spent a restless night gearing myself up for a heartfelt expression of gratitude for the exquisite frame, I'd waited all day to deliver it, and now it looked as though I would have to go on waiting.

Still, he did seem exhausted, as though he'd been on the go since dawn. He had spent so much time with me during the past week that I had forgotten about his other responsibilities. Apparently he had, too, and had tried to cram them all into a single marathon day. Once we were airborne, I called a flight attendant over and asked for a blanket. Bill didn't stir so much as an eyelid when I tucked it in around him.

I was much too keyed up to sleep, so I spent the time leafing through magazines and reading the novel I had brought along. After a while, I simply gazed out of the window at the moonlit clouds. I imagined Willis, Sr., examining his map, perhaps asking a law student to fetch a book or two down from the small library. I smiled again when I remembered his going-away gift to me. The smile grew broader when I thought of his characteristically precise description of it: "A topographic map . . . It shows the natural features and the elevations of the land surrounding the cottage."

The natural features and elevations . . .

With a sharp glance to make sure Bill was still asleep, I reached into my bag and pulled out the photograph, kicking myself for not having thought of this sooner.

A small clearing on a hill overlooking a broad valley. Beyond the valley, a series of hills, all of them of uniform height and shape. Excited now, I took out the topographic map. It would be child's play to locate the clearing if it was anywhere near the cottage.

Except that the cottage was smack-dab in the middle of the Cotswolds, which meant that it was *surrounded* by hills and valleys, and I hadn't learned enough from Willis, Sr.'s short lesson to be able to distinguish one hill from another. As soon as I opened the map, I saw that there were at least a dozen places that seemed to meet my requirements. I pored over the maze of curving lines, as though staring at it would force it to yield up its secrets, until Bill's voice broke my concentration.

"Planning a walking tour?" he asked, peering at the map with great interest. A scant two days ago, I would have bristled and told him to mind his own business. Now I tilted the map so he could see it better.

"A bon voyage present, from your father," I explained.

"You're kidding." He shook his head in disbelief. "Did you manage to keep a straight face?"

"More or less. Well, I mean, you're supposed to grin when you get presents, aren't you?"

"I wish we'd hidden a camera in the office. I would love to have seen his face when he saw *his* map."

"Thanks for remembering to smuggle it down." I refolded the topographic map, trying to recall the words I'd rehearsed the night before. "And, Bill, about the frame. I just want to say that—"

"What's this?" Bill was folding the blanket I had put over him, but he stopped and reached for something on the floor. When he sat up again, he was holding the photograph. "Is it yours?"

I nodded, too shocked by my own carelessness to speak.

"It must have fallen when you moved the map. Very pretty. Where is it?"

"England," I said. "It's . . . a place my mother visited. During the war."

"It must mean a lot to you," said Bill. "I have my mother's photo albums up in my rooms, and I go through them every once in a while. Do you do that?" He handed the photograph to me. I put it and the map in my carry-on and zipped the bag securely before answering.

"No," I replied, in a tone that persuaded most people to drop the subject.

"It was hard for me at first, too," he said. "I'd just turned twelve. I was away at school when the news came—she'd been hit by a bus and killed instantly. That's one of the reasons Father doesn't care for public transportation." He gave me a sidelong look. "I wasn't making that up, you know.

"It's never easy to lose a parent," he continued, "but at that age . . ." He creased the folds of the blanket carefully between his finger and thumb. "That's when I claimed Arthur's dome for my own. I think

part of me believed that if I looked hard enough through the telescope, I'd be able to find her." He unbuckled his seat belt. "Thanks for
covering me up, by the way. I'd hate to arrive in London with the snif-
fles." He stood up and stashed the blanket in an overhead bin.

"You're welcome." I hoped the interruption might turn his mind
to other things, but when he sat down again, he picked up where he'd
left off.

"When I went back to school after the funeral I felt like a freak.
The faculty had briefed the other boys not to say anything that might
upset me, so they ended up not saying anything at all. It confused the
hell out of me, as though my mother had done something that couldn't
be mentioned in polite company."

"You didn't want to talk about it, did you?" I said.

"No, but I didn't want a hush to fall over the room every time the
word 'mother' came up. It was a relief when Father pulled me out of
classes to go with him to England."

"That's when you met Dimity." I began to pay closer attention.

"We stayed at her town house in London. It was a fantastic place,
and I had the run of it. I spent most of my time in the attics, going
through dozens of dusty crates. I found gramophone records,
kaleidoscopes—even an old cat's-whisker radio that still worked.
And Dimity was . . . I don't know what I'd have done without her.
She didn't tiptoe around the subject. We'd be in the walled garden
and she'd ask what flowers my mother liked best. Then she'd fill bas-
kets with them and put them all around the house, just like that, as
though it was the most normal thing in the world. And every night,
she told me stories."

"Aunt Dimity stories?"

"No," said Bill, with a brief smile. "As far as I know, those stories
were created exclusively for you. Mine had a different heroine
entirely."

"But they helped, those stories?" I was intrigued in spite of
myself.

"Yes. They helped." He was silent for a moment. "I'd like to read
your stories someday. Perhaps we can work an exchange. How about
it?" He nudged my arm. "I'll tell you mine if you'll tell me yours."

"Only if you behave yourself," I said.

"I am a paragon of good behavior," he replied. "Father would have sent a chaperone to stand guard over you at the cottage otherwise. I was planning on staying there, if it's okay with you. There's plenty of room, apparently, and it'll be that much easier for me to run errands for you. Father suggested that I check into a local hotel, but I convinced him that his ideas of propriety weren't exactly au courant. We're hardly a pair of teenagers, are we?"

The challenge in his eyes was more than I could resist—and if necessary, I could send him on some extremely time-consuming errands. With a toss of the head, I replied, "Fine with me, as long as I can get my work done."

"You won't know I'm there." He took a fountain pen and a small, leatherbound notebook out of his pocket. "As long as we're discussing details of the trip, there are a few questions I'd like to ask before we land. Father said that your mother met Dimity Westwood in London during the war. Is that right?"

"Yes," I said. "My mother was sent over with a team of advisers before we'd even declared war on Germany, and she stayed on until VE Day."

"What did she do?"

"She was a clerk, a secretary—a paper-shuffler, as she put it. Now that I know about Dimity I'd like to see the city the way they saw it, go to the places they went."

"Such as?" He uncapped the pen and opened the notebook.

"Such as . . . Well, some of this may not make sense to you," I said. "They aren't places usually associated with the Second World War."

"But they *are* places you associate with your mother."

"She tried to see everything. You remember the story I told you and your father the night I arrived at the mansion? The one about the torch?" Harrod's went into the notebook, along with the zoo, the Tate Gallery, St. Paul's Cathedral, and several other museums and monuments that didn't require explanation. When I had run out of places, Bill capped his pen, then returned it and the notebook to his pocket.

"We'll see what we can do," he said.

I stifled a jaw-cracking yawn. "We may have to wait until tomorrow to start. I can feel jet lag setting in already."

"This isn't your first trip overseas?" Bill asked.

"Hardly," I replied. "But don't get me started on that. I've been known to bore strong men to tears with my hitchhiking stories."

He pulled a large white handkerchief from his breast pocket and regarded me expectantly.

"So this will be my fourth visit to London," I concluded. "The first was during the summer after my freshman year in college. I spent a week there that time, crashing in my sleeping bag on the floor of a flat belonging to two guys I'd met on the road. The second time was with my former husband. By then I'd had enough of sleeping on floors, so we booked a room at a B & B. It turned out to be an Earl's Court special, though, complete with an uncloseable window overlooking a train yard, and a mattress that sagged to the floor, so I ended up sleeping on the floor again anyway."

"You're joking," said Bill. "Exaggerating, at least."

"I am not. I had to hook my leg over the side of the bed to keep from rolling down into the middle. But we learned. The next time we went, we booked a room at a clean and quiet guest house in Sussex Gardens. Even with a bath up the hall, we thought it was heaven." I rested my head against the back of the seat.

Bill went through the motions of wringing out his handkerchief, then tucked it back into his pocket.

"Where are we staying this time?" I asked, closing my eyes.

"A hotel," he said. "Father and I stay there when we're in town. Dimity recommended it to us, in fact. It's a nice place. Clean. Quiet."

Ten

When the liveried doorman trotted out to open the door of our limousine, I began to suspect that Bill had indulged in some serious understatement. When I found myself standing beneath the venerable forest-green awning of the Flamborough Hotel, I knew it, and succumbed to momentary panic. There I was, wearing jeans which, although new, were still *jeans,* for pity's sake, about to walk into one of the world's most genteel hotels. The regular residents would probably strain their eyebrows.

"Clean and quiet, huh?" I said under my breath.

"Private baths, too," Bill murmured.

"Oh, goody. Now I feel right at home." I averted my eyes when my decrepit canvas bags were pulled from the limo, and stared when they were followed by an unfamiliar set of royal blue canvas carryalls. Bill saw what had caught my attention.

"Like my new luggage?" he asked as we entered the lobby. "Wonderful stuff, canvas. Durable, lightweight, easy to repair . . ."

I groaned inwardly. Evidently Bill had changed hats again. The amiable traveling companion was gone, the joker was back, and there was nothing I could do about it—except gird myself to face whatever other surprises he had in store in London.

Bill escorted me to a chair and I sank into its depths, peering timidly at my surroundings as he walked to the front desk. The lobby was all brass and wood, tall ferns and taller doorways, with writing desks tucked discreetly into alcoves, islands of comfortable chairs, and bellboys in spotless dove-gray uniforms. Elderly women sat or stood, draped in ancient fur stoles, pearls at their throats, tiny hats nestled in their silver hair, chatting with equally elderly gentlemen. I felt like a dandelion in a grove of stately oaks, a drooping dandelion at that, and I was relieved when Bill returned; his wrinkled tweed jacket was at least as disreputable as my jeans. He arrived in the company of a dignified, middle-aged woman, and I stood up as they approached, wishing I had a forelock to pull.

"Lori," said Bill, "this is Miss Kingsley. She takes care of Father and me when we're staying here."

"Miss Shepherd, how nice to meet you," said Miss Kingsley.

I shook her hand and nodded dumbly. She must have wondered if I understood English.

"If you will excuse me," said Bill, "there are some arrangements I need to make. You take it easy, Lori, and get some sleep. Why don't we meet here tomorrow morning, at ten o'clock? I'll see you then." Bill went back to the desk and I was left alone with Miss Kingsley.

"Shall I show you to your suite, Miss Shepherd?"

"Yes, please," I said. "And . . . would it be all right with you if you called me Lori? Bill's father is the only person in the world who calls me Miss Shepherd."

"Of course." Miss Kingsley summoned a porter to carry my bags and led the way, explaining that she would be at my disposal while I was in London. If I had any questions, problems, or special requests, I should feel free to contact her. She couldn't have been friendlier, but I found myself restraining the urge to curtsy when she left.

The suite consisted of a sitting room, bathroom, and bedroom, with windows that opened on to a courtyard garden. It was charming, but I was pooped. After a brief tour, I made a beeline for the bedroom, peeled off my clothes, dumped them in a heap on the floor, and fell into bed. The last thing that passed through my mind was the memory of my mother's voice telling me that the best way to deal with jet lag was to fight it. "Good idea, Mom," I murmured. Then I faded into sleep.

I awoke at three in the morning, of course, wide-awake and raring to go. Miss Kingsley, or some of her elves, had visited the room while I slept. The heap of clothes had vanished and a fluffy white robe had been placed on a chair near the bed. I slipped it on and noticed that my bags had been unpacked and my gear stowed in the wardrobe.

Wandering into the sitting room, I saw a tray of sandwiches on the table near the windows. Beside it was a lovely, floral-patterned tea service, complete with an electric kettle. And next to that was a guidebook, several London maps, and the current issue of *Time Out*. "Good grief," I muttered. "They could have ridden the Horse Guard through here and I wouldn't have noticed."

I thumbed through the guidebook and saw that someone had marked it in red ink. A handwritten list, keyed to the page numbers in the book, had been taped to the inside of the front cover. The list had been written on a page torn from a small notebook. Just like Bill's.

He was waiting in the lobby at ten o'clock, along with Miss Kingsley and a small, white-haired man in a dark blue uniform, whom Bill introduced as Paul.

"Paul will be our driver while we're in London," Bill explained, "and I can testify that he knows the city inside out."

"That's very kind of you, sir," said Paul. "And you, miss—young Mr. Willis here tells me that you'd like to see places having to do with the Second World War. Is that correct?"

"Yes," I replied.

"Did you know that you're standing in one?"

"The Flamborough?" I looked around the lobby with renewed interest.

"Paul is quite right," said Miss Kingsley. "The Flamborough was a famous watering hole in those days, or so I've been told. The young airmen thought of it as their unofficial headquarters. They used to come here to relax, to have a drink, to dance with their wives and girlfriends—"

"They came here to gossip," Paul put in with an authoritative nod. "Talked like there was no tomorrow, they did, miss, bragging and poking fun at one another. If there was any news to spread, it came to the Flamborough first. The Flamborough Telegraph, they used to call it."

"Please, come with me," said Miss Kingsley. "I think you might find this interesting."

She took us into the hotel lounge, a large, rectangular room with wine-red banquettes along the walls and a small dance floor. The focal point was a glorious traditional English bar, with mahogany frame-work that went right up to the ceiling. The bar was ornamented from top to bottom with carved scrollwork and brass fixtures, and an oval mirror etched with fruit and flowers stretched across the back of it. The room was dim and silent, not yet open for business.

"The Flamborough was fortunate to escape the Blitz," Miss Kings-ley said, "and the nature of our clientele precludes extensive renova-tions. The room appears now very much as it did during the war. Here, this is what I wished to show you."

The walls at the far end of the room were hung with photographs. They were snapshots rather than professional portraits; framed, black-and-white pictures of men in uniform or in flying gear, stand-ing beside their aircraft or sitting at camp tables, grinning.

"They're so young," I said, looking from face to face.

"And they stayed that way," said Paul.

Miss Kingsley frowned slightly at him, then turned to me. "These are the boys who didn't come back," she explained. "Their comrades put the pictures here, in tribute. We keep them here, to remember."

The faces of those boys remained with me throughout my time in London. My mother had always spoken of the war as a great adven-ture, a time of unforgettable sights and sounds, of strong friendships quickly made. She had never mentioned the friendships that had been even more quickly ended.

Bill seemed to hold the keys to the city. He got me into the building where my mother had worked—now just another maze of modern-ized corridors—and out on the roofs of St. Paul's, where she had seen the incendiaries fall. He found an elderly general to give us a private tour of the Cabinet War Rooms, the underground bunkers from which Churchill had conducted the war during the Blitz, and he somehow got permission for me to view Imperial War Museum photo archives that were usually reserved for scholars.

Bill was so solicitous, in fact, that he made me edgy. There was nothing I could point to, no overt act that embarrassed or annoyed me, but there was something in his manner. . . . Perhaps it was the re-turn of the same secret, knowing smile he had tried to hide during his tenure as my chauffeur in Boston. In London it gave me the feeling that something was up, that he was planning some monumental prank that would leave me flabbergasted.

As far as I could see, however, he only put his foot wrong once in London, and even that wasn't his fault. It was pure bad luck that brought us together with a guy who had frequented the rare book reading room at my university in Boston; a genuine, bona fide, one-hundred-percent-guaranteed creep named Evan Fleischer. Evan was in his late twenties, with stringy, shoulder-length black hair, thick glasses, and a hairy little potbelly that peeked out between the lower buttons of his ill-fitting shirts. I might have found him endearingly scruffy if it hadn't been for the fact that he was the single most ego-centric individual I had ever met.

I was never able to pin down Evan's area of expertise because he claimed to know everything. The word "important" was frequently on his lips, but he defined it rather more narrowly than the rest of the English-speaking world. If anyone else had a deadline to meet, it was inconsequential, and the same went for ideas: only Evan's were "important." One day in the reading room, when he referred to his laundry as "important," I laughed in his face. It didn't faze him. He simply explained, in little words that even I could understand, why doing *his* laundry was a service to humanity. Looking pointedly at his grease-stained tie, I conceded that he had a point, but the jibe was lost on him. He merely assumed I'd seen the light.

And how he loved to enlighten people. He gathered around him a coterie of emotionally disturbed undergrads who hung on his every word, which reinforced his self-image as an altruistic mentor. He led them on in order to feed his own ego, and that, when all was said and done, was what made him a creep rather than just another obnoxious jerk. I had no time to explain any of this to Bill when I heard Evan call my name in the lobby of the Tate.

"Lori? Lori Shepherd?"

I would have tucked my head down and sprinted for the exit, but Bill was already shaking Evan's hand, eager to meet another one of my friends.

"What a pleasant surprise," said Evan.

"You're half right," I muttered.

"I don't believe we've met before." Evan blinked owlishly at Bill. "I am Dr. Evan Fleischer. You may call me Evan, if you wish, although naturally I prefer Dr. Fleischer. Lori and I are old friends."

"It's very nice to meet you, Dr. Fleischer," said Bill. "I'm Bill Willis. Lori and I are——"

"I'm sure Evan doesn't have time for small talk," I interrupted.

"Only too true," said Evan. "I'm delivering an important paper on Dostoyevski's use of patronymics this coming Saturday at the British Museum. I'm sure you would find it instructive, though perhaps a bit esoteric. I find it difficult to write for a general audience, you see, because——"

"What a shame," I said. "We're leaving London on Saturday."

"Where are you off to?"

In full Mr. Congeniality mode, Bill piped up: "We'll be staying in a cottage in the Cotswolds, near a place called Finch."

"What about our change of plans?" I asked Bill urgently.

"What change of plans?"

"Oh, but you mustn't change a thing!" Evan exclaimed. "It's a fascinating area. I'm sure I can find the time to visit you there. I'm always eager to give foreigners the benefit of my extensive knowledge of the sceptered isle." Since Evan had been born and raised in Brooklyn, New York, his use of the word "foreigners" was highly suspect.

"I'd rather you didn't," I said. "Really, Evan, I'm going to be awfully——"

"It would be my pleasure." He checked his watch. "I'd love to tell you about my paper, but I have some important appointments."

"Picking up your laundry?" I asked.

"No, I had that seen to this morning," he replied. "Now I've really got to run. Where are you staying?"

"The Flamborough," said Bill.

"I'll be in touch." He strode off toward the exit, leaving me to glower at Bill.

"What's wrong?" he asked.

"Nothing much," I said. "Only that you've saddled us with a visit from one of the most obnoxious human beings on the face of the planet. Once he moves in, we'll never get rid of him. Oh, God," I groaned, "he'll probably try to read his paper to us."

Bill had the grace to hang his head. "I thought he was a bit of a pill, but—"

"I know. You also thought he was my friend." I sighed and took his arm. "Oh, come on. I'll tell you all about him while we look at William Blake's visions of hell. After a brush with Evan, they'll seem soothing."

Bill redeemed himself by showing up at my suite the next day with enough of the finest Scottish wool to keep Meg's knitting needles flying for a good long time. Impressed, I had to admit that he noticed far more than I gave him credit for.

I bought a few things I couldn't resist—a couple of sweaters, a book or two—and others I didn't even try to resist. A flashlight, for instance. From Harrod's, of all places. And I made sure to have a brand-new brolly handy when I went to the zoo. Even when I was caught up in shopping, Dimity and my mother were never far from my thoughts.

I kept seeing them in my mind's eye, sharing a bag of chips, riding bicycles, running for shelter during an air raid. I touched the shrapnel-gouged walls of buildings along the Embankment and tried to imagine what it had been like to hear the rumble of German aircraft overhead, to feel the sidewalk shake as the bombs struck home. There was one moment, driving past Hyde Park, when I thought I saw the greensward scarred with trenches, sandbags piled high, conical canvas tents staked out in rows across the fields. The image was startlingly vivid. I called out for Paul to stop the car, but before he could pull over to the curb, the vision was gone, the helmeted Tommies replaced by the usual lunchtime throng of trench-coated Londoners. When Bill started to question me, I only shook my head and asked Paul to drive on.

Because the zoo had gained an almost mythic status since I'd read the letters—I guess I subconsciously expected to find a brass plaque commemorating the day Beth Shepherd met Dimity Westwood—I'd saved it for last. Needless to say, it was a bit of a letdown to see it bathed in sunlight and crowded with noisy families.

Bill had arranged for me to speak with one of the keepers who'd been there during the war, a pink-faced, elderly man named Ian Bramble. We sat with him by the Grand Union Canal, and he sighed when I asked him what the zoo had been like in those days.

"A sad place," he said. "Terribly sad. Hated to come to work, myself. No children around, and the place all boarded up." He pulled a handful of corn from his pocket and tossed it to some passing ducks. "It was a strange time. People were afraid there'd be lions in the streets if a bomb fell in the wrong place, and they had enough to worry about without lions. So we put them down, the lions, and others as well. Perfectly healthy they were, too. It's not something we tell the kiddies, you understand, but perhaps we should. I sometimes think they'd be better off knowing it's not all crisps and candy floss during wartime."

Eleven

$\mathcal{P}$aul had been too young to enlist. "Not that I didn't try, mind you," he told us. "Lied like a rug, I did; used bootblacking to give myself whiskers. Board told me to go home and wash my face." We were speeding along a narrow, twisting lane, on our way to the cottage. We had left London very late in the afternoon the day after our visit to the zoo. I had wanted to leave earlier, but Bill had gone off to make some more of his mysterious arrangements and hadn't surfaced again until after tea.

"That's why I went to the Flamborough," Paul continued. "The bartender there was a chum of mine, and I liked to listen to the lads. We were taking such a pasting in London that it was good to hear the Jerries were getting some of their own back. Finch should be coming up shortly, miss." I had tried to break him of the "Miss Shepherd" habit, but he had been trained at the Old Servant's School of Etiquette and "miss" was as far as he would unbend. "The cottage lies about two miles beyond the village."

It was too dark and we passed through Finch too quickly for me to see much of it, but as we pulled into the drive, I could see that lights had been lit in every window of the cottage. It was exactly as I had pictured it. And it seemed to be waiting for me.

"Here we are," said Paul, switching off the engine. An absolute silence settled over us. We climbed out of the limo to stand on the gravel drive and I shivered as the cold night air hit me.

"Touch of frost tonight, I'd say." Bill blew on his hands and I could see his breath.

"A bit nippy for this time of year," Paul agreed. "You two run along in and get warmed up. I'll see to the luggage."

Paul unloaded the limo and Bill headed for the front door, scrounging through his pockets for the keys Willis, Sr., had given him. I started to follow Bill, then stopped on the path to confirm my initial impression that the cottage looked . . . as it was supposed to look.

It was just as my mother had described it in her story, a two-story stone house with a broad front lawn, sheltered from the road by a tall hedgerow. The yard light glinted from diamond panes of leaded glass and hinted at the golden glow the walls would have in sunlight. The slate roof, the flagstone path leading from the drive to the weathered front door, all was as I had envisioned it, down to the bushes that were already heavy-laden with white lilacs.

"Lilacs in April," I murmured. "They must bloom earlier here than they do at home."

Paul came to stand beside me. "Lovely old place this is, miss."

"Too good to be true," I said, searching the facade for some flaw that would jar it, and me, back into the real world. I didn't like the sense of belonging that was seeping into my bones. It made it too easy to forget that I was only a visitor.

But the yard light revealed no imperfection. With a shrug, I joined Bill on the doorstep. He seemed to be having difficulty with the lock.

"Let me try," I offered. I turned the key, and the door swung open to reveal a brightly lit hallway.

"Look at the place," said Bill. "It's lit up like a Christmas tree."

"The Harrises probably came by today to get things ready for us," I said. "They must have forgotten to turn off the lights."

"I'd talk to them about that if I were you, miss," said Paul, Old Servant's School disapproval in his voice. "The electric doesn't come cheap these days."

"Cheap or not, I'm glad they turned on the heat," said Bill. "Let's get inside before we all catch colds."

Paul set the bags in the hall and returned to the car for the last of them. As I stepped across the threshold, the cottage seemed to pull me into its warm embrace, and when the door swung shut behind me, I thought: I may be only a visitor, but I sure do feel like a welcome one.

There was a gentle knock at the door. The Old Servant's School again, I thought, rolling my eyes.

"For heaven's sake, Paul, you don't have to knock," I called out. "Come on in, it's open."

His muffled voice came through from the outside. "Sorry, miss, I can't budge it."

"What do you mean, you can't—" The door opened at my touch. Paul stood on the doorstep, a bag in each hand and a perplexed expression on his face.

"These old places do have their quirks, miss." He set the bags beside the others while Bill fiddled with the door handle.

"There doesn't seem to be anything wrong with it," Bill said, "but I'm not a locksmith. I think I'll ask the Harrises to have this checked out."

"Fine," I said. "Now, how about a cup of tea before you go back to London, Paul? Or would you like to stay here for the night? You're more than welcome."

"Thanks very much all the same, miss, but I'd best be getting back, if it's all right with you. Up early tomorrow, you know, can't keep the ambassador waiting." He offered to carry our bags upstairs, but we assured him that he had done more than his fair share of work for the day and walked him to the limousine. After he'd driven off, I turned in the still night air for another long look at the cottage.

The feeling of familiarity was uncanny. There was the shadowy oak grove and, there, the trellis ablaze with roses. Each item was in its proper place and the whole made a picture I remembered as clearly as the apartment house in which I had grown up. I probably would have stood there all night, lost in the déjà vu, but the crunch of Bill's shoes in the gravel reminded me that I was not alone. He held out his jacket and I pulled it around my shoulders, grateful for the warmth.

"You seem to be a million miles away," he said softly.

"More like a million years," I said. "One of my mother's stories has a cottage in it, exactly like this one. I feel as though I've been here before."

"It's a strange feeling," said Bill, "to see a legend from your childhood come to life."

"Mmm." I nodded absently. "I was a little worried, after the zoo. She told a story about that, too, and she made it sound like . . . like Disney World. And it wasn't like that at all—not during the war, at any rate. But the cottage is just as it should be."

"As she promised it would be," Bill murmured.

It was an odd comment, but I wasn't paying attention. I was already walking toward the door, curious to see if the inside of the cottage would be as true to the story as the outside was. Bill followed me into the hall, then stopped. He pointed to the ladder-back chair beside the hat rack. "I'll wait here. You go on ahead, get acquainted with the place."

"You don't mind?"

He shook his head. "It's your story."

I searched his face for a trace of mockery, but there was none to be found.

"I'll be right back." I handed him his jacket and started up the hall.

The two front rooms on the ground floor were the living and dining rooms. A study was just beyond the living room, to the rear of the cottage, and there was a pretty little powder room just beyond that, complete with lavender-scented hand soap and ruffled towels. I wasn't big on ruffles, as a rule, but here I couldn't imagine anything else.

Having completed a quick once-over, I returned for a more leisurely examination of the living room. I saw no sign of the renovation Willis, Sr., had mentioned until I found a television and a snazzy sound system hidden in the cabinetry along one wall. The room had to have been enlarged to accommodate these additions, but even so, I had no trouble picturing Aunt Dimity eating brown bread and drinking tea before that fireplace.

The room was spacious yet snug, with deeply upholstered chairs and a beamed ceiling. Bowls of lilacs had been placed here and there, filling the room with the scent of early summer. A bow window overlooked the front garden, and its window seat was fitted with cushions straight out of my mother's story.

Or were they? If I remembered the story correctly, Aunt Dimity's cat had spilled a pot of ink on one of the cushions (having already chewed the fern to bits, scratched the legs of the dining room table, and tipped over the knitting basket). Aha, I thought, feeling extremely clever, I've caught you. Surely, that had only been part of the story. Surely . . .

The ink stain was there. Someone had tried many times to remove it, and it had faded over the years, but it was still there, a defiant blue patch in the back corner near the wall. I gazed at it, then crossed the hall to check the legs of the dining room table. They bore the claw marks of a cantankerous cat. I glanced over my shoulder, half expecting him to stalk through the doorway, demanding a bowl of cream. No such thing happened, of course. The cat had undoubtedly gone on to harass his mistress in another world.

Even without the cat, the dining room was recognizably Aunt Dimity's. It mirrored the living room, with its fireplace, bow window, and cabinetry, though here the cabinets were glass-fronted and filled with delicate bone china and crystal. A door in one wall opened on to the kitchen and it was there that I found the first big discrepancy between the cottage of my mother's story and the one in which I stood. I also discovered that Willis, Sr., shared his son's fondness for understatement.

This was no "minor improvement." This was the most fully equipped modern wonder of a kitchen I'd ever seen, with everything from a microwave oven to a set of juice dispensers in the refrigerator door. As I opened doors and drawers and examined countertops, my first coherent thought was: This is a kitchen for someone who can't cook.

In other words, a kitchen designed with me in mind. It was a far-fetched notion, to say the least. My former husband had been as good a cook as my mother, and I had been too intimidated to learn, but even if Dimity had known of my culinary incompetence, she couldn't have revamped the kitchen for my benefit. I was only going to be here for a month, after all. The truth had to be that Dimity Westwood had been a lousy cook, too. It would certainly explain why Aunt Dimity seemed to subsist on brown bread and tea.

I wasn't one bit disappointed to find that the kitchen bore no resemblance to the primitive one of *Aunt Dimity's Cottage*. I loved the idea of an open hearth, but if I'd been forced to cook on one, I would have starved.

A second door led into a well-stocked pantry and a roomy utility area, and the third and last door led into the hallway. Directly across the hall was the book-lined study, and a white-painted, fern-bedecked solarium stretched across the back end of the cottage.

I paused to survey the study. A stack of papers sat on the desk that faced the ivy-covered windows, and I crossed the room to investigate. I thought it might be miscellaneous bits and pieces of the correspondence—selected letters, perhaps, related to the stories—but it proved to be the stories themselves. They had been written in longhand on fine, unlined paper, and the title page brought me up short.

"Lori's Stories," I whispered. It was as though Dimity had foreseen my reluctance to share my heroine with the masses, and had offered this title to reassure me: no matter how far afield these tales might travel in years to come, they would always be mine. I straightened the edges of the manuscript with hands that were none too steady, glanced idly at the bookcases—and found the correspondence.

Books filled several vertical sections of shelves, but the rest of the wall was reserved for row after row of neatly labeled archive boxes. Talking about the letters, reading about them, even thinking long and hard about them, hadn't prepared me for the impact of seeing them. More than forty years of my mother's life had been captured in those boxes and the sight left me feeling slightly dazed. Stan Finderman had once mentioned something called "the mystique of the manuscript" and I finally understood what he had meant. My mother had touched these pages, and in their presence, I felt hers. I wanted to pull down a box right away, but I held off. Not now, not yet. Not with Bill cooling his heels in the hall. After a moment's thought, I picked up the manuscript and headed for the front door.

Bill stood as I returned.

"That good?" he asked.

"Better," I replied with a grin.

"And there's still one more floor to go."

"You can come up with me, if you want," I offered. "Aunt Dimity never went upstairs in the story, so it won't change anything to have you there. Here, you can put this on your nightstand." I handed him the manuscript, grabbed my bags, and started up the stairs.

Bill stayed where he was. He looked down at the manuscript, then up at me on the stairs. "You're sure you want me to read these?"

"I'm sure," I said; then, more gruffly, "Well, don't just stand there. They're bedtime stories. They belong upstairs, next to your bed."

A full bath was at the top of the stairs, and two cozy bedrooms occupied the front of the cottage, each with twin beds, wardrobes, reading chairs, and fireplaces. I put my bags in one and Bill put his and the manuscript in the other.

"You wouldn't think they'd need so many fireplaces," Bill remarked as he emerged from his room. "The central heating seems to work well enough."

"But central heating doesn't warm the soul the way an open fire does. It's so"—I skirted around the word "romantic" and finished lamely with—"old-fashioned." Bill was about to reply when the sight of the master bedroom silenced him.

The master bedroom took up the entire back half of the second floor. A sliding glass door opened on to an outside deck, and another sliding door led to a bathroom that brought to mind the changing room in the Willis mansion. The main difference was that, instead of a simple whirlpool bath, it had a strange-looking Jacuzzi/steam-bath installation. Bill, of course, knew how it worked and showed me how to use it. A good thing, too—I would have parboiled myself if I had tried it on my own.

This room seemed to combine bits and pieces of all the other rooms in the cottage. Aside from the wardrobe and bureau, there were bookshelves, glass-fronted cabinets, and a desk, all of which appeared to be empty. Two overstuffed chairs were in one corner and a tea service had been placed on a round table between them.

The bed was the size of a small football field, and another grin broke across my face when I saw Meg's blanket folded atop a wooden chest at its foot. Seeing it there was like seeing an old friend. I began to say something about it to Bill, then noticed that he'd left me alone again so I could enjoy my discoveries in private. The bed faced yet another fireplace, in which a fire had been laid, but I was too distracted to contemplate that pleasure. For there, on the mantelpiece, was a vase filled with deep blue irises. My knees buckled and I sat, stunned, on Meg's blanket.

Bill reentered the master bedroom, carrying my bags. He placed them on the bureau, folded his arms, and declared: "*This* is your room."

"Bill," I said, "did you come here today?"

"No. Why?" He walked over to stand in front of me.

"I was wondering how those got here." I pointed to the flowers. Bill glanced over his shoulder. "So that's where they put them. With so much to look at, I nearly missed them. The Harrises must agree with me—about this being your room, that is."

"The Harrises?"

"I called them today and asked them to put some irises in the cottage for you. I thought they'd add a nice welcoming touch."

"So you've really never been here before?"

"Lori, I may have an odd sense of humor, but I've never lied to you. I have never set foot in this cottage before this evening."

I twisted a strand of the fringe on Meg's blanket. "I didn't mean to sound so . . ."

"Suspicious? Paranoid?" Bill suggested helpfully.

"It's just that, for a minute there—"

"You thought someone else had opened your birthday present."

I ducked my head. "It sounds pretty childish when you put it that way."

"What's wrong with that? I'd feel the same way if I found out that someone had been snooping around Arthur's dome. By the way"—he stepped aside to give me an unobstructed view of the flowers—"do you like them?"

"You know I do." I stood up. "But you haven't seen the rest of the place yet. Come on, I'll give you a guided tour." We were halfway down the stairs when I heard tires crunching on the gravel drive.

"Who on earth—" I backed up a step. "Oh, no . . . not Evan."

"You stay here," said Bill, squaring his shoulders. "I'll take care of this."

Twelve

*I*f Bill had his heart set on giving Evan the boot, he must have been disappointed when he opened the door. I know I was, but for very different reasons. Our unexpected guests turned out to be Emma and Derek Harris, and one look was enough to tell me that they couldn't possibly be the couple who had given my mother the photograph. They weren't the doddering, white-haired caretakers I had envisioned. In fact, unless my ears deceived me, Emma wasn't even English.

"You're American?" I asked, coming down the stairs.

"Yes, I am," said Emma, looking up from the doorway. She was shorter than I, a bit plumper and some years older, wearing a bulky hand-knit sweater beneath a lightweight parka, and a gorgeously mucky pair of Wellingtons. Dishwater blond hair hung to her waist and she peered shyly at me through a pair of wire-rim glasses. "But my husband is the real thing. Harrow, Oxford—he even plays cricket when he has the chance."

"Which is none too often." Derek Harris had eyes to kill for, the kind of deep, dark blue eyes that casting directors dream about and the rest of us don't really believe exist. Emma would have been justified if she had married him for his eyes alone. He was tall and angular, with salt-and-pepper curls framing a weatherworn face. Like Emma, he wore a lightweight parka and appeared to be in his late forties. "I scarcely have enough time to run my business, let alone practice my bowling." He eyed Bill speculatively. "I don't suppose you . . ."

"Sorry," said Bill, "speed-reading is my game." He gestured for the Harrises to come into the hall, closed the door, and made formal introductions. "By the way, Harris, my father wanted me to express his gratitude to you for keeping an eye on the cottage."

"Only too happy to help." Derek turned his blue eyes toward me. "Hope we haven't interrupted anything. Bill rang this morning to let us know you were coming out today. We spotted a car in the drive when we were coming back from town, so we thought we'd drop yours off."

"My what?" I asked.

"Your car," said Emma. "Bill asked us to lease one for you locally. It was no trouble," she added. "Our house is just up the road. We can walk back."

"Do you have to get back right away?" I asked. "If not, you're welcome to stop in for a cup of tea. It's the least I can do to thank you."

"An Englishman never turns down a cup of tea," said Derek with a smile. "Here, Em, let me help you with those." Emma took his arm and stepped out of her Wellies while Bill hung their jackets in the hall closet.

"I assume I have you to thank for stocking the pantry?" I said to Emma.

"I didn't want you to find the cupboards bare," she replied. "I hope I haven't forgotten anything."

"I don't think you have to worry about that. I doubt that we'll get through half of it before we leave. How about helping us tackle the crumpets tonight?"

Derek and Bill were all in favor, so I set them to work lighting a fire in the living room while Emma and I repaired to the kitchen to put the kettle on. She helped me locate a sturdy brown teapot and four stoneware mugs—"No need to use Dimity's best china with us," she assured me. She filled a tea ball with loose tea from the tin tea caddy in the pantry, then brought out a white ceramic sugar bowl, a squat cream jug, and four dessert plates, arranging them with the rest of the tea things on a polished wooden tray with brass handles.

"So this is a toasting fork." I was fascinated. "I've read about them, but I've never used one before. I hope you know something about the fine art of crumpet toasting."

"With a ten-year-old daughter and a fifteen-year-old son at home I've become something of an expert on crumpets. Oh, and before I forget . . ." Emma reached into the pocket of her brown woolen skirt. "I borrowed this yesterday and I wanted to return it. Peter and Nell prefer these even to crumpets and I can't say that I blame them." With a cheerful smile, Emma handed me a recipe for oatmeal cookies.

It was unmistakably my mother's. An index card, browned with age and stained with use; her looping scrawl——I could almost smell the nutmeg.

"Where did you get this?" I asked.

"The usual place." Emma went into the pantry and came back with a fat old dog-eared cookbook. "I used to borrow recipes from Dimity all the time. I've copied this one, though, so I won't be needing the original again."

I paged through the cookbook, culling card after card, until I held a fan of my mother's old standbys: tuna casserole, meat loaf, onion soup, cookies, cakes, even the champagne punch she had made to celebrate my college graduation. She had gotten that one from Mrs. Frankenburg downstairs, who was fond of fancy touches.

"Should I have waited for your permission?" asked Emma in a small voice.

I had forgotten she was in the room.

"No, no," I said. "It's not that. It's . . ." I tapped the fan into a pile and tried to collect myself. "These are my mother's recipes. All of them. I mean, she wrote them herself. She must have exchanged recipes with Dimity Westwood. And she . . . she passed away last year."

Emma looked stricken. "I'm so sorry, Lori. I didn't mean to spring it on you like that. I had no idea."

"Of course you didn't. It's all right, Emma, really. To tell you the truth, it's a . . . a pleasant surprise. I knew that her letters were here, but I——"

"Is that what those are? In the boxes in the study?"

"Yes——hers and Dimity's. I'm going to be reading through them while I'm here. Didn't Bill tell you?"

"Bill told us that he was bringing someone to the cottage, and that it had something to do with Dimity's will. Period. Derek and I have been referring to you as 'the Westwood Estate' all day." Emma took a bottle of milk from the refrigerator and with a steady hand began to pour off the cream into the squat jug.

"I'm not the Westwood Estate," I said firmly. "I wish I were. It'd be nice to take up permanent residence here, but I'm only staying for a

month. I'm going to be . . . doing a research project. You know—
exploring Dimity's old haunts."

Some drops of cream spattered the wooden surface of the table,
and Emma wiped them up with a spare napkin. "Are you? That sounds
interesting."

"You knew her, didn't you?"

"Oh, yes," said Emma. She put the milk bottle back in the fridge.
"We knew Dimity. That's the main reason we came over, in fact. We
thought . . . That is, Derek and I thought you might want to know—"
A shriek from the teakettle broke in on her words and as I was warm-
ing the pot, Bill put his head in the doorway.

"We can't get the fire going, Lori," he said. "Derek thinks you
should have a try."

"You've checked the flue?" I knelt on the hearthrug while Emma put
the tea tray on a low table. Bill stood behind me, and Derek sat on the
couch, his long legs crossed, very much at ease.

"It's open," said Bill. "The wood is dry, the tinder is in place, and
Derek says that everything is in working order."

I struck a match. "I used to be pretty good at this back in my hos-
teling days. . . ." It was like flipping a switch. The match touched tinder and the fire caught on contact. I tossed the spent match into the
flames. "Maybe you hit some rot or something. Wood can be funny
that way."

Emma glanced at Derek, then picked up a pair of toasting forks and
knelt beside me. "Watch closely and I'll show you how it's done."

She was a good teacher and we soon had a respectable pile of
beautifully browned crumpets to butter and munch. I hadn't burned
a single one, a first in the annals of my cooking experience.

"My father told me that you helped with the renovation work
here," said Bill.

"We did a lot more than help," said Emma. "Derek was in charge
of it. He's an independent contractor."

"I specialize in dying arts," Derek elaborated. "Thatched roofs,
stone walls, stained glass—"

"Everything that makes a place like this so special," Emma finished proudly. "I think the cottage is my husband's finest achievement."

"I can see why," Bill agreed, dabbing butter from his beard with a napkin. "It's magnificent. And you, Emma? What did you do?"

A self-deprecating smile played on her lips. "Dimity let me work in the garden."

"'Let you'?" Derek echoed indignantly. "Emma, she begged you to work on it."

"Oh, Derek . . ."

"You're a gardener?" Bill asked.

"Well . . ." When Emma faltered, Derek smoothly stepped in.

"My wife trained as a computer engineer at Caltech," he explained. "She was working as a project manager for a Boston firm when we first met and she feels compelled to describe herself along those lines, although she's nothing of the sort anymore. Oh, she still does the odd consulting job in London, but most of the time she's rambling round the countryside or tending her gillyflowers. Emma is a gardener through and through. Cut her and she bleeds sphagnum moss."

"It's true," admitted Emma. "When I'm working in a garden, I'm at peace with the world."

"Then you're in the right place," I said, refilling Emma's cup.

"What do you mean?" Derek asked, and his blue eyes were suddenly alert.

"'This other Eden, demi-paradise,'" I quoted loftily.

"Oh," said Emma, patting Derek's knee, "you mean *England*. Well, it's true enough. The English do love to dibble and hoe, but Dimity's garden is unusual, even for here." A faraway look came into her eyes. "Working on it has been quite an experience."

"The cottage, as well," Derek added. "Quite an experience." Waving away my offer of more tea, he returned his cup to the tray, contemplated the fire, then sat back, looking vaguely uncomfortable. "Actually," he went on, "we didn't come over tonight solely to deliver the car."

"Although we wanted to do that, certainly," said Emma.

"Yes, of course," said Derek. "But we were also wondering if . . ." He cleared his throat.

". . . if you had noticed anything," Emma put in. "Since you arrived, that is."

"Like what?" I asked.

"Oh . . . anything unusual," Derek said casually.

I thought for a second. "The lock's not working on the front door. I mean, it works sometimes, and sometimes it jams."

"Have you had any trouble with it, Lori?" asked Derek.

"No, but—"

"Anything else out of the ordinary?"

I shrugged. "All of the lights were on when we got here, but I assumed that you—"

"We didn't," said Emma. "You see . . . well . . . I'm not quite sure how to say this. It's not something I've had much experience with."

"There was the lady chapel in Cornwall," Derek pointed out.

"Yes, but that didn't involve someone we *knew*, Derek. This is completely different." Emma turned back to me. "Besides, we didn't know anything about you and we were afraid you might be . . . disturbed by it."

"Disturbed by what?" I asked warily.

"We simply wanted to tell you not to worry if you notice any peculiar things happening in the cottage," said Emma.

"Such as the front door lock," said Derek. "We've never had trouble with it before, but as you said, it will only open for you now. It stands to reason, of course. She had the whole place done up for you. She must feel protective."

"I'm sure that's why the lights were on, too. And the lilacs blossoming so early . . ." Emma gestured at the bowl of fragrant flowers on the piano. "She was always very fond of lilacs. There's the fire as well, but you saw what happened with that."

"Wait a minute," I said, as gently as I could. I put my cup on the tray and looked dubiously from Emma's face to Derek's. "Let me see if I've got this straight. By 'she' you mean Dimity?"

"Oh, yes," said Emma. "We're not sure why, but we're certain it's Dimity."

"You're telling me that the cottage is *haunted?*"

"I'm afraid so," replied Derek, and Emma nodded her agreement.

"Not that there's anything to be afraid of," Emma added.

"Bill, did you hear that?" But there was no reaction from Bill. Instead, a strange stillness had fallen over him, the stillness of a hunter waiting for his prey to step into the trap. I felt a pang of disappointment so intense that I nearly groaned aloud.

This was it, the monumental prank I'd been waiting for ever since we'd touched down at Heathrow. And I had to admire how carefully he had set it up. He'd drawn me out during the flight and behaved like a perfect gentleman in London, all in order to win my trust, to lull me into complacency, so that when the time came, I would . . . what? Scream and run out of the cottage? Fall fainting into his arms? What kind of a fool did he take me for? I had no doubt that Emma and Derek were in on the game, but I couldn't blame them. I knew how charming Bill could be.

"Thank you," I said, with a touch of frost in my voice. "I'll keep that in mind."

"As I said, it's nothing to worry about," Emma repeated earnestly. "It shook me a bit at first, but you'd be amazed at how quickly you get used to it." She looked uncertainly at Derek.

"Yes. Well." Derek drummed his fingers on the arm of the couch, then stood up. "Thank you very much for your hospitality. We'd best be going, Em. Vicar's roof tomorrow."

"First thing in the morning," said Emma. "They're forecasting heavy rain for the rest of the day."

We stayed with the safe subject of the weather until Derek and Emma walked out into the cold. I closed the door and leaned my head against it, willing Bill to admit that the whole thing had been his idea of a joke. If he had, I think I could have shrugged it off.

"Strange story," he said.

I straightened slowly.

"I can't imagine why they'd make it up, though," he added.

"Can't you?" I asked, still with my back to him.

"No. I'll have to speak to Father about it. He's not going to like—" He broke off as I swung around to face him. "Lori? You don't think I—"

"You don't want to hear what I think," I said. I darted past him and fled up the stairs to the master bedroom, where I slammed the door and locked it. I was not going to give Bill the satisfaction of seeing me cry.

Thirteen

Some people are lucky enough to look like Bambi when they cry. I look like Rudolph. I woke up the next morning with a headache and a shiny nose, and promptly blamed Bill for both.

I took a long, hot shower, then pulled on some jeans and a Fair Isle sweater I'd bought in London. When I slid open the door to the deck, a blast of wind nearly knocked me back inside. One glance at the overcast sky told me that this would not be my day for hill climbing, and as my breath condensed in the cold air, I wondered how often it snowed in the south of England in late April.

The back garden almost made up for the gloomy sky. It was spilling over with bright blossoms and the cold didn't seem to affect them at all—a pair of redbuds were just coming into leaf in the meadow beyond the stone wall. I recalled what Emma had said about the lilacs, but dismissed it when the first windblown splashes of rain sent me back inside to unpack.

I put my books on the shelves, set Reginald's shoebox in the bottom of the wardrobe, and stowed the rest of my gear in the bureau. I only had enough for three of the large drawers, so I decided to put the emptied canvas bags in the fourth one, and that's how I found the box. It had been shoved way back in the corner of the bottom drawer, and I would have missed it if it hadn't shifted forward when I jerked the drawer open.

I carried it to the windows, where a sickly gray light was beginning to leak into the room. Covered with smooth, dark blue leather and die-stamped with a curlicued *W*, the box fit easily in the palm of my hand, and when I saw a tiny keyhole on one edge, my heart fell. I didn't want to damage it, but I wanted very much to find out what was inside. If it held a picture of Dimity, it would be the first I'd ever seen.

"Damn," I said; then, "Oh, what the hell." I tried the lid and it opened without hesitation. The box held a locket, a gold locket in the shape of a heart, with flowers incised on the front. It hung from a fine gold chain. I lifted it gently from the box, slipped a thumbnail into the catch, and opened it.

It was empty. There were places for two small pictures, one in each heart-shaped half, but they held nothing. I closed the locket and regarded it thoughtfully. According to my mother, Dimity had been looking at albums of photographs when the neighbors had found her alone in the cottage, in a state of nervous collapse. Where were those albums now? What if the photograph that had been given to my mother had come from one of those albums, and what if the page had been labeled, and what if . . . I hung the chain around my neck to remind myself to search for Dimity's albums, then went to listen at the hall door.

The wind rattled the windows and the rain pounded the roof, but there was no other sound. I hadn't heard a peep out of Bill since the night before. With any luck, he'd have the good sense to move in with the Harrises for the rest of the month.

The lights had been turned off throughout the cottage, and a fire burned cheerfully in the fireplace in the study, proof, I thought, that Bill had given up on the ghost hoax. If he hadn't, he would have called upon my alleged magical powers to start the fire for him. I wondered if he had stayed up all night in the study, reading the Aunt Dimity stories and—I hoped—feeling ashamed of himself.

My experience with the crumpets, and the absence of witnesses, gave me the confidence to try an omelette for breakfast. To my great delight, and even greater amazement, the result was light and fluffy and oozing with melted cheese. I ate in the solarium, watching the rain cascade down the glass panes and hoping that the poor vicar's repairs had been finished in time. When the telephone rang, I went to the study to answer it.

"I do hope I've gotten the time change right." The line crackled with static from the storm, but Willis, Sr.'s thoughtfulness came through loud and clear. "I haven't disturbed your sleep, have I, Miss Shepherd?"

"No," I replied, "and it wouldn't matter if you had. It's wonderful to hear your voice."

"Thank you, Miss Shepherd. It is pleasant to speak with you as well. I take it that you have arrived in good order?"

"Paul drove us to the doorstep last night."

"And the cottage—it meets with your approval?"

"I'd like to wrap it up and bring it home with me," I said. "I'm in the study right now, looking out through the ivy with the rain pouring down and a fire in the grate. It's so beautiful . . . I wish you could see it. And we had a wonderful time in London, too. Bill was . . . um . . ."

"Yes, Miss Shepherd? You were saying?"

"Bill was fine," I said quickly, too quickly to fool Willis, Sr. I could hear his sigh even through the static.

"Would I be correct in assuming that my son has done something objectionable, Miss Shepherd?"

"Well . . ." I toyed with the phone cord. "Does trying to convince me that the cottage is haunted count as objectionable?"

"Pardon me, Miss Shepherd. Did I hear you correctly? Did you say *haunted?*"

"Hard to believe, isn't it?"

"Where my son is concerned, I no longer know what to believe. I really am going to have to speak with the boy."

"I don't think he meant any harm by it," I blurted, wishing I'd kept my big mouth shut. I didn't like the agitation I heard in Willis, Sr.'s voice.

"Nonetheless, this has gone far enough. He can have no excuse for such unprofessional conduct. If he cannot be trusted to carry out Miss Westwood's wishes, I shall order him home and appoint a suitable substitute. I am beginning to regret my failure to accompany you myself."

"You mustn't do that." Now I was thoroughly alarmed.

"I am Miss Westwood's executor, Miss Shepherd. It is my responsibility to—"

"It was just a joke," I insisted, "a silly practical joke. It didn't even scare me. Not for a second."

"You are quite sure?"

"Do I strike you as someone who believes in ghosts?"

"No. . . ."

"Then please don't give it another thought. I'll talk to Bill myself."

"Very well. But if he continues to——"

"I'll let you know, Mr. Willis."

"I shall count on you to do so." There was a moment of silence on the line and when Willis, Sr., spoke again, his voice had regained its customary calm. "Now, Miss Shepherd, if I might turn to a more pleasant subject before I go?"

"Yes, of course."

"I would simply like to express my heartfelt gratitude for your most thoughtful gift. I attempted to contact you in London, but you were out much of the time, and I did not like to convey my thanks through Miss Kingsley. I am most grateful. I have seldom seen such a fine example of cartographic art and I have never seen such a splendidly appropriate frame. My dear, it quite took my breath away." His warm words sent a rush of pleasure through me. I twirled the phone cord around my finger and turned a slow pirouette, like a little girl being lauded for a flawless piano recital.

And stopped.

Because there, looking up at me from the arm of one of the tall leather chairs near the fire, was Reginald.

Not *my* Reginald. *My* Reginald was upstairs in the master bedroom, in the wardrobe, in the shoebox, in pieces, and *this* Reginald was here, in the study, in the chair, sitting up as pretty as you please, with every stitch intact, two button eyes gleaming, and both ears on straight, as powder-pink as the day he'd been born.

Except for the purple stain near his hand-stitched whiskers.

"I have to go," I said abruptly.

"Pardon me, Miss Shepherd?"

"I really have to go," I said. "Right now. I'll call you back in a little while."

"Is there anything wrong?"

"I'll call you back," I repeated. I dropped the phone on the cradle, tore out of the study, pounded up the stairs, flung open the wardrobe, grabbed the shoebox, and flipped the lid onto the floor.

The shoebox was empty.

There was no way Bill could have known about Reginald. Not even Meg knew about Reginald. Having a stuffed bunny as a confidant isn't something a thirty-year-old woman readily admits to.

But someone had known about him. Someone who needed to get my attention.

I put the shoebox back into the wardrobe and gently closed the door. I descended the staircase in slow motion, stopped at the doorway of the study, and peeked in. The fire was snapping, the rain was drumming, a book of some sort was lying on the ottoman, and Reginald was sitting beside it. He had *moved*.

"Reg?" I called softly. "Is that you?"

His eyes glittered in the flickering firelight. I walked over to pick him up. With a trembling finger, I traced his whiskers and touched the purple stain on his snout, then cradled him in one arm and bent to pick up the book. It was bound in smooth blue leather, with a blank cover and spine; a journal, perhaps.

Slowly, I sat down with it in the chair and, even more slowly, I fanned through the pages. All were blank except for the first one, on which a single sentence had been written.

Welcome to the cottage, Lori.

Before I had time to digest that, another formed below it as I watched.

I'm so glad you are here, my dear.

I'm not sure how long I stopped breathing, but it was long enough to make my next breath absolutely essential.

"Dimity?" I whispered. "Is that you?"

Yes, of course it is, my dear. And let me say what a joy it is to make your acquaintance after all these years.

I clapped a hand over my mouth to suppress a quavering giggle. "It's nice to meet you, too." I cleared my throat. "Uh, Dimity?"

Yes, Lori?

"Do you suppose you could tell me what's going on here? I mean,

I know what's going on here, but what's *going on* here, if you catch my drift. I mean . . . what I mean is . . . I don't even know what I mean."

Perhaps you could be more specific?

"More specific. Right. Um . . ." My mind raced through the events of the night before. "Did you do the lock and the lights and the lilacs and the . . . the fire? Did you light the fire in here this morning?"

Why, yes, my dear. As Derek indicated, I wished to celebrate your arrival. You really should trust what he says about the cottage, Lori. He and Emma know it better than anyone. And you must stop blaming young Bill. I assure you, he had nothing to do with my arrangements.

"Well, thank you, Dimity, it was . . . lovely." I was reluctant to voice the other suspicion that had occurred to me. It was rather deflating, but it was also staring me in the face. "I should have known it'd take supernatural intervention to turn me into a good cook."

NO! I had nothing to do with the omelette!

"You mean it?" I asked. "You're not say—er, writing that just to make me feel better?"

I am telling you the truth. I did lend a hand with the crumpets, but that was only to build your confidence. You may take full credit for the omelette. You might try the oatmeal cookies next. I do so love the scent of cinnamon.

"Me, too," I said, with a nostalgic smile.

I had become so caught up in the give and take of our "conversation" that I had temporarily forgotten what was actually taking place. In fact, I had pretty much lost touch with reality altogether. When a log fell on the fire, I jumped, then looked slowly around the room, realizing the picture I would present to anyone peering in through the windows. I was sitting in an isolated cottage, the wind was howling, the rain was roaring, and I was communicating with the dead. I tightened my grip on Reginald and glanced nervously back at the journal as a new sentence took shape.

I know how strange this must seem.

"Now that you mention it, this is a little . . . no, this is a *lot* strange. I mean, you did say something in your letter about not coming back from the grave. And what about all those long chats with my mother?" I paused, almost afraid to ask the next question. "Dimity—how is she?"

I haven't seen Beth yet.

"You haven't? Why not? I mean, you're both in . . . the same place, aren't you?"

Not precisely. She's gone ahead.

"Oh. Well, she . . . went first, I guess. But you'll catch up with her, won't you?"

I hope so. A sigh breezed through the room. *You see, Lori, things are a bit muddled.*

A bit muddled? Was that what they meant by British understatement? My suspension of disbelief was about to snap.

It's my own fault, of course.

"What is?"

Oh, everything. I've known all along that I would never be forgiven.

"Forgiven for *what?*"

I simply don't deserve forgiveness. And this isn't such a terrible way to spend eternity, is it? I could think of much worse.

The handwriting stopped.

"Hello?" I said. "Are you still there? Can you hear me?"

Nothing more. I stared at the page until my head swam, then looked up, round-eyed, to see Bill standing over me.

Fourteen

"*D*on't let me interrupt." As his eyes traveled slowly around the room, he held out the manuscript of *Lori's Stories*. "I finished reading it this morning, up in my room, and thought I'd return it before . . . Lori? Lori, what is it? What's the matter?" He put the manuscript on the desk, then knelt before me. "You look like you've seen a—"

"Don't," I said. "Please, Bill, no jokes."

"But I'm not—" His eyes widened. "You mean, you actually *have* seen—"

"Not *seen*, exactly."

"Oh, my. . . ." Bill sat back on his heels. "Dimity?"

I gave a barely perceptible nod.

"So the Harrises were telling the truth." He pulled the ottoman over and sat on it, leaning forward, his elbows on his knees. "I thought they might be. When you first stepped into the cottage, I . . . I don't know how to explain it, but I sensed something. That's why I let you go on ahead without me. I felt like an intruder." He shook his head. "Sounds crazy, doesn't it?"

"No," I said. I let the journal fall shut in my lap. "I felt it, too. But I—I thought it was the central heating."

"That's what comes of being such a practical sort of person," said Bill. He brushed away a tear that had rolled down my cheek. "Tell me about it?"

Struggling to keep my voice level, I introduced him to Reginald. "I've had him since I was a kid, Bill, since I was really little, you know? I'd recognize him anywhere. But last year a burglar left him in pieces all over my apartment. I brought him to England in a shoebox and now—" I gulped for air.

"Now he's fully recovered." Bill took out his handkerchief and wiped away a few more tears that had managed to escape. "The burglar didn't hurt you, did he? Oh, now, Lori, come on, don't cry like that. There's no need to be frightened."

"I'm not f-frightened," I said, taking Bill's handkerchief and burying my face in it. "For Pete's sake, Bill, it's not as though headless horsemen are galloping through the living room. How could I be afraid of Dimity? I'm—I'm *ashamed* of myself. Here you are, being so nice to me after I behaved like such a jerk last night. I didn't even give you a chance to explain."

"I don't think I could have explained," said Bill. "And even if I had, there was no reason for you to believe me."

I caught my breath and blinked at him through my tears.

"Well, I *might* have tried rigging the cottage," he said. "In fact, I kind of wish I had. It might have been fun. Give me one good reason why I shouldn't have been your prime suspect."

"Because you promised," I said bluntly, twisting his handkerchief into a knot. "When we were at Meg's. You promised that you wouldn't . . . step over the line again."

"You have a point. And yes, it would have been nice if you'd remembered it sooner. Consider yourself castigated. But I refuse to stalk out of here in a huff, because if I do I won't get to hear what else happened this morning to convince you of my innocence. So let's skip over the recriminations and the apologies and go straight to the good stuff." Bill leaned closer and whispered, "Did she . . . manifest herself to you?"

"She *wrote* to me," I said with a sniff and a quavery laugh. I held up the journal. "A new form of correspondence. All the pages but one were blank when I opened it. Now look at it." I showed him the first page. "It's her handwriting, Bill. I'm sure of it."

"Does that mean it wasn't ghostwritten?" he murmured. He studied the page, then said, with great reluctance, "I know you don't want to hear this, Lori, but I have to confess that I—"

"You can't see it?" I took the journal from him. The sentences were still there, plain as day. I fought down a sudden surge of panic.

Bill took hold of my shoulders. "Calm down, Lori, and think about this. She's writing to you, not to me. I doubt if anyone else can see what you're seeing."

"But—"

"That doesn't mean I don't believe you," Bill stated firmly. "That doesn't make it less real. It doesn't make it less anything, except, well . . . less visible. Who knows? Maybe it's some sort of security system. A private line, open only to you. That would make sense, wouldn't it?"

"I suppose. . . ."

"Well, all right, then." Bill released his grip on my shoulders, took the journal from my hands, and opened it. "Please, Lori. Calmly and clearly and in the correct order, tell me what Dimity—" He glanced down at the journal and his eyes remained on the page, moving from left to right, as a ruddy glow rose from his neck to his hairline. He blinked suddenly, then snapped the book shut.

"What?" I said eagerly. "What did she write?"

"Nothing important," he said.

"Then why are you blushing?"

"You couldn't see it?" he asked.

"Private line," I replied.

"She was . . ." He averted his eyes. "She was complimenting me on my appearance."

I looked at him doubtfully.

"She *was*," he insisted. "She said that my teeth are nice and straight, as she always knew they would be."

"And what else?"

He looked away again and said, with studied nonchalance, "And that she was right in telling Father not to worry about my thumb-sucking."

"You were still sucking your thumb at *twelve?*"

"No," said Bill, "I *started* sucking my thumb at twelve. It's a common reaction to bereavement."

"Oh." The room grew very still. Bill watched the fire and I watched his profile until he turned in my direction.

"I don't anymore, if that's what you're wondering."

"What I was wondering," I said softly, "was why I didn't try it. A little thumb-sucking might have helped."

"It helped me."

"And your teeth are very straight," I added.

"Thank you."

"Bill," I said, "you know about Reginald, and I know about your thumb. I think that makes us even."

Some of the starch went out of his spine. "It's a start." Tapping the journal, he returned to the subject at hand. "She thinks of everything, doesn't she? It's a strange effect, though—how the words . . . appear. What did she say to you?"

I read through Dimity's half of the dialogue and supplied my side of it as best I could remember. When I finished, he let out a low whistle.

"Deep waters," he said.

"It's a metaphysical swamp, if you ask me. I don't even want to think about what her return address might be."

"What was all that about forgiveness?" Bill asked. "Forgiveness for what?"

"I don't know. That's when you came in."

"Why don't you try asking her again?"

"You mean just . . . ask?" With a self-conscious glance at Bill, I opened the journal once more. "Uh, hello?" I said. "Dimity? Are you there?" I touched Bill's arm as a new sentence appeared on the page.

Yes, of course, my dear.

"Good," I said, "because I want to ask you about what you said before, about needing to be—"

Do you like the cottage?

"Like it? I love it, Dimity. Derek did a fantastic job."

There are few craftsmen as gifted as Derek. I was fortunate to find him. Have you seen the back garden yet?

"Only from the deck."

Oh, but it's no good gazing down on a garden. You must stroll through it in order to see it properly.

"I'll do that," I promised, "as soon as it stops pouring. But, to get back to what I was saying before, could you explain what you meant when you said—"

It's nothing for you to concern yourself with, Lori.

"But I am concerned, Dimity. I mean, it's great to have a chance to talk with you like this, but——"

There's nothing you can do, you see. I want you to enjoy your time here. I want you to read the correspondence.

"I will, Dimity, as soon as——"

You must read the letters. Read them carefully. But please, take the time to make a batch of cookies for young Bill. You could find no better way to make amends. Oh, dear, it seems I must go now. Once more, Lori, I welcome you with all my heart.

I tried a few more questions, but when nothing else appeared, I closed the journal and leaned on the arm of the chair, lost in thought.

"She's stonewalling," I murmured.

"She's what?"

"She's shutting me out, just like she shut out my mother."

"What has this got to do with your mother?"

I handed the journal to Bill and got to my feet. "You stay right here," I said. "I have something to show you."

". . . So Dimity bottled something up all these years and now it's blocking her way to heaven?" Bill took off his glasses and rubbed his eyes. "The things they don't teach you in law school . . ."

He was sitting at the desk in the study, with the manuscript, the topographic map, the letters from Dimity and my mother, the tattered old photograph, and the journal arrayed before him. Reginald sat beside the journal, watching the proceedings with an air of benign detachment, while I paced the room, filled with nervous energy. I stopped at the desk and pointed to the photograph.

"And it must have happened here, in this clearing. The photograph reminded Dimity of it and that's why she keeled over. That's my working hypothesis, anyway. There's this, too." I pulled the locket from the neck of my sweater and showed it to Bill. "I found it upstairs this morning, in a box marked with the letter *W*—for Westwood. It's empty. See? No pictures. Where are they, Bill?"

"Maybe she never put any pictures in it."

"Not just *these* pictures." I perched on the edge of the desk. "Don't you remember? My mom said Dimity was looking at photo albums when the neighbors found her. I snooped around while you were in here reading the letters and——" I hopped off the desk. "Come upstairs and see what I found."

Bill put on his glasses and followed me up to the master bedroom. I moved Meg's blanket from the old wooden chest to the bed, then opened the lid of the chest. A row of photo albums bound in brown leather had been packed inside it, their spines facing upward. Like the archive boxes in the study, they had been labeled with dates.

"Neat little ducks, all in a row," I said, then pointed to a gap in the sequence. "Except that one has flown the coop, the one covering the years just before Dimity met my mom." I let the lid fall back into place. "So what did she do with it? And don't try to tell me that she stopped taking pictures all of a sudden, because——"

"Wait, Lori, back up a step." Bill sat on the chest. "What do you think happened in that clearing? What could be so terrible that it would follow Dimity into the afterlife? Are we talking about murder? Suicide? Are we going to find a body buried under that tree?"

"Don't say things like that," I said, suppressing a shudder.

"You've been thinking them, haven't you? I don't mean to sound ghoulish, but it has to have been something fairly drastic to cause Dimity this much grief. If we're going to go digging into the past, we should be prepared to uncover some unpleasant things."

"But . . . murder?" I shook my head. "No. I can't believe that. It's got to be something else—and don't ask me what, because I don't know. I'm going to call the Harrises again." I started for the telephone on the bedside table, but Bill blocked my way.

"You've already left four messages on their machine," he reminded me.

"But where can they *be?*"

"Still bailing out the vicarage is my guess. The storm hasn't let up." Bill patted the space next to him on the wooden chest. "Come here and sit down. The Harrises will call when they call, and not one minute sooner. You can't help Dimity by running in circles." He waited until I was seated, then went on. "We have no idea where the missing photo album might be. For all we know, Dimity might have burned it."

"A depressing possibility," I conceded.

"On the other hand, she may have kept it somewhere else—a bank vault, a safe-deposit box—somewhere special. Maybe it got mixed up with the rest of her papers. I'm sure that Father would be—"

"Your father!" I clapped my hand to my mouth. "Oh, my gosh, Bill. I was talking with him when I saw Reginald. I slammed the phone down on him. He must be worried sick." I rose halfway to my feet, then sat down again. "But he'll want to know why I hung up on him. What am I going to say?"

"That's easy," said Bill. "Tell him that you were distracted by another one of my stunningly clever stunts."

I shook my head. "No way. When I told him you were haunting the cottage, he threatened to recall you and fly over himself."

"I hope you talked him out of it," Bill said quickly.

"I did, but I don't want to risk stirring him up again."

"Definitely not. Tell him . . . tell him that you were distracted by one of my stunts, but that you've had it out with me. You've taught me the error of my ways and I've promised never, ever to do anything so childish again." He looked at me brightly. "How's that?"

"Will he believe it?"

"It's what he wants to hear."

"That always helps." I went over to dial the number on the bedside phone and Bill stood beside me, listening in. Willis, Sr., answered on the first ring.

"Ah, Miss Shepherd," he said. "So good of you to call back. I was beginning to become concerned. Was there an emergency of some sort?"

"No, no, Mr. Willis," I replied airily, "no emergency. Just another one of Bill's silly jokes. The last one, as a matter of fact. I've given him a . . . a stern lecture and he's promised to behave himself from now on." Bill signaled that I was doing fine, but I felt sure Willis, Sr., would hear the deception and guilt in my voice.

But he began to chuckle. "Well, well, Miss Shepherd, if my son has stubbed his toe on your temper, I've no doubt he'll watch his step in future."

I put my hand over the receiver and whispered, "Is he saying I'm bad-tempered?" but Bill waved the question away and hurried to the foot of the bed to point at the wooden chest. He mouthed the word "Photos."

"Uh, Mr. Willis?" I continued. "While I have you on the line, do you think you could answer a couple of questions for me?"

"I am at your service, Miss Shepherd."

"It's just that I found some old photo albums here in the cottage and one seems to be missing. I was wondering what could have happened to it. Did you come across anything like that when you were going through Dimity's papers? It's an old album, from around 1939. . . ." I listened to Willis, Sr.'s reply, said a polite good-bye, and hung up.

"Well?" said Bill.

"He doesn't think so. He'll check, though, and get back to me."

Bill nodded, but his mind was somewhere else. "Let's go back to the study," he said. "It just occurred to me that the answers we're looking for might be right under our noses."

I trailed after him. "If you're thinking of the correspondence, Bill, you're way off base. My mother had her antennae out. If Dimity had dropped the slightest hint, she would have told me."

Bill entered the study and approached the shelves. "True, but what if Dimity didn't mail all the letters she wrote to your mother? What if she couldn't bring herself to send some of them?"

I hadn't thought of that. Scanning the crowded shelves, I felt a flicker of hope. If Bill and I worked together, we could read through the letters in a matter of hours. If there were any clues to be found— to Dimity's past, or to the origins of the stories—we would find them. With Bill's help, I might be able to keep everyone happy. Still, I hesitated.

"Bill," I pressed, "have you thought this through? Looking for answers to my mother's questions could take a lot of time, more time than I have. I may not be able to write Dimity's introduction. Bill . . ." I tugged on his sleeve and he looked down at me. "Your father has gone to a lot of trouble to see to it that Dimity's wishes are obeyed. Won't he be furious with you for helping me disobey them?"

"He'd be dismayed, certainly. But I'm not helping you."

"You're not?" I blinked up at him, confused.

"No." He reached for the first box of letters. "I'm helping Dimity."

Fifteen

$\mathcal{I}$ don't know what made me think we could rush through the correspondence. There were sixty-eight boxes full, for one thing, letters from my mother interfiled with those from Dimity in strict chronological order, but it wasn't the quantity that slowed us down. It was the quality. I had expected the letters to be moving, fascinating, enlightening—and they were—but I had not expected them to be so entertaining. I found myself pausing frequently to reread certain passages, to translate my mother's handwriting for Bill when he had trouble with it, and to read the best parts aloud.

I also found myself watching Bill. He never caught me at it—the slightest movement on his part would send my eyes scurrying down to whatever I was supposed to be reading—but it happened time and time again. Of all the strange things that had happened that day, his presence in the study was perhaps the strangest. Only that morning I had been ready to throw him out of the cottage, and now he was sitting peacefully across from me, his jacket and tie thrown carelessly over the back of the chair, his collar undone and his shirtsleeves rolled up, calmly stroking his beard while he read his way through this most intimate correspondence, as though he belonged there. With each passing hour, it became more difficult to imagine journeying into my mother's past without him.

The seeds of the stories were scattered everywhere we turned. I think Bill was even more thrilled than I was each time a familiar situation or setting surfaced. He crowed in triumph less than an hour after we'd gotten started.

"I've found Aunt Dimity's cat!" he exclaimed. "Listen to this:

"*My Dearest Beth,*

"*My cat is terrorizing the milkman.*

"*You didn't know I owned a cat, did you? That's because I didn't, until a week ago. I do now. The only trouble is that I'm not quite sure who owns whom.*

"He showed up on my doorstep last Monday evening, a ginger tom with a limp and a very pitiful mew. A bowl of cream miraculously cured the limp, and after a night on the kitchen hearth, the mew was replaced by a snarl that caused the milkman to shatter a fresh pint all over my kitchen floor. I strongly suspect premeditation, since the cat promptly lapped it up.

"There's not a plant in the house that's safe from his depredations and he's learned to sharpen his claws on the legs of my dining room table. I've lost my temper with him a dozen times a day. I know I should put him outside to fend for himself, Beth, but I like him. There hasn't been a dull moment since he walked through my door, and he keeps my feet warm in bed. Surely that's worth the loss of a few house-plants. Or so I keep telling myself.

"I have dubbed him Attila."

Bill chuckled as he jotted the date of the letter in his notebook for future reference.

"Wait," I said. "Don't close that notebook."

"Why? What have you found?"

I shushed him and read aloud:

"My Dearest Beth,

"My dear, why do we put ourselves through Christmas? If the Lord had known what He was about, He surely would have announced His son's birth privately to a small circle of friends, and sworn them to se-crecy. Failing that, He might at least have had a large family and spaced their arrivals at decent intervals throughout the year. But no. In His infinite wisdom, the Almighty chose to sire but one Son, thus setting the stage for a celebration only a merchant could love.

"I have just returned from the vale of tears which is London the week before Christmas. Should I ever suggest such a venture again, you are encouraged to have me bound over for my own protection. Only the weak-minded would willingly enter the holiday stairwells at Harrod's, of all places.

"Picture a trout stream of packed and wriggling humanity; picture the rictus-grins of clerks exhausted beyond endurance; picture my foot beneath that of a puffing and alarmingly well-fed gentleman.

"And picture, if you can bear to, my chagrin at having survived it all, only to depart empty-handed. [Enter Greek chorus, cursing Fate.] The torch, my sole reason for braving the savage swarm, was not to be had, and I shall have to make do with candles until March, or perhaps June. Please God, the crowds will have thinned by then. . . ."

"No wonder your mother treasured this friendship," Bill said. "Can you imagine getting letters like that all the time?"

I told him the date of the letter and kept on reading. It was fun to run across those familiar-sounding passages, but I was even more captivated by the unfolding story of their everyday lives, and by their frequent references to the time they'd spent together in London.

"How do you like that?" I said at one point. "Dimity the matchmaker."

Bill started at the sound of my voice. "What's that?"

I glanced up. "Sorry," I said, "but I just found out that Dimity introduced my mom to my dad."

Bill blinked a few times, then grinned. "You don't say."

"It's right here in black and white: '. . . that night in Berkeley Square when I introduced you to Joe.' I knew they had met during the war, but not that Dimity was behind it. Well, they were a great match."

"Do you believe in that sort of thing?" Bill asked.

"What, matchmaking?" I paused to consider. It wasn't something I'd given much thought to. "I guess there's nothing wrong with it. If you know the people well enough, if you think it might work—why not bring them together? What harm could it do?"

"None that I can think of," said Bill.

"Why? Has your father tried it?"

"No," he said, going back to his reading. "He'd consider it impertinent, bless him."

It must be the "desiccated aunts," I thought, the ones he'd mentioned that morning in the guest suite. Did they parade their favorite nephew before a bevy of suitable females? It might explain why his fa-ther thought he was shy around women. I felt a touch of pity for him, but the temptation to tease got the better of me. "Bill?"

"Yes?"

"Does your matchmaker consider you a tough assignment?"

He put down the letter he was reading and pushed his glasses up the bridge of his nose. "Why do you ask?"

"Well, you're not married yet. Do *you* have something against matchmaking?"

Bill tilted his head to one side, as though debating whether to joke or give me a straight answer. I was a little surprised when he chose the latter.

"Not at all," he said. "There have been a few romances along the way, but nothing that stuck. It's a matter of time as much as anything. First college, then the Peace Corps—"

"You were in the Peace Corps?" I was impressed.

"For four years. I re-upped twice. Then came law school, then learning the ropes at the firm. No breaks for the son of the house, I'm afraid. And my job entails a lot of traveling, which makes it difficult to maintain any sort of ongoing relationship. But now that you mention it, maybe I am a tough assignment." He held up a frayed cuff and shrugged. "Let's face it. I'm not movie star material."

"But I think you're—" I broke off midprotest, realizing that I was on the verge of telling him that he was more attractive than any movie star and that the women who had rejected him had probably been shallow, vain, and dumber than doorstops. "I think you're forgetting," I said carefully, "that you were busy establishing yourself in your career."

"Mmm, maybe that was part of it. Anything else you'd like to know?"

"No, no, I was just, uh, wondering. . . ." I returned to my reading, but a short time later, I couldn't help looking up again. "Bill?"

"Mmm?"

"What did you do in the Peace Corps?"

"I gave puppet shows," he replied, still concentrating on the letter in his hand.

"Puppet shows?"

He put the letter down. "Yes. I gave puppet shows. I was sent to Swaziland—that's the place in southern Africa, by the way, not the place with the Alps—to teach English and after two years of using more traditional teaching methods, I added puppet shows."

"What a great idea." My mother had tried the same thing in her classroom.

"They were a big hit, education and entertainment in one neat package. I ended up traveling around the country in a Land Rover, giving shows in schools, churches, kraals, anywhere they sent me." He lifted his hand and began to talk with it, as though it were a puppet. *"Sahnibonani beguneni."*

"What does that mean?" I asked, delighted.

"Roughly? 'Good evening, ladies and gentlemen.' That's about all the SiSwati I remember after all these years. Oh, and: *Ngee oot sanzi, Lori."*

"What's that?"

Bill smiled. "Let's get back to work, Lori."

The news about my parents' meeting was the biggest revelation, but even the small ones fascinated me. After demobilizing, Dimity had remained in London: busy, happy, and unexpectedly up to her elbows in children.

My Dearest Beth,

You will think me quite mad, for I have decided not to return to Finch. Moreover, I have taken off one uniform and put on another. No, I have not taken holy orders—perish the thought!—but I have signed on with Leslie Gordon at Starling House, a quite sacred place in its own right.

I believe I told you of my friend, Pearl Ripley. She married an air-man, young Brian Ripley, who was killed in the Battle of Britain. She was a bride one day, a widow the next, and a mother nine months later. I once questioned the wisdom of wartime marriages—even you waited until after the Armistice to marry Joe—but I have since come to admire Pearl greatly for making what I now feel was a very coura-

geous decision. Surely Brian was fortified and comforted as he went into battle, knowing that he was so dearly loved.

Starling House is meant to help women like Pearl, war-widows struggling to support young children on a pittance of a pension. The kiddies stay there while their mothers work. Isn't it a splendid idea? Leslie asked only for a donation, and I have made one, but I think I have more to give these little ones than pounds sterling.

To be frank, I am not cut out to be a lady of leisure. Although I now have the means, I lack the experience. In fact, it sounds like very hard work. I suppose I could sit with the Pym sisters knitting socks all day, but I'd much sooner change nappies and tell stories and give these brave women some peace of mind.

Mad I may be, but I think it a useful sort of madness, a sort you understand quite well, since you suffer from similar delusions.

My mother's "useful sort of madness" had sent her back to college in pursuit of a degree in education. Despite exams, term papers, and long hours at the library, she managed to write at least twice a month.

D,

Midterms! Yoicks! And you thought D-day was a big deal!

I can't tell you how much I'm enjoying all of this. Joe says that I'm regressing and I do hope he's right. After all of those gray years in London, I think I've earned a second childhood, don't you?

I've put student teaching on hold while I study. I'm not happy about it, but there are only so many hours in the day and I have to spend most of them in the library. I miss the day-to-day contact with kids, though. Makes me wonder when on earth Joe and I are going to have our own. We're still trying, but nothing seems to work, up to and including the garlic you forwarded from the Pyms. Thank them for me, will you? And just between you and me —how would a pair of spinsters be acquainted with the secret to fertility?

The two friends talked about everything that touched their lives. As my mother grew increasingly despondent over the lack of a family of her own, Dimity wrote to her about "Mrs. Bedelia Farnham, the greengrocer's wife, who delivered healthy triplets—Amelia, Cecelia, and Cordelia, my dear, if you will credit it—shortly after her forty-third birthday" and exhorted her not to lose hope. When Dimity wondered how she could bear to see another war-torn family, my mother responded with characteristic common sense:

> *Does the word "vacation" mean anything to you? How about "holi-*
> *day"? I've copied the dictionary definitions on a separate sheet of*
> *paper, in case you have trouble remembering. Take one, and write me*
> *when you get back.*
>
> *I'm serious, Dimity. It's no good, wearing yourself down like this.*
> *It's not good for you and it's certainly not good for the children. I*
> *know I'm stating the obvious, but sometimes the obvious needs to be*
> *stated.*
>
> *So take some time off. Paddle your feet in a brook. Read a pile of*
> *books and eat apples all day. Remind yourself that there's joy in the*
> *world as well as sadness. Then go back to work and remind the kids.*

I fixed sandwiches for a late afternoon lunch, and Bill's disappeared so rapidly that I thought I had scored another culinary coup, until he happened to mention that he hadn't had any breakfast. I hastily made him another, a thick slab of roast beef on grainy brown bread, and sent him into the living room to eat it, ordering him to leave me alone in the kitchen until I called for him. The letters could wait. It was time for me to heed Dimity's advice and start making amends.

In no time at all, I produced a truly scrumptious double batch of oatmeal cookies. I was so proud that I was tempted to go upstairs and fetch my camera, to record the historic moment. It sounds foolish, I know, but if you'd burned as many hard-boiled eggs as I had, you'd understand.

I could almost hear my mother humming in the warm, cinnamon-scented air, and I hoped Dimity was around to enjoy it, but the best moment came when Bill took his first bite. A look of utter bliss came to his face and he closed his eyes to concentrate on chewing. Then, without saying a word, he picked up the cookie jar and carried it back with him to the study.

Later that evening, I tried my hand at onion soup and a quiche lorraine, and Bill seemed more than happy to test the results. He had three helpings of the quiche. Sometime after we'd finished our dinner break and gone back to our reading, he leaned forward and held a letter out to me. "Here's one I think you should read." He shook his head when I looked up expectantly. "Nothing to do with Dimity."

"Go ahead and read it aloud, then," I said.

"I think you'll want to read this one to yourself. Here, take it."

"But what's so special about—"

"The date, Lori. Look at the date."

The letter he was holding had been written by my mother on the day after my birth. I took it from him, bent low over the page, and inhaled the words.

> *D,*
>
> *She's here! And she's a girl! We got your cable, so I know you got ours, but I couldn't wait to write you a proper letter. Eight pounds twelve ounces, eighteen inches long, with a fuzz of dark hair, and ten fingers and ten toes, which I count every time she's within reach. Since you wouldn't allow us to use Dimity—I repeat, it is not an old-fashioned name!—we've named her Lori Elizabeth, after Joe's mom and me. She has my mouth and Joe's eyes and I don't know whose ears she has, but she has two of them and they're perfect.*
>
> *We got your package, too. What can I say? You are a whiz with a needle, but you know that already. How about this: Lori took one look at that bunny's face and grinned her first grin. Love at first sight if I ever saw it. He reminds Joe of Reginald Lawrence—remember him? that sweet, rabbit-faced lieutenant?—so guess what we've named him. On behalf of my beautiful baby girl: Thank you!*
>
> *Gotta run. It's chow time for little Lori and I'm the mess hall. I'll write again as soon as I'm home. In the meantime, here's a picture of my darling. Joe snapped it with the Brownie and it's a little out of focus, but so was he at the time. Yes, he's still working too hard, and yes,*

*he still smokes like a chimney—the nurses made him open a window
in the waiting room!*

Are we proud parents? Silly question!

All my love,

Beth

The rain slashed the windowpanes as the echoes of my mother's
voice faded into the distance. Staring into the fire, I examined my
feelings gingerly, the way you explore a cavity with your tongue.

"Isn't it great?" Bill said. "She sounds so happy. It's just blazing off
the page. I especially like the part about Reginald. We'll have to go
through your mother's photographs when we're back in Boston.
Maybe we'll find a picture of the rabbity Lieutenant Lawrence . . ."
Bill's voice trailed off.

I glanced at him. "You're right, this is a wonderful find. I never
knew that about Reginald."

Bill looked at me for a moment, then got up and cleared the ottoman of boxes. He pushed it over next to my chair and sat on it, waiting for me to speak. I had the feeling that he would wait patiently for
hours, if that was how long it took me to find the words.

I pointed to the closing lines of the letter. "My father died of a
stroke. He worked too hard, he smoked too many cigarettes. . . ." I
shrank from an irony I had been shrinking from my whole life: a man
who had survived Omaha Beach had been killed by a briefcase and a
bad habit.

"I'm sorry," said Bill.

"I never knew him," I went on. "I was only four months old when
he died, and I never . . . asked her about it." I knew so many things
about my mother. I knew her favorite color, her shoe size, her
thoughts on the French Revolution, but about this central experience
in her life I knew next to nothing. Of all the things I had never asked
her, this was the one I regretted most. "When she spoke of my father,
she spoke of his life, not his death." I brushed a hand across the letter.
"I suppose she thought it wouldn't help to dwell on it."

Bill nodded slowly. Then, his eyes fixed on the fire, he asked, "How
can you avoid dwelling in the past when the past dwells in you?" He

sighed deeply, still gazing into the flames. "Dimity said it to me one night while we were staying with her, when I told her about the way the boys at school had acted. She disapproved. She told me that the past was a part of me, and that trying to avoid it was like trying to avoid my arm or my leg. I could do it, yes, but it would make a cripple of me." Turning to me, he said, "I don't think your mother was a cripple, was she?"

"No," I said, "but I don't know how she managed to get over this." I held up the letter. "Here, she's on top of the world, and four months later her world collapsed. How does anyone get over something like that?"

"Would you mind another quotation?" Bill asked.

"From Dimity?"

"It's something else she said that night. She told me that losing someone you love isn't something you get over—or under or around. There are no shortcuts. It's something you go *through,* and you have to go through all of it, and everyone goes through it differently. I don't know how your mother did it, but I do know that you're wrong when you say that her world collapsed. She still had you—"

"A lot of good I was to her," I mumbled.

"And she still had Dimity. Look around you. What do you see?"

"Her letters." I felt my spirits begin to lift. "Oh, Bill, how could I be so stupid? Dimity must have been her lifeline."

"I can't think of a better person to turn to at a time like that," Bill agreed. He reached over and pulled a box onto his lap. "Let's go on reading. We'll soon find out if I'm right."

It was nearing midnight when I put the letters aside, rose to my feet, and left the study, too upset to speak. There had been no phone call from the Harrises, and we had yet to find the unsent letter we were searching for, but that wasn't what bothered me. Bill had warned me of the dangers of digging into the past and I had expected to learn some disturbing truths about Dimity—but I had not expected to learn them about my mother.

Bill caught up with me in the solarium. I stood with my hands on the back of a wrought-iron chair, and Bill hovered behind me, an arm's length away. It was pitch-dark outside and the rain was still fall-ing steadily.

"I know it's not what we expected, Lori, but——"

"It doesn't make sense." My hands tightened on the wrought iron. "My mother wasn't like that."

For four months after the joyful announcement of my birth, the letters from my mother had continued without interruption. Then they stopped cold. She sent one short note informing Dimity of my father's death, and that was it. For three years, not a Christmas card, not a birthday greeting, not so much as a postcard came from my mother. When I realized what was happening, I went back to that brief note in disbelief—I could almost hear the portcullis crashing down, could almost see my mother retreating behind walls of sorrow and self-absorption.

Dimity, on the other hand, had continued to write. And write. And write. For months on end, without response, Dimity sent off at least a letter a week—and I don't mean short, slapdash notes, but real letters: long, lively missives written—it seemed to me—solely for the purpose of letting my mother know that she was not alone.

And how did my mother respond to this outpouring of affection? With silence.

"She wasn't like that," I insisted. "She didn't crawl in a hole when things went wrong. She was strong; she faced things."

"Dimity said that everyone goes through it in their own way. Maybe your mother had to go through it alone."

"But that's why it doesn't make sense. She didn't have to go through it alone. She didn't *believe* in going through things alone. She . . ." Aching for her, I looked out into the darkness, searching for the words that would explain it all to Bill. "She was a schoolteacher, the kind whose door was always open. Her students used to come back to visit her all the time, no matter how old they got. You should have seen her funeral—the church wasn't big enough to hold every-one, and they all stood up and talked about her, told how they wouldn't be where they were if it hadn't been for her." A faint scent of lilacs took me back to that day. "Do you know the one thing they all remembered? That they could bring their problems to her, and she would *listen* to them, really listen, with her heart wide open. If anyone knew how important it was to reach out, it was my mother. So you tell me why, for three of the worst years in her life, she didn't—" I choked on the lump in my throat, swallowed hard, and went on. "And what about Dimity—left out in the cold for all those years?"

"I think Dimity must have understood," said Bill.

"Well, I don't," I said. "I keep thinking of my mom all alone with a crying baby, and the bill collectors banging on the door. There wasn't any Starling House for her, but she could have turned to Dimity." I rubbed my forehead. "God, I never knew."

"Lori," said Bill, "it's late, and a lot has happened to you today. Why don't you go to bed? We can go on with the correspondence tomorrow, when we're fresh."

"I don't know if I want to go on with it."

"Then I'll go on with it for you," Bill said soothingly. "For now, you just try to get some rest, okay? I'll see you in the morning."

I was too tired to protest, but I lay awake late into the night nonetheless, curled forlornly under Meg's blanket, listening to the wind howl mournfully across the rain-slicked slates. I was haunted by my mother's silence, afraid to imagine the kind of pain that would bring it on. The letters had thrown me into a world of hurt I was not prepared to face.

Sixteen

*A*s I gazed through the living room windows the following morning, I began to suspect that some local druid had objected to my arrival and conjured this unceasing rain to drive me away. The weather was not what anyone would call auspicious. The storm had continued almost without pause throughout the night and seemed likely, from the look of it, to continue into the next century. As a rule I was very fond of rain, but this kind of endless, cold, driving downpour was enough to put me off the stuff for the rest of my life. Dispirited, I went over to light the fire, hoping that a cheerful blaze would dispel the gloom.

The bedside phone had awakened me bright and early. It had been Emma, returning my calls. She and Derek hadn't gotten home from the vicarage until after midnight, and Derek had returned first thing in the morning to put the finishing touches on his repairs. She asked me to come over later that morning, after she'd dropped Peter and Nell off at school. Bill and I had breakfast, then filled a manila envelope with the items I wanted to show to Emma: the journal, the photo, my mother's letter to me. I threw in the topo map for the heck of it, and Reginald sat atop the envelope, ready to testify on my behalf. Bill stayed in the study to continue reading, while I filled a blue ceramic bowl with oatmeal cookies for the Harrises and killed time watching the storm. I had just finished lighting the fire when Bill called me into the study.

He was sitting on the desk when I came in. "It's occurred to me," he said, "that we haven't asked Dimity about the missing album."

"Why bother?" I replied. "I doubt that she'll discuss anything related to her problem."

"But we don't know for sure if the album's related to her problem," Bill pointed out. "If she evades the question, however . . ." He nodded toward the manila envelope. "It's worth a try."

I took out the journal and opened it to a blank page. "Dimity?" I said. "Hello? It's me, Lori. Do you have a minute?"

I always have time for you, my dear.

Wide-eyed, I glanced at Bill and nodded. "So, uh, how are you?"

As well as can be expected.

"You know, Dimity, Bill and I have been trying to figure out why you're . . . stuck wherever you are, instead of moving on to where you're supposed to be."

It is a very long story.

"I always have time for you, Dimity."

And I would prefer not to discuss it.

"Come on, Dimity, we want to help, but we don't know where to begin. Couldn't you just give us a hint? Like about the photo albums, for instance—"

Lori, I must insist that you drop this line of inquiry.

"You know me too well to think that I'll do that, Dimity."

In that case

Nothing more appeared on the page. I looked up at Bill and shook my head.

"Try again," he said.

I tried again, several times, but not another word was added. Finally I closed the book and put it back in the envelope.

"I guess that answers our question," said Bill.

"Or raises a few more," I said.

"Such as?"

"What if we've gone too far? What if Dimity's gone for good?"

Bill had nothing to say to that. With a pensive sigh, I left him to his reading. I brought Reginald, the manila envelope, and the bowl of cookies to the living room, and as I approached the hall closet to get my jacket, the doorbell rang.

"I'll get it," I called, and went to open the door, wondering who would come visiting on such an awful day.

Evan Fleischer was standing on my doorstep. He shook his greasy locks from his shoulders and sniffed. "Nice little place you have here," he said. "It's a shame about the modernization, but I'm sure that doesn't bother you."

Stunned, I took an involuntary step backward. The door flew past me and slammed in his face. If I'd had any presence of mind, I would have left it that way, but my politeness reflexes kicked in and I opened it again without thinking.

"Strong winds today," he commented as he brushed by me to inspect the hallway. "Yes, yes, very nice. Plebeian, but it suits you. Ooh." He shivered. "Drafty, though."

He was right. The indoor temperature had plummeted. I was at a loss to explain how that had happened, but I hoped against hope that the chill would drive Evan away.

Fat chance.

"I'll keep my coat on, since your heating is so primitive," he said, striding into the living room.

"You'll get everything wet," I protested.

"For heaven's sake, Lori, it's only water." Still bundled up in his sopping wet pseudo-Burberry, he sat and held his hands to the fire.

I stood poised in the doorway for a moment, decided not to hit him over the head with the poker, then marched to the study, which was as toasty as ever. Bill looked up as I entered. "I'll be in in a minute," he said.

"I think your services are required immediately, Mr. Facilitator. Your guest has arrived and I have to leave."

He looked perplexed for a moment, and then the penny dropped. "Evan?"

"Live and in person and dripping all over the—Good Lord, what's he done now?" Loud noises from the living room brought me running. The room was filled with smoke, and Evan was choking and coughing and banging at the windows, trying to get them open.

"Evan, you idiot, stop it!" I shouted. "If you break my windows I'll break your neck!"

I elbowed him aside to open the windows, and the smoke dissipated rapidly. Evan collapsed in a chair, panting and sputtering, while I checked the flue in the fireplace. It was closed. I opened it, then eyed Evan suspiciously.

"Were you messing around with the fireplace?" I demanded.

"I was not," he gasped indignantly. "I was sitting quietly when the room began to fill with smoke. The damned chimney is obviously defective. You should have it replaced at once. I could have suffocated."

"Welcome, Dr. Fleischer." Bill was standing in the living room doorway, smiling weakly. "So you've taken me up on my invitation. Lori said you might."

The arrogant smirk returned to Evan's face. "I wouldn't miss a chance to visit this part of England," he said. "I am, of course, intimately familiar with it. I once wrote a monograph on the Woolstaplers' Hall in Chipping Campden. It was never published—academic publishing is so political, so corrupt—but I should be only too happy to summarize it for you."

"I'd love to hear it," said Bill, "but unfortunately, you've come at a bad time. I'm afraid that Lori was just about to—"

"This piece is quite nice, actually," said Evan, running his fingers along the smooth leg of the table beside his chair. "A Twirley, unless I'm very much mistaken."

"Evan," I said, backing toward the hall, "I really have to be—"

"Aha," said Evan, now on his knees and peering closely at the bottom of the table. "There's his signature, a whirligig, you can see it quite clearly. Nice. Very nice. Augustus Twirley carved only twenty-seven of these tables, and thirteen of them are known to have been destroyed in fires."

"Fascinating," I said, although I was convinced that he was making it up as he went along.

"Not at all." Evan rose, brushed his palms lightly together, and seated himself once more. "Knowledge is a gift that must be given freely. I dare say you knew nothing of the treasure lying under your own nose." He sighed wistfully as he helped himself to a cookie from the bowl I'd left on the table. "It is my considered opinion that Americans have become blind to quality." He was about to dispense more pearls of wisdom when he bit into his cookie and let out a yelp of agony.

"Evan, what's wrong?" I asked in alarm.

"My toof!" he howled, grimacing horribly and gripping the front of his face with both hands. "I broke a toof!"

I raised a hand to my own jaw. If there is anyone for whom I have complete and instantaneous sympathy, it is someone with a broken tooth. The first time I broke one, I was a twenty-six-year-old, independent, and—in most other ways—mature human being, but I was so traumatized that I called my mother in tears, long-distance, right after it happened. I was shocked, therefore, to find myself suppressing a smile at Evan's misfortune.

I was also just plain shocked. Bill and I had both sampled the cookies and none had caused bodily harm. I took one from the bowl and bit into it cautiously. It contained nothing more tooth-threatening than some chewy raisins.

"Would you like me to call a local dentist?" Bill was saying. "It's a little early, but I'm sure—"

"Sod the local dentist!" Evan roared. "No country clown is going to touch a tooth of mine. I'm going back to London. I should never have left civilization in the first place." He pitched the remnants of his cookie into the fireplace and stalked to the front door. Another gust of wind caught it as he crossed the threshold and I think it may have helped hasten his departure with a gentle shove as it slammed shut.

I held my breath until I heard his car speed down the road, then turned to Bill, who was sitting on the couch, looking dumbfounded.

"What did you do to the cookies?" I asked.

"I was about to ask you the same thing."

We stared at each other, then spoke in one voice: "Dimity."

I shook my head, torn between pity and relief. "Poor Evan. Well, she tried to freeze him out, then smoke him out, but he wouldn't pay attention."

"Attending to others doesn't seem to be one of Dr. Fleischer's strong points. All the same, we owe him a debt of gratitude. Thanks to him, we know that Dimity hasn't left us."

"But she still won't talk to us." I fetched my jacket and an umbrella from the hall, then gathered up Reginald, the cookies, and the manila envelope. "Not about the album, at least, and that makes me more determined than ever to find it. You're sure you don't want to come along?"

"One of us should be here in case Father calls," said Bill, opening the door. "Besides, I'm making good progress with the correspondence. Who knows what the next letter will bring?"

The entrance to the Harrises' drive was less than a mile from the cottage, but the drive itself was a good half mile long, curving between rows of azalea bushes, then skirting the edge of a broad expanse of lawn. Ahead of me and to the left was what appeared to be a very soggy vegetable garden, while to the right stood a rambling three-story farmhouse built of the same honey-colored stone as the cottage. Low outbuildings clustered behind it, and the drive led into an open gravel yard littered with the debris of Derek's profession: sawhorses, a sandpile, bricks, fieldstones, ladders. As I turned off the ignition, raucous barking sounded from the house, and a moment later Emma appeared on the doorstep, wearing a rose-colored corduroy skirt and a pale green cowl-neck sweater. Her long hair billowed behind her as she came to welcome me, sheltered from the storm by a striped golf umbrella.

Clambering out of the car, I began to deliver a string of apologies for my cool reaction to her warning about Dimity, but she stopped me. "No need for that," she said, taking charge of Reginald. "I didn't accept it at first, either."

I cast an admiring glance at my surroundings. "This is an amazing place."

"Six bedrooms and four baths in the main house." Emma raised a hand to indicate the other buildings. "My potting shed, Derek's workshop, the children's lab—much safer to have it at a distance—the garage, and general storage. You never know what you'll find in there." A satellite dish lent an incongruous touch of modernity to the shingled roof of the children's lab, and a two-foot-tall stone gargoyle leered demonically from the half-open door of the storage building. When we reached the doorstep of the main house, Emma stopped. "Do you like dogs?"

"Very much."

"Good. We couldn't have heard ourselves speak if I'd had to lock up Ham. He'll calm down once he's finished saying hello." The low doorway led into a rectangular room with a flagstone floor, where we were greeted by an ebullient black Labrador retriever. He wagged his tail, grinned, and barked exuberantly, while I scratched his ears and told him what a handsome hound he was.

"My daughter found him when he was still a puppy," Emma explained, "trussed up and tossed on the side of the road not far from here. She brought him home, we nursed him back to health, and she named him after her favorite tragic hero."

"Hamlet?" I hazarded.

"As Nell is fond of pointing out, he always wears black." Emma handed Reginald back to me, then put our umbrellas in a crowded stand beside the door and hung my jacket on a row of pegs with many others. Wellington boots, hiking boots, sneakers, and clogs lay in a jumble beneath a wooden church pew that stood against the far wall, and fishing poles, walking sticks, and four battered tennis rackets leaned in one corner. "We call this the mudroom, for obvious reasons. Come into the kitchen. I've just filled the pot."

A brightly colored braided rug covered most of the kitchen floor, burgeoning herb plants trailed over the windowsills, and copper pots hung on hooks near the stove. From a crowded shelf on a tall dresser, Emma took cups, saucers, and a hand-labeled mason jar, placing them beside the teapot on the refectory table in the center of the room. Ham leaned against my leg adoringly as I sat in one of the rush-bottom chairs.

"Oh, Ham, stop flirting." Emma ordered the dog to his blanket by the stove, then sat across from me. Her eyes lit up when I presented her with the bowl of oatmeal cookies. "Derek and the children will be so pleased. They've been after me to make some, but I simply haven't had the time. You don't mind if we talk in here, do you?"

"I can't think of a better place."

Emma handed me a steaming cup of tea, then pushed the mason jar toward me. "Raspberry jam I put up last summer. Try some in your tea."

I stirred in a liberal dollop, took a sip, and sighed with pleasure. "Yum. Now, about our mutual friend. Would you like me to go first?"

Emma smiled. "Derek says that my orderly mind drives him crazy sometimes and right now I understand what he means. I can hardly wait to hear what's happened to you, but . . ."

"First things first," I said.

"I'm afraid so. And I'm terrible at making long stories short."

"Take all the time you need," I said. "I'm in no hurry."

Emma gathered her thoughts, then leaned forward on her elbows. "Derek and I moved to Finch five years ago. Although we knew of Dimity through a mutual acquaintance, we had met her only in passing. It didn't take us long to learn more about her, though. According to the baker, she had been born and raised in the cottage. According to the vicar, she continued to live there after her parents had died. And according to the greengrocer, she joined up the day war was declared, and served in London until the Armistice.

"That was when Dimity came into her inheritance. It was left to her—according to everyone—by a distant relative, and the money enabled her to return to London, purchase her town house, and become involved in charity work. After that, she rarely returned to the cottage. It was a simple country cottage then: two up, two down, no electricity, and rudimentary plumbing. It must have seemed fairly primitive compared to her digs in London.

"At any rate, I was clipping the azaleas one day when Dimity's Bentley pulled into our drive. Derek had done some restoration work on the church in Finch, so Dimity knew of his skill as a builder, and she'd come to ask him to do some work on the cottage. Derek thought she meant a simple renovation and he jumped at the chance." Emma laughed. "As you can tell, he landed up to his chin.

"Dimity's 'simple renovation' lasted for two years. Derek had to turn down scores of other jobs, and I cut way back on my consulting work in order to do what I love best. Dimity gave me a free hand with everything except the front garden."

So that it would match the cottage in the story, I mused silently, offering Emma another cookie and taking one for myself.

"But the rest was mine," Emma continued, "and it was heaven. Derek was as happy as I was. He loved the challenge Dimity threw at him: rebuild the cottage, expand it, update it, but keep its soul intact.

It was the biggest project he'd ever undertaken and it seemed to get bigger as he went along. Dimity would stop by once a month, each time with another suggestion to make. Derek began referring to the cottage as our own private Winchester House.

"But during that whole time, we never knew why Dimity was doing it. We thought at first she might move in permanently, but she just shook her head when we mentioned it. We doubted that she'd ever sell it, so what was the point? There it stood, like . . . like Sleeping Beauty, waiting for her handsome . . . Lori? Are you okay?"

I finished choking on my cookie and took a swallow of tea. "Yes, of course. Please, go on."

"Just before Dimity died, we ran into all sorts of problems with the project. Building materials weren't delivered on time, the ones that arrived were substandard, and some of the workmen decided to disappear when the weather turned ugly. It drove Derek mad. Dimity was quite ill by then and he had his heart set on finishing the work before she died. Dimity called it the ultimate deadline." Emma began to smile, then stopped and blushed self-consciously. "I'm sorry. That must seem heartless. But if you'd known Dimity . . ."

"I can imagine," I said. "It's a good line. I'll bet she thought it was funny."

"She had a wonderful sense of humor. And she never worried about whether the cottage would be finished in time or not. She arranged it so that Bill's father would oversee the financing of the renovation after her death and she told Derek to do the best possible job and not to worry—if she didn't see it then, she'd see it . . . later."

"Little did you know. . . ." I murmured.

Emma nodded. "Her attitude helped Derek cope with the fact that she died before the renovation was complete. But that's not all that helped." Emma rested her chin on her hand, a puzzled expression on her face. "We didn't notice it at first, but gradually everything about the project began falling into place. Derek said he didn't think he could hit his thumb with a hammer if he tried. And the garden!" Her voice was filled with wonder. "I'd drop a seed on the ground and I could almost watch it take root. But, as I said, we didn't notice. We just went along from day to day, feeling very proud of our progress.

"Which may explain why the accident happened. Or rather—didn't happen. Perhaps we had become overconfident and careless. Whatever the reason, Derek dropped his welding torch in a pile of paint-soaked rags. They should have gone up in smoke and taken the cottage with them, and Derek, too." She tightened her hold on her teacup. "But nothing happened! Nothing. Derek ran out into the garden to find me and I went back inside with him to see. There wasn't so much as a scorch mark anywhere.

"We were both shaken up, and as we sat there that afternoon, we began to remember all sorts of things that we had dismissed as they were happening, little things—warped boards that straightened overnight, tools that were always at hand when we needed them, boxes of nails that never seemed to run out—all sorts of things that we could explain in all sorts of ways, except when we added them up. When we did that, we had to admit that, as impossible as it seemed, something—or someone—was . . . helping us. I thought it sounded preposterous, until Derek reminded me of an even stranger experience we'd had in an old chapel in Cornwall. In the end, I was forced to agree that something extraordinary was taking place."

It sounded so familiar; all the little, easily explained happenings that added up to something inexplicable. I realized that I was sitting there with my mouth hanging open, so I closed it, then said, "Well, at least she's a friendly ghost."

Emma laughed. "Yes, we were pretty sure we knew who was helping, but we didn't know why."

"Until Bill's father called you."

"Almost a year after Dimity died, the cottage was as complete as we could make it. Soon after that, Mr. Willis contacted us to ask us to get it ready." Emma stood and rummaged through another shelf on the dresser until she found a tin tea caddy similar to the one at the cottage. Prying off the lid, she sat down again. "The day before you arrived, I went over to the cottage to stock the pantry. In the middle of the kitchen table I found this." She pulled from the caddy a single piece of pale blue stationery. The note read: *Thank you.* By then I knew the handwriting as well as I knew my own.

"I can see now why you wanted to warn me," I said.

Emma put the note back in the caddy and returned the caddy to the shelf, giving me a sidelong look. "Our motives weren't entirely selfless. If all of that had happened to the bit players, we couldn't wait to see what would happen to the star. I take it that there have been further developments?"

"You could say that." I reached for the manila envelope.

Because of her previous experiences, Emma took the story of Reginald and the journal in stride. She was far more intrigued by my mother's account of Dimity's collapse.

"That's a new one on me," she said. "Dimity never breathed a word about it to us, and if anyone in Finch knew of it, I'm sure we would have heard by now. As for the location of the clearing . . . I think I may be able to help you there. I discovered orienteering when I moved to England. It's taught me the value of recognizing landmarks." She noticed my blank expression and explained, "It's a kind of cross-country race, using a map and compass."

"Is that what Derek meant when he said you were always off roaming the countryside?" I asked.

"I'm afraid my husband doesn't share my enthusiasm for the sport," she replied. "But Peter and Nell and I belong to a club in Bath. It frequently holds meets in this area." She pointed to one of the distant hills in the photograph. "It's hard to say for sure—places like this change so much over the years—but I think . . . I think that's the ridge Peter fell from last summer. No damage done, but it took a while to get him back up to the top. We came in last that day. Let me get some of my maps and—"

"Will this do?" I offered her the topographic map.

"Oh, yes, that will do nicely," said Emma. "Now, let me see. . . ." Her eyes darted back and forth from the photo to the map, as her finger moved along the curving lines. "They have contests like this in the orienteering magazines," she commented. "I must say that I never expected to . . ." Her finger stopped. "I think . . . yes, that has to be it. I should have recognized it right away. It's much steeper and more heavily wooded than most of the hills around here. It's called Pouter's Hill."

"It's right behind the cottage?"

"It's part of the estate," Emma explained. "I've never been up there myself, but it's the correct orientation to give you this view of those hills."

"Is that a path?" I asked, touching a broken line that ran up the hill.

"Yes," said Emma. "It starts on the other side of the brook out back." She pointed. "Here. From the way it's marked I'd say that it was pretty rough going. I wouldn't try it today if I were you."

"Just knowing where it is is enough for now." I started as a cold nose nudged my hand. Ham had come to claim a reward for his good behavior and he'd certainly earned it, curled patiently on his blanket while the humans had chattered endlessly. "Hello, you sweet thing." I scratched behind his ears and glanced at Emma for permission to give him a treat from the table.

She shrugged. "Why should you be any different?" Ham approved of my oatmeal cookies, too, and wolfed down three of them before Emma called a halt. "Would you like to have a look round the place?" she offered.

By then I was glad of a chance to stretch my legs, and Ham was more than ready for a romp. He frisked at our heels as Emma took me from room to room. "The house was badly run-down when we bought it—a handyman's dream, as we say in the States, and therefore an ideal home for Derek. We've battled dry rot and mildew, but our worst enemy has been our predecessors' bad taste. Please don't ask me to describe the wallpaper we found in the parlor. It took us a whole summer to get rid of it."

The parlor walls were now plain whitewashed plaster, but the furnishings were eccentric, to put it mildly. The television sat atop an antique and worm-eaten altar, and the coffee table was an intricately carved wooden door overlaid with glass. A pair of elegant Louis XIV chairs faced a plain-as-dirt horsehair sofa, and a Chinese black-lacquered desk held a Victorian globe lamp, a brass pig, and a human skull. "Derek comes home with all sorts of things," Emma explained, "and we thought that the family room should be furnished by the family." She pointed to the television. "That's Derek's little joke, and the chairs were Nell's idea. I don't know who brought the skull in here, but Peter chose the desk."

The parlor reflected an active family life. It was littered with books and magazines, a forgotten shoe peeked out from under the couch, and a bowl half-filled with cherry pits graced a marquetry chest beneath the windows. When I saw the chest, I realized that I had forgotten to ask Emma about the missing photo album. When I put the question to her, she nodded thoughtfully.

"Nell was working on a project for school last spring, something about the role of women in the Second World War. Dimity loaned her some pictures for it, but I thought she'd returned them." She glanced toward the hall. "But let's make sure." With Ham galloping ahead, we went upstairs to what I thought was a second-floor bedroom. When I hesitated, Emma said reassuringly, "We're not about to invade my daughter's inner sanctum. This is the children's study."

In marked contrast to the parlor, the study was sparely furnished and orderly, with heavy-laden bookshelves, filing cabinets, and a pair of desks facing opposite walls. "I'm happy to say that the children take their schoolwork very seriously. They may make a shambles of the rest of the house, but they're neat as a pin in here. Nell's half is on the left." Emma scanned the bookshelves on that side of the room while I went through the drawers in her daughter's desk. Five minutes later, Emma came up trumps.

"Is this it?" She handed me a brown leather photograph album labeled *1939–1944*.

Too excited to speak, I nodded, then opened the album on Nell's desk and flipped rapidly through it. There were three or four pictures on each page, all of them affixed with black paste-on paper corners. Dimity had written brief captions beneath each of them: names, dates, places. I turned past pictures of Dimity posed alone or with groups of other women in military uniform, catching my breath when my mother's young face appeared in the crowd, until I came to the end.

"Damn," I muttered, "there's nothing missing."

"What do you mean?"

"If the photograph from Pouter's Hill came from this album, there'd be an empty space somewhere. But there isn't."

"Oh, I see." Emma half sat on the edge of the desk, her arms folded. "What a shame."

"No, wait. Maybe I'm just jumping the gun again." Sitting in Nell's chair, I switched on her desk lamp, reopened the album, and began going through it slowly, spreading it flat at every page. "I used to work with rare books, and one of the things I had to check for was vandalism—theft, really. There's a big market for old woodcuts and engravings."

"Like those framed botanical illustrations you see in antique stores?" Emma asked.

"Right. Some come from books that are too far gone to salvage, but some . . ." I turned the fifth page, spread it flat, and stopped. "Some are razored out of perfectly sound volumes. Like this." Emma bent low for a closer look as I thumbed a series of quarter-inch stubs, all that remained of twelve black pages.

"You don't think—" I began, but Emma shook her head decisively.

"Not Nell. Not in a million years."

I sighed, closed the album, and brought it back downstairs to the kitchen, where Reginald eyed me sympathetically and Emma looked once more at the photograph of the old oak tree.

"There's still hope," I said wistfully. "Maybe Bill's father will find the missing pages."

"I wonder who could have given this to your mother," Emma mused. "The couple we bought this place from passed away several years ago, and I don't know of any other . . . May I read your mother's description?"

I had told her about it earlier. Now I dug out the letter and handed it to her. She read it intently.

"But this doesn't say anything about a couple," she murmured. "It only says 'two of Dimity's neighbors.' 'Elderly . . . not terribly coherent. . .'" Suddenly she looked up, her eyes sparkling. "I think I know who you're looking for."

Seventeen

"*The Pym sisters?*" I exclaimed. "The sock-knitting Pym sisters? Are they still alive?"

"And kicking," Emma replied. "Decorously, of course." She went on to say that Ruth and Louise Pym were the identical twin daughters of a country parson. No one knew how old they were, not even the vicar, but most guesses placed them over the century mark. They had never married and had spent all of their lives in Finch. "I think they know more about what goes on in the village than most people would like to believe," Emma concluded. "I'm sure they're the ones who gave the photograph to your mother, and if they didn't, they'll know who did."

"How do I get to meet them?"

"Invite them to tea, of course. They'll be dying to meet you. I'll ask them for you, if you'd like."

"Yes, please. And you'll come, too, won't you?"

"Why don't I come early to help you set up?"

"That would be terrific."

Emma accompanied me to the mudroom, where I donned my jacket and gave Ham a last few pats.

"You'll have to come over when the sun is shining so I can show you the grounds." Emma held Ham's collar while I opened the door. "Be sure to let me know if you find out anything about those missing pages, and I'll call as soon as I've set things up with Ruth and Louise."

I unfurled my umbrella, then reached out to clasp Emma's hand. "Thank you. I don't know if you realize how much this means to me, but—"

"I think I do." She smiled. "Derek and I loved Dimity, too."

Bill was asleep in the study when I got back, his feet up on the ottoman, the date-filled notebook dangling from his fingertips. I woke him up by dropping Reginald in his lap, then sat on the ottoman and repeated everything Emma had told me that morning. I showed him the stubs in the photo album and he shared my disappointment, but agreed that Willis, Sr., might come through for us yet. He was delighted by the thought of meeting the Pym sisters, but the mention of tea made us both realize that we were ready for lunch. Greatly daring, I tried a spinach soufflé. It was flawless.

I couldn't bring myself to face the correspondence after lunch. The things I had learned about my mother had spooked me and I shied away from learning any more. True to his word, Bill soldiered on in silence while I returned scattered archive boxes to their proper places on the shelves. I was sitting at the desk, paging through the photo album when he spoke up.

"Listen!"

"I don't hear anything."

"That's what I mean. It's stopped raining!"

I could scarcely believe my ears. The steady drumming of the rain had been replaced by a stillness as heavy as Devonshire cream, and when I leaned forward to look through the windows I saw that a dense fog had settled in the storm's wake.

Bill closed the notebook and put it in his pocket, then walked over to have a look for himself. "Ah, the glories of English weather."

"I'll bet it's a big relief to Derek and the vicar. You think it'll clear by tomorrow?"

Bill shrugged. "Something tells me that we're going up that hill tomorrow even if it snows. You have many virtues, my dear Miss Shepherd, but patience is not one of them."

"I'm always halfway up the block before I know where I'm going," I admitted. "My mother used to say—" I broke off and looked out at the fog again. "I've been meaning to thank you, by the way."

"For what?"

"For believing me when I told you about the journal, even before you'd seen it with your own eyes. If you had come to me with a story like that, I would have—"

"Wait," said Bill. "Let me guess." He put his hands on his hips and his nose in the air and launched into what I feared was an accurate imitation of me at my indignant worst. "'Bill,' " he said with a sniff, "'What kind of a fool do you take me for? I don't believe in ghosts!' " He relaxed his stance, then raised an eyebrow. "Did I come close?"

"A direct hit." I winced. "I've been pretty impossible, haven't I?"

"No more than I," said Bill, "and you had a much better excuse. Finding yourself alone in a very strange situation, I can understand why you'd be on guard."

"On guard, maybe, but not hostile," I said. "I don't know—maybe I acted that way because I was confused. I didn't understand why you were being so . . . friendly." I dusted an invisible speck from the edge of the desk. "To tell you the truth, I still don't understand it."

"Can't you just accept it?" he asked.

"It's hard for me to accept something I don't understand," I said.

"Like your mother?" he said gently.

I planted my hands on my hips and shot a fiery glare in his direction, then realized what I looked like and sank back in the chair, deflated. "Yes, like my mother." I pointed to a picture in Dimity's album. "That's her. That's my mom."

Bill put one hand on the back of my chair and watched over my shoulder as I paged through the rest of the album. It was filled with pictures of my mother, in uniform and in civilian dress, her dark hair pulled back into a bun or braided in coils over her ears. "She wore it that way to keep her ears warm," I said. "She said that coal rationing in London during the war meant chilly offices. She had beautiful hair, long and silky. She used to let me brush it before I went to bed, and every night I prayed that my curls would straighten out and that I'd wake up in the morning with hair just like hers." I ran a hand through my unruly mop. "It didn't work."

"You have her mouth, though," said Bill. "You have her smile."

"Do I?" The very thought brought a smile to my lips. It had been a long time since I had talked to anyone about my mother, and now it seemed as though I couldn't stop talking about her. "Yes, I guess I do. See this one, where she's making a face? She used to make that same face at me, wrinkle her nose and cross her eyes, and it killed me every time, just laid me out flat, giggling. We used to have pillow fights, too, and she'd chase me all over the apartment until Mrs. Frankenberg banged on her ceiling with a broom handle. She'd made up this whole set of holidays. I was in kindergarten before I realized that no one else celebrated Chocolate Chip Tuesday." I turned the page. "Other mothers seemed like cardboard cutouts compared to her."

"Were you in any of her classes?" Bill asked.

"Never. She knew what kids could be like, so she enrolled me in another school entirely."

"PTA nights must have been tricky."

"Tricky? Try being in two places at once sometime. But she always managed to take care of everyone." I closed the album and sighed. "Everyone but herself."

"Lori——" Bill began, but the telephone cut him off. He snatched it up before it could ring again.

"Yes?" he said. "How are you, Father? Good, good. Of course I'm behaving myself. You don't think I want to go through *that* again, do you? Yes, in some ways she's very much like my old headmaster, though she lacks his little mustache, of course. . . . Yes, she's been hard at work on the correspondence." Bill glanced at me, then turned away. "I'm sorry, Father, but I don't think she can come to the phone right now. Would it be possible for you to call——"

"It's all right, Bill," I said. "I'll take it."

"One moment please, Father." Bill covered the receiver with his hand and said to me, "This can wait."

"I know. But I'm all right. I'll talk to him."

Bill gave me a measuring look, then spoke into the phone again. "You're in luck, Father. She's just come down. Here, I'll give you to her now. Yes, I will. Good to speak with you, too." He passed the phone to me.

"I'm so glad to have caught you, Miss Shepherd," said Willis, Sr. "I looked into the matter we discussed yesterday, as you requested. There are photographs with Miss Westwood's papers, but I regret to say that none of them were taken before the year 1951. They are official portraits, having to do with her role as founder of the Westwood Trust."

"That's a shame," I said, shaking my head at Bill, "but thanks for checking it out."

"You are most welcome. My son tells me that you've made great progress in your reading. Since that is the case, I wonder if I might trouble you to answer a few of Miss Westwood's questions?"

"Questions? Oh—you want to ask about the letters," I said, tapping Bill's breast pocket. I had forgotten all about our question-and-answer sessions. If I'd been attending to my research, it wouldn't have mattered, but as it was, I was relieved to see Bill pull out his notebook and open it, poised for action. "Why, certainly, Mr. Willis. Fire away."

"The first concerns the letter in which Miss Westwood's cat is introduced. Have you run across it in your reading?"

"Aunt Dimity's cat?" I said. Bill consulted his notebook, ran his hand along the rows of archive boxes, and took one down. "Yes, that one appeared fairly early on."

"Excellent. Miss Westwood wished for you to explain to me the ways in which the original anecdote differs from the finished story. Would it be possible for you to do so?"

"The differences between the story and the letter," I said. "Let me see, now. . . ." Bill located the letter and handed it to me. I scanned it, then closed my eyes and ran through the story in my head. "The story is more detailed, for one thing. The letter doesn't mention the cat overturning the knitting basket or spilling the pot of ink on the window-seat cushions."

"Yes," said Willis, Sr., with an upward inflection that suggested I wasn't off the hook yet.

"And in the letter, the cat is named Attila. In the story, he's just called 'the cat.'"

"Very good," said Willis, Sr., but I got the feeling that I was still missing something. I put the letter down and tried to concentrate.

"In the story," I said, "the cat is a monster. Honestly, he has no redeeming qualities. He's played for laughs, but he's— Just a moment, please, Mr. Willis. *What?*" This last was to Bill, who was waving wildly to get my attention. He had opened the manuscript of the stories and was now pointing urgently to a page.

"Wrong answer," Bill whispered. "Look—right here."

Still holding my hand over the phone, I bent down to skim the page. It was the conclusion of the *Aunt Dimity's Cottage* and as I read through it I realized that I had gotten it wrong. Confused, and a little shaken, I straightened and spoke once more to Willis, Sr.

"That is to say . . ." I cleared my throat. "What I meant to say is that the cat has no redeeming qualities *at first,* but then, when you get to the end of the story—and the letter—he turns out to be kind of a sweetie. I mean, he still does all sorts of awful things and he still makes Dimity lose her temper, but he also amuses her, and he . . . he keeps her feet warm in bed."

"Thank you, Miss Shepherd," said Willis, Sr. "If you have no further commissions for me, I shall ring off. I have no wish to impede your progress."

"No, no further commissions. I'll talk to you again soon." I hung up the phone and looked down at the story. "I don't understand this. . . . I thought I remembered every word."

"Did Dimity change the ending?" Bill asked.

"No. That's what's so strange. As soon as I began reading it, the words came back to me, exactly as they're written on the page."

"So your memory slipped up a bit. I wouldn't worry about it."

But I was worried. I had been utterly convinced that I knew these stories inside out, but it seemed as though I had been wrong. I felt disoriented, bewildered. What else had I forgotten? I turned to the beginning of the manuscript and began reading.

Eighteen

We were fogbound for three days.

Emma swore she had never seen anything like it. She dropped by to let me know that Ruth and Louise Pym had accepted my invitation to come to tea on Saturday, and to reiterate her warning about Pouter's Hill. "It may not be Mount Everest," she said, "but it can be just as hazardous in weather like this." I confounded Bill's expectations by agreeing with her, and confounded them further by postponing the trip for another twenty-four hours after the sun finally appeared on the morning of the fourth day. I figured it wouldn't hurt to give the hill a chance to dry out—a path mired in mud would be no easier to climb than one covered in fog.

Our time wasn't wasted, though. Bill finished a first read-through of the correspondence and handed me a complete index of letters that related in one way or another to the Aunt Dimity stories. I was amazed at the speed with which he had completed his reading, but he shrugged it off, saying that it was a breeze compared to reading contract law.

He failed to find so much as a hint about Dimity's problem, but he set to work compiling a list of the people mentioned in her letters, everyone from Leslie Gordon of Starling House to Mrs. Farnham, the greengrocer's wife. If Ruth and Louise Pym didn't pan out, we would go down the list until we found someone who did.

While Bill was busy with the correspondence, I continued to pore over the manuscript, testing my memory against the written text. All too often, my memory fell short, and the ways in which it did were disturbing. I clearly remembered the very large man who had stepped on Aunt Dimity's foot at Harrod's, for example, but what happened next had somehow been edited from my recollection.

With profuse apologies, the very large man turned to Aunt Dimity and offered her his very large arm. "I am so very sorry, Madame," he said, in his very large voice, "but the crush is quite impossible today. Won't you take my arm? Perhaps we can make better progress if we face the crowds together."

And Aunt Dimity did take his arm, and they did face the crowds together, and he escorted her to the train afterward and said a cheery farewell. And, although she left without the torch, the bright memory of the kind man lit the way home.

All I had remembered was her squashed foot. It was as though I had twisted the story to fit an entirely different view of the world, one which was harsher and more harrowing, and the same was true of almost every story in the collection. Disquieted, I said nothing of it to Bill, but I wondered—when had I grown so bitter?

When I had finished the stories, I made a careful search of the cottage, starting with the utility room and going from there through every cupboard, cabinet, drawer, and shelf, looking for the missing photographs, a personal diary, anything that might help us figure out what had happened to Dimity. I went so far as to try tapping walls and floorboards to discover hidden recesses—a procedure that amused Bill no end—but my hunt proved fruitless.

I used Bill's index to cull from the correspondence all of the letters related to the stories, then used them as an excuse to drive into Bath. I told Bill I was going there to find a photocopy shop, and he agreed that it made sense to work with copies of the letters rather than the originals. It was a plausible story—I believed it, too, until I found myself browsing through the dress shops. That's when I decided that I had *really* gone to Bath to find something to wear to tea on Saturday. After all, it was my duty as a hostess to show up in something more presentable than jeans and a sweater.

So, after wandering through the splendid arcades and elegant crescents of the prettiest of Georgian towns, and after duly copying the letters, I did a little shopping. Maybe more than a little. Once I'd found the dress—a short-sleeved blue silk one, with a dainty floral print—I had to find the shoes to go with it, and then came all the bits in between, and by the time I was finished, I had squeezed my supply of personal cash dry, Why I didn't ask Bill for an advance was a question I avoided like the plague.

I tiptoed upstairs to stash my new clothes in the master bedroom, then floated innocently back down to the study, photocopies in hand. When Willis, Sr., called, late in the afternoon on the fourth day of our hiatus, I greeted him with the self-assurance of someone who knows that all the bases are covered.

"What's it to be this time, Mr. Willis? Do you want to know about Aunt Dimity's adventures at Harrod's? Or maybe we'll stick closer to home—Aunt Dimity setting aside a patch of garden for the rabbits."

"I am heartened to hear the enthusiasm in your voice, Miss Shepherd," said Willis, Sr. "It is reassuring to know that Miss Westwood's wishes are being carried forward with such zeal. My question, however, has to do with Aunt Dimity's experiences at the zoological gardens. Can you recount for me the original version of that story?"

"*Aunt Dimity Goes to the Zoo*," I murmured, leafing patiently through the photocopies. "Let's see. That should be here somewhere. . . ." But it wasn't. I double-checked Bill's index, but the end result was the same: there had been no reference to the zoo in any of Dimity's letters. Reluctantly, I admitted as much to Willis, Sr. "I don't know what to say. There doesn't seem to *be* an original version of that story."

"Precisely, Miss Shepherd. Thank you very much. Have you had an opportunity to look about you yet? Though your work comes first, of course."

"As a matter of fact, we've been having some pretty wet weather since we arrived," I said. "It's cleared up a bit today, though, and I think I may get a chance tomorrow to use the map you gave me."

"I envy you, Miss Shepherd. England in the springtime is not a thing to miss. I would suggest a longer outing, but, alas, the work needs must be done." And with a pleasant good-bye, he hung up.

I put the receiver back in the cradle, then turned to Bill, who was still laboring over his list of names. "Why didn't Dimity write to my mother about the zoo?" I asked. "She talks about Berkeley Square and that rabbit-faced lieutenant, but in all her wartime chatter there's not one word about the zoo."

"Another uncomfortable memory?" he suggested. "Your mother did find her there, wandering about in a daze."

"As though whatever happened had happened recently," I said. "And Dimity went there . . . why?"

"Because she'd been happy there? Because it reminded her of better days?"

"What a shock it must have been to find it deserted, boarded up. . . . Yet she used it as the setting for one of her most cheerful stories." I riffled through the manuscript. "You know, Bill—Dimity said she wrote these for me and for my mother. I'm beginning to wonder if she wrote them for herself as well."

I rose early the next day, showered, then put on a pair of shorts, a T-shirt, heavy socks, and my hiking boots. I tied the arms of a sweater around my waist, in case the sun decided to hide its face again, and tucked the topographic map and the photograph in my back pocket. After a light breakfast, I was ready to face the great outdoors.

Bill, on the other hand, didn't look ready for anything more strenuous than a stroll across a putting green. He met me at nine o'clock in the solarium dressed in his usual tweed sportcoat, button-down oxford shirt, and corduroy trousers. The only thing out of the ordinary was the absence of a tie.

"Don't you have any other clothes?" I asked.

"You sound like my father," he said, shifting impatiently from foot to foot.

"You should listen to your father. But I'm not talking about matters of taste at the moment. I'm talking about survival." I looked doubtfully at his smooth-soled leather shoes. "Even a pair of sneakers would have better traction than those, and I think you're going to swelter in that jacket. Didn't you ever climb any hills when you were in Africa?"

"I had a Land Rover," Bill replied evenly. "Besides, Emma said there was a path."

"A rough path, in a roughly vertical direction." I poked the bulging canvas bag he'd slung over one shoulder. "What's in there?"

"A few necessities. Let's see. . . ." He opened the bag and rummaged through it. "A bottle of water, a loaf of bread, some cheese, a few bars of chocolate, the emergency lantern from the car, a throw rug, a trowel from the utility room, a camera—"

"We're not going on safari," I protested. "Trust me on this, Bill—that bag is going to weigh a ton before we get to the top. You're going to wish you'd left some of that stuff behind."

"You let me worry about that." Throwing open the solarium door, he strode out into the garden. "What a glorious day!"

He was right about that much, at least. It felt so good to be outside that I had to restrain myself from taking off at a run. A sheep meadow stretched green and serene to the west, the oak grove stood to the east, and ahead of us rose Pouter's Hill.

We crossed the sunken terrace of the back garden, then went up the stairs and through the gate in the gray stone wall and out into a grassy meadow. A graveled path led us between the pair of redbuds I had seen from the deck, to a willow-shaded brook that ran along the foot of the hill. The rustic bridge that spanned it practically pointed to an opening in the trees. We consulted the map, decided it was the path Emma had pointed out, and started up. I fell silent, saving my breath for the climb, but Bill spent enough for both of us.

"Birdsong, bluebells, and bracken," he rhapsodized. "Soft breezes to speed us on our way. Good, honest sweat, the heady scent of spring, and a winding path beneath our feet." He paused to take off his sportcoat and mop his brow. "Ah, Lori, it's wonderful to be alive."

"Right," I said, and kept on walking. As the good, honest sweat began cascading down Bill's face, his lyric interludes grew fewer and farther between. Halfway up, there was no sound from him but labored breathing, and he began muttering something about chain saws when the pretty, soft little plants that had invaded the lower part of the path were replaced by great hulking thornbushes.

Three-quarters of the way up, I had mercy and took the shoulder bag, but by the time Bill had dragged his scratched and aching body up the last stretch of path, he was muddy, sweaty, and pooped and seemed to have a very clear idea of why it was called Pouter's Hill. He looked ready to sulk for a week.

Until we saw what lay before us.

The path had deposited us in a glade that overlooked the land beyond the hill. A wide valley opened out below, a patchwork of bright yellow and pale green and deep, rich brown; of freshly planted fields and newly turned earth crisscrossed with low stone walls and woven together by the meandering course of a stream which glinted silver in the sunlight. Sheep grazed on distant hillsides and a pair of hawks soared in wide, sweeping arcs across the flawless blue sky. It was the clearing in the photograph, come to life.

"My God," Bill murmured, his voice hushed with awe.

The scene below looked as though it hadn't changed for a hundred years. I sensed a stillness in the clearing, in myself, that I had never felt before, a tranquillity as timeless as the hills that rolled away to the horizon. I knew as surely as I knew my own name that whatever terrible thing had happened to Dimity hadn't happened here.

I took the photograph from my pocket and held it up, glancing at it as I moved slowly across the open space. "This is where the picture was taken," I said, coming to a halt.

Bill came over to where I was standing, looked down at the photograph, and pointed. "There's the ridge Emma's son fell from. And there's the tree."

The gnarled old oak tree stood by itself at the edge of the clearing, and we walked over, drawn to its cool circle of shade. I set the bag gently on the ground, not wishing to disturb the stillness, and Bill dropped his jacket on top of it, then gazed out over the land below. He turned, startled, when I uttered a soft cry.

A heart had been carved into the old tree. It was darkened with age, and the bark had grown back over some of it, but the initials it encircled were still plainly visible.

"*RM & D—*" I looked at Bill. "RM and Dimity Westwood. RM. Who's RM?"

"Someone who came up here with her," Bill guessed, "and took pictures to commemorate the day? Maybe someone who went to the zoo with her as well?" He traced the heart with a fingertip. "Clearly someone she loved."

I sank to the ground at the foot of the tree, and Bill sat beside me. He took the water bottle from the bag and we each had a drink. Pouring some water into his cupped hand, he cooled his face, then recapped the bottle and put it away. He sat with his back against the rough bark while I watched the hawks glide gracefully through the air.

Whose hand had carved that heart? What had happened to him? I closed my eyes and sensed . . . something. A dream of distant laughter, a memory of voices, a whisper of sweet words echoing down through time; the stillness at the center of a raging world.

"Lori?"

Bill's voice came to me from a long way off. Closer, much closer were those other voices, low voices murmuring, whispering, echoing, then snatched away by a roaring wind. I strained to hear them, but the roar of the wind was followed by silence. I felt a sadness, an intense longing, a sense of loss so powerful that it struck me like a blow. Who had come with Dimity to this still and peaceful place? Whom had she lost to the chaos that surrounded it?

Bill put his hand on my shoulder.

"A soldier," I said, unaware that I was speaking the words aloud. "RM was a soldier, a boy Dimity loved, who joined up early and was killed."

"Was he?" said Bill.

"I . . . I don't know." I opened my eyes and put a hand to my forehead, squinting against the sun's sudden glare. "I don't *know*, but I thought I heard . . . Did you hear it?"

"All I hear is the wind in the trees."

"The wind . . ." The wind of death had silenced the voices in the clearing, as it would one day silence all voices. I rubbed my eyes and tried to shake the cobwebs from my mind.

"RM—a soldier?" Bill mused. "It makes sense. There was a lot of dying being done in those days, and a lot of hearts were broken. It would explain why Dimity was so shaken when your mother met her. It might even explain why she never married. But why would she get rid of the photos? If she loved him, why would she try to erase his memory?"

I ran my fingers along a twisted root, still touched by a sorrow that was, and was not, my own. "Sometimes it hurts to remember."

Bill let the words hang in the air for a moment. "It hurts worse to forget. Because you never really do, do you?"

"No," I murmured, "I suppose you don't."

"Dimity didn't. If we're guessing right, she may have tried to forget, but . . ." He looked up at the heart on the tree. "RM wouldn't leave her alone. She's still hurting, still in pain over . . . something that requires forgiveness. I don't understand why she would need to be forgiven for the death of someone she loved."

"I do," I said, in a voice so low that Bill had to lean forward to catch my words. "Sometimes you feel guilty after someone dies."

"For what?"

"For . . . all sorts of things. Things you did and things you didn't do."

"Like suspecting a perfectly innocent man of playing ghost?" said Bill archly.

"Something like that." I glanced at him, smiled briefly, then plucked a blade of grass and wound it around my finger. "My mother used to do that—say silly things to pull me out of a lousy mood."

"Did she?"

"She used to tease me all the time, the way you do. I was pretty impossible with her, too."

"I find that hard to believe," said Bill.

"It's true, though. She never said anything about it, but . . ." I shook my head. "I don't think I grew up to be the daughter she had in mind."

"Who do you think she had in mind?"

"Someone who wasn't stupid enough to study rare books, for one thing." I began to shred the blade of grass into tiny pieces. "Someone who could manage to keep a marriage together. Someone who wasn't so damned pigheaded. But I've always been that way. That's why . . ."

"That's why what?" coaxed Bill.

"Nothing." I tossed the bits of grass to the wind. "We're supposed to be talking about Dimity."

"We'll come back to Dimity. Right now we have to talk about something else. That's why *what*, Lori?"

"That's why . . ." The wind had ceased, and not a leaf was stirring. It was as though the old tree were holding its breath, waiting for me to go on. "She asked me to come home, Bill. She pleaded with me to come home. But I was too proud, too stubborn, too set on proving . . . I don't know what. And that's why . . . that's why I wasn't there when . . ."

Bill put his arms around me and pulled me to his side. He held me quietly, caressing my hair, then murmured softly, so softly that I could scarcely hear his words, "Did your mother ask you to come home for her sake or for yours?" I stiffened, but he tightened his hold, waiting for the tension to ease from my body before going on. "You shouldn't have stopped reading those letters when you did. You might have learned a thing or two." His fingers feathered lightly down my cheek. "You inherited more than your mother's mouth, you know. You have her chin, too, and it's a very determined one. That's how your mother described it, at any rate. I don't recall her ever using the word 'pig-headed.' 'As strong-willed as I am,' were the words she used."

I shook my head in protest, but Bill continued on, regardless.

"Do you think your mother joined the army because it was a good career move? Do you think she sat down and weighed the pros and cons? She didn't, Lori. She saw the war as a grand, romantic adventure, and she saw the same romantic streak in you. Why else would you study something as impractical as old books? She didn't think you were foolish, though. She would've supported anything you did, as long as you were following your heart. You know that, don't you?

"As for your marriage—she understood that, too. She had doubts about it from the beginning, and she was proud of you for discovering your mistake. Yes, she wanted you to come home then, but it was because you seemed lost. She thought *you* needed *her* help. She never wanted yours."

"Because she knew I was useless," I said bitterly.

Bill's fingers dug into my arm. "Stop it. You know that's not true."

"But—"

"Your mother, Lori Shepherd, was just as pigheaded as you are. She never asked *anyone* for help. That's why she clammed up after your father's death. It took Dimity a long time to knock some sense into her."

"And did she?" I sat up, my heart racing. "Did she talk about it?"

"Yes, after Dimity did everything but send a brass band through the mail." Bill pushed a stray curl from my forehead. "Yes, your mother finally came out with it, all of it, all of the pain and the loneliness she'd gone through, along with the joy she'd found in you. She told Dimity all about it, eventually. But she would have saved herself a lot of heartache if she'd spoken of it sooner."

"I wish she'd told me about it," I whispered.

"She should have. She should have explained what a nightmare it is to lose someone you love. She should have told you that it took her a long time and a lot of work to wake up from it."

"Maybe she was trying to protect me," I said loyally.

"I'm sure she was. But she ended up hurting you. Dimity warned her about it—I'll show you the letter when we get back. She said you'd grow up thinking that your mother was the Woman of Steel, that you'd want to be just like her. Dimity said there'd be trouble when you found out you weren't as tough as you thought you should be."

"When my mother died . . ."

"You found out that you weren't made of steel. You had no way of knowing that *no one* is made of steel. How could you? You had no one to tell you otherwise."

"You had Dimity."

"And your mother had Dimity." Bill raised his eyes to the distant hills. "But who did Dimity have?"

I followed his gaze. Bill's words had fallen like balm on my wounded spirit, but the thought of Dimity's unnamed sorrow reawakened the sense of anguished longing I had felt upon seeing the heart. The clearing itself seemed to change when he spoke her name, as though something were missing, or out of place. The sunlight had become harsh and a cool breeze chilled me. The ground felt rough against my legs and when I searched the sky for the soaring hawks, I could not find them.

Bill reached for the bag and stood up, then stretched out a hand to pull me to my feet. "It's time to go back to the cottage."

I spent the rest of that day in the study, catching up on the correspondence.

Bill spent it in the Jacuzzi.

Nineteen

$\mathcal{I}$ would have made a fortune if I'd had the foresight to sell tickets to *Tea with the Pym Sisters*. It was better than anything playing in the West End.

It helped a lot to have Mother Nature as set designer. It was another sunny day and when Emma showed up it seemed only natural to suggest tea in the solarium. With the aid of Dimity's cookbook and my ever-growing self-confidence in the kitchen, I baked an array of seedcakes and meringues and strawberry tarts. While Bill set out Dimity's best china and linen, Emma decked every nook with freshly picked flowers, even seeing to it that Reginald's ears were adorned with a diminutive daisy chain. By the time she announced the arrival of my guests, the solarium looked like something out of an Edwardian novel.

As did the Pym sisters. They were identical, from the veils on their hats to the tips of their lavender gloves. They looked so tiny and frail that I wondered how on earth they had managed the walk from Finch to the cottage, until I noticed a car parked behind the one we had leased. Like them, it was both ancient and pristine.

As remarkable as the Pym sisters were, I was pleased to note that Bill found me even more distracting. His jaw dropped when I descended the staircase, dressed in my teatime finery, and Emma had to introduce him to the Pyms twice before he remembered to say "How do you do." Even then, he said it without taking his eyes from me. I, of course, gave my undivided attention to my guests.

"Thank you so much for your kind invitation," the one on the right said.

"Yes, indeed. Such a lovely day for a drive," the other added. Even the voices were identical—not just the tone, but the rhythm as well.

Emma had cautioned me not to tackle the subject of Dimity head-on. The sisters' sense of propriety would not permit them to gossip.

They were, on the other hand, perfectly willing to *reminisce* for hours if given half a chance, so I invited them to take a look around the cottage. I hoped that a tour would spark memories of their longtime neighbor.

"How kind."

"How lovely. Emma tells us . . ."

". . . it has changed quite a bit . . ."

". . . since our last visit."

It was like watching a tennis match. As I led the way through the ground-floor rooms, the Pyms kept up a steady flow of point-counterpoint commentary in my wake. After a while, I was able to distinguish one voice from the other: Louise's was softer, and she seemed more timid. The minute they closed their mouths, however, I couldn't tell one from the other.

After we had seated ourselves around the wrought-iron table in the solarium, Emma excused herself to make tea. The Pyms chatted on about the weather and the garden and the vicar's new roof, and just as I'd begun to think my memory-sparking tour had fizzled, both sets of eyes came to rest on the heart-shaped locket which still hung on its chain around my neck.

"Oh, my . . ." said Ruth softly.

"How very curious. Might we ask . . ."

". . . how you came by this piece of jewelry?"

"I found it upstairs," I replied. I held the locket at the length of its chain for the sisters to examine more closely. "It was in a little blue box. I think it belonged to Dimity."

"Indeed it did," said Louise. "She acquired it in London, during the war, and she wore it . . ."

". . . always. We never saw her without it. We had been given the impression, in fact . . ."

". . . that a young man had given it to her."

My heart leapt and Bill leaned forward eagerly, but the Pyms seemed unaware of the impact of their words.

"Dimity was always a very kind . . ."

". . . very generous . . ."

". . . very good-hearted girl. And a great . . ."

". . . judge of character."

"Yes, indeed. She was quite a . . ."

". . . matchmaker and not one of her matches . . ."

". . . ever failed."

"Yes," I said. "I know about that. She introduced my mother to my father, didn't she, Bill?"

"What?" He looked up from what appeared to be a minute inspection of his teaspoon. "Oh, yes." He cleared his throat. "She did."

"And were they happy together?" asked Ruth.

"Extremely happy," I said.

"Well, there you are," said Ruth, and beamed with pleasure. "Dimity grew up in this cottage, you know."

"And she never left . . ."

". . . until the war."

"A most tragic affair. Here, dear, let me help you with that." When Louise turned her attention to helping Emma pour, Ruth took up the narrative thread on her own—more or less.

"She was engaged to a young officer very early in the war." I held my breath. "Young Bobby MacLaren." I looked at Bill with exaltation and he gave me a covert thumbs-up.

"Did you ever meet Bobby?" he asked.

"Indeed, we did." Ruth accepted her cup of tea with a distracted air, her face reflecting a long-forgotten sadness. "Such a fine boy, and so courageous. We lost so many. . . ." Her voice trailed off.

I took my cup of tea from Emma and placed it on the table, wondering how many young boys Ruth's old eyes had seen march off, first to one war and then to another. She sat motionless, and I could almost see their faces as she saw them, the faces of boys who would never grow old, who would always be young and fine and courageous. A memory flickered at the back of my mind, but a jay's angry chatter from the back garden extinguished it.

Ruth drew herself up and went on. "Dimity brought him to visit us once when they came to Finch on leave. He was such a lively boy, so energetic, and he had such lovely manners." She sipped her tea. "When he died, Dimity was . . ."

"Devastated." Louise had finished helping Emma.

"Quite devastated. She would have worked herself to death in London. But her commanding officer saw what was happening and ordered her to rest up for a month. She returned here, to the cottage, looking like a . . ."

"Ghost."

"A pale ghost, a shadow of herself. Louise and I thought it would be best if we came over regularly, to sit with her and look after the garden. We didn't like to leave her alone, you see . . .

". . . not after the first time."

"The first time we stopped by . . ." Ruth paused and her eyes widened. "My, but these seedcakes are lovely," she said. "Did you make them yourself? Might I ask for the recipe?"

"Y-yes, of course," I stammered, startled by the abrupt change of subject.

"I'll copy it out for you," Emma offered, and went into the kitchen to pull out the dog-eared cookbook. I sent a silent blessing after her.

"Oh, that is most kind of you. It is so difficult these days to find *real* seedcake." For a second it looked as though Ruth might stop there, but after a sip of tea, she continued. "The first time we stopped by, we found Dimity curled up on the couch, as cold as ice, staring and staring at that lovely photograph. It didn't seem healthy to leave it with her. We don't think she noticed . . ."

". . . when we took it. And she didn't seem to miss it. We brought it home with us and kept it safe. We thought that one day . . ."

". . . it might be precious to her." Ruth looked up as Emma returned, recipe in hand. "Thank you so very much, dear. Tell me, are you still having trouble with your *Alchemilla mollis?*"

Emma was halfway through her reply before I realized they were talking about a plant. I'm not sure if Bill actually saw me gripping the edge of my seat, but he seemed to sense my agitation because he decided to lead the witness for her own good. He waited for a pause, then leaned slightly toward Ruth. "Can you tell us about Bobby?" he asked.

"So full of life," mused Ruth in reply. "He wasn't a local boy, you know, but he loved it here at the cottage all the same. He said that he could imagine no place more beautiful than Pouter's Hill, and he could think of nothing more wonderful than to return there after the war. He and Dimity spent hours up there, the way young lovers do. A valiant young man, and so proud of his wings."

"So very proud," Louise echoed. "I believe the bluebells are out on Pouter's Hill." Ruth and Louise turned their bright eyes upward. "What a lovely sight."

The fact that I survived the afternoon is amazing, but it's nothing compared to the fact that the Pym sisters emerged unscathed. After the initial burst of information, their progress was sporadic at best. They'd move toward adding another tidbit about Bobby and then meander onto some wholly unrelated topic, usually having to do with food or flowers, and every time they did, I was torn between having an apoplectic seizure or committing Pymocide. Now I knew why my mother had described them as not very coherent. But Bill and Emma kept their cool and guided the conversation with admirable dexterity. By the time the Pyms took their leave—in stereo—we had learned quite a lot about the sequence of events following Bobby MacLaren's death.

When Dimity was strong enough she'd returned to active duty, but she remained dazed, heartbroken, and inconsolable. The next time Dimity came down, a year later, it was as though a cloud had lifted from her soul. The reason became clear when she introduced them to her new friend: my mother. Seeing at once how close the two women were, the Pyms entrusted my mother with the photograph, knowing that she would give it to Dimity when the right time came.

They were worried that they might not live long enough to do it themselves. No matter how lighthearted Dimity seemed, the Pyms saw a darkness in her eyes that showed she was grieving still. Unlike the other villagers, they were not surprised by the fact that Dimity seldom came back to the cottage after coming into her fortune.

Shortly after we had pieced the story together, Emma left for home, carrying my heartfelt thanks and a selection of goodies for her family. Bill and I loaded the dishwasher, then sat in the solarium, watching the dusk settle. Reginald sat in the center of the table, his daisy chain lopsided and wilting.

"Your mother was a remarkable woman," Bill commented. "It sounds as though she turned Dimity's life around completely."

"Not completely," I said, "but enough to get her back on her feet again and moving forward. My mother was a great believer in moving forward, in looking on the bright side of things." I plucked a red rose from a vase and leaned it between Reginald's paws. "I suppose . . ."

"What do you suppose?" Bill asked.

"Give me a minute, will you? This isn't easy for me to say." I got up and opened the door. The sound of crickets wafted in on a soft breeze. "I've done some thinking about what you said up on the hill—some thinking and some reading, too."

"You went back to the correspondence?"

"Yes, while you were soaking your . . . sore muscles in the Jacuzzi. Well, after all those things you said, I had to. I was up pretty late last night, reading through letter after letter, and I noticed something. My mother never says anything that isn't cheerful. Even when she's talking about things that must have bothered her tremendously—like taking ten years to have a baby, for instance—even when she's talking about that, she's cracking jokes, as though it didn't *really* bother her. And that's how I remember her—happy all the time." I turned and held a hand up. "Don't get me wrong. That's not a bad way to be. I mean, look at what it did for Dimity." My hand dropped and I looked back out into the garden. "But I'm not sure it was all that good for me. It's not . . . human. As you said, she didn't teach me how to be *un*happy." I shook my head. "And that's hard for me to handle. I didn't think she had any weaknesses."

"Do you mind finding out that she did?"

I sat down again, leaning toward Bill with my elbows on the table. "That's the strangest part, Bill. I don't mind at all. It's a relief, in fact. It's not easy being the daughter of a saint."

Bill smiled ruefully and nodded. "Being the son of one is no fun, either. That's why I constantly remind myself of each and every one of Father's faults. It's a depressingly short list, but it helps. Did you know, for example, that he has a secret passion for root beer?"

"Is that a fault?"

"For a man raised on Montrachet? One might even call it a serious character defect. He'd be drummed out of his club if word got around. Please don't let on that I told you."

"I wouldn't dream of it." We shared a smile, then I lowered my eyes to the wrought-iron tabletop. "You know, Bill, I might not have gone back to the correspondence if it hadn't been for you. Thanks for giving me a shove."

"You're welcome." The sound of the crickets rose and fell as the dusk turned into darkness. Bill took the rose from Reginald's paws. "Excuse me, old man, but you don't mind if I . . ." He handed the rose to me. "I didn't get the chance to tell you how beautiful you look. The color suits you."

I couldn't be sure if he was referring to the cornflower blue of my new dress or the blush that had risen to my cheeks, so I changed the subject. "Ruth and Louise were very helpful, weren't they?"

"Yes, indeed." Bill sat back in his chair. "RM. Robert MacLaren."

"More commonly known as Bobby—an airman who was killed in action late in the year 1940, just before my mother met Dimity. A call to the War Office would confirm all of that, I suppose."

"But they wouldn't be able to tell us about this." My heart did a flutter step as he reached over to touch the locket. "The War Office doesn't keep track of that sort of thing. Whatever is tormenting Dimity, it's not just grief over losing Bobby. Something must have happened between them, something terrible." Bill stood up. "What we need is someone who knew Bobby and Dimity." He strode off down the hallway.

"Where are you going?" I asked, scrambling after him as fast as my brand-new pumps would allow.

"Upstairs to pack," he called from the stairs.

I followed him up. "To pack? Why?"

"I'm going to London." At the top of the stairs, he turned to face me. "Lori, think about it. Bobby was an *airman*." He went ahead into his room.

"So?" I stood frowning on the stairs, then hit myself in the forehead, feeling like a complete fool. "Of course! The Flamborough!"

Bill stuck his head out of his door. "Bingo."

"I thought of the Flamborough when we were talking with the Pyms, but then it slipped away." I climbed the last few stairs, then stood in Bill's doorway while he tossed a few things in a bag.

"I'm going to pay a visit to the redoubtable Miss Kingsley," said Bill, pulling a shirt off a hanger in the wardrobe, "to find out if anyone still knows how to operate the Flamborough Telegraph. They might be able to put us in touch with some of Bobby's friends or fellow airmen." He folded the shirt and placed it in the bag, then opened a drawer in the dresser.

"Why do you keep saying 'I'? You mean 'we,' don't you?"

Bill pulled a pair of socks out of the drawer and shook his head. "Not this time. You have to be here to field calls from Father." The socks went into the bag.

"Oh. Right." Bill's plan made perfect sense. I could trust him to ask the right questions, to discover all there was to discover. There was no need for me to accompany him. So why did my heart sink when he zipped the bag shut?

He left the bag on the bed and came over to where I was standing. "I'll call as soon as I find anything out," he said.

"I know," I mumbled, looking at my shoes.

"I'll call even if I don't find anything out."

"Fine."

"I'll give you the number at the Flamborough, Miss Kingsley's private line, so you can reach me night or day."

"Okay."

He bent slightly at the knees and peered at me through narrowed eyes. "So what's the problem?"

I couldn't stand it any longer. Scowling furiously, I grabbed hold of his lapels and planted a kiss firmly on his lips. "There, all right? I don't want to stay here. I don't want to be away from you. I'm packing my own bag and coming along and that's final, end of discussion, no debate. Okay? Satisfied? Does that answer your question?"

He closed his eyes and stood very still for a moment. Then he released a long breath. "Yes, thank you."

Looking somewhat dazed, he made his way back to the bed,

bumped into the nightstand, knocked the lamp to the floor, picked it up, dropped it again, then left it where it was and came back to the doorway to pull me into his arms.

"I just want to be sure I understood you correctly," he said. "You know how lawyers are. . . ."

By the time we were both ready to leave, everything was clear enough to satisfy the Supreme Court.

Twenty

We didn't lose our heads entirely. I took the precaution of calling Willis, Sr., before we left. It was the middle of the night in Boston, so I left a message informing him that I was so far along in my reading that I had decided to spend a few days exploring the countryside, with Bill in tow to look after things. I added that we would telephone him the minute we got back to the cottage.

Bill phoned ahead and Miss Kingsley responded with characteristic efficiency. Our rooms were waiting for us when we arrived, and a late supper was ready in one of the Flamborough's private dining rooms. At Bill's invitation, Miss Kingsley joined us, and she lived up to her redoubtable reputation by remaining undaunted even by the vague nature of our quest.

"Robert MacLaren?" she said. "Well, the name certainly doesn't ring any bells, but I'm a relative newcomer. I've only been at the Flamborough for fifteen years. I'm sure we'll be able to find someone who can tell you something about the old days, though. Retired military gentlemen are our mainstay. I shall make some inquiries, and I should be very surprised if I have nothing to tell you by tomorrow evening."

Miss Kingsley's inquiries took a little longer than that—two days, to be precise—but the results were spectacular. Archy Gorman was worth a whole army of retired military gentlemen. He was a stout man with a magnificent head of wavy white hair and a drooping handlebar mustache, and before opening his own public house, he had spent seventeen years as the bartender at the Flamborough—including the war years. Archy had long since retired from bartending, but Paul had kept in touch with him, and Miss Kingsley had been able to reach him at his flat in Greenwich. Paul drove the limousine round to pick him up, and the two of them met us in the Flamborough lounge two hours before opening time. The polished dance floor shone in the light from the fluted, frosted-glass wall lamps as we gathered at one of the round wooden tables near the bar. Paul sat with us, but Archy immediately made his way to the taps and began pulling pints for the assembled group.

"Have to keep my hand in," he explained, with a wink at Miss Kingsley, "and I never was a stick-in-the mud about the licensing laws, was I, Paul?"

"No, you weren't, Archy. And there's many an airman who thanked you for it."

"Here you are, now." Bill got up to carry the tray of drinks to our table and Archy joined us there, puffing slightly with the effort. "To happier days," he said, and raised his glass. I watched over the top of my own as he expertly avoided dipping his mustache into the foam.

"Now, you might be wondering why I was here at the Flamborough for the duration instead of out there doing my duty," Archy began, folding his hands across his ample stomach. "The plain and simple fact is, they wouldn't have me. Rheumatic fever and a heart murmur and no-thank-you-very-much said the board." He thumped his chest. "But here I am, closing in on seventy and never a day's bother with the old ticker. Never understood it, why they sent the healthy lads off and left the tailings at home, but there you are. You can't expect common sense from the military, can you, Paul?"

"Not a bit of it, Archy."

"What was it that Yank told us that one time? Snafu, he called it— you remember, Paul?"

"'Situation Normal, All Fouled Up,'" Paul recited dutifully.

"That's your military, the world over." Archy took another long draught, then set his glass on the table. "Now, tell me again about this chap you're looking for."

When I had recounted the little we knew about Bobby, Archy pursed his lips. "He must have flown during the Blitz," he said. "The Battle of Britain, they called it. Not many survived to tell the tale, did they, Paul?"

Paul shook his head soberly. "After a while, it was hard to strike up friendships with the lads. They were gone so fast, you see."

"Here today, and gone tomorrow, that's the way it was, eh, Paul?"

"A truer word was never spoken, Archy."

"You don't happen to have a snap of this MacLaren fellow, do you?" asked Archy. "The old memory is sharp as a tack, but there were so many boys through here . . ."

"No," I replied, "but I do have some pictures of his girlfriend." I handed him several photographs from Dimity's album. "This is Dimity Westwood," I said.

"Dimity Westwood, you say? Well, there were a lot of girlfriends coming into the old Flamborough in those days. It was a lively place back then, not the museum piece it is now—begging your pardon, Miss K."

"That's all right, Archy, no offense taken," said Miss Kingsley. "Things are rather quieter around here nowadays."

"Dull as dishwater," Archy muttered, with a conspiratorial wink at Paul. Stroking his mustache, he looked carefully at each picture. "I couldn't say that I recognize . . ." He paused. "Wait, now . . ."

The rest of us craned our necks to see what had caught his eye. He had come to one of my favorite pictures, a shot of Dimity standing in front of a shop with shattered windows. She had reached inside to touch the dress on a toppled mannequin, and was grinning mischievously at the camera. Archy contemplated the photo for a moment; then his eyebrows shot up and he slapped the table with his hand. "The belle of the ball," he exclaimed. "You remember, Paul—the beautiful belle of the ball—that's who she is."

"By heavens, you're right, Archy. That's who she is," said Paul. "The sweetest girl you'd ever want to meet . . ."

Archy cupped a hand to his mouth and in a stage whisper explained, "Paul took a fancy to her."

"Look who's talking," Paul retorted. "I seem to remember you being rather fond of her yourself."

"So I was, so I was," Archy conceded. "But who could help being fond of her? She was . . . something else. Something you don't find every day, I can tell you. You may know her as Dimity Westwood, but we called her Belle. She came in here all the time, on the arm of that Scottish fellow. Frightful accent, mind you, but how he could dance. Bobby . . . yes, Bobby and Belle. What a pair."

"Lit up the whole place when they came in," said Paul.

"I kidded them about spoiling the blackout—you remember that, Paul?"

"I do, Archy."

Archy put his arm around Paul's shoulders and the two men gazed, misty-eyed, at the photograph before Archy returned it to me. They emptied their glasses, and stared stolidly into the middle distance.

"It's easy to remember the happy times," Archy said. "No one likes to think of the rest, but it was there all the same, wasn't it, Paul?"

"It was, Archy."

"I remember the last time Belle came in here. She was on her own that night and I could tell just by looking at her what had happened. I'd seen it so many times before, but my heart broke for her all the same. I gave her the message and off she went, without saying a word. She never came back after that."

"That's how it was in those days," said Paul. "Dancing one minute, and the next—"

"There was a message?" I said.

"Oh, yes," Archy replied. "The chaps were always leaving messages with me here at the Flamborough, billets-doux for their sweethearts and the like."

"That's why they called it the Telegraph," said Paul.

"Do you remember what the message was?"

Archy was taken aback. "I never opened it," he said. "It wouldn't have been proper."

My face must have fallen, because he pushed his chair back and lumbered to his feet. Raising a crooked finger, he said, "Now, you come over here, and I'll show you something. It's not something I show to everyone, mind you. You can be sure I didn't show that young bloke who came in after me. He got very snippy when I tried to show him the ropes—you remember him, don't you, Paul?"

"A regular Mr. Know-All," said Paul.

"So I said to him, 'Fair enough, Mr. Know-All, figure it out for yourself.' But seeing as you have a personal interest in all of this . . ."

I followed him to the bar, and the others drifted over from the table. Archy lifted the hatch and motioned for me to go inside, then closed it behind him as he came in after me. He spread his hands flat on the smooth surface of the serving counter, looking very much at home.

"They called it the Telegraph," he said, "but in point of fact, it was more like a post office. It was a sight more efficient than your official post office, and Paul here will vouch for that."

"It was," said Paul, "especially in those days, with so many house numbers disappearing, thanks to Mr. Adolf-bloody-Hitler—oh, excuse me, miss." He covered his mouth with his hand and looked a good deal more shocked than anyone else in the room.

"No need to excuse yourself," Archy declared. "Now, about the Telegraph . . ." Archy ran his hand lovingly up one of the pillars that supported the decorative woodwork overhead, every square inch of it covered with scrolls and flourishes. "I was the postman, you see, and this"—he pointed up to a knob that had been camouflaged by the elaborate carving—"was the postbox. That's where I used to put all the messages the boys left with me. Didn't want them getting wet, so I had Darcy Pemburton—where's old Darcy got to these days, Paul?"

"Living in Blackpool with his sister."

"Blackpool? What's he want to live in Blackpool for?"

"Says he likes the donkey rides."

"The *donkey*—You're having me on, Paul."

"That's what he says."

"Then he's having *you* on. But never mind. . . . Darcy was a fine cabinetmaker in his day, and I had him fit this little box up for me to keep the notes and such out of harm's way. You see, you just give the knob a twist and the door swings—" Archy's mouth curved into an unbelieving grin as a cascade of papers rained down on his leonine head.

It took us a while to gather them all up, and a little while longer to persuade Archy to let us read them. Piled neatly on the bar were folded note cards, sealed envelopes, and slapdash notes scrawled on scraps of napkins, train schedules, betting cards, whatever had been at hand, it seemed. Most were brief ("Pru: Bloody balls-up at HQ. Can't make our date. Will call. Jimmy.") and not all concerned romance ("Stinky: Here's your filthy lucre, hope you lose your ration book"—unsigned, but accompanied by a faded five-pound note). A few were cryptic ("Rose: You were right. Bert.") but some were all too clear ("Philip: Drop dead. Georgina.").

"I can't understand it," Archy muttered, twirling one end of his drooping mustache. "I might have left one or two behind, but never this many."

"Archy?" Paul said softly.

"Doesn't make sense," Archy continued. "The new man didn't know about the Telegraph, so how could he manage it, eh? Tell me that."

"Archy?" Paul repeated, a bit more loudly.

"Not as though he'd do a favor for—"

"I did it!" Paul declared.

Archy turned to Paul, shocked. "You, Paul?"

"I did it for the lads, Archy." Paul's eyes pleaded for understanding. "The notes kept coming in after you left, and someone had to look after them, so I did. Then Mr. Know-All caught me behind the bar one day and booted me out of the lounge, and after that I . . . I must've lost track of time."

"I'll say you did." Archy looked from Paul to the notes and back again. "Poor old Stinky went short five pounds because of you."

"I know, Archy," Paul said miserably.

"And let's hope this one hasn't caused more serious mischief." Archy bent down to retrieve a white envelope that appeared to have a raised coat of arms on the flap. Archy examined it closely, then, without saying a word, handed it to me.

"It's addressed to Dimity." I locked eyes with Bill. Archy came up with a polished breadknife, and I used it to slit open the envelope. The others clustered around me as I pulled out a single sheet of paper and read:

Miss Westwood,

It is my duty to inform you that I recently came into possession of a certain object that belonged to my late brother. Please contact me immediately, so that we may discuss its disposition.

A.M.

"It's dated July 15, 1952," noted Miss Kingsley. "Imagine, it's been sitting here all these years."

"Have I caused a terrible mess?" Paul asked in a low voice.

I leaned across the bar to squeeze his arm. "You were doing your best, Paul, and it wasn't your fault that that jerk kicked you out of here. You've helped us enormously today, and we really appreciate it." Bill echoed my words, but it wasn't until Archy reached across to pat Paul's shoulder that the smaller man finally perked up again.

"There's no return address," I said, looking once more at the white envelope.

"If we assume the writer to be *A. MacLaren,* that and the coat of arms should be enough," said Miss Kingsley. "Let me check my files." She reached the door of the lounge in time to head off the Flamborough's current bartender, a slender man with flowing blond hair.

"Having a party?" he asked.

"We are having a private conference," replied Miss Kingsley tartly, "and I'll thank you to wait outside until I call for you."

The man clucked his tongue at the empty glasses on the table, but he was no match for Miss Kingsley and left without further comment. Archy leaned on the bar and watched as the door closed behind the two. "A fine figure of a woman," he said, his voice filled with admiration. "Now, would anyone say no to another round? Bring those empty glasses over here." While Paul gathered up the letters and Archy was busy at the tap, Bill and I walked over to look at the framed snapshots arrayed upon the wall.

"I wonder if Bobby's here," I said. "It's so strange to think that we might be looking right at him and not know it." I called over to the bar, "Archy—do you know if Bobby MacLaren's picture is here?"

"'Course it is. His chums brought it in and I hung it there myself. Let me see, now." Pint of stout in hand, Archy came over, with Paul at his heels. "That's Jack Thornton," said Archy, as his large hand moved slowly across the wall. "Brian Ripley. Tom Patterson. Freddy Baker. He was a wild one, old Freddy. Always getting himself put on report."

"They never found fault with his flying, though," Paul pointed out.

"No, Paul, they never did. Ah, it brings 'em all back, this wall does. They were none of them saints, but they were there when we needed them. Here, now, here's Bobby." Archy unhooked one of the pictures and handed it to me, and the four of us looked down upon a young man in flying gear, standing beside a fighter.

"That's his Hurricane," said Paul. "Proud of it, he was. Said it streaked through the sky like a falcon. The picture doesn't do him justice, though."

"Hard to do that in a snap, but you're right," Archy agreed. "His eyes were brighter, and his smile . . ."

"Yes," said Paul. "His smile."

Sighing, the two men returned to the bar. Bill took Bobby's picture from me and stared at it for a long time before hanging it back in place. "So many of them, and each one of them left someone behind." He took a deep breath, then cleared his throat and looked down at the letter. "I think our next step is to contact A.M., if Miss Kingsley can discover who he is. I'd be interested to know if Dimity ever received word about this"——he tapped the letter——" 'object' that belonged to Bobby."

"Me, too, but what are we going to say to A.M.?"

"You leave that to me."

Archy had not quite topped off Paul's glass when Miss Kingsley returned, a piece of paper in her hand and a gleam in her eye.

"Mr. Andrew MacLaren is sixty-six years old, unmarried, and still living on the MacLaren estate in the mountains west of Wick," she informed the table. "Quite far north, actually. He had only one sibling, a brother, Robert, whose death made Andrew the sole heir to the family fortune, which is extensive—wool, whiskey, and, lately, North Sea oil. He's something of a recluse, apparently, seldom sets foot off of the estate. I have his telephone number, if you'd like it."

"Bless you, Miss Kingsley. Where would we be without you?" said Bill, as Miss Kingsley handed him the number. "I'd love to have a look through those files of yours someday."

"I'm afraid they are held in the strictest confidence," she replied with a smile. "Would you like to come into my office to place the call? Yes, Archy, you and Paul may stay here and enjoy your drinks, but I'll have to allow Bjorn to open the doors to the rest of our patrons as well."

Archy snorted in disgust. "I might have known," he said. "What's a chap named Bjorn doing at the Flamborough, that's what I'd like to know. Sign of the times, eh, Paul?"

"Yes, Archy, a sign of the times."

Bill and I left them there and went with Miss Kingsley into her office. Bill sat at the desk, dialed the number, then began to speak in a voice that was businesslike, mature, authoritative—in short, completely unrecognizable. Listening to him, I began to understand how he had gained access to the Imperial War Museum archives.

"Good morning," he said. "This is William A. Willis speaking, of the law firm of Willis & Willis. I am calling in regards to a certain matter pertaining to the disposition of the Westwood estate—yes, the Westwood estate. I am the estate's legal representative and I would like to speak with Mr. Andrew MacLaren, if he is available. Yes, William A. Willis. Thank you, I'll wait." Bill covered the phone with his hand. "Don't look so astounded," he said to me. "This is my professional manner. Or did you think I didn't have one?"

"I was just wondering if the 'A' stood for—"

"Admirable? Astute? Articulate? Modesty prevents me from saying, 'All of the above.'"

Andrew MacLaren must have come on the line at that moment because Bill turned his attention back to the telephone. As he did, Archy Gorman came into the office. "Don't bother your young man," he said. "I just popped in to say I'd be on my way." He held up the assembled notes. "Have to go home and sort this lot out. My duty as the postman, you know."

"Paul's driving you, isn't he?" I asked.

"'Fraid not," he said. "Has no head for lager, our Paul. He'll be asleep in the lounge if you need him."

"You wait out front, Archy," said Miss Kingsley. "I'll have another driver for you shortly. As for Paul . . . will you excuse me, Lori? I think my presence is required in the lounge."

I turned to Archy and thanked him for all his help.

"Don't give it a second thought," he said. "You've given me a chance to finish up a job I should have finished years ago. I'm the one who should thank you." He nodded in Bill's direction. "You tell your young man I said cheerio, will you? He's a nice fellow and the two of you make a fine couple. I'm very pleased to have met you both. You be sure to stop and visit if you're ever passing through Greenwich." He shook my hand, winked, and was gone.

Bill hung up the telephone.

"Well?" I asked.

"MacLaren invited us both to come up to his estate." When my eyes lit up, he raised a cautioning hand. "It was a strange invitation. He was ready to hang up on me until I mentioned the long-lost letter. Apparently he doesn't share Archy Gorman's enthusiasm for chatting over old times."

"He did lose his brother," I said. "It must be a pretty painful memory."

"Yes, but . . ." Bill stroked his beard. "No, never mind. Let's wait and see if you get the same impression." He stood up as Miss Kingsley returned.

"If anyone had told me that one day I would see our Paul dead drunk before noon . . ." She shook her head.

"He's a lot smaller than Archy," said Bill. "I suppose it goes to his head faster. And now, Miss Kingsley, I have another favor to ask of you."

By seven o'clock that evening, Bill and I were on board a private jet bound for Wick.

Twenty-one

Andrew MacLaren was at the airport to meet us. As tall as Bill and broader across the shoulders, he walked with a pronounced limp and used a cane, yet he seemed surprisingly agile. Certainly he was more fit and trim than I'd have expected for a man of his age, not to mention a man with a handicap.

He must have read the question in my eyes, and it must have been a familar one because he tapped the cane lightly against his leg. "Polio. Grew up with it. Doesn't slow me down." His nonchalant manner put me at ease and by the time we had reached the parking lot, Andrew's lopsided gait seemed as unremarkable as Bill's steady stride.

He led us to a dilapidated Land Rover. Uh-oh, I thought as we climbed in, an aristocrat on the skids. I wondered if that might explain his reluctant invitation; perhaps he was ashamed to have houseguests. But that theory went out the window as we approached MacLaren Hall. When the road narrowed from a one-lane gravel drive to a rutted track, I realized that Andrew's choice of transport was merely practical.

"I'm sorry about the road," he said. "We have a perfectly usable drive, of course, but this is faster and, as it's getting late, I thought you might be in need of supper."

There was no need for him to apologize. We were far enough north and it was still early enough in the year for there to be a good deal of daylight left even at that late hour, and the scenery more than made up for the jouncing, jostling ride. We were surrounded by some of the wildest, most desolate country I'd ever seen, with mountains looming on all sides, barren, craggy, majestic. They took my breath away, but also left me feeling uneasy. This was a harsh, unforgiving place. I suspected it would not deal kindly with weakness and, given half a chance, it would kill the unwary.

MacLaren Hall did nothing to soften that impression. It was an enormous, intimidating old place faced in weathered red brick, with dozens of chimneys and deep-set, shadowy windows. It stood on a rocky hillside above a loch—magnificent, but terribly lonely, over-looking the black water in bleak isolation.

As if to compensate for the somber surroundings, Andrew had ordered his housekeeper to lay on a huge spread, including venison from a deer he had bagged himself and whiskey from the family dis-tillery. While we ate, he regaled us with the history of MacLaren Hall. He was obviously proud of his ancestral home and he seemed to have a story about every family member who had ever lived in it. Except for Bobby. It wasn't until we had retired to the library, whiskeys in hand, that Bill was able to broach the subject. On the flight up I had agreed to leave the questioning to him.

"As I mentioned on the telephone, Mr. MacLaren," Bill began, "we found something in Miss Westwood's papers that piqued our curios-ity." From his breast pocket he took the letter we had found at the Flamborough and handed it to Andrew. "The envelope was still sealed when we found it. We were wondering if the matter you mentioned was ever resolved."

Andrew glanced briefly at the letter. "It was settled long ago," he said. Then he crumpled it into a ball, and with a flick of the wrist, threw it on the fire. I started up from my chair, aghast, but Bill mo-tioned for me to remain seated and continued on as though nothing had happened.

"Might I ask what it concerned?" he said.

"Some property. It's unimportant now. As I say, the matter was settled years ago."

"You relieve my mind," said Bill, seemingly unconcerned. He raised his glass to the light. "This is from the family distillery? It's marvelous. Tell me, do you use oak barrels for the aging process or do you prefer . . ." With unshakable aplomb, Bill led the conversation on a circuitous route. By the time he got back to Bobby, Andrew had tossed back three glasses of whiskey in quick succession and his mood had mellowed considerably.

"Was Bobby your elder brother?" asked Bill.

"By two years," Andrew replied. "There was only the pair of us."

"You must have been very close."

"We were." Andrew stared moodily into the fire, as though mesmerized by the dancing flames.

I wondered how long it had been since he had spoken of his brother. I wondered if it came as a relief to him to say Bobby's name aloud, or whether it fell like a hammerblow every time. How much more whiskey would it take before he could say the name without flinching?

"I worshiped him," Andrew went on. "You might think I'd feel a dram of jealousy or envy, with Bobby being the elder son and healthy to boot . . ."

"But you didn't?" said Bill.

"Never crossed my mind." Andrew emptied his fourth glass, then set it on a table beside his chair. "What you must understand is that Bobby treated me as an equal. When I couldn't walk, he carried me up into the hills to see the falcons' nest, or out to fish in the loch. He taught me how to track, how to use my eyes and my brain to compensate for the weakness in my legs. I'd have been bedridden for years longer if Bobby hadn't lured me out to explore the world."

"He must have been a fine young man," said Bill.

"They come no finer," said Andrew. "The curious thing was that he made me love the place much more than he ever had. He was so full of life himself that our barren crags left him feeling hungry for . . . something kinder, less austere, I suppose, something more like himself." Andrew picked up the empty glass and held it out to Bill.

"It must have been very hard on you when he joined up," said Bill. When he handed the glass back, it was filled only halfway.

"He was too young, much too young," Andrew said with a note of bitterness. "But they didn't question matters too closely in those days. There was a great demand for air crews and he was keen as mustard, so . . ."

"They took him on."

"They did. He was stationed at Biggin Hill. God help me, I was so proud of him. It never occurred to me that he could be killed. My brother was young and strong and invulnerable. He was . . ." Andrew's voice faltered, but another swallow steadied it. "He was shot down over the Channel on the ninth of September, 1940. His wing-man saw the plane hit the water, but there was no parachute, and Bobby . . . The body was never recovered," he finished gruffly.

"My God," I whispered.

Andrew raised a hand to smooth his thinning gray hair. "It was a common enough occurrence during the war," he said, bowing his head to stare into his glass, "but I'll admit that it was an uncommon blow to me. It may sound foolish, but I sometimes go into the chapel to be with him."

"The chapel?" Bill asked. "But I thought . . ."

Andrew looked up. "It's a family tradition," he explained. "A family as old as ours has left its share of unburied sons on many battle-fields. When Bobby died, we added his name to the memorial tablet. I like to think I can sense his presence down there. MacLarens are canny that way." Andrew was silent for a few moments. Then he asked: "Would you like to see it?"

"Thank you," Bill replied. "We would be honored."

Carrying a lantern to light the way, Andrew led us to the family chapel, a narrow Gothic structure attached to the west wing of the hall. Generations of MacLarens were entombed there, and I'd never seen a darker, damper place in all my life. The weeping granite walls seemed to close in upon us, and the chill air made me wish I'd worn something warmer than my short-sleeved tea-party dress. I couldn't imagine how anyone could rest in peace there. I could almost hear their bones rattling from the cold.

Footsteps echoing on the uneven stone floor, we wound our way past recumbent lords and ladies to the far side of the chapel, where a large bronze plaque had been set into the wall. Many names had been inscribed on it, and many dates, and down in one dim corner Bobby's name and birth date appeared above the words: LOST IN DEFENCE OF THE REALM, 9 SEPTEMBER 1940.

"My brother had just turned twenty," Andrew said. His voice rang hollowly in the chamber. On impulse, I bent down to touch the in-scription, and when the locket slipped from the neck of my dress to hang glinting in the lantern light, I heard a sharp intake of breath and felt Andrew's eyes on me.

"I'm sorry," I said, straightening quickly, "I didn't mean to—"

He passed a hand across his face and seemed to shrink in on himself. "If you will excuse me . . . I have had a very tiring day." Slowly, painfully, all agility gone, he made his way back to the entrance. His valet and the housekeeper were waiting there, as though Andrew's visit to the chapel were a nightly ritual. Andrew leaned heavily on the strong arm of his valet, a stocky young man with broad shoulders.

"I will show you to your rooms now," said the housekeeper. She was a sharp-eyed older woman in a starched black dress, and her words seemed to be a statement of fact, not a suggestion.

"Yes," said Andrew. "You go ahead with Mrs. Hume. We'll speak again in the morning." He started off, then hesitated, and turned to Bill. "There's good fishing nearby, if you're up early enough."

"I wouldn't want to impose—"

"It's no imposition," said Andrew. "Colin and I are usually up at first light. We'll find a rod for you, young man, and a pair of waders."

"In that case, Bill would be happy to accept your invitation," I said, treading lightly on Bill's foot.

"Uh, yes," he said. "Yes, thank you, I'd be delighted."

"Good," said Andrew, with a wan smile. "Colin will rouse you bright and early, and perhaps we'll have fresh salmon for breakfast." With one hand on Colin's shoulder and the other on his cane, Andrew made his way slowly down the hall.

The housekeeper led us up the dark-paneled main staircase to adjacent second-floor bedrooms overlooking the loch. She indicated the location of the nearest lavatory and bathroom, then added, in a cold, unfriendly voice, "Mr. MacLaren sometimes has difficulty sleeping. It would be appreciated, therefore, if you did not disturb his rest while you are here. Should you require assistance during your visit, you may use the bellpulls in your rooms to summon one of us." She paused, and her brown eyes narrowed to slits. "There is always someone awake in MacLaren Hall. Good night."

We nodded obediently; then Bill went into his room and I entered mine. I half expected to hear a key turn in the lock, shutting me in for the night. Mrs. Hume's words had sounded more like a warning than an offer of hospitality: you are being watched; don't stray from your rooms. Creepy, but also tantalizing. Someone was afraid to let us roam MacLaren Hall unattended.

My room had a funereal charm to it, with shoulder-high wainscoting, a single dim brass lamp, and grim Victorian furniture. Dark green velvet drapes blocked the view, and a green brocade quilt covered the rock-hard bed. Everything was spotless, though, and well maintained. Museum pieces, I thought, fingering the black tassel on the bellpull. When enough time had elapsed for Mrs. Hume to go back downstairs, I tiptoed over to knock at Bill's door. He opened it, grabbed my arm, and pulled me inside. He seemed somewhat peeved.

"*Waders?* At *dawn?* What have you gotten me into?"

"Keep your voice down." I steered him over to sit on a low, burgundy plush couch at the opposite end of the room. "I have a feeling that Mrs. Hume's hearing is excellent."

He glared belligerently at the door, but lowered his voice. "Lori, I'll make a fool of myself out there. I don't know the first thing about fishing."

"I have complete confidence in your ability to fake it," I said cheerfully. "Playing fisherman can't be all that much harder than playing chauffeur."

"Are you still mad about that? Lori—"

"I'm not mad about anything. You'll do fine. Just take your cues from Andrew and let Colin bait your hook. And while you're out there, suggest a walk around the grounds, maybe a hike up to the falcons' nest."

"More hiking?" Bill groaned and buried his face in his hands. "I still have blisters from Pouter's Hill."

"Then put on an extra pair of socks," I said sternly. "Listen, Bill, do whatever you can to keep Andrew and Colin away from the house tomorrow."

"Don't tell me." Bill raised his head from his hands. "While I'm out there drowning, you'll be in here searching for whatever it was that Bobby left to Dimity."

"You saw what Andrew did with the letter," I said. "Why would he destroy it if he was telling us the truth? It was an incredibly stupid thing to do, don't you think? Like shouting 'I'm innocent' before we'd even accused him of anything. He must have known it would arouse our suspicions."

"I don't think MacLaren's thinking very clearly," said Bill. "That's why I kept a certified copy."

"What?"

"Keep your voice down," said Bill, his good humor fully restored. "Remember Mrs. Hume."

"You rat," I whispered. "Why didn't you tell me?"

"I wanted one of us to have an authentic reaction. I'm a lawyer, so he wouldn't expect one from me, but—"

"But authentic reactions are my specialty. Thanks a lot."

Bill stretched his legs out and tucked a fringed throw pillow behind his head. "I thought something might be up when I talked to him on the telephone. He wanted nothing to do with us at first, but as soon as I mentioned the letter, he couldn't invite us up here fast enough. It seemed odd to me. There's a photocopy machine in Miss Kingsley's office, and Miss K counts among her many talents those of a commissioner for oaths. That's a notary public, to you."

"Then you agree with me? You think he's hiding something?"

"I do. What's more, I think it might be out in the open and he must think it's something we'd recognize on sight. Otherwise, Mrs. Hume wouldn't have dropped her leaden hint about staying in our rooms."

I nodded slowly, then got up and walked over to the windows. Pulling the drapes aside, I looked into inky darkness. Not a glimmer of starlight reflected from the lapping waves of the loch. With a shiver, I turned back to Bill. "Why'd he invite you to go fishing, then? You'd think he'd want us out of here as soon as possible."

"Who knows? Maybe he's lonely. Maybe he's tired of hiding. Or maybe he feels safe with the dragon lady to watch his back. How do you plan to get around her?"

"Mrs. Hume doesn't know it yet, but she's going to give me a tour of the hall."

"Is she?"

I returned to the couch. "You heard the way Andrew talked about the place—he's bound to want to show it off, and if you persuade him to take you on an excursion, he'll have to deputize someone. My guess is that it'll be Mrs. Hume. If she's going to be breathing down my neck anyway, I might as well make use of her."

"Thus, by a process of elimination . . ."

"Whatever she doesn't show me tomorrow must be what we want to see. That's why I need you to keep Andrew away as long as possible. This is a big place and I'm going to insist on seeing all of it." I paused for a moment in silent thought, then asked, "What did you think of the chapel?"

Bill snuggled his head deeper into the pillow and shuddered. "Pouter's Hill it most certainly is not."

"No. No light, no warmth, no open space." I frowned. "It doesn't seem right, somehow, that Bobby's only monument should be a plaque in the damp corner of a mausoleum in the middle of nowhere. I find it very hard to believe that Andrew can sense his presence down there. Everyone we've talked to—his brother included—remembers Bobby as bursting with life, vibrant."

"Dancing, laughing, lighting up the room."

"Exactly. Bobby's name seems out of place in that cold hole. And did you notice that Andrew never once mentioned Dimity? Not once. Do you suppose he was jealous of her? Afraid she would steal Bobby away from him? Is that what this is all about?"

"I've got a better one for you. Why doesn't Dimity take care of it herself?"

I looked at him blankly.

"Lori, if she can fix Reginald and write in journals and send Evan packing, why can't she just swoop in here and get whatever it is Bobby meant for her to have? For that matter, why can't she just fly straight into Bobby's arms?"

"I—I don't know."

Bill tented his fingers and looked thoughtfully at the ceiling. "I think it's because she loves you."

"But she loved Bob—"

Bill's hand shot up. "Hush. My theory, such as it is, requires patience." Folding his arms, he went on. "Dimity loves you. You're her spiritual daughter, so to speak. Every single manifestation of her supernatural power has been for your benefit, from lending a hand in the kitchen to helping Derek finish the cottage on time. This much we know for sure."

"Yes, but—" Bill gave me a sidelong glare and I subsided.

"We also know that she loved Bobby, probably as much as she loves you, if the Pym sisters are to be believed. Regardless of that, her . . . spirit . . . is unable to connect with his. Why? If she loved both of you, why can she make contact with you but not Bobby?"

I shrugged.

"I think it's because her bond of love with you was never broken."

"But her bond with Bobby was?" I ventured.

"In a way that required forgiveness." Bill took off his glasses and rubbed his eyes. "A theory. Only a theory. One step at a time, and I don't know about you, but my next step is going to be toward the bed." His head moved from the pillow to my shoulder. "Now, about the sleeping arrangements . . ."

"They will stay as they are." I nudged his head back onto the pillow and got to my feet. "We don't want to scandalize Mrs. Hume."

"I think Mrs. Hume could use a nice juicy bit of scandal."

"Be that as it may," I said, heading for the door, "you need your rest. Your fishy friends will be waiting at the crack of dawn." Halfway out the door, I said over my shoulder, "Besides, Bill, we're *hardly* a pair of teenagers, are we?"

I ducked as the throw pillow sailed past me into the hall.

Twenty-two

There was fresh salmon at breakfast, but Andrew and I had to start without Bill. He was up in his room, changing into dry clothes.

"I warned him to watch his step," said Andrew, "but he became overexcited when he saw the falcons. I don't suppose he sees many in America."

"No, I suppose he doesn't," I said, accepting another cup of tea from Mrs. Hume. She hovered silently between us, filling cups, removing plates, and generally overseeing the meal.

The night's sleep and the morning's outing had done little to refresh my host. His eyes were shadowed, his face drawn, and his thoughts seemed to wander at times, yet he seemed oddly bent on helping us to enjoy the rest of our stay.

"He asked if we could go up to the nest after breakfast," Andrew continued. "He seemed so keen on it that I didn't have the heart to refuse. I've loaned him some clothes, as his aren't particularly well suited to our Highland terrain, and we'll be starting up directly after breakfast." He addressed the housekeeper. "Mrs. Hume, will you please see to it that a picnic lunch is prepared? It may take us some time to complete the expedition." Mrs. Hume gave him a curt nod and left the room. "With Colin's help, I can still clamber up there and back," Andrew added, "but not as speedily as I once did. You're welcome to join us, if you like, Miss Shepherd."

"Thank you, but I think I'll stay here. I'm not nearly as outdoorsy as Bill." I cast an admiring glance around the room. "And it's not often that I find myself in a place like MacLaren Hall. We don't have anything like this in America, either."

"Then you must have a look round while you're here," Andrew offered.

"Really?"

"You're more than welcome. Mrs. Hume is nearly as well versed in the hall's history as I am. I'm sure she can take some time off from her morning duties to escort you." When he put the proposition to Mrs. Hume, she agreed to it with her usual economy of words.

Bill entered the dining room a short time later, and I had to hand it to him—he was much better at concealing his emotions than I was. He must have been ready to throw me into the loch, but his greeting was as genial as ever. He made light of his dunking, waxed rhapsodic about going up to the falcons' nest, and graciously expressed his gratitude to Andrew for his new apparel—a pale gray cashmere turtleneck beneath a navy pullover, and heavy wool knee socks tucked up into a pair of tweed plus-fours. He even dared to call a cheery good-morning to Mrs. Hume.

"Mr. MacLaren has promised me a pair of hobnailed boots for the climb." He displayed a stockinged foot. "It's going to be a while before my own shoes are dry enough to wear. Coffee, if you please, Mrs. Hume. I don't think the tea is quite strong enough to take the chill away." When he bent his head over the steaming cup, I noticed that his hair was curling in damp tendrils behind his ears. "Tell me, Lori, how do you plan to spend your time while the menfolk are away in the hills?"

"Mrs. Hume is taking me on a tour of the hall."

"What a splendid way to spend the day," said Bill, with more heartfelt sincerity than either Mrs. Hume or Andrew could have realized. "How I wish I could be here with you."

MacLaren Hall was massive, but it seemed to grow even larger as I trailed behind Mrs. Hume, who was impervious to small talk and met any attempt at humor with a stony stare. More like a dour professor than a tour guide, she plodded methodically from room to room, giving a set speech about the contents of each, and achieving with ease the remarkable feat of turning a Scottish lilt into a monotone. If she expected to dull my wits, she was in for a disappointment. She took me past smoky oil portraits and marble-topped pedestal tables, rosewood étagères and musty tapestries, from the dim and dusty attics to the spotless kitchens—she even showed me the linen closets—but there were three places in which we did not set foot. As we passed by Andrew MacLaren's private suite and the staff apartments, Mrs. Hume merely gestured at the closed doors, as though no more needed to be said on the subject.

But one closed door, the fourth one up the hall from my bedroom, won neither gesture nor comment. We had passed it several times on our way to and from the main staircase, but Mrs. Hume acted as though it were invisible. I dutifully kept my eyes front and center.

After a late afternoon lunch, Mrs. Hume escorted me to the library, where she left me with a selection of dusty books about the history of the MacLaren family. At any other time they would have intrigued me, but at that moment my mind was on other things—such as breaking and entering. I sat for fifteen minutes by the ormolu clock on the mantelpiece, then opened the door to see if the coast was clear.

Mrs. Hume looked up from polishing the time-darkened oak wainscoting that lined the hallway. "Yes, Miss Shepherd? May I help you?"

I gave her a frozen grin, then managed, "I wonder if I might trouble you for a cup of tea?"

"Of course." Mrs. Hume put down her cloth and walked off in the direction of the kitchens, while I closed the door and thought fast. If I went up to my bedroom she'd probably move her polishing operation right along with me. There were miles of wainscoting to polish in MacLaren Hall. What I needed was a diversion. I scanned the room, spied a telephone, and a plan clicked into place. Hurriedly, I dialed, and began speaking the moment I heard Willis, Sr.'s voice.

"It's Lori," I said in low, urgent tones. "I can't explain now, but I need you to do a favor for me. A really big favor, right away. Do you have a pen and paper?"

"Yes, Miss Shepherd."

"Then write this down." The phone number of MacLaren Hall was printed on a small card affixed to the phone. "Did you get that?" I asked, glancing at the door. He read it back to me and I raced on before he could ask any questions. "I need you to call that number in about twenty minutes and ask for a Mrs. Hume. That's *H-U-M-E*. She's a housekeeper at a big old place way up in northern Scotland. Keep her on the line for as long as you possibly can, and don't mention my name or Bill's or anything about Dimity Westwood. Don't tell her who you are, either. Can you do that?" Every muscle in my body tensed as I waited for him to give the matter his due consideration.

"I suppose I could present myself as an American relation," suggested Willis, Sr., finally. "I could, perhaps, be in the midst of conducting an investigation into the genealogy of my family."

"Perfect!" I said. "You're a genius, Mr. Willis—and thanks. I'll explain soon and, remember, give me twenty minutes. I have to go now." I hung up the phone and was back behind the pile of dusty books in plenty of time to assume a suitably studious appearance. When Mrs. Hume arrived with the tea trolley, I closed the book I had opened at random, and yawned languorously.

"Gosh," I said, rubbing my eyes. "I'm sorry, Mrs. Hume, but I don't think I'll have that tea after all. To tell you the truth, what I really need is a nap. I believe I'll go up and stretch out until the men come back."

Mrs. Hume's lips tightened, but she conducted me up the main staircase without comment, pausing only to pick up her basket of polishing supplies.

"Is there anything else you require, Miss Shepherd?" she asked when we arrived at my room.

"Thank you, Mrs. Hume, but I think I've bothered you enough for one day." I yawned again, and hoped I wasn't overdoing it. "Thanks again for the tour. This is a marvelous place."

Mrs. Hume's head turned at the sound of footsteps on the staircase. A red-haired girl in a maid's uniform approached, then proceeded to astonish me by dropping a curtsy to the housekeeper.

"Please, ma'am," said the girl, "there's a telephone call for you. A trunk call."

"A trunk call?" Mrs. Hume queried sharply. "For me? You're certain?"

"Yes, ma'am," said the girl. "And Mr. Sinclair has come about the stove."

"Very well." Mrs. Hume's knuckles went white on the handle of the basket. "Tell Mr. Sinclair to wait in the kitchen. I will attend to him presently." The girl bobbed a curtsy once again, and left. Mrs. Hume turned back. "I trust that you will have a restful few hours, Miss Shepherd. I shall be up again shortly, to make sure you have everything you need. You will excuse me."

"Of course, Mrs. Hume. Good luck with the stove." When both sets of footsteps had faded into the distance, I sprinted up the hall. I placed a trembling hand on the doorknob, sent a quick prayer to the god of locks, and followed it with thanks when the knob turned. Slipping into the room, I closed the door gently behind me, then leaned against it to catch my breath. I felt so much like a little kid playing hide-and-seek that I wanted to giggle, but when I turned to view the room, the laughter died in my throat.

It was a boy's room, still and silent, washed in the golden light of the late afternoon sun. A stuffed badger peered down from the top of the wardrobe, and the shelves above the bed were crowded with clockwork tanks, lead soldiers, and gleaming trophies. A battered leather binocular case dangled from the gun rack in the corner and schoolbooks were arranged in ranks upon the bookshelves. Above my head a squadron of model airplanes hung at dramatic angles. An unfinished one, made of balsa wood and tissue paper, sat on a table against the wall, still waiting for its wings. I turned a slow circle to take it all in, then crossed the room.

The desk was covered with pencil drawings of gentle hills, a patchwork valley, a rose-covered cottage with a slate roof. The smiling face of Dimity Westwood looked out from a graceful silver frame that had been placed to one side. I looked from the portrait to the softly shaded drawings and knew that this was Bobby's room, preserved in amber. The center drawer of the desk held pencil stubs, bits of eraser, a broken ruler—and a tattered exercise book that bore the name ROBERT MACLAREN. Burning with a sudden flush of shame, I closed the drawer and turned away.

This was no game. Blinded by my own cleverness, I had forgotten that we were dealing with death and loss and wrenching grief. I had betrayed the trust of my host, and I had invaded what must have been, for him, a shrine. My very presence felt like a desecration. If this was what it took to help Dimity, then I would have to fail her. I got up from the desk and headed for the door.

I was halfway there when it opened.

Twenty-three

*A*ndrew MacLaren stood erect in the doorway for a moment; then his shoulders drooped. I feared for a moment that he would collapse, but he called upon some inner reserve of strength, pulled himself to attention, and entered. Bill followed, closing the door behind him.

"I see that you have found my brother's room," Andrew said in a soft, tired voice. "When I saw Mrs. Hume, I suspected . . . but no matter. Had you waited, I would have brought you here myself." He pulled the chair from the desk and sat down, gesturing for us to sit in two others. He raised his eyes to the model airplanes overhead. "I have tried to keep it the way it was during his last visit. The last time before . . ." Andrew rubbed a hand across his weary eyes. "Perhaps I have tried to keep too much unchanged."

He reached over to pick up the photograph of Dimity, and the words he spoke were spoken to her. "I have tried to keep my anger unchanged, but it has been hard, so very hard. You cannot warm yourself at the fire of anger without chilling your soul. I am an old man now, and it seems that the fire has died. All that is left is sorrow, and guilt, and the cold and certain knowledge that I was wrong." He pulled a silk handkerchief from his pocket, gently dusted the frame, then returned it to the desk, taking care to place it in exactly the same position. He twisted the handkerchief absently for a moment; then his hands relaxed and he folded them calmly on top of his cane.

"You wish to hear of Dimity Westwood," he said. "Dimity, my brother's bonny Belle. He met her at the Flamborough and, for Bobby, one meeting was enough. He knew at first sight that he had found all that his heart desired. He told me he'd proposed to her on a hill overlooking heaven, that he planned to return there after the war, to the place he had first discovered love. He asked me to look after his beautiful Belle if anything should ever happen to him, and I promised, upon my oath as a MacLaren, that I would do as he wished.

"It was such an easy promise to make. His love for Dimity enveloped him in a"—Andrew passed a hand through the dust motes dancing in the sun—"a golden haze. I had never seen such happiness before, and I have never seen it since. It was exquisite, the kind of love that admits no envy, no jealousy. I was dazzled and warmed by it and felt sure that Dimity would feel as I did, that it would be worth any sacrifice to keep that golden aura glowing."

Andrew placed his cane on the floor, opened the bottom drawer of the desk, and withdrew a bundle of papers bound with a pale blue ribbon. Untying the ribbon, he took out a single photograph. He gazed at it for a long time before handing me a picture of a handsome young man in uniform, sitting in the shade of a gnarled oak tree. He nodded at the bundle of papers.

"It was in among Bobby's personal effects at Biggin Hill," he explained. "I was mistaken about Dimity, you see. The night before his final mission, Bobby called me from the base, saying that she had broken off their engagement." With a shaking hand, he raised the papers toward me. "She'd returned his letters, his pictures, his ring, everything that might remind her of their time together. She'd told him that they must stop seeing one another. I was outraged, incensed. I couldn't understand how she could be so blind, so willfully cruel. But Bobby remained undaunted.

"'She thinks she's being practical,' he told me, without a trace of rancor. 'She thinks it's foolish to make plans in such uncertain times.' He laughed then. 'She's wrong,' he said. 'This is when you need to make plans, dream dreams. This is when you need to believe that there will be a tomorrow to fly to. I'll convince her of it, I know I will. She's returned the ring to my keeping, but she and I both know that it's hers forever. As I am.'"

Andrew picked up the ribbon and tied it once more around the papers. He gave the bundle to me, then let his hand fall limply to his knee. "It was the last time I ever spoke with my brother. He was shot down the following day.

"I could not comprehend it. I could not accept that his death had been a mere twist of fate, a misfortune of war. My brother had always flown like a falcon. What had tripped him up? The question tormented me night and day, until, finally, I knew the answer." Andrew's hand closed into a fist. "I kept my promise to him. I deposited his share of our inheritance in Dimity Westwood's account. I cannot be accused of betraying that trust.

"But I . . . I also wrote her a letter. Bobby had told me that, should I ever need to communicate quickly with Dimity, I should write in care of the Flamborough. He said that everyone there knew who Belle was.

"When I got word of his death, I wrote to her, telling her that the money was hers to do with as she pleased, but that if she tried to return it, we would throw it to the winds because my family wanted nothing more to do with her. I told her that Bobby's mind had been clouded by thoughts of her betrayal, that his reflexes had been dulled, and I . . . I accused her of being responsible for . . ." Andrew pressed his fist to his mouth.

A chill went through me. What must Dimity have felt? She must have been half-mad with grief, consumed with guilt, all too willing to believe Andrew's vicious accusation. The words must have seared into her soul, and she had carried that great and secret sin with her to the grave.

"She never touched the money," Andrew went on, "not until she began her work with Starling House. She invested it, then, on behalf of the children, as though seeing to their welfare would right the wrong she had done. She was a canny businesswoman and she made a tidy sum, I'll grant her that. But how I hated her for it.

"I wrote to her once more, a letter I hoped she would never receive. Although the war was over, I sent it to the Flamborough, with no return address, and I used her proper name, hoping no one would recognize it. I knew that I was breaking faith with Bobby, but I did not care. When the years passed and I received no reply, I felt well satisfied.

"That was when the nightmares began." Andrew bowed his head and touched his fingers to his temples. "They did not come every night, but often enough to make me afraid to sleep. You cannot imagine their vividness, their power. They always begin with the same hellish vision. I am spinning out of the clouds toward an iron-gray sea. I watch as the waves grow closer and closer, but I can do nothing to stop myself. Sometimes the impact awakens me, and I cry out, gasping for breath, terrified. And sometimes the gray waves pull me under, and that—that is the true nightmare, when I am pulled down into the chill, black depths of the sea and left there, alone and wandering, searching for, but never finding, my way home." A shudder racked Andrew's body, and when he opened his eyes, his face was haggard.

"I lied when I told you that I sensed my brother's presence in the chapel. It is in these visions that Bobby comes to me. For years I've told myself that he came to keep my rage alive, to remind me of the horrible way he had died. But in the chapel last night, my certainty began to crumble." He raised his eyes to mine. "The locket you're wearing—it was Dimity's, was it not?"

"She treasured it," I said. "She was never without it."

"It was my grandmother's. Bobby gave it to Dimity. She must have worn it the day she broke off their engagement, and that's why Bobby knew . . . She didn't return everything, you see; she kept back one token of their bond, and when I saw it last night, I knew that Bobby had been right, that, regardless of her actions, she had never stopped loving him." Andrew bowed his head and moaned softly. "If I'd been wrong about that, was it not possible that I'd been wrong about everything else? My brother was not given to anger—why would his visions encourage it in me? Perhaps he sent them for another reason. Perhaps they were sent to tell me that, as long as Dimity suffered, my brother's spirit would find no peace."

He faced the desk once more, opened a narrow side drawer, and withdrew a small box. He gazed at the box, turning it between his fingers as he spoke.

"Shortly after my brother's plane was shot down, a member of the Home Guard was patrolling the waterfront in the coastal village of Clacton-on-Sea. He found a map case that had floated ashore. In it, he found this." Andrew passed a gentle finger over the lid of the box, then handed it to me and gestured for me to open it. It held an elaborately carved gold ring.

"The man who found it must have been scrupulously honest," Andrew continued, "because he turned it in to the local constabulary. It took some years, what with the war and all, but they eventually traced it back to its owners by identifying the MacLaren crest.

"The ring belonged to Bobby," he said. "He had it with him when he died. He sent it back to her, not to me. He must have known what was in her heart."

I stared at the ring wordlessly, knowing that the last piece of the puzzle had finally fallen into place. Bobby had known what was in Dimity's heart. He'd sent the ring home to reassure her, to comfort her, to show her that he had never lost faith in her love. He'd sent the ring home, but it had gone to the wrong home, waylaid by a brother's misguided love. MacLaren Hall had been Bobby's birthplace, and the birthplace of his ancestors, but it was not his heart's home. He had been struggling desperately ever since to find his way back to that place where he had been most vibrant, most alive.

The aching loneliness that filled Andrew's nightmares had been Bobby's. It had been Bobby's voice I'd heard on Pouter's Hill, his longing I'd felt, a longing to return to the place where he had spent the most precious moments of his brave, brief life, to return to the woman he loved and convince her to take his love and keep it, believe in it, no matter what the odds, no matter how short the time.

Andrew seemed to read my mind. "Bobby trusted me to get the ring to Dimity, but I betrayed him. I did what I could to deprive her of this token of my brother's love. Can you imagine what I feel, knowing that, by keeping the ring from Dimity, I have prolonged my brother's suffering? I should have celebrated Bobby's memory by living as he would have lived, with honor and kindness and greatness of spirit. But I have spent my life on the pyre of anger, and now there is nothing left but ashes. I make no excuse. And now it is too late. . . ." Andrew covered his face with his hands.

I couldn't take my eyes from the ring. The light from the setting sun glinted off the gold, making it look warm and alive. I closed my hand over it.

"It's not too late," I murmured. The old man raised his head and I repeated, more loudly: "It's not too late, Andrew. Bobby's been out there all this time, searching for a beacon to bring him home. I promise you, Andrew, I'll bring him home."

Twenty-four

$\mathcal{A}$ndrew allowed us to help him to bed, where he fell into what may have been the first sound sleep he'd had since the ring had come into his possession. Looking down on his peaceful face, I knew that his nightmares were at an end, and I was glad for him. I couldn't be angry. There had been too much anger already.

When we came downstairs, Mrs. Hume was still on the telephone in the library, diligently recounting the ill-fated marriage of a couple named Charlie and Eileen. She seemed to be enjoying the conversation—it was the first time I'd seen her smile. I murmured a brief explanation of the scene to Bill.

"Why did you bring my father into it?" he asked in a low voice. "I would have thought Miss Kingsley—"

"Bill," I said, "can you think of anyone more capable than your father of charming Mrs. Hume?"

Bill called Mrs. Hume away from the phone for a few moments, and I picked up the receiver. "It's me again," I said quietly. "You can wrap up your conversation when Mrs. Hume comes back."

"Did I fulfill my commission, Miss Shepherd?" he asked with an air of mild curiosity.

"Admirably. I'll tell you all about it as soon as I get a chance."

"I look forward to your explanation."

Colin was kind enough to drive us to the airport. The moon was rising when we left MacLaren Hall and it was nearing midnight by the time we landed in London. Bobby's ring was tucked safely into a deep pocket in my jacket, and we flew in silence for a time, sorting through the bundle of papers that Andrew had given to us. The missing pages from the photograph album were there, folded with care so as not to damage any of the pictures. The photos were of Bobby, and all but five had been taken atop Pouter's Hill. The rest showed him with his Hurricane and his fellow airmen at Biggin Hill. The bundle contained some handwritten notes as well, the kind that would have fit easily into Archy Gorman's "postbox" at the Flamborough. Bill picked one up, but I stopped him before he opened it, murmuring, "These aren't for us to read."

It was Bill who found the pictures I'd been searching for. Cut from a larger photograph, the two small heart shapes bore two familiar faces. Dimity's dark hair was swept back and up off her face, held in place with a ribbon that might have been pale blue. Bobby was smiling his warm, engaging smile, and wings gleamed on the collar of his uniform shirt. As I fitted them into the locket, I said, "Remember the marking on the blue box? The *W* for *Westwood* was really an *M* for *MacLaren*."

"You read it upside down," Bill said with a wry smile. He held up a page from the album and pointed to one of the captions. "Did you notice this? Their first date. Just over a month before Bobby's plane went down. He must have proposed right after they met."

"My dad proposed to my mom on their second date," I said, "and she accepted on their third. Things happened faster in those days. I guess they had to." Gathering the pages together, I laid them flat on the seat across the aisle. "When we get to the cottage, we'll put them back where they belong. We'll put back the picture my mother gave me, too." I put the folded notes into a pile, tied the ribbon around them, and put them in my carry-on bag.

Bill gazed pensively out of the window at the star-filled sky. "Poor Andrew," he said. "Barricading himself in his mansion on the hill, all alone with his anger and his grief."

"And his love," I said, "his terrible love for his brother. That was at the root of everything that followed."

"Mmm." Bill nodded absently, and when he looked at me, his eyes were troubled. "Did Dimity really believe she'd killed Bobby?"

I switched off the overhead light and looked past him at the stars. "You were right when you said that it had to be something pretty drastic to cause her this much grief. Dimity must have convinced herself—with Andrew's help—that Bobby had died because of her cowardice, and she never forgave herself."

"Cowardice?" Bill said in surprise. "What cowardice?"

"She chickened out of the engagement, Bill. It's my guess that she didn't want to end up like the women at Starling House, married one minute and widowed the next, so she tried to play it safe. She was so afraid of things ending that she never let them begin."

Bill shook his head. "I hate to think of her that way, leading a life filled with secret misery."

"I don't think there's any way around it." I put a hand on the ring in my pocket. "If Dimity had let herself off the hook for a minute, Bobby's spirit would have touched her, his ring would have gotten to her, somehow, and she would've known that everything was all right."

"As it was . . ."

"Bobby never stood a chance. Dimity's guilt blocked him like a brick wall. She never talked or wrote about him, she only went back to the Flamborough once, and she rarely went back to the cottage. She probably wore the locket to remind herself of the pain she'd caused him. We'll never know for sure if Bobby 'visited' her the way he 'visited' Andrew, but even if he tried—"

"She'd have misinterpreted his message," Bill said. "She'd have filtered it through her guilt, the way Andrew filtered it through his anger."

"And twisted its meaning as badly as he did."

Bill stroked his beard, then asked doubtfully, "Then guilt can be stronger than love?"

"I didn't say that." I let go of Bobby's ring and took Bill's hand. "Oh, Bill, haven't you figured anything out? You're just too sane, I guess. It might help if you were a bit more neurotic."

"I'll work on it," he said, "but in the meantime, I'll defer to an expert." He made a half bow in my direction.

I ducked my head sheepishly. "Yeah, so I have been sort of . . . crazed. So was Dimity. So was Andrew, for that matter. Grief can make you believe things that never happened and forget things that you know for sure."

"The way you forgot your mother's pride in you?"

"And a lot of other things as well. You remember what I did with Aunt Dimity's cat? I did the same thing with the rest of the stories. It wasn't until I had them shoved in my face that I began to remember the way things really were, the whole of it, not just the disappointments. Dimity handled it a lot better than Andrew and I did, though. She didn't let pain cut her off from the world."

"She had your mother to help her," Bill reminded me.

I squeezed his hand. "Let's say they helped each other."

Bill nodded thoughtfully, then scratched his head. "So guilt can overwhelm you—"

"But love is stronger. It's in the process of triumphing, remember? It just took a little time for the right messenger to come along."

"Dimity's spiritual daughter."

I nodded. "There's nothing between Dimity and me but love, and I think I know a way to bury her guilt, to get Bobby's message through to her once and for all. That's what we were sent here to do."

"Who sent us? Bobby?"

"Yes." I reached into the bag at my feet and pulled from it the battered old photograph of the clearing. "We were sent by Bobby, and by my mother, and Ruth and Louise, and your father, and Emma and Derek—even Archy and Paul helped. We were sent here by everyone who ever loved Dimity."

Bill nodded slowly. "So what do we do now?"

"Wait and see," I said. "And in the meantime, help me think of something to tell your father."

I had called Emma and Derek from MacLaren Hall to give them an update and they were waiting for us at the cottage, flashlights in hand, when we drove up. I fetched the one I had purchased at Harrod's and Bill took the emergency lantern from the car. The three of them exchanged looks, but asked no questions as I led them through the back garden to the path up Pouter's Hill.

The woods had been dim in full daylight; now they were black as pitch. We had to stop frequently to search for the path and the beams from our flashlights danced like will-o'-the-wisps as we swung them from side to side. I could hear Bill puffing behind me, and the faint rustling noises of night creatures running for cover. I wondered what they made of our peculiar expedition.

As we reached the top of the hill, the gray predawn light was beginning to filter through the swirling mist that had settled in the clearing. When I pulled up short at the eerie sight, Bill walked into me and then Derek and Emma bumped into him, so our entrance was more in character with the Marx Brothers than the Brontë sisters, which was okay by me.

I led the way to the old oak tree and swung my carry-on bag to the ground. Kneeling, I pulled out a trowel and began to dig between two gnarled roots. Emma and Derek and Bill switched off their lights and watched in silence, and when the hole was deep enough, I paused to look up at the heart Bobby had carved so long ago. They followed my gaze and, one by one, knelt beside me, eyes alight with understanding.

I took from the bag the folded notes, still tied with the pale blue ribbon, and placed them at the bottom of the hole. From a pocket I took the blue box, then unclasped the chain from around my neck. I slipped Bobby's ring onto it; it clinked softly as it touched the locket. I placed them together in the blue box and set it gently atop the bundle of notes. Bill troweled the dirt back in and as he patted the last scattering into place, the sun rose.

The clearing glittered with dew-diamonds and a lark sang out the first sweet song of morning. The mist rolled back from the valley floor, and the fields and hills emerged, flushed pink and peach and golden. It may have been a trick of the light, and I've never confirmed it with the others, but I'm willing to swear that the heart on the old tree shimmered as I stood up.

The scene was complete now; nothing was missing or out of place, and I knew that when the sun was high, the hawks would rise again to ride the thermals.

Twenty-five

$\mathcal{I}$'m not sure if the mind at work was that of a son or a lawyer, but Bill managed to come up with a fairly convincing story for me to give to Willis, Sr. It had to do with running into old friends during our country ramble, being invited to visit them at their home in northern Scotland, and getting drafted into arranging a surprise party. It sounded farfetched to me, but Willis, Sr., seemed willing enough to accept it. I figured that sort of thing must be routine in their circle.

Much to my surprise, Willis, Sr., was also willing to go along with my request to end our question-and-answer sessions. He seemed to understand when I told him that they weren't needed anymore, that I was ready to begin writing. I called Bill into the study to say hello, and when he had hung up the phone, I pointed to the door. "Now go away," I ordered. "I have an introduction to write."

From that moment on, Bill was like a second ghost haunting the cottage. Sandwiches and pots of tea mysteriously appeared and the empty plates and pots seemed to vanish on their own. At one point, a cot showed up in the study, then an electric typewriter, with Reginald perched jauntily on the keys. Needless to say, my memory of those days is hazy at best, but nine drafts later, with a week left to the end of the month, the introduction to *Lori's Stories* was finished.

I slept for fourteen hours straight, then typed it up and went looking for Bill. He was upstairs on the deck, luxuriating in the sun. He squinted up at me, then waved. "Hello, stranger. I've been meaning to ask you, have you talked to Dimity lately?"

"Yes, but there was no reply. I didn't expect one. She had a lot of catching up to do. Have a look at this, will you?" I handed the pages to him, then stood by the railing to wait while he read them.

I had put into them all that I had learned since I had come to the cottage. I wrote about pain and loss and disappointment; about splendid plans going tragically awry. And I wrote about courage and hope and healing. It wasn't hard to do—it was all there already, in the stories. There were no names mentioned, of course, and the sentences were simple, and that had been the most difficult part: to say what I needed to say, in a voice that would speak to a child.

I also tried to speak to the adult that child would one day become. I urged her not to let the book lie dusty and forgotten on a shelf, but to keep it nearby and to reread it now and again, as a reminder of all the good things that life's trials might tempt her to forget.

I had added a final paragraph, one that I would not include in the next and final draft because it was intended for one pair of eyes only. In it I wrote of the terrible, wonderful power of love; how it could be used to hold someone captive or to set someone free; how it could be given without hope of return and rejected without ever being lost. Most of all, I wrote of how vital it was to believe in the love offered by an honest heart, no matter how impractical or absurd or fearful the circumstances. Because all times were uncertain and the chance might never come again.

Bill seemed to take forever to finish reading it, but when he did, the look in his eyes told me that it had done what I had hoped it would do. "It's good," he said. "It's very good. I think the critics will be writing about this instead of the stories."

"As long as the children remember the stories."

"If they pay attention to what you've said here, they'll remember them all their lives." Bill left the typed sheets on the deck chair and came over to me. "That last part might be a little tricky for them, though. It's beyond the scope of the assignment, isn't it?"

"It's not part of the assignment."

"I see." Bill's hand reached out to cover mine, where it rested on the railing. "And did you mean what you wrote?"

"Every word."

"In that case . . ." He got down on one knee and looked up at me. "Lori Shepherd, I have nothing to offer you but . . . well . . . the family fortune and a slightly warped sense of humor. And my heart, naturally. Will you marry me?"

"An interesting idea," I said judiciously, "and one to which I have given much thought. After due consideration—"

"You're enjoying this, aren't you," Bill grumbled, shifting his weight from one knee to the other.

"After due consideration," I repeated, "I have decided that I will accept your proposal, with two conditions."

"Name them."

"First, that you tell me what the 'A' stands for in William A. Willis. Does it really stand for Arthur or am I just imagining a family resemblance?"

"I prefer to think of it as an affinity with a great, imaginative mind," Bill said haughtily, "but yes, you're right. Quick now, before my leg falls asleep—what's the second condition?"

"That we spend our honeymoon here at the cottage."

Bill's face fell, and this time there was nothing theatrical about it. "Lori, you know I'd arrange it if I could, but it's impossible. The cottage has already been sold. The new owner is moving in at the end of the month."

My gaze swept out over the back garden. Emma's skillful hands had woven a glorious tapestry of colors, textures, scents, and I hoped that whoever lived here next would pause to savor its loveliness. Every petal seemed to glow, every leaf fluttered spring-green and shining. The shallow pond reflected clouds of roses in a crisp blue sky, and tiny purple blossoms cascaded over the gray stone walls. The oak grove loomed cool and inviting, and the meadow beyond the sunken terrace was awash in daffodils. I looked from their bright yellow trumpets to Bill's anxious face.

"In that case," I said, "I guess I'll have to accept your proposal without any conditions at all."

"You will?"

"Of course I will. Rise, Sir Knight, and claim your lady." I reached down to take his hand, but he stayed where he was.

"Then you accept?" he asked.

"Would you like me to write it in blood?"

"I would like you to say yes."

"*Yes,* William Arthur Willis. I will marry you."

I expected him to rise to his feet and sweep me into a passionate embrace. Instead, he sat back on his heels and let out a whooshing sigh of relief. "Thank God," he said. "I thought I'd never pry it out of you."

"You didn't seriously think I would refuse, did you?"

"No, but you had to say yes. You had to say that particular word, and I didn't think you would ever say it." He stood up and began to put his arms around me, but I held him off.

"Wait a minute," I said. "Why that particular word? Why do I get the feeling that there's something you're not telling me?"

"Because you're right. I couldn't tell you before, but now I can." He leaned forward on the railing. "You remember those stories I told you about, the ones Dimity told me when Father and I were staying at her town house in London?"

"Yes."

"I never told you who the heroine was. She was a feisty, irrepressible, entirely enchanting little girl, and her name just happened to be . . . Lori."

"You're not saying——"

"All I'm saying is that I never got her out of my mind, especially after Dimity promised that I'd get to meet her one day. She said I'd meet her and fall in love with her and that she would fall in love with me, too, though it would take her a while to realize it. And she said that I couldn't tell her anything about any of this until I'd won her heart and hand."

"*Dimity?* Dimity was *our* matchmaker?"

"Now, Lori, you said yourself that you have nothing against matchmaking. And we have it on the very highest authority—that of the inestimable Pym sisters and the experience of your own parents—that Dimity was the best."

"But . . . but . . ." I gave up and shook my head. "No wonder they call twelve an impressionable age."

"I'm sorry for pushing all those clothes on you, by the way. I should have known it would be too much too soon. But I'd waited so long and I was so happy. . . . And, uh, there's one other thing I should probably clarify as long as I'm at it." He pulled a small box from his pocket. It was covered with dark blue leather. He held it out to me and said, "*Ngee oot sanzi, Lori.*"

I blinked up at him in confusion and searched my memory. "Let's get back to work? But I've finished—"

"Wait. That's not what it means. What it actually means is what I've wanted to tell you all along. It means, I love—"

Before he could get the last word out, the sound of tires on gravel wafted through the air from the front of the cottage. He grimaced. "What a perfect time for Emma to bring the kids over to meet the Cookie Lady."

"Oh, come on," I said, tugging his arm. "I've been wanting to meet Peter and Nell. It won't take long."

"It'd better not," he said, but he allowed himself to be dragged to the front door.

We swung it wide, and to our mutual astonishment beheld none other than Willis, Sr., climbing out of the limo with the ever-helpful Paul at his elbow. Paul waved and tipped his cap at me, unloaded Willis, Sr.'s luggage, then backed the limo onto the road and sped off. Willis, Sr., meanwhile, stood on the flagstone walk, his eyes fixed on the cottage, deep in thought.

"Father! Why didn't you call? I would have come to pick you up."

"Mr. Willis, if I'd known you were coming early, I'd have—"

"Curious," Willis, Sr., said, half to himself. "Most curious." He became aware of our dumbfounded presence and shrugged helplessly. "I assure you that I share your surprise at my early arrival. I am not at all certain that I can explain it."

"I think I can," Bill muttered as he went to get his father's luggage. I had to bite my lip to keep from laughing out loud.

By the time we were settled in the living room—Bill beside his father, and me perched on the window seat—Willis, Sr., had given us as much of an explanation as he could. It wasn't much. He had simply canceled all of his appointments for the day, boarded a Concorde, and come straight to the cottage, drawn by an urge as irresistible as it was inexplicable. "Whatever will Mrs. Franklin think? And Mr. Hudson? Two of our most valued clients. Oh, dear me . . ."

"Father, I think that Lori and I will be able to explain this to you." Bill put a reassuring hand on his father's impeccably tailored shoulder.

"Will you?" Willis, Sr., asked doubtfully.

"Yes, though you may find our explanation a little difficult to believe," I said.

"It could scarcely be more incredible than the present circumstances. To change one's routine so abruptly is really quite . . ." His gray eyes focused on me. "My dear, please forgive this inexcusable intrusion. I beg of you, do not interrupt your own work on my account."

I dismissed his apology with a wave. "I'm always glad to see you, Mr. Willis. As a matter of fact, I was going to call you today to let you know that I've finished the introduction. If I had to, I could leave right now."

"Now, Miss Shepherd? You wish to depart today?"

If I had been honest, I would have admitted that there was nothing I wished less. My eyes wandered from the fireplace, with its neat pile of fine white ash, to the lilacs, still fresh and fragrant in their bowls. I touched the ink stain in the corner of the window seat, and looked through the diamond panes at the rose petals fluttering in the breeze. I would miss this place, I would cherish it in my memory, and I didn't want to leave it. But I knew that I could. It was better, much better, to leave now, with my head up, than later, looking back over my shoulder.

"Yes," I said decisively. "I don't need to stay here any longer."

"I see." Willis, Sr., regarded me in silence, then added, "Your mind is quite made up on that point?"

"It is."

"I see." Willis, Sr., pursed his lips, raised his eyebrows, then seemed to reach a decision. "Well, in that case, I see no reason to delay carrying out Miss Westwood's final instructions."

"There's no need to do that, either, Mr. Willis," I said. "I'd feel guilty taking a penny of the commission. My work has been a labor of love."

"That is a very noble sentiment, Miss Shepherd, and I shall honor it, if you so desire. But I am not speaking of the commission."

"You're not?"

Willis, Sr., asked Bill to fetch his briefcase from the hall. When

Bill returned with it, Willis, Sr., withdrew a leather portfolio and examined its contents soberly. He nodded once, then closed the portfolio and folded his hands on top of it.

"My dear Miss Shepherd," he said, "there is one last question I must put to you. Would you please tell my son and me the story entitled *Aunt Dimity Buys a Torch?*"

I folded my legs beneath me on the window seat and told the story again, the correct version this time, with the bright memories as well as the trodden-on foot. As I told it, I seemed to travel back in time to the night I had arrived at the Willis mansion. I saw myself standing on the doorstep in the dark, cold and alone and angry at the world, and it was like looking at a stranger. That person could never have believed in ghosts or happy endings. That person could never have fallen in love with the Handsome Prince. I felt a great tenderness for her, and when the door opened and the warm light drove away the darkness, I wished her well.

". . . and Aunt Dimity went home to warm herself before the fire and feast on buttered brown bread and a pot of tea, smiling quietly as she remembered the very large and very kind man she had met that day at Harrod's."

Willis, Sr., let the silence linger for a time, then nodded slowly. "Thank you, Miss Shepherd. Most beautifully told." He opened the portfolio and cleared his throat. "I am now empowered to inform you that the cottage, the land surrounding it—in fact, the entirety of Miss Westwood's considerable estate, are to come into your sole possession at the conclusion of the allotted month's time. I am afraid there is no way to speed that along, my dear, but I am certain that such a delay will not—"

"Mine?" I whispered, afraid to say the word aloud. "The cottage is mine?" My astonishment was mirrored in Bill's eyes. Apparently his father had not discussed with him this detail of the case.

"Yes, Miss Shepherd. Your answer to Miss Westwood's final question was more than satisfactory. In fact—"

"Mine?" I repeated faintly, as the full beauty of the scheme unfolded before me. Dimity and Beth, those two remarkable women, guiding each other through rocky terrain, then reaching out to pull me from my isolation and show me another way. They had seen my downward spiral; they had brought me to the cottage to open my closed mind; and they had given me a month to read their words, to hear what they were trying to tell me, so that I would not use Dimity's considerable estate as a shield, a fortress, a lonely mansion on a hill.

Dazed, I rose from the window seat and walked out of the room. Bill started to follow me, but Willis, Sr., must have restrained him, because I left the cottage alone. Without quite knowing how I got there, I found myself in the clearing at the top of Pouter's Hill.

The words I exchanged with the gnarled old oak tree must remain between the tree and me. Suffice it to say that the tree proved to be as good a listener as Bill.

Epilogue

*E*mma planted flowers there later that summer, and according to Willis, Sr., they bloom all year round. He sits beneath the old oak tree for hours whenever he visits and he visits as often as he can. He nearly gave *me* a heart attack the first time he tackled the climb, but it seems to have done him good. His heart hasn't bothered him since.

I have to depend on his reports about the clearing because I don't get up there as often as I'd like. Between unearthing rare books for Stan, visiting Uncle Andrew in Scotland, and shuttling the little Willises between cottage and mansion several times a year—and they say that D day was a big deal!—I'm kept pretty busy.

Not one single person was surprised by the news of our engagement, least of all Willis, Sr., who had placed a special order with his tailor immediately after hearing of my first visit to Arthur's dome. "It has been a long-standing dream," he explained, "to see my son married in a morning coat, and I thought that perhaps you, Lori, might be able to persuade him. . . ." I did.

Miss Kingsley chartered flights to bring our Yankee guests over for the wedding, I baked the three-tiered cake from page 265 of the dog-eared cookbook, and the reception was held under the vicar's new roof amid hundreds of blue irises. Reginald took it upon himself to preside over the bouquet of fragrant white lilacs that had arrived without a card. And I only wanted to smack Bill once the whole day, when he announced in stentorian tones that he was marrying me for my cookies. Archy Gorman's interpretations of his remark sent Paul into paroxysms of glee and confused the Pym sisters no end.

Meg and Doug commissioned a portrait as our wedding present, which Meg unveiled with a flourish and a sneaky grin. The oil painting of the bearded knight in shining armor hangs above the fireplace in our living room now, and hardly anyone notices that he's wearing glasses. And on our first anniversary a new blanket arrived, made from the finest Scottish wool and big enough to cover two.

Oh, and I guess I forgot to mention it, but instead of giving me an engagement ring when he proposed, Bill gave me a heart-shaped locket. Two different faces smile up at me when I open it, and the feelings they engender are about what you'd expect from perfect happiness.

Beth's Oatmeal Cookies

1 cup butter (or margarine)
1 cup granulated sugar
2 jumbo eggs
5 tablespoons raisin water (see below)
2 cups all-purpose flour
1 teaspoon baking soda
1 teaspoon salt
1 teaspoon cinnamon
1/2 teaspoon nutmeg
2 cups old-fashioned rolled oats
1 cup raisins
2 cups water
1/2 cup chopped walnuts (optional)

Preheat oven to 350 degrees.

In small saucepan, combine raisins with water and bring to boil; lower heat and simmer uncovered for 5 minutes. Set aside to cool. When cool, reserve 5 tablespoons raisin water, then drain raisins in colander.

In large mixing bowl, cream shortening and sugar. Add eggs and raisin water and mix well. Blend dry ingredients into creamed mixture. Add nuts, if desired. Add raisins and combine well.

Drop by heaping teaspoonful, 2 inches apart, onto greased baking sheets. Bake 10–15 minutes, or until golden brown and firm on top when touched with your finger. Cool on racks.

Makes approx. 6 dozen cookies.

Aunt Dimity and the Duke

For
Leslie J. Turek,
Consulting Gardener

Prologue

"Come back, Master Grayson!"

"Master Grayson! Stop!"

"Grayson Alexander! When I get my hands on you—"

His father's roar was swallowed by the rising wind as the boy ran down the terrace steps and sprinted for the castle ruins. Shirttails flying, he ran, heedless of the servants' cries and headlong from his father's wrath, intent only on escape. Black clouds boiled overhead and a cold wind whipped in from the sea, surging mournfully up the cliffs and snatching at his hair as he dodged through gaping doorways, past tumbledown walls, feet pounding, lungs pumping, heart breaking. Tear-blinded, tripped by a half-buried granite block, he sprawled, lay panting, then pushed himself up and ran on.

He reached the green door and flung it wide, stumbled down the stone steps into Grandmother's walled garden. A building stood there, high on the jagged cliffs above the cove, rock-steady in the wind. They called it the lady chapel, though it was sacred to no one, except perhaps to the boy. It straddled the rear wall, pointing out over the storm-lashed sea like a ship riding the crest of a wave; a small, rectangular building—rough-hewn gray granite, peaked roof, rounded door with time-blackened hinges. Moss-covered and ancient, it rose from the ground as though it had grown there, its roots buried deep in Cornwall's dark past. Reaching up to release the latch, the boy put his shoulder to the door and let himself in. Panting, he pushed the door shut behind him.

Stillness. Silence.

Light?

Uncertainty gripped him. A candle burned where no candle should be, there on the ledge beneath the stained-glass window—the jewel-hued lady window that overlooked the sea.

"Hello, Grayson." The voice was calm and soothing. "Let's see what we can do about that knee, shall we?"

A woman sat in the front row of wooden benches. As she turned her head, the candle's luster illuminated white hair, gray eyes, a softly wrinkled face, and when she smiled, he remembered: Grandmother's friend, the woman for whom Crowley reserved his deepest bows, around whom even Nanny Cole spoke gently. She was the teller of tales who brought all the servants clustering round the nursery door. Miss Westwood, at first, but later:

"*Aunt Dimity?*" Blinking back his tears, he made his way up the center aisle to her side.

"A rough night, I fear," she commented, removing her pearl-gray gloves. "A full-blown Cornish gale brewing. Still, we'll stay dry as tinder in here."

A capacious tapestry handbag lay at her feet. From its depths she produced a hand towel, a small bottle, a length of white gauze. "Sit down, my boy," she ordered. "This will sting a bit." With deft hands she cleansed and bandaged the knee he'd scraped stumbling in the ruins, tied the gauze neatly, returned towel and bottle to the handbag, then sat back, hands folded, waiting.

"Why didn't you come?" he asked.

"I didn't know" was the prompt reply.

Of course. Grandmother's funeral had been a shabby affair. Father would not have announced it.

"I'm so sorry, Grayson," she added. "I know how badly you must miss her."

Grayson scrubbed at his eyes with the back of a muddy fist, then stared, unseeing, at his clenched hand. Crowley, gone. Newland, Bantry, Gash. Nanny Cole would be next. She and little Kate would be sent away from Penford Hall just like the rest of the staff, and he would lose them forever.

Slowly at first, then with an urgency born of anger and despair, he told Aunt Dimity all about it. There was no one else to tell. With Grandmother dead, the village deserted, and the servants dismissed, ten-year-old Grayson was the sole witness to his father's treachery.

"No one's left at Penford Hall," he finished sadly. "And now he's . . . selling things." The low-voiced confession was spoken to the flagstone floor. "Grandmother's jewels, her paintings . . . her harp."

"Oh dear." Aunt Dimity sighed. "Charlotte's beautiful harp . . ."

"He's sold the *lantern.*" Grayson's finger stabbed accusingly at the granite shelf below the stained-glass window, where the candle now stood. "How will we hold the Fête without the lantern?" He bowed his head, ashamed of a father who knew no shame.

Frowning slightly, Aunt Dimity asked, "Are you quite certain of that?"

The boy's head swung up.

"Are you absolutely certain that the lantern has been sold?" Aunt Dimity asked again. "I rather doubt that Charlotte would have allowed that particular item to leave the family, don't you?"

"Then where is it?" Grayson asked bluntly.

"I don't know." Aunt Dimity's gaze swept the stained-glass window and the dimly lit walls of the chapel, then she drew herself up and looked down at the boy. "But the Fête's a long way off, and we have more pressing problems to attend to. Your face, for example." Clucking her tongue, Aunt Dimity retrieved a fresh hand towel from the bag and began wiping the tear-streaked smudges from Grayson's cheeks. "I know how distressing these changes must be for you," she murmured, "and I won't tell you to be a man about it. Grown men too often forget their dreams, and some dreams are worth holding on to."

Tilting the boy's chin up, Aunt Dimity examined his face critically, then brushed his honey-blond hair back from his forehead. "You do have dreams for Penford Hall, don't you?" she coaxed. When the boy maintained a sullen silence, Aunt Dimity persisted. "You mean, there's nothing you love at Penford Hall? No one?"

All that I love is here, Grayson thought. *I would do anything to save it, anything to keep Kate here and bring the others back.* Aloud, he muttered, "What's the use? It'll all be gone soon and it'll never be the same again."

"Tush. Stuff and nonsense. Twaddle." Aunt Dimity sniffed disapprovingly. "My dear boy, if you expect me to pat you on the head and say, 'There, there, what a hopeless muddle,' then you've mistaken me for quite another person—someone with whom I would not care to be personally acquainted. I've no patience with such foolishness and neither would your grandmother. Your father won't always be the duke, you know. One day Penford Hall will be yours."

"It'll be empty by then."

"Then you must fill it up again."

"It'll be years before—"

"If it's worth having, it's worth waiting for."

"But—"

"And worth working for," Aunt Dimity stated firmly. "If you were not overwrought at the moment, you would see it as plainly as I do. Then again," she added, half to herself, "perhaps I'm not making myself clear." Staring thoughtfully at the lady window, Aunt Dimity put her arm around the boy, her fingers smoothing his windblown hair. "*She* would not have lost hope," Aunt Dimity said, her gray eyes fixed on the lady's brown ones. "And she faced far worse things than you're facing. Do you know the legend of the lantern?"

With a nod, Grayson dutifully recited the words he'd heard so many times before: "Once, long ago, a lady fair did love a captain bold—"

"Great heavens!" Aunt Dimity exclaimed. "Is that what Nanny Cole taught you? A lady and a captain? Dear me. Why do they fill children's heads with such piffle? She was no lady, my boy, but a hard-working village lass who served as a parlor maid at Penford Hall. And her love wasn't a captain, but the duke's son, shipped off as a common seaman. The only thing Nanny Cole got remotely right is that they loved each other." The halo of white hair nodded slowly. "Listen closely, Grayson, while I tell you the *true* story of the lantern. Perhaps then you'll understand why you must go on loving Penford Hall, come what may."

Grayson doubted that a story would save Penford Hall, or bring the servants back, but Aunt Dimity's arm was warm around his shoulders, and he had nowhere else to go. The boy nodded, then leaned against Aunt Dimity, his bandaged leg swinging listlessly.

"It is seldom wise," Aunt Dimity began, "for a poor girl to fall in love with a duke's son. Love may be blind, but fathers most certainly are not, and the duke was not amused at the prospect of having a parlor maid as a daughter-in-law. He loved his son too well to forbid the match—I'll grant him that—but he decided to test the boy's devotion, for both his son's sake and the family's." She glanced down at the boy, saw that his leg had stopped swinging, then went on.

"The maid was sent back to the village and forbidden to set foot within sight of Penford Hall. The son was sent away for a year and a day, to sail the wide oceans as a common deckhand. The duke hoped that a taste of hard labor would cure the boy of his infatuation.

"But this was no mere infatuation. The duke's son had found his heart's desire and he vowed that his first journey would be his last. 'If you are here when I return,' he promised the girl, 'I will never leave you again.' And with that, he rowed out from Penford Harbor to meet the great four-master that awaited him in the safe waters beyond the Nether Shoals."

Grayson had turned his face to the one that hovered above them. The lady's eyes blazed suddenly as a streak of lightning split the sky, and the boy flinched at the crack of thunder that followed. Aunt Dimity's arm tightened about him protectively as she went on.

"One year passed," she told him, "and one day, and on the night of the son's return a storm blew up at sea. It was a fearful, rollicking gale, with waves as tall as Penford Hall and winds strong enough to shred the stoutest sails. Huddled safely around their hearths, the villagers knew that no ship would risk approaching the Nether Shoals that night."

"But *she* wouldn't listen?" guessed Grayson, his eyes upon the window.

"She would not," confirmed Aunt Dimity. "Though her mother begged her to stay at home, the lass would not be swayed. 'I must be there when he returns,' she said. And with that, she took up her lantern—a plain, shuttered lantern, no more than ten inches tall, the kind used in every village house—and set out for the cliffs, where she could watch for her love's return."

The boy tensed and drew closer to Aunt Dimity, envisioning the treacherous cliffs just beyond the chapel's rear wall, and the long fall to the churning sea below.

"It was a terrible journey," Aunt Dimity continued, her voice pitched menacingly low. "She could not take the easy path, for it wound within view of the hall, and the hard path was very hard indeed. Rain pounded like hammers, wind snatched at her cloak, waves crashed before her, and dark shapes swirled on every side. A dozen times she fell, and a dozen times she pulled herself back up . . . and up . . . and up . . . until she stood upon the wind-lashed cliffs."

"And then?" Grayson breathed.

"Then it happened. The thing no one can explain. As she held the tiny lantern high, it began to glow with an unearthly light, softly at first, then more brightly, then blindingly, until it blazed forth like a beacon, piercing the curtain of darkness like a white-hot bolt of lightning." Aunt Dimity let the words linger, let the image of the blazing lantern fill Grayson's mind, before continuing, more quietly.

"In the first gray light of dawn she saw the ship, the great four-master bearing spices and gold and the treasure of her heart, floating in the safe waters beyond the Nether Shoals. From it came a tiny boat, gliding like an arrow across the rolling waves, straight for Penford Harbor."

"He met her on the quay," whispered Grayson, back on familiar ground.

"And he told her of the light that had guided his ship to safety. And she told him of the lantern. . . ."

"And together they told the duke. . . ."

"And the duke was filled with wonder," said Aunt Dimity. "From that moment on, he loved the lass as dearly as he loved his son. To honor her, he built this chapel, on the very spot where she'd stood, and he brought craftsmen to make the stained-glass window bearing her likeness. And in the chapel he placed the lantern, to remind his descendants of the miraculous light that had saved his son, a light that blazed forth bright as lightning, fueled by the power of a young girl's love." Aunt Dimity looked down on the tousled head at her shoulder. "And once every hundred years . . ." she prompted softly.

"And once every hundred years," the boy murmured, "the lantern shines of its own accord, and the duke of Penford must fête the villagers, in memory of the village lass, or Penford Hall will crumble and the Penford line will fade forever from the face of the earth."

"You must find the lantern, Grayson," urged Aunt Dimity. "You must save Penford Hall. Look, Grayson. Look at the lady."

Grayson stared up at the window. The lady's raven hair swirled wildly around the hood of her pale-gray cloak, but her chin was up and her shoulders were back. She thrust the lantern defiantly into the face of the storm, and her liquid brown eyes were fixed on something that remained forever out of reach. Grayson rose to his feet, pulled upward by the strength and courage in the lady's eyes.

Aunt Dimity's voice seemed to come from a long way off: "Neither mother's cry nor duke's command could stay her, neither wind nor wave could sway her, for her heart was true, her hope undying. Tell me, young Master Grayson, shall you be any less steadfast?"

Lightning flashed and thunder cracked and rain pounded down like hammers, but Grayson Alexander, who would one day be the fourteenth duke of Penford, stood unflinching.

One

"All of the good men are either married or gay," Rita declared. "And now Richard's married." She closed the file drawer with a bang.

Emma Porter touched a finger to her wire-rim glasses and cast a furtive glance at the freesias atop the file cabinet, gathered fresh from her garden that morning. The vase wobbled, but remained upright, and Emma quickly lowered her gaze to the keyboard of her computer. Bending forward, she let her long hair fall like a shield on either side of her face, determined to avoid the same, tedious conversation she'd had every day for the past six weeks.

"Not that Richard was a good man," her assistant continued, scooping up another armload of files. "I'd've scratched his eyes out if he'd run out on me like that. No eyes, no cameras, no sweet young things to drool over." *Clang!* Another drawer took the brunt of Rita's disapproval.

"Please, Rita—the freesias."

"I'm sorry, Emma." Rita's voice trembled with outrage. "But when I think of Richard dumping you like that, after fifteen years—"

"We weren't married," Emma pointed out.

"But—"

"We lived in separate houses."

"Still—"

"We were two independent adults."

"You were a *couple!*" Rita marched back to stand before Emma's desk. "For fifteen years you did everything together. You even planned your big trip together. Then he . . . he . . ." Tears welled in Rita's eyes.

Without looking away from the computer screen, Emma reached for the half-empty box of Kleenex on the windowsill behind her and handed it to Rita, silently reminding herself to buy a fresh box on her way home. It seemed as though half the women in Boston had stopped by to commiserate since the wedding and each one had ended up in tears.

"Oh, Emma," Rita managed, trying to stem the flow before it ruined her mascara, "how can you be so *brave?*"

Burying her face in a handful of tissues, Rita retreated to her own desk, just outside Emma's office. When the other women in the department began to cluster around, Emma got up and closed the door firmly. The past six weeks had taught her that a firmly closed door was the only way to keep her sympathetic underlings at bay.

Sighing, Emma reached out to the vase on the file cabinet, plucked a fragrant blossom, and held it to her nose, wishing that her coworkers would mind their own business. It wasn't as though she and Richard were facing a messy divorce. She'd had no more desire than he to be tied down by marriage vows. Theirs had been a practical relationship, separate but equal, and it had outlasted most conventional marriages. Richard had his town house in Newton; she, her Cape Cod cottage in Cambridge. He'd pursued his career in photography and she'd pursued hers in computer science. They'd been a couple for fifteen years and now they weren't. That was all there was to it.

The light on her telephone began to blink, and Emma glanced at her watch. Time for Mother's morning pep talk, she thought wryly. Returning to her desk, she tossed the freesia blossom into the wastebasket and reached for the phone.

"Hello, Mother." Emma swiveled her chair to face the windows, where the bleak Boston skyline was etched against a lowering April sky.

"Hi, Emma. Heard from that rat yet?"

Emma's gaze traveled up along the tangled strands of ivy framing the window. She reached for her pair of scissors. "No, Mother, I haven't heard from Richard, and I don't expect to." Pinching the phone between her neck and shoulder, Emma stood and began pruning the tendrils of ivy. "I'm sure Richard is much too busy with his new life—"

Her mother snorted. "His new *wife,* you mean. I told you a thousand times to marry that rat."

"And I've told you that I don't see how marrying Richard would have changed the situation," said Emma.

"It would have given you some leverage in court! As it is—"

"As it is, I own my own home, I have a very lucrative position as an executive at CompuTech, and I enjoy my freedom. I don't think I have too much to complain about, Mother, do you?"

Her mother sighed. "Honestly, Emma, I never expected a daughter of mine to just sit back and take it."

"What would you like me to do, Mother?"

"Get angry! Throw his picture against the wall! *React!* That's what normal women do. But not my daughter. I mean, Emma, honey, I know you're trying to put on a brave face, but did you really have to go to the rat's wedding?"

"That had nothing to do with bravery," Emma explained, for what seemed like the hundredth time. "It was simply a matter of facing reality."

"I'll tell you about *facing reality,*" her mother echoed scornfully. "When a thirty-nine-year-old woman gets dumped for a twenty-two-year-old ditz, she doesn't just shrug it off. You're going to have to deal with your anger, dear heart, or you're going to come apart at the seams!"

"I'm sure you're right, Mother."

There was a pause, followed by: "Okay. Have it your way. But just tell me one thing, Emma. Did you love that rat?"

Emma winced as a long strand of ivy came away in her hand. "Mother, I'm afraid I have to go now. The Danbury project is due before I leave for England, and—"

"Uh-huh. I thought so."

"Good-bye, Mother." Emma hung up the phone and put the scissors away, afraid there'd be nothing left of the ivy if she continued to prune it in her present state of mind. Trust her mother to ask the most *impossible* questions. Emma was no starry-eyed idealist. She'd known from the start that her career would leave little room for a demanding emotional life. Marriage and motherhood were out of the question, and she'd given her heart to Richard, in part, because he'd understood that. Richard hadn't been perfect—his twin passions for bad sci-fi movies and heavy-metal rock music were two reasons to be glad they'd lived apart—but he'd respected her self-sufficiency. Her mother could say what she liked; Emma had nothing—*nothing*—to complain about.

Taking a calming breath, Emma sat down, swiveled her chair to face the desk, and leaned her head on her hands. In two weeks she'd be in England. She couldn't wait to leave.

Granted, she hadn't counted on leaving alone. Emma pulled her long hair back into a ponytail, then bent down to retrieve the file of travel brochures that filled the bottom drawer of her desk. She leafed through them until she came to the map, which she spread over the installation specs for the Danbury project. Cupping her chin in her hand, she gazed at it eagerly.

There was Cornwall, protruding like a broken branch from the southwestern tip of England, a jagged, irregular peninsula with the Atlantic Ocean to the north and the English Channel to the south. Emma had been to England many times and toured many gardens, but she'd never seen the gardens of Cornwall. She ran a finger along her intended route, pausing at the circled names: Cotehele, Glendurgan, Killerton Park, and the rest, private estates given over to the National Trust and open now to the pound-paying public.

Richard had planned to close up the studio for the summer, to lay aside fashion photography in favor of a more serious—some might say pretentious—pursuit: a black-and-white photo essay on the neolithic standing stones that dotted the Cornish landscape. Emma had been so absorbed in planning his trip as well as her own that she'd felt nothing but relief when he'd disappeared from her life for a few weeks.

She'd had no reason to worry. Theirs had been an open relationship, of course, and Richard had a long track record of short-lived flings. There'd been no reason on earth to suspect that this one would be any different.

Then the travel agent had called, informing her that Richard had canceled his airline tickets. Next, Richard had telephoned, telling her that he'd met someone special. Finally, the wedding invitation had arrived, proof positive that Richard had disappeared from her life for good. Emma had shocked her friends and appalled her mother by attending the wedding, but she'd wanted to go. She'd needed to see the fairy princess with her own eyes.

Emma refolded the map, smiling faintly. The fairy princess—that's what Rita had dubbed Richard's bride, and Emma had to admit that it was an apt description. Graceful, slim, and twenty years Richard's junior, with hair like silken sunlight and eyes like summer skies, the fairy princess hadn't walked down the aisle, she'd floated. And Richard had been waiting for her, rotund in his cummerbund, a sheen of perspiration on his balding pate, beaming at his wife-to-be with a smile that was disturbingly paternal. Emma blushed at the memory. It had been pathetic to see her free-spirited Richard succumb to something as trite as a midlife crisis.

Yet there it was. A fifteen-year relationship had ended with neither bang nor whimper, but with the whispery sound of an envelope slipped through a mail slot.

She'd spent a long time in her garden after the wedding, raking over the compost and wondering why she felt so . . . numb. Emma wasn't given to expressing strong emotions, but even she had been surprised by the stillness that had settled over her. Was she in shock, as her mother insisted? Or was she merely going through a natural transition that would lead, ultimately, to a mature acceptance of her new situation? Emma preferred the latter explanation. She knew that there were some things in life she couldn't change.

But there were some she could. She'd gone back into the house and spent the rest of the evening gathering up the odds and ends Richard had left behind—a worn bathrobe, a broken tripod, a stack of CDs and rock videos. As she dropped the garish video boxes in the Goodwill bin, she thought wryly that Richard's taste in music had been as juvenile as his taste in brides, and the small joke had heartened her. It seemed to prove that she was ready to face the world without Richard.

Her friends—and her mother—remained unconvinced. They thought of her as a victim and expected her to behave like one.

It was ludicrous. Why couldn't her friends be honest with her? Why couldn't they just come out and say what they were really thinking? "You're no kid anymore, Emma. You're forty, fat, and frumpy, and your chances of landing another man at this stage of the game are nil. We understand, and our hearts go out to you."

The faint smile returned as Emma put the map back in the bottom drawer. What a surprise it would be if she came home from England with a new man in tow—a six-foot-tall stunner with sapphire-blue eyes, broad shoulders, and . . .

Emma's pleasant daydream faded as common sense reasserted itself. She didn't need her mother to remind her that men—of all ages—preferred mates who were younger than themselves, girls who were graceful and slim, with hair like silken sunshine and eyes like summer skies. She knew that the doors of romance were more often than not slammed in the faces of plump, plain-looking women approaching middle age.

Emma was proud of her ability to accept the truth, and she prepared for the trip accordingly. Come May, she would be in Cornwall, where she would feast on cream teas, explore pretty fishing villages, and, best of all, enjoy the springtime spectacle of massed azaleas in full bloom. She would do everything her heart desired. Except fall in love.

"Never again," she murmured, stifling a wistful sigh. "When I come back from Cornwall, I'll buy a hammock for the garden and settle down to a life of industrious spinsterhood. But as for love—never again."

On that same day, in an Oxford suburb an ocean away, Derek Harris wiped the last trace of rain-spattered mud from the headstone on his wife's grave. He could have left the task to the sexton, but Derek had worked with his hands long enough to know that, if you wanted a job done right, you did it yourself.

He tucked the dirty rag into the back pocket of his faded jeans and rose to tower over the grave. He was a tall man, just over six feet, and his deep-blue eyes were shadowed with grief as he read the dates he'd carved into the roseate marble. It had been just over five years since pneumonia had taken her from him. The thought made his heart swell until he could scarcely breathe.

"Ah, Mary," he whispered, "I miss you."

The spiderweb tracery of budding trees stood black against a darkening sky, and a chill April wind moaned low among the gravestones. Derek shivered, and thought of going back to the house. Peter would be home from school by now, and Nell would be back from her play group, and their Aunt Beatrice would be stopping by to check up on them.

Still he lingered by the grave, unwilling to face Beatrice's barrage of questions. She'd already begun to nag him about his plans for the coming year. He wondered, not for the first time, how his sweet Mary could have had such a harridan for a sister.

Wasn't it a shame that Derek had wasted his first in history— taken at Oxford, too, more's the pity—and gone into this mucky business of restoration? You'd hardly know he was an earl's son, such an embarrassment to his family and such a keen disappointment for poor Mary. His university friends were respectable gentlemen by now—financiers and politicians, most of them—and here was Derek, at forty-five, still messing about with leaky thatched roofs, crumbling stone walls, and nasty old brasses. It had turned her hair gray to think of her only sister living in such a higgledy-piggledy household.

And now it was turning her hair white ("as the driven snow, the cold and driven snow") to think of poor Peter and Nell. Couldn't Derek see that men weren't meant to raise children? It was unnatural, unhealthy, and—"mark my words, nothing good will come of it." Surely he must see that Peter and Nell would be better off in a stable home, with an aunt and uncle who adored them and had only their best interests at heart. Surely . . .

Angrily, Derek ground a clump of mud beneath the heel of his workboot. He'd promised Mary he'd keep the family together and nothing would make him break that promise. Mrs. Higgins was a splendid housekeeper, more than capable of looking after things when Derek was away. Thanks to her, the house was immaculate, the children were well kept, and Beatrice, search as she might, could find no solid ground for complaint. He made a mental note to put a little something extra in Mrs. Higgins's pay packet before he and the children left for Cornwall.

"Thank God for Grayson," Derek murmured, blowing on his wind-reddened hands. The duke's proposal had arrived last month—a stained-glass window to restore at Penford Hall—and, with it, an invitation. *Bring Peter and Nell,* his old friend had written. *Spend the summer.* It'd mean taking Peter out of school before the end of term, but Grayson had promised a governess to see to the boy's lessons, and Beatrice, dazzled by Grayson's title, had been unable to object.

Luckily, among Beatrice's many shortcomings Derek could not, in all honesty, include a fondness for the tabloid press. Beatrice thought the scandal sheets "common" and thus remained blissfully ignorant of the dark rumors and innuendo that had surrounded the scion of Penford Hall five years ago. Fortunately for Derek, Mrs. Higgins, whose passion for the rags was second only to her devotion to the Sunday radio broadcasts of *The Archers,* was not on speaking terms with the beastly Bea.

Derek had to admit to a certain amount of curiosity about the affair, and about Grayson, as well. Theirs had been an odd friendship, blossoming briefly during the summer Derek had spent touching up the ceiling in Oxford's Christ Church Cathedral, where Grayson, still a student, had been the organist for the local Bach chorale. Grayson had expressed a keen interest in Derek's work, and they'd had a number of lively discussions over pints of ale at the Blue Boar. But at the end of the summer, when the old duke had died, the younger man had been off like a shot, never bothering to finish his degree. Derek hadn't been the least bit surprised. He remembered how Grayson's eyes had softened whenever he'd spoken of his boyhood home, how they'd blazed when he'd described his plans for its restoration.

In the ten years that had passed since then, Derek had often wondered if his young friend's grandiose plans had come to fruition. Well, soon he would find out. Come May, he'd be in Cornwall, restoring the window in the duke of Penford's lady chapel.

And after that? He balked at thinking beyond the summer. Somewhere, tucked into a far corner of his mind, was the thought that Peter and Nell should have a mother to look after them, but it was a thought he was not yet ready to contemplate.

He doubted he would ever be ready. He knew he couldn't bring himself to marry someone "for the sake of the children." The idea made his blood run cold. No, if he married again, it would be because he'd found someone to love, truly and with all his heart. And how could he do that, when his heart lay buried at his feet?

"Never again," he murmured, turning, stone-faced, for home. "Never again."

Peter Harris threw the scraps out for the cats and said aloud, to no one in particular: "The first of May. On the first of May, Dad'll take us to Cornwall and everything will be all right."

Thus reassured, Peter closed the back door, put the breakfast dishes in the sink, wiped the crumbs from the table, and swept the kitchen floor. Mrs. Higgins should've put the place to rights before retiring to her room—that's what Dad paid her for, wasn't it?—but Mrs. Higgins had spent most of the afternoon snoring on the settee in the parlor. He trembled to think what might have happened had Auntie Beatrice caught her at it.

"It'll be over soon," he murmured happily, and he believed it. Dad had shown him on the map—Penford Hall was a long way away from Auntie Beatrice.

Peter capped the milk and put it in the fridge, checked to make sure the shepherd's pie was in the cooker—Mrs. Higgins forgot sometimes—and took the box of soap flakes from the cupboard beneath the sink.

Since his mother's death, Peter had learned to clean the dishes and fold the linen and wash Nell's hair without getting soap in her eyes. He'd learned to do the shopping and sort the bills and remind Dad to pay them. He'd learned that it was best to get Nell off to sleep before beginning his schoolwork, and he'd learned—the hard way— that Auntie Beatrice *always* checked under the beds for dust. Over the course of the past few years, Peter had learned what it was to be bone-tired and burdened and constantly alert.

He'd never really learned what it was to be a little boy.

Ten-year-old Peter pushed the step stool over to the front of the sink, climbed up, and turned on the tap. He was short for his age and slight of build, with his father's deep-blue eyes and his mother's straight dark hair. He'd inherited his mother's sober manner as well, and perhaps that was why no one had noticed the changes wrought in him.

Peter himself was unaware of the change. He'd accepted his lot from the first, hoping that a reason for it would one day be made clear to him. And with the arrival of the duke's letter, the reason had appeared at last.

It was the window. The window would be the most important job Dad had ever done, the most important job imaginable, and Peter had to make sure that nothing interfered with it. Because only when it was completed would Mum be truly at rest. Then Peter could rest, too.

Peter turned off the water, then paused, distracted by a strange thumping noise in the hall. The sound was familiar, but he couldn't quite remember where he'd heard it before. Puzzled, he stepped down from the stool and crept to the hall door to peek out. The sight that met his eyes made his stomach knot with dismay.

It wasn't his usual reaction. Unlike most big brothers, Peter was fond of his five-year-old sister. Dad called Nell his changeling, be-cause of her odd ways and fair hair, but she reminded Peter of a paint-ing he'd seen in one of Dad's picture books, a rosy-cheeked cherub with sparkling blue eyes and a mop of curls like Dad's, only Nell's were golden instead of gray. Admittedly, none of the cherubs in the picture books had carried a small, chocolate-brown teddy bear, but Peter could no more imagine his sister without Bertie than he could picture an angel without wings. And now the sight was making his stomach hurt.

"Where did you and Bertie find those clothes, Nell?" Peter asked.

"I am Queen Eleanor," Nell announced, clutching Bertie with one hand and pinching the hem of her skirt with the other, "and this is Sir Bertram of Harris, and we do not speak with pheasants."

"That's *peasants,* Nell." Peter had known it would be a mistake for Dad to read the King Arthur stories to her, but that was not the immediate problem. The immediate problem was that Nell had dressed Bertie in Mum's favorite silk scarf and herself in Mum's pink flowery dress and white high-heeled shoes, and Dad was due home at any minute.

"You must call me Your Majesty," Nell corrected him. "And you must call Bertie Sir Ber—"

"Nell, stop playing."

"I am Queen—"

"*Nell.*"

"Auntie Bea?" Nell spoke in her own voice, her eyes darting to the parlor door.

Peter shook his head, relieved. Nell was cooperative enough once he got her attention, but Queen Eleanor could be stubborn as a mule.

"No," Peter explained, "those clothes. It'll make Dad sad to see them."

"Will it?" Nell conferred briefly with Bertie before asking the inevitable: "Why?"

"Because they're Mum's. They'll remind Dad of her."

"And that will make him sad?"

"Yes," Peter replied patiently, "that will make him very sad." He considered telling Nell about the window, but decided against it. Queen Eleanor might turn it into a royal proclamation. "Come along, Nell. Help me pack those things up again and I'll find you and Bertie something else to play with."

"Something beautiful?"

He nodded. "Something beautiful." Peter unwound Bertie's scarf, then helped Nell step out of the high heels and slipped the dress up and over her head. He was pleased to see a kelly-green jumper and blue dungarees underneath. With Nell, he was never sure what to expect.

He followed her back to the storeroom, where she'd pried open one of the boxes in which Dad had packed Mum's things. After folding the dress and scarf, he laid them reverently on top of the other clothes, dusted the bottoms of the shoes on his pantleg, and placed them, soles up, atop the scarf. He closed the box, then turned to scan the storeroom.

"Nell," he said, as a plan began to take shape, "do you and Bertie remember the story Dad read about the Romans?"

"And the lions?" Nell asked, brightening. "And the chariots and the swords and—"

"And the noble Romans in their beautiful white gowns?"

"Yes, we remember." Nell nodded eagerly.

"Well," said Peter, plucking a clean sheet from the stack on top of the tumble dryer, "those gowns were called *togas*. Only the richest and most beautiful Romans were allowed to wear them." Peter thought he might be stretching the truth a bit here, but never mind. He draped the sheet over Nell's left shoulder, then swept it around to her right one.

"And they wore them to see the lions," Nell said dreamily, reaching for a pillowcase with which to adorn Bertie, "and the chariots and the swords and . . ."

Peter backed out of the storeroom as Nell's eyes took on that familiar, faraway look. That should hold her until supper. He could refold the linen after she and Bertie had gone to bed.

Peter paused on his way back to the kitchen. Turning slowly, he approached the door to his father's workroom. Sometimes he needed to look in, to remind himself of the reason Dad had left so much of the work to him. Carefully, quietly, he turned the knob, opening the door just far enough to peek inside.

There were the racks of colored glass Dad planned to use in the duke's window, and the packet of photographs the duke had sent. His father had shown him the photographs of the window, explaining how he would clean it up and make it good as new. His father hadn't explained all of it, but he hadn't needed to, because Peter understood.

Peter had heard the rector explain it to some visitors, not long after Mum had died, how the soul was like a window with God's light shining through. Auntie Beatrice had got it wrong, saying that Mum's soul would spend eternity in heaven. Peter knew that it was only waiting there, waiting for Dad to make this place for it on earth, this perfect place of rainbow colors, where God's light would shine forever.

Two

Bransley Manor was the first stop on Emma's meticulously planned itinerary. She'd learned of Bransley at a gardening seminar and toured its grounds once before, with Richard. She'd been enchanted by the avenue of monkey puzzle trees, Richard by the hedge maze beyond the pond. Bransley Manor wasn't known for its massed azaleas, but Emma had included it on her tour nonetheless. A one-hour visit would break up the drive from London to Plymouth.

Emma parked her rental car beside an ancient black Morris Minor, the sole occupant of the manor's small parking area. Bransley was an inconspicuous British gem, well off the tour buses' beaten track, and after a whirlwind week of theater in London Emma relished the prospect of having the grounds to herself. Removing her neatly printed itinerary from her shoulder bag, she made a careful X beside the first entry, then took a moment to savor the scene.

The monkey puzzles were just as she remembered them, thorny and twisted and eccentrically grand. The fritillaria borders were new, though, and she wasn't sure she approved. The spiky topknots seemed too dramatic for the setting, and that particular shade of orange clashed resoundingly with the buttery tones of the stone gateposts. If she were head gardener here—

"Everything all right, ma'am?"

Emma started. A young man was standing a few yards away from her car, hunched over and peering at her, a mud-encrusted trowel dangling from one hand.

"Can I help you, ma'am?" He was wearing a tan shirt and tight jeans, and his auburn hair glinted penny-bright in the sun. He was no more than twenty, brown-eyed, freckle-faced, and well muscled, and his voice held the detached politeness that a well-brought-up young man might show to the elderly or infirm. It was the constantly reiterated "ma'am" that did it. He might as well call me "Granny," Emma thought.

"Are you lost, ma'am?" he inquired.

"No, thank you," said Emma. "I know exactly where I am."

"Good enough," the young man said. "Hope you enjoy your visit, ma'am." With a courteous smile, he walked past Emma's car and disappeared between the gateposts. Watching the sway of his narrow hips, Emma felt a wave of self-pity wash over her. Would it have been such a terrible moral compromise, she wondered dismally, to have touched up her mousy-brown hair with something livelier, blonder?

Catching sight of herself in the rearview mirror, Emma paused to take stock. Was her nose a bit too long, her jaw a touch too strong to be called beautiful? Had long hours in the garden traced fine lines across her forehead, crow's-feet around her clear gray eyes? Were her wire-rim glasses dowdy and out of date? Was she?

We can't all be fairy princesses, she thought glumly. *Nor would we want to!* As self-pity veered toward anger, Emma closed her eyes, inhaled deeply, and sought refuge in wry humor. "Well, Granny," she murmured, glancing at her watch, "better get out your cane and start cracking. Time waits for no woman."

Bransley's airy profusion of wallflowers, columbines, and tulips should have sent Emma's spirits soaring, but the longer she strolled its paths, the lower her spirits sank. By the time she reached the hedge maze, tucked away beyond the pond, it was as though a gray cloud had settled over her. She stood in the entrance to the maze, remembering Richard's shout of triumph when he'd reached the center, and knew that her return to Bransley Manor had been a mistake.

The obvious remedy was to leave at once and never come back, but as she turned to go, the young man with the trowel appeared on the far side of the pond. Emma gasped, then scurried into the maze, paying no attention to its twists and turns, thinking only that she'd rather spend the summer lost among the hornbeams than face the young man's polite smile again.

Once safely out of sight, though, Emma began to enjoy herself. She had a retentive memory and was fond of puzzles. In no time at all, she was entering the small clearing that marked the center of the maze, where she looked up in triumph, blinked, and shook her head to clear it.

She was losing her mind. First she'd let a muscle-bound boy send her into an emotional tailspin, and now she was seeing double. Removing her glasses, she passed a weary hand over her eyes, then ventured another look into the clearing.

They were still there: two frail, elderly women who were more alike than any two peas Emma had ever encountered in any one pod. They were dressed identically, from the tips of their white crocheted gloves to the toes of their sensible shoes. They held matching handbags—the word "reticules" flitted through Emma's mind—and wore matching straw sunhats tied with wide lavender ribbons. They were seated side by side on the stone bench beneath the chestnuts, looking at Emma with bright bird's eyes and smiling identical smiles.

"Good afternoon," said one.

"Such a lovely day," said the other.

Was it possible to *hear* double? The women's voices were as indistinguishable as their faces. "Y-yes, it is," Emma managed. "A lovely day."

"I am Ruth Pym and this is my sister . . ."

". . . Louise." Louise patted the bench encouragingly. "Won't you join us? There's room enough . . ."

". . . for three." As Emma sat between them, Ruth continued, "We're from a small village called Finch and we're here for the day . . ."

". . . with the vicar. It is a bit far for us . . ."

". . . to drive on our own. Our motorcar, you see, is somewhat . . ."

". . . antiquated."

Emma waited to be sure it was her turn to speak, then introduced herself.

"You are an American?" Ruth inquired. "And you have come all this way to see Bransley? How splendid. Are you by any chance . . ."

". . . a horticulturalist?" Louise finished.

"An amateur," Emma replied. "I have a garden at home and I love it dearly, but I pay for it by working with computers."

"But that is fascinating!" Ruth exclaimed. "You must be a very intelligent . . ."

". . . and capable young woman."

"Thanks," said Emma, vaguely comforted by the thought that, in the eyes of these two elderly maidens, she was still a young woman. "It's an interesting field, but I need something else to balance it. That's why I started gardening."

"I can well believe that," said Ruth. "Computers, we have heard, are so frightfully . . ."

". . . clean."

"A thing that cannot be said of gardens!"

The two sisters chuckled at Ruth's small joke and Emma laughed with them, relaxing as they began a steady stream of garden gossip. They asked where she'd been and where she planned to go, eagerly soliciting her opinions on pesticides, mulches, and garden designs, but offering few of their own. The Pyms were so friendly, their interest was so genuine, and their enthusiasm so contagious, that well over an hour had passed before Emma even thought to glance at her watch.

"I've really enjoyed meeting you," she said, getting reluctantly to her feet, "but I have a long drive ahead of me and I really should be going."

Ruth smiled reassuringly. "Of course you should, dear."

"And may we say what a pleasure it has been to have this little chat with you," said Louise. "Ruth and I do so enjoy coming to . . ."

". . . Bransley Manor. One meets such . . ."

". . . interesting people."

"I love Bransley, too," agreed Emma, "yet, even here—"

"Ah, you noticed." The sisters looked at her expectantly.

"The fritillaries?" Emma asked. She sat back down again. She'd been dying to get this off her chest. "It'd be hard not to notice them. *Fritillaria meleagris* might've worked in a pinch, but *imperialis?* That shade of orange—" Emma pulled herself up short, put a hand to her mouth, and blushed. "I'm sorry. That must sound pretty pretentious, coming from me. I'm sure the head gardener had a good reason for making the change."

"If he did, he was unable to explain it to us," said Louise firmly. "The *Fritillaria imperialis* was . . ."

". . . a grave error in judgment. We have spoken with the head gardener . . ."

". . . dear Monsieur Melier, and he quite sees our point."

"We hope . . ."

". . . indeed, we expect . . ."

". . . to find them replaced with something more suitable next year."

Emma would have given a lot to have eavesdropped on the Pyms' conversation with dear Monsieur Melier. She suspected that the poor man had caved in before he knew what had hit him. Gallic spleen would be no match for the Pyms' relentless British politeness.

As the sisters lapsed into a comfortable silence, Emma changed her mind about leaving. Keeping to her schedule seemed suddenly less important than sitting quietly with these two pleasant spinsters, watching the linnets dart in and out of the hornbeams while the shadows grew longer and the afternoon slipped away. Besides, she could always make up the lost time tomorrow.

"You are presently traveling to Cornwall?" Ruth inquired after a few moments had passed.

Emma nodded. "I have the whole summer ahead of me and I've never been there before and I . . . I thought some fresh horizons would do me good."

"Of course they will," said Ruth. "Cotehele is particularly lovely at this time of year."

"And Killerton Park," Louise added. "You must not miss the azaleas at Killerton Park. Great banks of them, my dear . . ."

". . . around an oriental temple."

"Most striking."

"The azaleas at Killerton Park are on my itinerary," Emma confirmed.

Another silence ensued. Again, Ruth was the first to break it.

"Might we recommend one other garden?" she asked.

"It is not well known," said Louise.

"It is not, in fact, open to the public," admitted Ruth.

"Then how would I get in to see it?" Emma asked.

"The owner is a friend of ours, my dear. Young Grayson Alexander . . ."

". . . the duke of Penford. A delightful young man. We met him quite by accident. His automobile ran off the road . . ."

". . . directly in front of our house . . ."

". . . straight through the chrysanths . . ."

". . . *and* the birdbath. So exciting." Louise sighed with pleasure. "He sent buckets of chrysanths to us afterwards, as well as a new birdbath, and . . ."

". . . kind Mr. Bantry to roll the lawn and Mr. Gash to repair the wall. We later discovered . . ."

". . . that we had a dear friend in common. Most unexpected . . ."

". . . for ours is a very small village."

"We have kept up with him ever since."

"It was unfortunate about his papa, of course."

"Poor as a church mouse . . ."

". . . and proud as a lion."

"Gone now, poor man . . ."

". . . and now Grayson has the title . . ."

". . . and the estate . . ."

". . . and the worries that come with it. You really must stop by . . ."

". . . as a favor to us. Penford Hall is on your way . . ."

". . . and you would do us a great service if you would bring him word of our . . ."

". . . continued warm regard."

"Penford Hall?" Emma asked, her eyes widening. "Isn't that where—"

"Yes, my dear," Ruth broke in, "but that was long ago and it has all been sorted out . . ."

". . . as we knew it would be. Such a thoughtful young man could not possibly be guilty . . ."

". . . of truly serious wrongdoing. Here, we'll send a note with you . . ."

". . . a little note of introduction."

Ruth opened her handbag and produced a calling card, while Louise opened hers and withdrew a fountain pen. They each wrote something on the back of the card, then handed it to Emma.

"Now, you must promise us that you will look in on our young friend."

"And you must visit us on your way back to London."

"The vicar will be able to find Finch for you on one of his maps."

"He will be able to direct you to Penford Hall as well."

"He is clever with maps. He has scores of them in his glovebox . . ."

". . . and he used every last one to bring us down from Finch today."

"Come along," said Ruth. The Pym sisters stood and Emma stood with them. "Let us find the dear man."

Emma accompanied the two ladies to the car park, where they found the vicar dozing peacefully in the backseat of the Morris Minor. He insisted on presenting Emma with an ancient roadmap, so creased with use that she was afraid it might fall apart in her hands, upon which he marked the location of Penford Hall.

She thanked them all, promised to stop in Finch on her way back to London, and waved them off in a flurry of maps as they began their return journey. When they'd passed from view, Emma looked down at the card in her hand. On the back, the sisters had written:

This is our dear friend, Emma.
She knows gardens.

The parallel lines of curlicued script were identical.

Three

"*I*sn't that where Lex Rex died?"

Mrs. Trevoy, the matronly widow who ran the guest house where Emma had spent the night, leaned so far over the breakfast table that the frills on her apron brushed the top of Emma's teapot. She answered Emma's question in a confidential murmur, presumably to avoid disturbing the honeymoon couple breakfasting at the far end of the small dining room. Glancing at the self-absorbed pair, Emma thought that nothing short of cannon fire would have distracted them, but she appreciated Mrs. Trevoy's sensitivity and kept her own voice down.

"Five years ago," Mrs. Trevoy hissed. "Went down just outside Penford Harbor, the whole drunken lot of them." She leaned closer to add, with obvious relish, *"Drowned like rats."*

"Drowned?" Emma said, alarmed.

Mrs. Trevoy nodded. "Served 'em right," she went on, her ruby-red lips pursed censoriously. "Stole His Grace's yacht, didn't they? And that rubbishy noise they called music . . ." Mrs. Trevoy rolled her eyes. "Enough to make you spew. Bit of a to-do when it happened. Newsmen thick as fleas on a dog's fanny. One of the cheeky buggers wanted to stop here for the night, but I sent him on his way. My sister-in-law lives in Penford Harbor, and what Gladys don't know about human nature would fill a fly's pisspot. If she says His Grace is a nice boy, that's good enough for me." Straightening, Mrs. Trevoy plucked at the ruffles on her apron. "But that's all over now. Well, it's been five years, hasn't it? Story's as old as last week's fish, and twice as rotten. More eggs, dear?" Smiling weakly, Emma declined, and Mrs. Trevoy tiptoed from the room, casting motherly smiles on the young couple at the other table.

Emma stared out of the window. No wonder Penford Hall had sounded so familiar. Richard had been one of Lex Rex's biggest fans.

And probably his oldest. Richard had plastered his studio with the rock singer's lurid photographs, watched and rewatched the videos, cranking up the sound to such earsplitting levels that Emma had fled to her garden for respite. Richard had followed Lex's meteoric rise and been devastated by his death. He'd talked of the yachting accident for weeks, mourning the loss as though the world had been deprived of a young Mozart.

In Emma's personal opinion, the loss of Lex Rex had been a major victory in the battle against noise pollution. Still, she had to admit that she was intrigued. There was the spice of scandal surrounding the rock singer's death, and a certain shivery fascination at the prospect of seeing the actual spot where the yacht had gone down. Glancing at the honeymooners, Emma couldn't help feeling the tiniest bit smug at the thought that, but for the fairy princess, Richard could have seen it, too. Perhaps she would send the happy pair a postcard from Penford Hall, to show that there were no hard feelings.

But first she had to get there. None of her travel brochures had mentioned Penford Hall, nor could she find it in any of her guidebooks. The only proof she had of its existence was the vicar's out-of-date map, with his spidery *X* and the words "Penford Hall" written in his elegant, old-fashioned hand. Emma took the vicar's map from her shoulder bag and opened it gingerly.

There was the *X*, almost on top of the fishing village of Penford Harbor, where Mrs. Trevoy's insightful sister-in-law currently resided. A single road gave access to the coast at that point, a narrow, "unimproved" lane that turned upon itself like a wriggling snake. Very slow going. The drive there would certainly ruin her schedule and possibly rob her of the chance to see Killerton Park's azaleas in full bloom.

Emma refolded the map, finished her toast, and gulped her tea, then headed upstairs to grab her bags and pay the bill. If she left Mrs. Trevoy's guest house immediately, she'd arrive at Penford Hall in time to see the gardens gilded by the afternoon sun.

Emma passed the turnoff twice before creeping slowly by a third time. The sign for Penford Harbor was obscured by weeds, but at ten miles an hour it was visible, and she turned onto a rutted road that was every bit as narrow as she'd feared it would be.

It was not a scenic drive. Hawthorn hedges blocked her view on either side, and the situation straight ahead wasn't much better, since there was no straight ahead. Inching gingerly around one bend after another, Emma tried to skirt the deepest potholes or, when that proved impossible, to ease the car through them gently.

When the hedge on her left parted to reveal a paved and sheltered parking area, Emma pulled into it. The track continued westward, but Emma's teeth had been rattling for close to an hour and she was ready to give up on Penford Hall. No garden was worth this much trouble.

The parking area was protected by a pitched roof of corrugated metal and nearly filled by two rows of shiny new cars. Emma doubted that the owners ever used the road she'd just survived, but the sight of the cars filled her with hope. Perhaps the vicar's map would prove reliable after all.

The only available parking space was in the front row, next to a wheelless white van set up on blocks. Emma carefully nosed in beside it, released her death grip on the steering wheel, and leaned back against the headrest. The enveloping silence was a balm for her jangled nerves.

Settling her glasses more firmly on her nose, Emma reached for her shoulder bag, got out of the car, and edged her way past the van to the car park's southern edge. She was in a narrow, densely wooded valley. Somewhere to her right, hidden by bushes and overhanging trees, a fast-moving stream tumbled and splashed, while below her, at the foot of the valley, lay the village of Penford Harbor.

Emma murmured a heartfelt apology for ever doubting the vicar's map. The village hugged the edge of a natural harbor formed by the embracing arms of towering gray granite cliffs. A beacon flashed from the barren headland to the east, warning of treacherous waters below, while the western promontory seemed to be littered with blocks of gray stone, as though a castle or a fortress had once risen there, now tumbled into ruin.

Four fishing boats bobbed gently in the half-moon cove and fishnets were spread on the gray granite quay, where seagulls roosted in search of easy meals. The stepped and cobbled main street was lined with whitewashed houses, the doors and shutters painted with a Crayola palette of colors—lemon yellow, sky blue, tangerine. Fuchsias trailed from window boxes, pansies filled clay pots on doorsteps, and geraniums topped old barrels along the quay.

The sounds of village life floated upward on the wind. A cloud of gulls hovered over a fishing boat just entering the harbor and Emma could hear their raucous cries as clearly as though she were standing on the deck.

Then she heard another sound, a low, tuneless whistling that seemed to be coming from somewhere in the region of her ankles. Looking down, she saw a pair of legs emerge from beneath the front bumper of the white van. The legs belonged to a chubby, white-haired man in a royal-blue jumpsuit who was lying flat on his back on a low, wheeled platform—a creeper, Emma thought it was called. The man was holding a wrench in one hand and an oily rag in the other, and when he saw Emma, he stopped whistling.

"Hello," he said. "Lost your way?"

Emma bridled slightly. The boy at Bransley Manor had made the same assumption and the question was beginning to annoy her. "No," she replied firmly. "I'm looking for Penford Hall. I believe it's very near here."

The chubby man slipped the wrench and the rag into the breast pocket of his jumpsuit, rolled off of the creeper onto all fours, then slowly got to his feet. "Not as young as I used to be," he commented, rubbing the small of his back. "Lookin' for Penford Hall, you say?"

Emma took the Pyms' calling card from her shoulder bag and presented it to him. "My name is Emma Porter. I was sent by some friends of the duke."

The man examined the card, then bent to unzip a pocket in the leg of his jumpsuit. When he stood up again, he was holding a palm-sized portable telephone. He flipped the mouthpiece down, pushed a few buttons, then held the telephone to his ear.

"Gash here," he said. "Got a visitor for His Grace. Name of Emma Porter. Sent by"—he consulted the card—"Ruth and Louise Pym.

Something to do with gardens. Right. I'll wait." He covered the mouthpiece with his hand and winked at Emma. "Handy gadget, this," he whispered.

It was also extremely expensive. To see such a pricey piece of hardware emerge from the zippered pocket of a mechanic's jumpsuit was a bit unexpected.

Gash was speaking again. "Right," he said. "I'll bring her up straightaway." Gash folded the telephone and stowed it once more in his pocket, then gestured toward Emma's car. "Hop in," he said. "I'll drive."

As he maneuvered the car out of the tight parking space, Emma commented on the lamentable state of the road. "Don't get used much," Gash replied. "Not since His Grace laid in the new one. Easier on the villagers, he says. Some folks still get round by boat, o' course. Or by chopper, but that's for emergencies, mainly."

"Did you say helicopter?" Emma clarified.

"Yes, well, Dr. Singh had to have one, and since the village needed him, His Grace got him his chopper." As though suddenly remembering his manners, Gash turned to extend a pudgy hand to Emma. "I'm Gash, the mechanic up at Penford Hall."

Formalities concluded, Gash backed Emma's car out of the parking area and drove westward, beyond the point where Emma had given up. They crossed a stone bridge, then turned a corner where, mercifully, the potholed track became a ribbon of smooth asphalt climbing out of the valley. At the top, they came to another, broader road that ran along the crest of the western headland. Gash turned toward the sea.

When Emma saw the gates of Penford Hall, she very nearly changed her mind about visiting. Tall, black, and forbidding, the gates were set into imposing granite posts flanked by thick walls and topped with surveillance cameras that swept the road in steady, unrelenting arcs. She was further unnerved when a small door in the gate opened to reveal a stocky old man strikingly attired in a black beret, a khaki army sweater, camouflage trousers, and highly polished black leather boots.

"Newland," Gash murmured, by way of introduction. "Nice enough feller, but you won't get a handshake out o' him. I expect it's on account of his job."

"What *is* his job?" Emma asked, noting the wire that ran from beneath Newland's black beret to the sleek two-way radio hooked to his belt.

"Gatekeeper," Gash replied. "Newland lets the good 'uns in and keeps the bad 'uns out. Makes him a bit antisocial, if you know what I mean."

Newland squinted at them, raised a hand to his beret in a brief salute, then slipped back through the small door. A moment later, the gates swung wide and the black-topped road became a graveled drive bordered by twin banks of white azaleas, shoulder-high and exploding into full bloom.

Gash spoke again, but Emma was unaware of his words, or of the smile that had stolen across her face, or of anything except the fluttering white blossoms, fragile as butterfly wings, that seemed to beckon her onward. The walls enclosed a delicate, dark woodland carpeted with a smoky haze of bluebells and lit now and then by the hawthorn's snowy boughs and the blushing pink petals of cherry trees. Emma had scarcely drunk it in when Gash jutted his chin forward, announcing, "There's the hall."

Emma peered curiously at the gray granite edifice that had come into view on the horizon. There was no telling how old Penford Hall was or how many rooms it contained. It spilled across the headland, bristling with balconies, chimneys, and conical towers, a seemingly haphazard collection of parts that formed an eccentric and somewhat forbidding whole. Emma, who leaned toward the precise geometry of neoclassical pillars and porticoes, found the domain of the duke of Penford a bit too Gothic for her taste.

The landscape, at least, showed the touch of an orderly hand. A pair of yews flanked the broad stairway leading to the hall's main entrance, and germander hedges extended on either side to the stables, which had, by the looks of it, been converted into a single vast garage. Gash's domain, Emma thought, just as the gatehouse was Newland's.

Gash swung around the circular drive and parked at the foot of the stairs, where a pair of elderly men stood waiting. Both wore old-fashioned black suits with stiff collars and cuffs. The taller of the two was nearly bald and slender as a rake, while the shorter, round-shouldered man wore thick horn-rimmed glasses.

"The scarecrow's Crowley," Gash explained. "Crowley's head butler. The chap with the specs is Hallard, the footman. Hallard'll look after your bags."

"My bags?" Emma was about to explain that she hadn't intended to impose on the duke's hospitality, but Hallard had already removed her luggage from the trunk, and Crowley had opened the car door, saying, "Please come with me, Miss Porter."

Flustered, Emma obeyed.

Four

The entrance hall's plaster walls were hung with oil portraits in heavy gilt frames. The beamed ceiling had been ornamented with gold leaf, and the marble floor was a pristine cream-and-rose checkerboard. A pair of feathery tree ferns in brass pots flanked a splendid mahogany staircase that divided in two at a landing.

The landing's wall was adorned with a frieze of slender figures in diaphanous robes, painted in shades of ivory, peach, pale green, and gold. Emma blinked when one of the figures appeared to move, and it was then that she saw the woman, a flawless beauty in a gossamer gown, with hair like silken sunlight and eyes like—

Emma wrenched her gaze away. Since when had she started seeing Richard's bride in every skinny blonde that crossed her path? Besides, she thought, daring a second look, *this* skinny blonde is *famous*.

Emma might not know much about the world of fashion, but she knew enough to know that face. It had appeared on too many talk shows, shown up on too many magazine covers—and Richard had sung its praises far too often. It had been out of the limelight for some years, but, nevertheless, only a cave-dwelling hermit could have failed to recognize the model known as Ashers, the English Rose. The queen of the fairy princesses.

"What have we here?" Ashers asked, gliding weightlessly down the stairs and across the marble floor to where Emma stood.

"A guest to see His Grace," Crowley replied shortly.

Ashers looked down her delicate nose at Emma's beige corduroy skirt and loose-fitting white cotton pullover, and sniffed when she saw Emma's walking shoes. "Charming," she commented. "An outdoorswoman, I take it?" She leaned forward to peer at Emma's face. "If I were you, darling, I'd start ladling on the sunscreen."

Emma's cheeks flamed and she looked at the floor.

"Susannah!"

Emma glanced up. The cry had come from a man walking briskly across the entrance hall. He reminded Emma of the duke of Windsor: thirtyish, compact, elegant, with small, neat hands and finely chiseled features. He wore a dark tweed hunting jacket over a russet waistcoat and beige trousers; his shoes had the muted gleam of glove leather. His honey-blond hair was straight and conservatively cut, and his eyes were a deep, liquid brown.

"Welcoming my guest, Susannah?" he asked when he reached them. "How thoughtful of you. As you've no doubt discovered, this is my good friend Miss Emma . . ." He faltered.

"Porter, Your Grace," Crowley supplied, confirming Emma's guess that this was, indeed, the duke of Penford.

"Miss Emma Porter, of course. May I present my cousin, Miss Susannah Ashley-Woods?"

"So pleased to meet you," said Susannah. She favored the duke with her dazzling smile. "It's about time you balanced the table, Grayson."

"Quite," said the duke, with an uneasy grin. "Now, if you'll excuse us, Emma and I have some business to discuss." The duke took Emma by the elbow. "Crowley, please see to Miss . . . ah . . ."

"Emma will do," Emma put in hastily.

"Just so," said the duke. "Please see to it that Emma's bags are placed in the rose suite, and have Gash return her car to the office in Plymouth."

"Very good, Your Grace."

"But, Your Grace," said Emma, "I hadn't planned to—"

"You must call me Grayson," chided the duke. "Crowley calls me Your Grace because he knows it embarrasses me. Perfectly gorgeous day, what?" The duke swept Emma across the entrance hall, around several corners, up one short flight of stairs, and down another, chattering nonstop all the while.

"I couldn't help but notice you noticing the frieze on the landing. It was done by Edward Burne-Jones. Great-Grandfather was mad for the Pre-Raphaelites, invited the chap down for a long weekend, and Eddie whipped up the painting as a thank-you. Much nicer than the usual note card, I've always thought."

The duke led Emma into an enormous dining room and, closing the door behind them, finally came to a stop. "Sorry about the quickstep," he said, leaning against the door, "but I wanted you out of reach of Susannah's claws. I do hope you'll forgive her. She was raised by wolves, you know."

"Isn't she—"

The duke nodded gloomily. "Ashers, the English Rose. The face that's launched a thousand product lines. A somewhat distant and distaff twig of the family tree, but a twig nonetheless. The last time I saw Susannah, she was a scrawny twelve-year-old with two plaits down her back and a brace on her teeth."

"She's changed," Emma observed.

"Not enough," said the duke. "Now, Emma, my dear—"

"Grayson," Emma said quickly, "about my luggage and my car. I really hadn't intended to impose—"

"Impose?" cried the duke. "Nonsense! We've scads of rooms at Penford Hall and more cars than we know what to do with. If you need transport, give Gash a ring, and if you need anything else, call for Crowley. Now, come along, Emma, come see the garden. We've only an hour of good light left." As he spoke, the duke ushered Emma across the dining room to a pair of French doors that opened onto a balustraded terrace, where a flight of steps descended to a broad expanse of manicured lawn. The lawn ended, much to Emma's delight, at the front wall of a ruined castle.

"It *is* a castle," she murmured.

The duke had already reached the bottom of the terrace steps. At her words, he turned, smote himself on the forehead, and bounded back up to stand by Emma's side, saying ruefully, "Forgive me. I forgot that you hadn't seen the place before." He waved a hand toward the ruin. "Yes, yes—started out as a fortress, of sorts. The first duke was a bit of a blackguard, and a blackmailer as well. Got the title in exchange for a promise to stop preying on Her Majesty's shipping lanes and start protecting them."

"He was a pirate?" Emma asked with a smile.

" 'Fraid so. Must've been frightfully good at his chosen profession, to get a hereditary title as a retirement gift. Wish he'd got a bit of arable land as well, but one can't have everything. Nothing left of the original pirate's keep, of course, but . . ." The duke rattled on, telling of the castle's rise and its gradual fall as later dukes reclaimed its massive blocks to build Penford Hall—"Recycling at its finest," proclaimed the duke.

All that remained of the magnificent edifice were the four massive outer walls and a random collection of interior walls—"with the odd staircase and hearth thrown in for dramatic effect." Within the ruins, Bantry—"head gardener here, splendid chap"—had created half a dozen garden "rooms." Emma nodded her understanding, having seen something similar, at Sissinghurst, in Kent, where the gardens were laid out among the ruined walls of an Elizabethan manor.

"Admittedly," the duke concluded, "the castle rather spoils the view from the dining room, but it's a marvelous windbreak, don't you think?"

Emma nodded. Like the woodland she'd just driven through with Gash, the lush green lawn could not have existed without protection from the scouring wind. East and west, the lawn had been enclosed by ten-foot walls that extended from the hall to the castle. A dozen pleached apple trees hugged the warm gray stones, basking in the sunlight.

"End of history lesson," said the duke, "and on to botany." Flashing an engaging grin, he took Emma by the elbow and guided her at a brisk pace down the terrace steps and across the lawn toward the arched entryway of the ruined castle. "I hope you won't mind if we bypass Bantry's garden rooms and head straight for the chapel garden. I'm rather eager for you to see it." He held up his hand. "Not that you'll be rushed. You must take all the time you need." The duke smiled so warmly that Emma half expected him to hug her. "Thank heavens Aunt Dimity heard my prayers and sent the Pyms to find you."

Emma was on the verge of protesting that she'd never met the duke's aunt, but they'd passed under the arch and into the cool shadows of the castle's interior, a bewitching collection of fragmented walls and roofless arcades, gaping doorways and stairways leading to open sky.

Glancing through an opening on her left, Emma saw the first of Bantry's garden rooms, a grassy courtyard surrounded by a deep perennial border. Madonna lilies, delphiniums, and bellflowers beckoned and Emma turned toward them, but stopped when the duke held up a cautioning hand, pointing to a cluster of white wicker lawn furniture at the far end of the courtyard.

"Afternoon, Hallard," called the duke.

Hallard, the bespectacled footman who'd taken charge of Emma's luggage, was seated on a cushioned armchair, tapping steadily at the keys of a laptop computer. At the duke's salutation, he slowly raised his head, blinking at them from behind his thick glasses. "Hmmm?" he murmured. "Your Grace requires my assistance?"

"Not at all, old man," the duke replied cheerfully. "Just passing through. Carry on."

"Very good, Your Grace." Hallard nodded vaguely, then focused once more on the computer screen. The sound of tapping keys resumed.

"What's he working on?" Emma ventured.

"Chapter six, one hopes, but it wouldn't do to ask. Come along, Emma, right this way."

Chapter six? thought Emma, but before she could frame an appropriate question, the duke had swept her into a grassy corridor that seemed to pass through the center of the ruins. On either side of the corridor a series of gaping doorways revealed ancient, roofless chambers that had been transformed into flourishing gardens, but the duke passed them by without comment, hustling Emma down the grassy corridor until they came to what must have once been the banquet hall.

It was now a vegetable garden. Rows of cabbages, carrots, and turnips were interplanted with marigolds, poppies, and nasturtiums, and staked tomato vines grew along the walls. The layout reminded Emma of her garden at home, with one extremely large exception.

At the center of the hall, rising high above the walls, was a domed treillage arbor, a soaring, oversized birdcage of fanciful wrought iron covered over by a healthy crop of runner beans. It was the most extravagant trellis Emma had ever seen.

The duke chuckled at the expression on her face. "Grandmother gave parties here in the old days," he told her. "Long-necked ladies in beaded dresses, gents in white tie and tails, a gramophone playing in the moonlight. Bantry made it into a kitchen garden, and very useful it is, too."

"It's impressive," Emma agreed.

"Bantry's magical with plants. Veggies and flowers will sit up and sing for him, but he lacks . . . imagination. That's why he hasn't tackled the chapel garden. Can't find Grandmother's planting records, and without them he's lost." Humming a few bars of "Anything Goes," the duke strolled along a graveled path past the birdcage arbor to the opposite side of the banquet hall. As he lengthened his stride, Emma was forced to scurry to keep up.

It was a frustrating chase. Emma caught tantalizing flashes of pink and blue and yellow and red, glimpses of clematis clambering up walls and violets peeping from the shadows, but the duke gave her no chance to savor anything. She was working up the courage to call a halt when they came to the southernmost reach of the castle, the part nearest the sea.

They were facing a tall, green-painted wooden door, the first door Emma had seen since entering the ruins. The green door was set into a sturdy, level wall that stretched east and west for a hundred feet or so. The drabness of the gray stone had been relieved by a series of niches set into the wall at irregular intervals and planted with primroses.

Gazing upward, the duke explained, "Grandmother had this wall built from leftover bits of the castle. It's twelve feet tall and three feet thick, to protect that which she held most dear." He reached for the latch. "No one's looked after it for years," he added. "Bantry's had so much else to do. . . ." He glanced beseechingly at Emma. "What I mean to say is, I'm sorry it's such a cock-up, but it'd mean a great deal to me if you could see your way clear to . . ." He gripped the latch firmly and took a deep breath. "You see, this place meant everything to my grandmother, and she meant everything to me."

The duke smiled a wistful, fleeting smile, then lifted the latch. As the door swung inward, Emma stepped past him and down ten uneven stone steps. At the foot of the stairs she stopped.

"I'll leave you alone for a while, shall I?" murmured the duke.

Emma didn't notice his departure. For a moment she forgot even to breathe, and when she remembered, it was a slowly drawn breath exhaled in a heartbroken moan.

Five

*E*mma stared at the ghost of a garden. The shriveled stalks that shivered in the breeze held no bright petals or sweet scents, and the withered vines that stretched like cobwebs across the walls would never blossom again. The chapel garden was a tangle of decay and desiccation, yet it held within it the sweet sadness of a place once loved and long forgotten.

Two tiers of raised flowerbeds, deep terraces set one above the other, encircled a rectangular lawn. In each corner rounded ledges rose, like steps, almost to the top of the wall. To her right lay the dried bed of what had been a small reflecting pool, and a wooden bench rested beside it, bleached silver by the sun. The garden had been beautiful once, but now the ledges were crowded with cracked and crumbling clay pots, the raised beds dotted with dried flower-heads, the rectangular lawn matted with bindweed and bristling with thistles.

A curious building straddled the center of the long rear wall, one end facing out to sea, the other planted firmly in the garden. Stubby, oblong, built of the same charcoal-gray granite as the castle, it had no belltower, no arches, nothing to entice the mind or enchant the eye. Its only decoration was a thick mat of moss on its steeply pitched slate roof, and a golden dapple of lichen above the low, rounded door. A flagstone path led from the door to the stairs, neatly bisecting the lawn.

On impulse, Emma dropped to her knees in the damp grass, parted the weeds, and dug her hand deep into the soil. She grabbed up a fistful of moist earth, sniffed at it, rubbed it between her palms, and let it fall through her fingers. "Anything will grow in this," she marveled, and felt a flicker of hope. With work and perseverance, the ghosts could be banished from this place, and the flowers that belonged here could be restored in all their glory.

When she had risen, Emma walked slowly to the door of the stubby building. She put her shoulder to the darkened wood and shoved, then caught her breath as she beheld the chapel's sole adornment.

It was like stepping into a jewel. The stained-glass window flooded the chapel with color and light, drenching the rough stone walls, the flagstone floor, and the beams overhead with rich and vibrant hues. Five feet in height, perhaps, and three feet wide, the window rendered all other decoration superfluous.

A border of red roses framed the figure of a woman. She stood against a swirling background of scudding clouds and storm-tossed trees, one hand clasping the collar of her billowing black cloak, the other hand thrust defiantly skyward, gripping a lantern that glowed with an unearthly radiance. Wind-whipped tendrils of raven hair flew wildly from the black cloak's hood, but the woman's face was as still as the surface of a cavern pool. Emma gazed up into her fierce brown eyes, then stumbled back across the threshold and through the rounded door. She leaned there for a moment, blinking dazedly in the sunlight, and when she looked up again, the garden had come to life around her.

She smelled the scent of lavender that framed the chapel door, saw the bed of irises, the splash of poppies, the glowing cluster of pink peonies backlit by the sun. Old Bourbon roses cascaded down the gray stone walls, coral bells rose from a cloud of baby's breath, and still water sparkled in the small reflecting pool.

Emma knew that she was dreaming in broad daylight, but she didn't want the dream to end. The images came to her as vividly as a memory of home and, sighing, she felt as though she'd returned to a place she'd left years ago and longed for ever since. She leaned against the chapel and watched the seasons change, until a sound caught her attention. The garden faded, the pool went dry, and she straightened, embarrassed to be found daydreaming by the duke.

But it was not the duke.

It was another man entirely. This man was tall and lean, with broad shoulders and a long, weathered face. His jeans were faded, his navy-blue pullover stained in places, his workboots scuffed and comfortably broken in. The leather tool belt slung around his hips held a hammer, some chisels, and several pairs of oddly shaped pliers. An unruly mop of salt-and-pepper curls tumbled over his high forehead, and his eyes were the color of sapphires.

"Sorry," said the man. "Didn't mean to disturb you. I was looking for Grayson."

"Grayson?" Emma said faintly.

"The duke," the man replied.

"The duke?" Emma echoed.

"I was told he'd be out here," the man elaborated. "Have you seen him?"

Emma tried to swallow, but her mouth had gone dry. "Yes," she managed, "but he's not here now."

"Ah." The man nodded. A few moments passed before he asked, "Will he be coming back?"

"I think so," Emma replied, adding helpfully, "In a while."

"I'll wait for him, then." The man walked with unhurried ease down the uneven stone steps and over to Emma's side, where he pulled the chapel door shut, then stood, looking at the decay that surrounded him. "A restful place," he commented.

Emma mumbled something, then wiped the back of her hand across her forehead, which had suddenly become damp.

"Pardon me," said the man. He pulled a handkerchief from his back pocket and offered it to Emma. "You've . . . um . . . ." He gestured toward his own forehead. ". . . left some dirt behind."

"Have I?" Mortified, Emma took the handkerchief and scrubbed at her forehead. "Is it gone?" she asked anxiously.

"Not quite. Please, allow me." The man eased the cloth from her hand and with gentle fingers tilted her head back until she was looking straight up into those eyes. "There's just a tiny smudge—"

"What have we here?" asked a voice. "Frolics in the garden?"

The man swung around, flushing crimson when he saw Susannah Ashley-Woods observing them from the top of the stone stairs. Fashionably shod in three-inch stiletto heels, the duke's cousin carefully negotiated the uneven steps and came to stand beside the tall man.

"Imagine my chagrin," Susannah drawled. "I've been after Derek all week to show me his beastly window and now I've teetered out here all on my own, risking life and a pair of heavily insured limbs, only to find another woman in his arms."

"There was dirt on my face," Emma tried to explain.

"A bit further down as well," Susannah noted, gazing pointedly at Emma's skirt.

With a sinking feeling, Emma looked down to see two large stains on her beige skirt, where her knees had met the damp grass.

"I'm sure there's no permanent harm done," Susannah cooed. "Corduroy is such a *durable* fabric." Running a long-fingered hand through her silky hair, she looked from the man's face to Emma's. "What? Cats have your tongues? Don't tell me—my cousin has been remiss in his introductions. Allow me. Emma Porter, meet Derek Harris."

Derek offered his hand and Emma reached out to take it, saw that her own was smeared with mud, and snatched it back.

"Glad to meet you," she muttered, her eyes on Derek's tool belt.

"Uh, yes," said Derek, his hand stranded in midair. He smiled slightly, then raised his hand to rub his chin. "Pleasure's mine."

"Derek's here to work on the window," Susannah went on. "What about you, Emma?" She leaned forward and asked, with a mischievous smile, "Come for a peek at Penford Hall's claim to fame?"

Emma stared at Susannah blankly.

"Lex Rex?" Susannah prompted. "The pop star? Don't tell me you've never heard of him."

"Of course I have," Emma mumbled defensively. To prove it, she added the first song title that popped into her head. "'Kiss My Tongue.'"

Emma blushed to her roots while Derek stared stolidly into the middle distance and Susannah smirked.

"Yes," Susannah confirmed, "that was one of Lex's more memorable videos. If you climb up those corner ledges you can see where he sank Grayson's lovely yacht. Surely, that's why you're—" She broke off as the garden door opened again and the front end of a wheelbarrow rolled slowly into view. "Ah," said Susannah, "Bantry has arrived."

The barrow was wielded by a short, stocky man with a wrinkled, nut-brown face and a tussock of white hair blown helter-skelter on the top of his head. Even on this fine day, he wore heavy wool trousers, a tattered argyle sweater-vest, an oiled green cotton jacket, and a mud-stained pair of black Wellington boots.

Derek strode over to offer a steadying hand as the old wheelbarrow, tightly covered with a patched oilcloth, clanked loudly down the steps. The thick wooden handle of a grub hoe and the bent handle of a scythe protruded from beneath the cloth.

When the two men had guided the barrow to a safe landing at the bottom of the stairs, Bantry pushed it a few feet to one side, then stood back to survey the group.

"Much obliged, Mr. Derek, sir," he said. His gaze traveled quickly past Susannah and came to rest on Emma. Grinning broadly, he crossed over to her and, before she could stop him, seized her muddy hand and pumped it vigorously.

"Bantry, head gardener, at your service," he said. "Very pleased to meet you, Miss Emma. His Grace told me you'd arrived." He indicated the tool-filled barrow with a jerk of his head. "Thought I'd make a start. Won't turn a clod without your say-so, o' course. Ah, you've been at it already, I see." He looked down at the damp soil that had been transferred from Emma's palm to his own. "Wonderful stuff Her Grace laid in here. Don't know what she did to make it so rich. She never told Father or Grandfather and she never told me." He touched the muddy tip of his little finger to his tongue, looked thoughtfully skyward, then turned his head and spat, missing Susannah's toes by inches. "Gull shit, I think."

"Oh, my Lord," Susannah said faintly. "How very rustic." She glanced up at the garden door and said, more loudly, "Grayson, darling, did you know that Bantry's acquired a taste for guano?"

"I should think it would be an acquired taste," Grayson replied. He ran nimbly down the stairs to join the little group. "Everyone's met everyone, I trust? Good. Now, if you'll all be lambs and give me five minutes alone with Emma, I'll be forever in your debt."

Bantry climbed the stairs and left the garden without demur, and when Susannah began to protest, Derek quickly cut her off.

"Come with me, Susannah. You'll be much more comfortable in the drawing room with a tall drink."

"As long as it's accompanied by a tall man, I won't complain." Susannah took Derek's arm and Emma watched, unaccountably hurt, as another skinny blonde walked off with the man of her dreams.

It took the duke several tries to regain her attention. "I realized how off-putting my cousin can be," he said, with an understanding smile. "But you mustn't let Susannah drive you away."

"Drive me away? Oh, no." Emma stared at the green door, her face hardening as she thought, *Not this time.*

"Wonderful!" exclaimed the duke. "Now, about the chapel garden," he went on. "You needn't tell me your plans—"

"Plans?" Emma turned to the duke, feeling as though she'd missed a vital part of the conversation.

"Your plans for the chapel garden, my dear. I simply want you to know that it's yours to do with as you like. Every resource shall be made available to you. If you need a backhoe or a teaspoon, you need only say the word. And you're to consider Penford Hall your home for as long as you wish."

"But, really, Grayson, I-I don't—" Emma stammered.

"I know what you're thinking," the duke broke in. "You're thinking there must be a catch somewhere, and you're absolutely right. You see, my dear, the chapel garden must be in some sort of shape by the first of August." Emma's jaw dropped, but the duke waved her to silence. "It doesn't have to be perfect. All I ask is that you make a start in restoring this place to the way it was while my grandmother was alive."

"But, Grayson, I—"

"Don't worry," he insisted. "You were selected by two infallible judges—Aunt Dimity couldn't have chosen better—and Bantry will be here to lend a hand." The duke seemed to take no notice when Crowley, the elderly head butler, appeared at the top of the stairs.

"Supper's at nine," he went on. "Drinks in the library, eight thirty-ish." His eyes never leaving Emma's face, he added, "Please escort this gracious lady to her room, Crowley, and see to it that she has everything she requires. I don't wish to lose her, now that I've finally found her."

Six

The rose suite was located somewhere between the second and third floors of Penford Hall. Crowley had explained, in a deferential murmur, that the hall was basically three stories in height, but that, owing to various quirks and fancies of former dukes and duchesses, a few half stories crept in now and again. There were the cellars and attics, of course, but one didn't really include them, and the towers, which threw one's calculations off completely, but basically, Penford Hall had three floors. Emma had listened carefully, but by the time they'd arrived at the rose suite, she wasn't at all sure how she'd reach the library at the appointed hour.

The view was lovely, at any rate. From her balcony Emma could look out over the great lawn and the castle ruins. She wasn't quite high enough to look down into the ruins, but a few fortuitous gaps in the walls revealed the wrought-iron finial of the birdcage arbor. The dome-shaped finial was almost as elaborate as the arbor itself. It looked like a smaller birdcage set atop a much larger one, and it, too, was liberally embellished with decorative ironwork. She could see the roof of the chapel as well, pointing like the prow of a ship over the vast sweep of the Channel, where a bank of dark clouds was blowing in from the west, filling the air with the scent of rain.

Emma leaned on the balustrade and sighed. She didn't know what to make of Penford Hall. The chapel, the castle, the wonderful arbor, even the odd, stiff collar worn by the storklike head butler, all hailed from an earlier era. Yet every time she turned around she saw evidence that the twentieth century was alive and well at Penford Hall—Hallard's laptop computer, Newland's hip-slung radio, Gash's pocket telephone. Emma felt as though she stood with a foot in two worlds, and knew that she didn't belong in either.

She certainly didn't belong in such a lovely room. The rose suite was aptly named. The nightstand, the four-poster, and the writing desk, adorned with a discreet burgundy telephone and a jeweled enameled clock, were made of rosewood. The creamy walls were hung with framed botanical illustrations, hand-colored woodcuts depicting roses from bud to blossom. The quilted satin coverlet on the four-poster was embroidered with a sprinkle of crimson rosebuds, and the pair of plump chairs before the tiled fireplace were upholstered in a pattern of blowsy grandifloras.

A dressing room and bathroom adjoined the bedroom. Emma's skirts had been hung in the wardrobe; her sweaters placed in the cedar-lined drawers of the dresser. Her plastic comb and brush had been carefully arranged beside a silver-backed brush and a tortoise-shell comb on the skirted dressing table. Her travel bottles of shampoo and hair conditioner had been set within reach of a deep tub boxed round with mahogany.

Closing the balcony door against the freshening breeze, Emma looked at the beautiful bedroom, and groaned. Clearly, an error—a whole string of errors—had been made. The duke had misread the Pyms' message, misunderstood the reason for her visit, and mistaken her for someone else. If he hadn't hurried her so, she'd have explained that she hadn't been sent by his aunt to restore the chapel garden.

Not that she didn't want to. The pleasure of touring a garden couldn't compare with the joys of creating one. It was an impossible task, of course. Even a professional gardener would need more than three months to bring the chapel garden back to life again, regardless of the high-tech gardening gadgetry the duke might see fit to supply. Still, she thought wistfully, it would have been an unforgettable three months.

Her reflections were interrupted by a knock at the door, followed closely by the entrance of a petite blond teenager who was, unmistakably, the maid. Her starched white apron, dove-gray uniform, and white cap, with its ribbons and lace, looked as though they'd been borrowed from the BBC's costume department, and her curtsy was equally anachronistic. Emma's thoughts swerved from space-age gadgets to Edwardian manners, and once more she had the jangled sensation of coming slightly unstuck in time.

"I'm Mattie, miss, Crowley's granddaughter," the maid announced shyly. Mattie showed Emma a luxuriant blue terry-cloth robe in the wardrobe, then went soberly about her tasks, drawing a bath, closing the drapes, and laying a fire, while Emma changed out of her soiled skirt.

Mattie came to life only once, when Emma asked for her advice on what to wear for supper. After surveying Emma's limited wardrobe gravely, she selected the one nice dress Emma had packed, a calf-length jersey in teal, with long sleeves and a cowl neck. As she laid it out on the bed, Mattie turned the hem up to examine the stitching.

"Quality fabric, this," she murmured, and Emma, hoping to put the girl at ease, asked if she was interested in clothing.

"I love designing things," Mattie replied. "When I found out I was coming here to work with Nanny Cole, I made this." With quiet pride, she raised a hand to the ribbons of her extraordinary cap.

"It's very becoming," Emma said diplomatically. "It must be exciting for you to have Ashers staying at Penford Hall."

Mattie's face lit up. "Oh, yes, miss. Have you seen her? Isn't she lovely?" Her pretty smile dimmed for a moment as she added confidentially, "Mind you, Granddad and the others don't care for her. Well, she's always going on about that old business—"

"What old business is that?" Emma asked, walking over to warm her hands at the fire.

Mattie's eyes shifted to the hall door. "That awful singer and his band," she replied shortly. "No one wants to hear about him anymore, not after all the trouble he caused." The girl gathered up Emma's corduroy skirt and moved to the door, where she paused, with one hand on the porcelain knob. "I don't mind so much. Ashers isn't like you and me, miss. She's got what you'd call an artistic temperament. Besides, she's promised to have a look at my sketches." Mattie's radiant smile returned. "Can you imagine, miss? It's a dream come—" Mattie jumped guiltily as a knock sounded at the door.

"Mattie? Is that you?" called a woman's voice. "Be a dear and open up, will you? My hands are full."

After smoothing her apron and straightening her cap, Mattie opened the door to a dark-haired woman whose arms were wrapped awkwardly around what appeared to be a portable drafting table. A T square and a clear plastic box filled with drawing supplies were propped precariously under her chin.

"Give us a hand, Mattie," the raven-haired woman managed. She was in her late twenties, fine-boned and fair-skinned, wearing a hand-knit crewneck sweater over a well-cut pair of pleated wool trousers. When she and Mattie had finished setting up the table, she sent Mattie on her way, then turned to regard Emma with a pleasant, level-headed gaze. "The drafting table's just for midnight insights," she explained. "For the real work, you'll have the library and whichever drawing room suits you." She paused before adding carefully, "I do hope Mattie hasn't been boring you about our visiting celebrity. Did I hear something about an artistic temperament?"

"A word or two," Emma admitted.

"Well, Susannah does have a temperament, but I'm not sure I'd describe it as artistic. And then there's Syd."

"Syd?" Emma asked.

"Syd Bishop, Susannah's manager. You'll meet him at supper. He's an American, too, from Brooklyn, and he's . . . unique. At least, one hopes he is." Extending her hand, the woman crossed over to Emma. "Hello. I'm Kate Cole, Grayson's housekeeper. Sorry I couldn't come down to greet you earlier, but Mattie and I were up here, getting your room ready. Is it all right?"

"It's great, but . . ." Emma glanced at the drafting table, then plunged ahead, eager to unburden herself. "But I'm not sure I should be in it." She gestured toward the armchairs. "Can we talk for a minute, Kate? I'm afraid there's been some sort of a mix-up."

Kate sighed. "There usually is, when Grayson gets one of his brilliant ideas." As they settled into the overstuffed chairs, she went on sympathetically, "I imagine Grayson's rushed you off your feet without bothering to mention silly things like salaries and contracts and—"

"It's not that," Emma said hastily. "I'd work on the chapel garden for free, if I thought I could do the job, but, frankly, I don't think I can. I'm not a landscape designer, Kate. I'm just an ordinary backyard gardener."

Kate's brow furrowed. "But the Pyms sent you, didn't they?"

Emma explained patiently that she hardly knew the Pyms. "I only met them the day before yesterday. We spent the afternoon at Bransley Manor, gossiping about gardens."

"Ah," said Kate, relaxing. "That would explain it. They've known for months that Grayson's been searching for someone to work on Grandmother's garden. As for your qualifications . . ." Tilting her head to one side, she asked, "Did you talk for a long time with Ruth and Louise? Did they ask you a lot of questions?"

Emma pursed her lips thoughtfully. Even at the time, she'd thought her conversation with the Pyms curiously one-sided. Replaying it in her mind, she realized that it had been a fairly thorough interrogation. She raised a hand to her glasses and asked doubtfully, "Are you telling me that my conversation with the Pyms was a . . . a *job interview?*"

Kate grinned. "I know how odd it must sound, but it's exactly the sort of thing they'd do: select an out-of-the-way place like Bransley—the kind of place only a certain type of gardening enthusiast would visit—where they could lie in wait for a likely candidate, then run her through her paces."

Emma's sidelong glance still expressed doubt, so Kate tried another tack. "What line of work are you in?" she asked.

"I'm a project manager at CompuTech Corporation, in Boston," Emma replied. "I work with computers."

"All right, then, who's the most brilliant computer scientist in Boston?"

"Professor Layton, at MIT," Emma replied without hesitation. "He taught me everything I know, at any rate."

Kate gave her a quizzical look. "If Professor Layton at MIT recommended someone for a job at your company, you'd hire that person, wouldn't you?" Smiling reassuringly, she went on. "Ruth and Louise may not be professionals, like your Professor Layton, but they've been gardening since before you and I were born. I think we can trust their judgment."

Emma took a deep breath, then let it out slowly before speaking. She was accustomed to thinking in straight lines. If you needed a gardener, you looked in the phone book. You didn't sit in the middle of a hedge maze, waiting for the right one to come along. And you certainly didn't hire someone selected by such a random process. Did you?

Perhaps you did, at Penford Hall, where no one seemed to think in straight lines. The gatekeeper thought he was Che Guevara, the footman thought he was Dickens, the maid thought she was the next Chanel, and the duke seemed to think he was Father Christmas, showering the villagers with new roads and flying doctors, his servants with laptops and cellular phones. Emma's own way of thinking was beginning to bend under the influence. For a moment there in the garden, she'd thought she was Marilyn Monroe, ready to do battle with the delectable Ashers for the blue-eyed Derek of her dreams. She might as well pretend to be Gertrude Jekyll for the summer. Who would notice?

I would, thought Emma, sheepishly. I'm no more a femme fatale than I am a long-dead gardening genius, and I can't work in the chapel garden as an impostor. If I stay on at Penford Hall, she decided, it won't be under false pretenses. She vowed silently to tell the duke the truth about herself at the earliest opportunity.

"Oh, and one other thing," Kate added, as Emma walked her to the door. "Mattie's only been here for a few months and, unlike her grandfather, she can be a bit overdramatic about Penford Hall's . . . colorful past. I wouldn't pay too much attention to what she says about that pop singer, if I were you."

Emma's understanding smile faded as soon as Kate had left the room. Great, she thought. Here I am, without a car, in a Gothic heap full of loonies, being warned off the subject of Lex Rex. What have the Pyms gotten me into?

Thanks to Crowley, who'd knocked on her door at precisely eight twenty, Emma arrived in the library as the case clock in the corner chimed the half hour. She was relieved to see that she was neither the first nor the last to arrive. The duke was nowhere in sight, but Susannah had Derek pinned in a bay window beside a tall and quite beautiful harp, where she was lecturing him on—God help us, thought Emma—spirituality and good nutrition.

Derek had exchanged his worn jeans and blue pullover for an open-necked shirt and corduroys, and replaced his workboots with a pair of tired loafers. He seemed unable to tear his gaze from Susannah, who was wearing something black, strapless, and ankle-length that clung like paint to the places where most women had curves. Her makeup was flawless, her sleek blond hair pulled into a chignon at the nape of her spindly neck, and diamond studs glittered from her delicate earlobes. Neither she nor Derek seemed to notice Emma's arrival.

Her entrance didn't go entirely unremarked, however. Crowley had barely ushered Emma into the room when a shout rang out. "Hey! You the gal with the green thumb we been hearin' so much about? Syd Bishop's the name. Suzie's manager. What're you drinkin'?"

Syd Bishop was a paunchy American in his midsixties, with faded red hair plastered in long strands across his freckled scalp. His accent reeked of Brooklyn, and his voice was so loud that it almost drowned out the rumble of thunder as the first rush of rain spattered the windows. Syd's tuxedo was black—Emma gave him credit for that much good sense—but the crimson trim on the wide lapels didn't quite match the vermillion bow tie and cummerbund, or the pink-edged ruffles on the front of his white shirt.

Syd sat next to Kate Cole on a burgundy brocade couch. Kate's wine-colored velvet gown had a tight-fitting bodice and a flowing skirt, a high collar and long sleeves. Syd Bishop looked as out of place beside her as a plastic gnome in the Chelsea Flower Show.

"I'll have a sherry, thank you," Emma replied.

Syd snapped his fingers at the bespectacled footman, who stood to one side, near the drinks cabinet. "Hallard, my man, a sherry for the lady."

Emma crossed the room to sit in one of a cluster of leather armchairs facing the sofa. She tried not to gawk at Syd, but she must have failed, because, the moment she sat down, he let loose a loud guffaw.

"I know," he said, with a self-deprecating grin. "Hey, a big-time operator like me, I should know what's what in fashion, right? Wrong. Me, I'm a nice boy from Brooklyn. What I know is business. So I leave the glamour to Suzie and she leaves the bottom line to me. It works. You met Kate Cole yet?" He winked at Kate. "She's the duke's genera- lissimo. Great gal. If she had six inches more leg, she coulda been a contender."

Midway through Syd's speech, Hallard had come to stand beside Emma's chair, carrying a glass of sherry on a silver tray. He remained there, staring myopically at Syd, long after Syd had fallen silent.

"Hallard," Kate Cole said softly.

"Mmmm?" Hallard replied in a faraway voice.

"I believe Miss Porter would like her drink now."

"Ah." Hallard looked down at the tray, as though surprised to find it in his possession, then bent to offer the sherry to Emma. He re- treated to his place at the drinks cabinet, blinking slowly and mur- muring to himself, ". . . coulda been a contendah, coulda been a contendah . . ."

"What that guy needs is a long vacation," Syd muttered.

"Kate," Emma said, "I meant to ask you earlier—Mattie men- tioned that she was working with a Nanny Cole. Are you related?"

There was a snort from across the room as Susannah glanced in Kate's direction. Kate colored, but replied calmly, "Nanny Cole is my mother. She's been at Penford Hall most of her life. I suppose you could say that Grayson and I grew up together."

Again, Susannah interrupted her monologue with Derek. "Weren't you and your dear mother sent into exile, darling?"

Kate's lips tightened. "We lived in Bournemouth for a short time," she acknowledged.

"Ten years seems on the long side to me," Susannah commented, and this time Kate bridled.

Emma spoke up quickly, hoping to defuse a potential argument. "Penford Hall must have been a wonderful place to grow up in."

"You said a mouthful, little lady," said Syd. "I was just tellin' Kate, a classy joint like this'ud make a helluva set for a shoot. Whaddya think?"

Emma let her gaze travel slowly around the dark-paneled, high- ceilinged library. A thick Persian carpet covered the floor, and a pair of Chinese vases flanked the marble fireplace, where a fire blazed.

Above the mantelpiece hung a portrait of an imperious, white-haired woman in a floor-length silver gown. Adorned with square-cut emeralds, she was seated beside a harp very like the one in the corner.

A mahogany staircase led to a broad gallery that ran the length of one wall. Arched floor-to-ceiling windows pierced the gallery's walls, and the glass-enclosed shelves on both levels held thousands of volumes. Here and there, a book's title, inscribed in gold leaf on a dark leather binding, gleamed in the firelight.

"So? Whaddya think? Am I right or am I right?"

Before Emma could answer, the hall door flew open and the duke rushed in. "Sorry, all," he said breezily. "Beastly rude of me to totter in so late, do forgive me. Will you listen to that downpour? Makes one glad to be indoors, what? Syd, how kind of you to dress for dinner." The duke, Emma noted, was wearing a tasteful but decidedly informal pair of flannel trousers and a fawn-colored cashmere turtleneck. "Emma, you are a vision in blue, and your hair! Your hair is like a soft mist rolling in off the sea." Gesturing toward the portrait over the mantelpiece, he added, "My grandmother. As you can see, her interests were musical as well as horticultural. She played the harp beautifully."

Syd's voice rang out. "Those are some emeralds your grandma's got on."

"Her wedding jewels," the duke explained. "My grandfather had a great fondness for emeralds." He turned to the bay windows. "Susannah, you look ravishing. And treating Derek to a talk about—which diet deity is it this week? Never mind, I'm sure it's a jolly fascinating one. Dreadfully sorry to interrupt the fun, but a higher power has informed me that our presence is required in the dining room."

"Hey, Duke," Syd said, rising to his feet, "I was just tellin' Emma how you could make a bucket rentin' this joint to the right people."

"How enterprising you are, Syd," the duke said easily.

"I got a card—"

"I believe we've accumulated quite a collection of your cards, Syd," the duke broke in. "So generous . . . Not one member of the staff has been overlooked. Emma, my dear, would you allow me the honor?"

With a shy smile, Emma placed her sherry glass on the table at her knee and crossed the room to take the duke's arm. Syd offered his to Kate, Susannah latched on to Derek's, and the three couples made their way up the hall to the dining room, Syd's voice booming, Susannah murmuring, and Emma raising a hand to rub her temple. It was shaping up to be an exceptionally long evening.

Seven

A candle-filled chandelier lit the dining room, and the silver-and-green velvet drapes had been drawn to reveal the rainswept fa-çade of the ruined castle, dramatically lit by concealed floodlights. "It's better on a clear night," the duke murmured, as he took his place at the head of the table.

Emma sat on the duke's right, Susannah on his left; Kate was at the foot of the table. Syd sat between Kate and Emma, tucking his napkin into his shirt collar and beckoning to Crowley to fill his wine-glass. Derek, who had yet to acknowledge Emma's presence, sat across the table from Syd, beside Susannah.

Shadows danced across the molded ceiling, and the table was a fairyland of twinkling crystal and gleaming silver. Quite a lot of silver, Emma noted. Aware of Susannah's coolly amused gaze on her worried face, Emma resolved to follow the duke's lead and hope for the best.

"Speaking of higher powers, Susannah," the duke was saying, "I'm almost willing to believe in one, now that Emma's here. She's an answer to my prayers, sent by a pair of angels in human form, who— Ah, Madama, what culinary magic have you worked for us tonight?"

A door had opened in the wall behind Emma, admitting a tiny old woman in a plain black dress, followed by Crowley, bearing a silver soup tureen, and Hallard, carrying a ladle. The old woman led the two manservants to the sideboard, where she carefully filled a soup bowl, then stood back. Hallard placed the bowl on a silver tray, and Crowley presented it to the duke. "Wild mushroom, Your Grace, with a touch of port wine."

The duke tasted the soup, then bowed his head. "Perfection," he declared.

The old woman's wrinkled face was instantly wreathed in smiles, and she departed the room in triumph, leaving Hallard and Crowley to serve the duke's guests.

"She does it every night," Susannah commented to Emma. "I find it positively medieval." She turned her gaze to the foot of the table. "But, then, so much about Penford Hall has a feudal air. It must be a special treat for you to dine with your betters, Kate."

Emma flinched, but Kate Cole merely nodded complacently.

"It is," Kate agreed. "I feel quite privileged whenever the Reverend and Mrs. Shuttleworth invite me to dine with them at the rectory in Penford Harbor. Mrs. Shuttleworth sets a shining example for us all."

Outmaneuvered, Susannah subsided.

"Now, where was I?" said the duke. "Ah, yes, my guardian angels. You would adore them, Derek. They live in a tiny Cotswolds village called Finch and they're the most incredibly identical——"

"You don't mean Ruth and Louise Pym by any chance, do you?" Derek interrupted.

"Derek, you astound me," said the duke. "Don't tell me you know them."

"I do, as a matter of fact. Worked on the church in Finch last winter, uncovering some whitewashed frescoes. Twelfth-century. Interesting." Favoring Emma with a brief glance, he asked politely, "How are the ladies?"

Candlelight glittered in sapphire eyes, and Emma's soup spoon slipped from her fingers, clattering loudly on the leg of her chair as it made its way to the carpet. She started to retrieve it, but the duke put out a restraining hand to keep her from knocking heads with Hallard, who was already bending to remove the offending utensil, while Crowley replaced it with a clean one, which Emma promptly swept from the table with her elbow.

Hallard and Crowley went into action again, Susannah tittered, and Emma blushed a shade of pink that made her grateful for the dim lighting. The duke came to her rescue, signaling Crowley to serve the next course, and continuing as if there'd been no interruption.

"But how else would they be, dear boy? There are few things in this world one can rely upon absolutely, and the Pym sisters——and I say this advisedly——are one of them."

"Tell them how you met," said Kate.

The duke obliged. "Front right tire went pop directly in front of their cottage. The road turned and I didn't. Came to a rest atop their birdbath, if memory serves. They were perfectly charming, of course. Took me in, fed me soup, gave me a kitten to play with—like being back in the nursery with Nanny Cole. Been thick as thieves ever since. Never go to London without looking in on them."

"And you, Miss Porter?" Derek asked.

"A m-maze," Emma stammered, still shaken by her mishap with the spoon.

"Know what you mean," agreed the duke, helping himself to the marbled salmon and sole Hallard offered from a silver serving dish. "But who wouldn't be? The first time I saw them, side by side, peering through my windscreen, I thought I'd bunged my head on the steering column."

"I don't suppose you'd care to tell me who you're talking about," Susannah put in, looking peevishly at the duke.

"Ruth and Louise Pym, my dear Susannah, are antique, inestimable, and identical twin sisters."

"I knew a pair of twins once," said Syd. The duke waited for him to go on, but Syd simply stared into the middle distance, a reminiscent smile playing on his lips.

"Identical twins?" Susannah grimaced. "How ghastly. I would dread having a twin."

"The thought is an unsettling one," the duke agreed smoothly. "I would venture to say—"

"*In* a maze," Emma said abruptly. The dinner party froze as all heads, including Crowley's, turned in her direction.

"I beg your pardon?" said the duke. "I didn't quite catch—"

"I met them *in* a maze. The Pyms. A hedge maze. At Mansley Bran—" Emma cleared her throat. "At *Bransley Manor*."

"Ah, Bransley Manor." The duke nodded. "Kate and I visited there as children, with my grandmother, when the Saint Johns were still in residence. That was many years ago, of course. It is a National Trust property now, I believe?" With infinite patience, the duke guided Emma through a description of the gardens at Bransley Manor, then gracefully changed the subject, giving her a chance to recover her composure. His solicitude reminded Emma that she had a confession to make, and as Crowley served the noisettes of lamb, she turned to the duke.

"Grayson?" she said softly. "I'm afraid there's been a slight misunderstanding."

"I knew it!" the duke exclaimed. "I knew the rose suite wouldn't do. Crowley, would you please—"

"Oh, no," Emma broke in. "It's not the rose suite. It's me." She riveted her eyes on the rim of his wineglass as the words came spilling out. "I'm not who you think I am. I'm just a tourist, and I met the Pyms by accident, and I came to Penford Hall to *look* at the gardens, not *work* on them."

There was a moment of heavy silence as the duke stared at her, uncomprehending. "Do you mean to say that you have to get back to your proper job by next week or something? If that's the problem, I'm sure Kate can arrange—"

"No," Emma said quickly. "It's not that."

"What is it, then? I'm sorry if I seem obtuse, but—"

"I'm not qualified to do the kind of work you have in mind," Emma explained. "I'm *not* a professional gardener."

"I see." The duke nodded thoughtfully, then rubbed the tip of his nose with his thumb. "Good heavens, Emma, how you unnerved me," he said gently. "For one earth-shattering moment, I thought the Pyms had made a mistake. My dear . . ." Susannah began a lecture on the evils of meat-eating, but the duke focused solely on Emma, leaning toward her, speaking softly, his warm brown eyes alight with understanding. "Kate tells me you work with computers, and I must believe her, but that, I think, is merely what you do for pay. Gardening, though—digging and planting, hoeing and weeding, watching the seasons change and feeling you're a part of the cycle—that's something altogether different, is it not?"

Emma nodded slowly, and the duke nodded with her.

"The thing that we love most is the thing that we do best," he murmured. "And you, my dear, love nothing quite so well as a garden. The Pyms discovered that, surely, and I saw it in your face this afternoon, just as clearly as I see it now. You could no more turn your back on the chapel garden than I could walk away from Penford Hall. Give me your hands."

Emma's hands seemed to float across the snowy linen to rest in the duke's outstretched palms. He gazed down at them in silence, then raised his eyes to Emma's once again.

"Just as I thought," he said. "Callused, strong, and exquisitely capable. All the qualifications I require. I've no doubt whatsoever that these two hands"—he enclosed Emma's in his own—"will bring the chapel garden back to life."

"Wow," said Syd, through a mouthful of lamb. "You gotta real way with words, Duke."

"Treacle," sneered Susannah, tossing back her glass of wine.

The duke took no notice of them, and Emma was aware of no one but the duke. Warmed by his touch, mesmerized by the light in his brown eyes, she felt her self-doubt melt away. At that moment, she would have followed Grayson to the ends of the earth.

"Well," she began, a bit breathlessly, "if you're sure . . ."

"I'm sure," said the duke, raising her hands to his lips, then releasing them with a radiant smile.

With a fluttering heart, Emma folded her hands in her lap. She felt as though she'd been seduced in public, but, oddly enough, she didn't seem to care. Plans began to take shape in her mind, and they kept her in a pleasantly preoccupied haze until the warm cappuccino soufflé was served, when the words "Lex Rex" pulled her sharply back to earth.

"Never replaced the yacht, have you, Grayson?" Susannah was saying. "Surprising, really, now that you can so easily afford one." Draining yet another glass of wine, she swayed toward Emma. "Wasn't always such a showplace, Penford Hall. Bit of a shambles when my mother and I came calling."

"The hall has seen its share of troubled times," Grayson acknowledged.

"Not anymore," said Susannah, waving her wineglass at the chandelier. "So why haven't you replaced the yacht? You were so fond of sailing, so good at it, too. Not like poor old Lex."

Syd looked up from his plate. "Give it a rest, huh, Suzie?"

"It's all right, Syd," said the duke. "It's true that I was once very fond of sailing. But I somehow lost my taste for it after Lex and the others died."

"Spoilt the day for you, did it?" Susannah drawled. "Spend a night or two crying in your pillow for poor old Lex?"

"Really, Susannah," said Kate, her eyes flashing.

"Lex's death spoilt quite a few days for me, actually," the duke replied tightly. "It may interest you to know, dear cousin, that drowning isn't the easy death it's made out to be. It is, in fact, nightmarish. Try, if you can, to imagine someone you care for sinking beneath the waves, helpless, struggling, gasping for breath—"

Derek stood abruptly. His face was pale and a fine line of perspiration beaded his brow. "Sorry," he said gruffly, staring down at the table. "Seems a bit close in here. Think I'll head upstairs."

Emma had no idea what had provoked Derek's reaction, but the pain in his eyes lanced through her like a knife. Almost without thinking, she, too, rose to her feet, then stood in awkward silence, not knowing what to say, embarrassed to have drawn attention to herself yet again.

Once more, the duke rescued her. Tossing his linen napkin on the table, he pushed back his own chair and stood. "I've just had the most splendid idea," he announced. His voice was light, but the look he gave Susannah was nothing short of murderous. "It's Emma's first night at Penford Hall. Why not have a little celebration? Crowley, Dom Pérignon to the music room, if you please, and open the piano. Nothing like a spot of Mozart and a tot of bubbly to brighten a rainy night." Without missing a beat, he added, "You'll join us, of course, Derek."

Derek slowly raised his head to look, slightly puzzled, at Emma. He lowered his eyes, then shrugged. "Perhaps one glass," he agreed.

Eight

One glass of champagne led to another, and when Emma awoke shortly after dawn the next day, she still felt a bit tipsy.

The evening had turned out well enough, in the end. The duke had proved to be a gifted pianist, and Susannah, deprived of the spotlight, had retired early, taking Syd and a good deal of tension with her. In her absence, the duke had played with renewed vigor, interspersing the promised Mozart with jaunty selections from *H.M.S. Pinafore*.

Still, Derek had never really shaken off the morose mood that had seized him at supper. He'd sipped his champagne and listened attentively to the music, but he'd said very little and smiled even less.

What had set him off, Emma wondered. Had he, too, known Lex Rex? Had the discussion of the rock singer's death reopened an old wound? Perhaps Kate had warned her off of the topic in order to avoid just such a scene. Clearly, the duke placed a high premium on his guests' well-being. Why, last night he'd made Emma feel . . .

. . . like a moonstruck teenager, she thought wryly, just as Derek had done in the chapel garden. This would never do. She had a job of work ahead of her at Penford Hall, and lying in bed, blushing like a schoolgirl, wouldn't get it done.

Throwing off the covers, Emma reached for her glasses, then pulled on the blue robe and made her way out onto the balcony. The rain had fallen steadily throughout the night, but the storm had finally blown itself out, leaving a handful of fleecy clouds in its wake. Shreds of gray mist drifted across the great lawn and swirled among the castle ruins, like graceful ghosts from one of Grandmother's moonlit parties. The mist would be gone by midmornmg, Emma thought. It promised to be a beautiful day.

After a quick bath, Emma dressed in a denim skirt, a short-sleeved cotton blouse, and her trusty walking shoes. She'd have to stock up on work clothes, but this morning she wanted nothing more than to have the chapel garden all to herself for an hour or two. Emma pulled her long hair into a ponytail, then boldly decided to find a back door to Penford Hall on her own.

Twenty minutes later, she was forced to admit defeat. It was galling, but she would have to retrace her steps and wait impatiently in her room until Mattie or Crowley or some other native guide materialized. She turned to go back the way she'd come, then jumped as a woman's voice exploded in her ear. *"What the HELL do you think you're doing here!"*

Emma was halfway through a terrified apology before she realized that the question had not been directed at her. The bellow had come from behind a closed door a few steps down the hall, and she could now make out the sound of a softer voice answering. Cautiously, Emma approached the door and bent her head to listen.

"No, you may bloody well *not* tidy up my blasted room, and if I catch you dusting under the beds in the nursery one more time, I'll tear your arm off and beat you with the bloody stump! *Have* I made myself clear?"

Emma flattened herself against the wall as the door flew open and a dark-haired, frail-looking little boy scooted out. He was pursued by a woman who was at least as old as Crowley, a head taller than Emma, and built like a Sherman tank. Her short white hair was tightly curled and trailing multicolored bits of thread. Snippets of bright-red yarn were scattered over her tweed skirt and twin set, a pincushion bristled on her wrist, and a tape measure dangled around her neck. The woman pointed a pair of pinking shears at the boy and bellowed, "Scat!"

The boy stood his ground. He was as neat as a pin, in navy-blue shorts and knee socks, a white polo shirt, and running shoes, and he regarded his formidable adversary with a look of nervous defiance.

"What about our lessons?" the boy demanded.

The hand pointing the pinking shears dropped to the woman's side. "Lessons?" She scratched her head, sending a shower of thread to the floor. "You had some yesterday, didn't you?"

"We're supposed to have them every day, Nanny Cole," the boy said doggedly.

"*Every day?* How in God's name am I supposed to finish Lady Nell's ball gown if I have to see to your dratted lessons every day? I want you outside, right now, quickstep march, and none of your cheek. Fresh air and sunshine are your lessons for the day, Peter-my-lad. Now, march!"

Scowling, the boy turned to go, but paused as he caught sight of Emma. His dark eyes narrowed for a moment; then he tucked his chin to his chest and stalked off down the hall without a backward glance. Emma cowered against the wall as Nanny Cole's belligerent gaze came to rest on her.

"Who the hell are you?" Nanny Cole barked. She thrust her face toward Emma's. "Not lurking, are you? Not snooping, like that underbred sack of bones?"

"No," Emma said hastily. "I'm Emma Porter and I was—"

"Ah." Nanny Cole straightened, put a finger to her lips, and nodded. "The garden lady from the States. Should've guessed. You have that look about you. Solid. Close to the earth." Rocking back on her heels, Nanny Cole bellowed, "Turn round, turn round, let's have a look at you. Haven't got all day."

Bewildered, but not daring to disobey, Emma turned a slow circle in the hall while Nanny Cole whipped a gold pen out of her pocket and began jotting something on the inside of her wrist.

"Mmm," muttered Nanny Cole. "Full figure, strong chin, fine head of hair. Eyes . . . gray? Yes. All right. That'll do. You can go now."

"Er—" Emma began.

"Good Lord, woman, get a grip. I can't spend all bloody morning standing in doorways."

"I was trying to get to the chapel garden and—"

"The chapel garden? What would the chapel garden be doing up here?"

"It's all right, Nanny Cole. I'll take her."

A little girl stepped out from behind Nanny Cole. She wore a short, fluttery pleated skirt and a white middy blouse trimmed in pale blue. In one arm she cradled a small chocolate-brown teddy bear in its own sailor suit, complete with bell-bottom trousers and a round, beribboned cap. In her free hand she held a plump, juicy strawberry.

"Good girl, Lady Nell," said Nanny Cole. "But mind how you go in that outfit. Took me all night to finish those dratted pleats. What a bloody way to start the day . . ." Still grumbling, Nanny Cole slammed the door.

As Lady Nell raised the strawberry to her lips, Emma wondered why the duke hadn't mentioned having a daughter. She was a pretty child, with pink cheeks, a cupid's-bow mouth, and a halo of loose golden ringlets. She might have been insipid had she been less self-possessed, but she carried herself with the dignity of a prima ballerina, and her limpid blue eyes gave Emma the uncanny sensation that a far older and wiser woman was looking out of them, taking her measure.

"We've been waiting for you," Nell declared.

"Have you?" Emma responded, surprised.

"Aunt Dimity said you'd come, but we didn't expect to wait such a long time. I'll be six in September, and Peter's *very tired,*" Nell stated firmly.

"I'm sorry, Lady Nell." Emma wondered if she should curtsy. "I'm afraid I don't know your aunt, and Grayson—that is, your father—must have forgotten to tell me."

"Aunt Dimity's not my aunt, my name's not Lady Nell, and Grayson's not my father," Nell informed her calmly. "My aunt's name is Beatrice, Papa's name is Derek, and I'm Nell Harris. The boy who was here before is my brother, Peter." Nell looked down at her bear. "This is Bertie. There's four of us—Auntie Bea doesn't count. But don't worry. Mummy's dead." Nell took another bite out of her strawberry.

Mummy's dead? Emma blinked at the impact of Nell's announcement. *Derek is a widower with two children?* By the time the rest of Nell's words had registered, the child was walking away. Emma scrambled to catch up.

"Nell?" she asked. "I'm very sorry to hear about your mother. . . ."

"She died a long time ago," said Nell. "I was just a baby. Now, turn left at the dog, then straight on to the big fat cow."

Emma looked up in alarm, then realized that Nell was referring to the paintings that covered the corridor's walls. From Nell's point of view, the scruffy-looking mongrel peering out from under the table was no doubt the most memorable feature of a hugely complicated family scene, almost certainly seventeenth-century and Dutch. The "big fat cow" was some eighteenth-century landowner's prize breeder, done in the unmistakable wooden style of George Stubbs. It was such a simple means of navigation that Emma kicked herself for not having thought of it sooner. She began to pay attention to the paintings they passed, and by the time they reached the staircase leading down to the entrance hall, she felt as though she could find her way back to Nanny Cole's room unaided. Not that she had any intention of doing so in the near future.

Halfway down the main staircase, Emma tried again. "Nell, what did you mean when you told me not to worry?"

Nell's only response was a reproachful, sidelong glance that seemed to say, "You know very well what I meant." Cowed by the truth, Emma decided to ask no more questions.

Nell led the way through the labyrinth of first-floor corridors to an airy storeroom piled high with linen, where she opened a door and stepped out onto the great lawn. Emma paused to thank Nell for her help, but the little girl kept walking, picking her way delicately through the wet grass, still nibbling on her strawberry.

Emma watched with dismay as Nell headed for the castle ruins. She hadn't planned to spend her first, precious morning sharing the garden with anyone, much less babysitting. When they reached the arched entrance in the castle wall, she stopped. "Thank you," she said, kindly but firmly. "I think I can find my way from here."

Nell turned on her a look of weary tolerance. "Emma," she said, "Bertie and I don't talk a lot and we don't need looking after by anyone but Peter."

"But I didn't say . . . That is, I'm sure your brother is . . . ." Much too young to be in charge of a nearly-six-year-old like you, Emma thought, but she bit back the words. She wasn't at all sure she could win an argument with Nell. "I guess I don't know many children like you," she said defensively.

"We know," said Nell, "but we can fix that." She turned to call a greeting to Hallard, the nearsighted footman, who was back in his wicker armchair, tapping at his keyboard, then proceeded down the grassy corridor toward the banquet hall, with Emma trailing slowly in her wake.

The banquet hall was deserted. Some of the vines on the birdcage arbor had been knocked loose by last night's rain and Emma paused to tie them up again, looking over her shoulder to see if Bantry was around. She felt ill-equipped to deal with Nell's unnerving pronouncements on her own.

By the time Emma finished retying the vines, Nell had left the banquet hall. Emma hoped that the little girl had decided to go somewhere other than the chapel garden, but her hopes were dashed when she rounded a corner and saw Nell lifting the latch on the green door. Emma was still several yards away when the door swung wide.

Nell made no move to enter the garden. She stood in the doorway, clinging tightly to her bear, and Bertie's black eyes peered imploringly over her shoulder, as though pleading with Emma to hurry up.

"Nell?" Emma called, hastening to the child's side. "What is it? What's—" Emma froze as she saw Susannah Ashley-Woods sprawled facedown in the grass at the bottom of the uneven stone steps, very near the old wheelbarrow. Her blond hair lay like a silken fan around her head, a gleaming black heel dangled from one shoe, and a thin trickle of blood trailed from her shell-like ear.

Kneeling in the doorway, Emma turned Nell to face her. "There's been an accident," Emma said, amazed by the steadiness of her voice. "Susannah's shoe broke and she fell down the stairs. You understand?"

Curls bobbing, the child nodded.

"I want you and Bertie to run back to the hall as fast as you can. Tell the first grown-up you see to call for a doctor. Can you do that for me?"

Nell gave another emphatic nod, then darted back up the corridor, with Bertie flopping limply, clutched in a dimpled fist.

Emma rushed down the steps to kneel at Susannah's side. She breathed a sigh of relief when she pressed a hand to Susannah's neck and detected a pulse. Bending lower, she saw that Susannah's eyes were closed and her left cheek was pillowed in a blood-soaked clump of grass.

"Warm. I have to keep her warm," Emma muttered. She grabbed blindly for the oilcloth on the old wheelbarrow, but it was no longer there. Frantically scanning the ground, she saw it lying a few steps away on the flagstone path. She scrambled to retrieve it, then spread it over Susannah's prone form and waited.

"*My God . . .*" Grayson stood at the top of the stairs, his face ashen. "Is she dead?" he whispered hoarsely.

Emma shook her head. "Have you called for an ambulance?"

Before the duke could answer, Kate Cole appeared beside him, carrying a heavy wool blanket. She hurried down the stairs, spread the blanket on top of the oilcloth, knelt, and with a practiced hand lifted Susannah's eyelid. She nodded, then took hold of the woman's wrist. "She's still with us," Kate confirmed, "but Dr. Singh had better get here quickly."

"Should we take her into the hall?" Emma asked.

"Best not," said Kate, gently placing Susannah's limp arm beneath the coverings. "There's not much blood, but there's a nasty bruise on her temple, and no telling what the fall might've done to her neck." She rose to her feet and regarded Susannah grimly.

Her gaze fixed on the bloodstained grass, Emma backed away until she bumped into the chapel door. There she stood, clasping and unclasping her hands, watching Kate direct the action as more people crowded into the grassy space at the foot of the stairs.

Crowley arrived with another blanket, and Hallard was next, carrying a first-aid kit. The distant sound of a helicopter reached Emma's ears just before Bantry stepped past the duke. The head gardener paused when he saw Susannah, then hurried down the stairs to confer quietly with Kate. Crowley joined them, and Emma caught something about "the men from the village" and "alerting Newland at the gate" before Crowley nodded and left.

"Dr. Singh'll be here straightaway," Bantry announced.

Still at the top of the stairs, the duke pointed downward. "It's those damned shoes," he said. Susannah's broken high heel protruded from the edge of the oilcloth. "If she hadn't insisted on wearing such absurd footwear, this never would've happened."

After checking Susannah's pulse once more, Kate went up the stairs to take hold of Grayson's hands. "We'll have to prepare a statement," she said.

"Of course," said the duke, and, *"Damn."* Turning to Bantry, he asked, "Is Lady Nell all right?"

Bantry nodded. "Mattie's lookin' after Lady Nell, and Mr. Harris is out lookin' for young Master Peter. Seems the boy's disappeared."

Emma wanted to tell them all that Nanny Cole had ordered the boy outside to play, but her teeth were chattering so badly that the most she could manage was a strangled squeak.

"Here, now, Miss Emma." The head gardener stripped off his oiled green jacket and walked over to where she stood. "You've had quite a shock. You come with me to the kitchen and we'll have Madama make you a nice cup of tea. There's a good girl, now, come along." As he spoke, Bantry draped his jacket around Emma's shoulders. It was still warm and smelled comfortingly of compost and pipe tobacco. The head gardener put a wiry arm around her shoulders as well, guiding her up the stairs and past the green door. Emma turned in the doorway to look once more at the nightmarish scene, and saw Grayson fire a questioning look at Kate, whose only reply was a minute shrug.

Nine

In the kitchen, bacon sizzled on a griddle, an outsized teakettle sent a plume of steam toward the vaulted ceiling, and Madama stood at the massive stove, using a wooden spoon to stir a row of bubbling stockpots and to direct the activities of a trio of white-aproned girls who scurried back and forth from the stove to the long oak table in the center of the cavernous room.

The girls were busily replenishing the breakfast plates of a dozen men in workboots and thick sweaters who sat at the table, talking in a low rumble among themselves while they ate. Like Newland, the gatekeeper, each wore a radio unit on his hip and an earphone in one ear.

Nell sat at the far end of the table, calmly devouring a large bowl of plump strawberries and heavy cream. Beside her, Mattie stared down at her teacup. Nell merely nodded when Emma and Bantry came into the room, but Mattie half rose from her chair. "Is she—?"

The girl's breathless question silenced the room, and every face turned to look expectantly at the new arrivals. Emma pulled Bantry's jacket around her self-consciously and looked across the sea of unfamiliar faces to Mattie.

"Susannah was still unconscious when we left her," she said, "but she was alive."

"Dr. Singh's flyin' her into Plymouth," Bantry added.

"Thank the Lord." Mattie leaned forward on her hands for a moment, then pushed back her chair and stood upright. "I should pack a bag for Miss Ashers," she said. "Mr. Bishop can bring it to her. She'll be wanting her own things when she wakes up."

"Run along, then," said Bantry. "I'll see to Lady Nell."

Mattie hurried from the room and Bantry exchanged sober greetings with the men as he and Emma made their way down the length of the table to sit on either side of Nell. Two of the serving girls peered curiously at Emma, and she overheard one of them murmur "the garden lady" before Madama rapped the stove sharply with her spoon and sent them back to work. The rumble of voices and the clatter of crockery resumed, and a moment later one of the girls placed a cup of strong, sweet tea before Emma, followed quickly by a plateful of fried eggs, sausages, bacon, and grease-drenched toast. Emma glanced at the plate, shuddered slightly, and reached for the tea.

"You can have strawberries, if you like," Nell suggested helpfully.

"I'll just have tea for now, thank you," Emma murmured.

The noise subsided once more as Derek came into the kitchen, his arm around Peter's shoulders. Derek looked haggard, but the boy's cheeks were flushed, his eyes bright, and he walked with a bounce in his step.

"You're sure you heard nothing?" Derek was asking.

"I told you, Dad. I was out on the cliff path, reading. I didn't even know she was there until everyone started to shout."

"All right, son, all right." Derek pulled the boy to him in a rough, sideways hug, then let him run to Nell's side.

"She's not dead," Nell informed her brother bluntly.

"I know," Peter replied, "but she's gone." The boy glanced over at the stove. "Madama, may I have strawberries, too, please?"

"Miss Porter? If I might have a word?" Derek gestured to the fireplace, where a tall settle offered a degree of privacy. Emma slipped out of Bantry's jacket and returned it to him with a murmur of thanks, then joined Derek on the high-backed wooden bench.

"Miss Porter," he began. "Emma. Want to thank you for looking after my daughter. Traumatic experience for such a young child. Not sure—" Derek stiffened as a thin, high-pitched scream sounded in the distance, then was abruptly cut off.

Knives and forks clattered to the tiled floor as the men at the table sprang to their feet and streamed through the kitchen door. Derek rose, too, and stood looking distractedly from the door to his children until Bantry waved him on.

"Go, man, go," Bantry urged. "I'll keep an eye on the young 'uns."

Pausing only to drop a kiss on the top of Nell's head, Derek raced from the room, with Emma hot on his heels, following the thud of re-treating workboots to the entrance hall.

Emma felt as though she'd stumbled into a war zone. The chubby mechanic, Gash, was holding the front door open and the roar of an idling helicopter thundered through it on the wind. Newland, with his black beret tilted at a rakish angle, was barking orders to the group from the kitchen. Two men in windbreakers were wheeling Susannah toward the open door on a collapsible stretcher, her neck strapped in a padded brace, her head swathed in bloodstained ban-dages, and Syd Bishop trotted alongside, carrying the overnight case Mattie had packed.

Mattie lay at the foot of the main staircase, her head cradled in Kate Cole's lap. Beside them knelt a bearded man in a white turban and caftan, brown socks and sandals, and a black leather bomber jacket. Crowley hovered nearby, white-faced, while the duke patted his shoulder, and Hallard stood to one side, observing the scene with intense concentration.

"What's happened?" Derek asked.

"She's fainted," replied the bearded man. "Some people do, at the sight of blood." Standing, he reached over to touch Crowley's arm. "Not to worry. Get her to bed and keep her warm. She'll be up and running again after a few hours' rest."

"Very good, Dr. Singh," Crowley replied.

Syd had followed the stretcher-bearers out to the waiting heli-copter, and Dr. Singh ran to catch up with them. The men from the kitchen had dispersed, and Newland and Gash, after conferring briefly in the doorway, had headed out after the men, closing the door behind them.

The duke knelt beside Mattie. "Poor child," he murmured. "Hal-lard, please fetch the brandy and bring it up to Mattie's room. Ask Madama to send up a pot of tea, as well." As Hallard sped off in the di-rection of the kitchen, the duke lifted Mattie's slight form in his arms and carried her up the main staircase, with Crowley close behind.

Kate Cole hung back. Looking worriedly from Derek to Emma, she said, "I'm afraid that Grayson and I must leave for Plymouth shortly, to prepare for a news conference there this afternoon. We'll want to keep the press away from the hall, you understand, so we may have to stay on a few days, until things settle down."

"Using Grayson as a decoy?" Derek asked.

"More like a lamb to the slaughter," Kate confirmed. "You've no idea what we went through when Lex died. Photographers behind every bush. So we may be away for some time. I hate to leave you short-handed, but with Crowley looking after Mattie—"

"We'll be fine," Derek assured her. Kate nodded gratefully, handed Derek a card with a phone number where she could be reached in Plymouth, and turned to run up the stairs. Dr. Singh's helicopter roared briefly overhead, then faded in the distance.

The entrance hall was suddenly silent. Derek looked down at Emma. "Library?" he suggested hesitantly. "Drink?"

"Maybe two," she replied.

Emma rested her elbow on the arm of the brocade couch in the library and ran a finger around the rim of her glass. It was almost ten A.M., and she wished she'd eaten breakfast. The first sip of the duke's single-malt whiskey had steadied her nerves, and the second had cleared her head, but a third, taken on an empty stomach, would probably put her under the table.

She glanced over at Derek. He sat at the other end of the couch, legs crossed and arms folded, frowning silently at the empty hearth. He hadn't moved since Bantry had stopped by to ask if Master Peter and Lady Nell might go with him to Madama's kitchen garden. Even then he'd only nodded.

He wasn't worrying about Susannah, Emma knew. He'd responded to Emma's words of consolation with a blank stare, followed by a shrug and an automatic "Bad show," as though he'd momentarily forgotten who had been injured.

Was he still brooding over his children? Emma honestly didn't think he had much to worry about on that score. Nell seemed to be handling the situation very calmly, and Peter appeared unfazed. Emma suspected that the children were more resilient than their father gave them credit for.

Emma, too, had recovered quickly, not only from the morning's shocking events, but from her brief infatuation with Derek. She was no longer tongue-tied and clumsy in his presence, at any rate, and she thought she knew why: Whether widowed or divorced, a single man raising a family was invariably looking for someone to mother his children. And since motherhood, even by proxy, had never been one of Emma's career goals, Derek was indisputably out of bounds. The realization came as a relief; Emma was tired of making a fool of herself over a pair of handsome blue eyes.

"Derek," she said, putting her glass on the end table, "I think I'll step outside. I need a breath of fresh air."

Derek surprised her by immediately unfolding his long limbs and rising from the couch. "I'll come with you," he said. And then, as they were strolling slowly across the great lawn, he surprised her again by saying that it was his first visit to Penford Hall.

"I thought you and Grayson were old friends," Emma said.

Derek pursed his lips. "We met in Oxford ten years ago," he said. "I was touching up some plasterwork in the cathedral and he was practicing a Bach cantata on the organ." Derek stopped walking and swung around to face the hall. "Haven't really been in touch since then." Raising a hand to shield his eyes from the sun, he tilted his head back and let his gaze travel slowly along the irregular roofline. "A hodgepodge," he muttered, "but a structurally sound one." He looked over his shoulder at Emma. "You wouldn't call Penford Hall a ruin, would you?"

Pointing at the fragmented façade of the castle, Emma replied, "*That's* a ruin."

"But he was talking about *that*." Derek gestured to the hall. "Natural enough, given my line of work."

"Which is . . . ?" Emma prompted.

"Hmmm?" Derek looked at her vaguely, then nodded. "Ah, yes. I'm, um . . ." He patted the unbuttoned breast pocket of his shirt, then began to search through the pockets of his jeans. He extracted a penknife, a keychain, a few coins, a tape measure, miscellaneous rubber bands and bits of string, and what looked like the remains of a roll of duct tape before coming up with a crumpled and lint-covered business card, which he handed to Emma. "Don't use the cards much," he muttered. "I work out of my home and, well, it's a word-of-mouth sort of trade."

"*Harris Restoration*," Emma read aloud, smoothing the card as best she could. She noted the Oxford address and phone number, then tucked the card into the pocket of her denim skirt. "You do restoration work?"

"Right. Rotted timbers, damaged frescoes—"

"Stained glass?" Emma put in.

Derek gave her a sharp glance, then lowered his eyes and resumed walking. "Only natural that Grayson would tell me about his plans to refurbish the hall. Roof leaked like a sieve, he said, and damp had buckled the floorboards. Fact is, he left me with the distinct impression that the place was a bit of a shambles."

"But that's what Susannah said last night," Emma exclaimed. "You remember—at supper?"

"Yes. She also said he was a sailor." Derek rubbed his jaw, then turned to look down at Emma. "Busy tomorrow?"

"I-I don't know," Emma stammered. "It depends on—"

"Good." Derek pointed to the balustraded terrace. "Meet me there, say, eleven-ish? Got something I'd like to show you. Need to know—" He broke off, and the worried frown returned to his face. "No. Wait till tomorrow." And without saying another word, he swung around and strode swiftly back into the hall.

Emma turned to look up at Penford Hall. As far as she could tell, the octagonal slates on the roof were all present and correct, the forest of chimneys stood strong and tall, and the leaded glass sparkled in the many and variously shaped windows, not a pane cracked or missing. People sometimes spoke disparagingly of their own homes, especially when they were stuck with a place that didn't suit their taste or their style of living, and Susannah might ridicule her cousin's home out of sheer spite. But Grayson seemed to love the rambling, Gothic sprawl. If he'd called Penford Hall a ruin, Emma suspected that he hadn't been speaking figuratively.

"You there! Miss Porter!"

Emma looked up and saw Nanny Cole leaning out of a second-floor window some twenty feet to her left. In one massive arm Nanny

Cole held a brown-paper parcel; with the other she beckoned to Emma. Obediently, Emma strode over to stand beneath the open window.

"Where the hell is everyone?" Nanny Cole bellowed. "And what was the quack doing here?"

"The duke's cousin fell and hurt herself in the chapel garden," Emma called back. "The doctor came to take her to the hospital in Plymouth and—"

"Never mind," barked Nanny Cole. "I can guess the rest. Brats all right?"

"Fine," said Emma.

"Loving every minute of it, I'll wager, the bloodthirsty little beasts. Where's Mattie?"

"In her room," said Emma. "She fainted—"

"Yes, yes," Nanny Cole broke in impatiently. "Dratted child. That's what comes of hero worship. Well, I can't spend all day running a blasted delivery service. This is for you. Catch!"

The parcel was bulky but soft, and Emma caught it easily. When she looked up again, the window was shut. Curious, Emma carried the parcel over to the terrace steps, where she sat and opened it. It contained two pairs of generously cut denim trousers, with elastic waistbands and padded knees, and two violet-patterned gardening smocks with deep pockets and hammer loops. Emma stared in puzzlement at the smocks for a moment, then shrugged, gathered up the discarded wrapping paper, and headed into the hall to change, murmuring wryly, "If ever there was a sign from heaven . . ."

Ten

*A*ll I need now are work gloves, Emma thought as she stepped into Madama's kitchen garden. It was late morning, the mist had cleared, and the sun was shining brightly overhead. Squinting skyward, Emma reminded herself that a sunhat might not be a bad idea, either. She was about to add a pair of wellies to her mental shopping list when she stopped midway down the rows of radishes, to gape at Bantry.

The old man had lurched out of a shadowy doorway a few yards away, brandishing a stalk of celery and growling ferociously. A bit of rag bound a pair of carrots to his head, like horns, with the greens trailing behind in a verdant, ragged mane. Emma took one look at Penford Hall's head gardener and burst out laughing.

Bantry's growling ceased as he stood up. Grinning good-naturedly, he untied his makeshift headband, put one carrot in the bib pocket of his canvas apron, and offered the other to Emma, who accepted it gratefully.

"Just havin' a bit o' fun with the kiddies," he said. "Tryin' to, anyway. Not really their cup o' tea, I don't think."

"Don't they like vegetable monsters?" Emma asked.

"Oh, I dunno." Bantry glanced over his shoulder. "Master Peter tries, but it shouldn't be so much of an effort, now, should it? And Lady Nell, she's just gone half the time." He touched the side of his head. "Up there. Talkin' half to that bear o' hers and half to herself. Never know what she's goin' to say next, that one." Bantry eyed Emma's new attire shrewdly. "So you're startin' in today, are you? Well, and why not? Constable Trevoy's been up from the village to take his snaps. He says it's clear enough what happened, and it's not as though the young lady's passed on." He turned as the sound of whispering came through the veil of vines on the birdcage arbor. "All right, you two," he called, "come on out. Miss Emma needs our help in the chapel garden."

Emma touched the old man's arm and shook her head. "I don't think Derek would approve of the children going in there so soon after the accident," she said.

"May be you're right," Bantry acknowledged equably, "but you could fill a barn with what Mr. Derek don't know about young 'uns." He bit into his celery stalk and chewed for a moment before adding decisively, "Won't do 'em a bit o' harm to go in there. Best for 'em to face it fair and square, or the bogeyman'll move in and they won't want to face it at all."

Peter and Nell were waiting expectantly on the steps of the wrought-iron arbor. Nell and Bertie had exchanged sailor outfits for matching cherry-red sweaters and scaled-down bib overalls. Peter still wore his white polo shirt, but had traded his short pants for a pair of neatly creased khaki trousers. Bantry beckoned to them to follow as he and Emma crossed the banquet hall, and the four of them entered the grassy corridor together.

An unanticipated flutter of dread ran through Emma as they drew closer to the green door, and the children, who'd been talking quietly as they walked, fell silent. Bantry must have sensed their rising unease because, when they reached the door, he turned to address the children. Bending down, his hands braced upon his knees, he said, "You both know about Miss Susannah bumping her head this morning, right? Well, now, I'm not goin' to lie to you. There might very well be a splash o' blood or two where she fell, but there's no need—"

"Like when the lions tore the Christians limb from limb," Nell put in with a knowing nod. "Or when Lancelot stabbed the Black Knight to the heart."

"Or when Professor Moriarty smashed on the rocks at the Reichenbach Falls," Peter added thoughtfully, but Nell objected that the water had probably washed *that* blood away, so it didn't really count.

"What about when Duncan Robards knocked his tooth out at football?" Peter proposed. "He was bleeding all over the place."

Bantry gave Emma a sidelong look and stood upright, muttering, "Don't know why I bother. . . ."

Bantry pulled the green door open, and for a moment they stood together, peering down at the grassy space at the bottom of the stairs. The oilcloth had been removed and a pair of stout planks had been placed on the stairs—a ramp for the wheeled stretcher, Emma thought. But the main focus of her attention, the damp grass near the tool-filled wheelbarrow, where Susannah's battered head had lain, had been obliterated by the passage of many feet.

Nell turned a reproachful eye on Bantry. "No blood," she said, somewhat testily.

"Wait," said Peter. He leaned forward slightly, then ran down the planks to point triumphantly at a dark stain on the handle of the grub hoe.

"Let me see." Nell shouldered her way between Bantry and Emma and joined Peter beside the wheelbarrow. Brother and sister bent low over the stain, discussing it with an almost clinical detachment.

"She must've whacked her head on the hoe when she fell," Peter reasoned, and Nell nodded.

"That's as may be," Bantry said, walking briskly down the planks, "but *we'll* be whackin' weeds with it." He picked up the grub hoe and the scythe and carried them over to the chapel.

"What are you doing, Mr. Bantry?" asked Peter.

"Movin' the tools into the chapel," Bantry explained. "Remember the rain we had last night? Might come back again tonight, and as we'll be needin' the barrow, and as I don't want my tools to get rusty, I'm goin' to put 'em inside where it's dry."

"But Dad won't want the chapel cluttered up," Peter objected.

Bantry shifted the load in his arms and looked curiously at Peter's worried face. "Don't your father look after his tools?" he asked. "That's all I'm doin', son. Your father won't begrudge us a bit o' roof. Now, you come over here and see that it's all stacked tidy."

"It's all right, Peter," said Nell. "Bertie says that Papa won't mind."

Peter glanced at his sister and seemed to relax a bit as he strode over to lend Bantry a hand. When the barrow was empty, Bantry looked up at Emma and asked, "Where do you want us to begin?"

The rest of the morning passed quickly. Bantry and Peter stripped dead vines from the walls, Emma turned the soil in the raised beds, and Nell trotted to and fro, carrying armloads of debris to the wheelbarrow, while Bertie sat on an upturned bucket, supervising.

Bantry and Emma took turns wheeling the barrow up the ramp and tipping its contents in a windswept, rocky meadow outside the east wall of the castle. A broad path cut through the meadow, a bright-green ribbon of moss running through the gorse bushes and clumps of tamarisk, and beyond the path the land fell away abruptly, dropping nearly two hundred feet to the foaming waves below.

"The cliff path," Emma said. She turned to Bantry. "Isn't that where Peter was this morning?"

"Aye," said Bantry, "but Master Peter knows not to go beyond the path. And Lady Nell's not allowed outside the castle walls on her own."

Emma nodded absently, listening as Peter called to Nell to bring him the pruning shears. Only fifty yards separated the cliff path from the east wall of the chapel garden. If Susannah had cried out, Peter almost certainly would have heard her. She must have fallen silently, Emma thought with a shudder, and quickly thrust the matter from her mind.

It was nearing one o'clock when a heavyset man with a bristly red mustache appeared in the doorway of the chapel garden. Emma recognized him as one of the men she'd seen eating breakfast in the kitchen. Like the others, he had a radio clipped to his belt, but at the moment he was also burdened with a large wicker hamper.

"Mr. Bantry, sir," he called respectfully, coming down the stairs, "Madama thought you might be wanting a bite to eat."

"Madama was right, Tom," said Bantry. He stepped down from the low retaining wall and walked over to take charge of the hamper. "Everything peaceful?"

"So far," the man said. He nodded pleasantly to Emma and the children before leaving.

Emma stuck her pitchfork in the ground, Peter tossed a last handful of dead vines in the wheelbarrow, and Nell went to fetch Bertie before joining them on the stairs. Once Bantry had handed plates and glasses around, he set out a jug of cider, a bunch of grapes, a round of cheese, a long loaf of crusty bread, a covered bowl filled with rose-mary chicken, and a dozen strawberry tarts topped with shredded coconut.

"God bless Madama," Bantry said reverently, and Emma mur-mured a heartfelt "Amen," smiling when Nell's hand darted toward the tarts. Bantry clucked his tongue and the hand hesitated, then picked up the bunch of grapes instead.

"Who was that man?" Emma asked, opening the cider. "The man who brought the hamper."

"Tom Trevoy," Peter informed her. "He's the chief constable in Penford Harbor."

"He's the *only* constable in Penford Harbor," Nell added.

"Trevoy?" said Emma. "I think I met a relative of his. She runs a guest house where I stayed, near Exeter."

"That'll be Tom's Aunt Mavis," Bantry confirmed.

"Why's Tom wearing that thing in his ear?" Nell asked.

"That's a radio," Peter explained. "It's so he can talk with the other men. Isn't that right, Mr. Bantry?"

"Aye," Bantry said shortly. "Now, who wants a nice bit o' cheese?"

Emma finished pouring the cider, then put the jug down and leaned back to survey the results of the morning's work. Clearing away the dead growth had given her a better idea of the chapel gar-den's basic shape and structure. There were more weeds to pull, more vines to remove, but her next step would be to the drafting table, to make some preliminary sketches. When the meal drew to a close, she declared a half holiday.

"You've earned it," she said, plucking twigs from Nell's curls. "You're hard workers and I want you both to know that I really appre-ciate all your help."

"No one works harder than Peter," Nell informed her. "At home, when Papa's away, Peter——"

"Would you like me and Nell to take the hamper back, Mr. Bantry?" Peter interrupted, getting to his feet.

"Miss Emma and I'll see to that," Bantry said. "Run along and play, now, the both of you."

"But I wanted to tell Emma——" Nell began.

"Here, Nell, have the last tart," said Peter, thrusting it toward her as he hustled her up the steps. "You heard Mr. Bantry. We're supposed to *play* now."

Bantry waited until the children were out of earshot, then shook his head. "'We're supposed to *play*, now,'" he mimicked gruffly. "Lad acts like it were an order." Piling dishes into the hamper, he went on. "Has a bee in his bonnet about keepin' busy, that one. Left him alone in my pottin' shed for five minutes last week, and when I came back, he'd swept the floor."

Emma nodded. "Nanny Cole seems to be having the same problem," she said. "She was reading the riot act to him about it this morning."

"Somethin's frettin' at him." Bantry looked thoughtfully at the closed door and rubbed the back of his neck. "Don't know what it is, but somethin's got him all wound up. Here, pass me that glass, will you?"

Emma shook the last drops of cider from her glass. "Maybe he's not used to having men patrol the house he's living in," she suggested. She caught Bantry's eye as she passed the empty glass to him. "That's what Newland and Chief Constable Trevoy and those other men are doing, isn't it?"

Bantry didn't answer until the hamper had been repacked and the lid closed. Then he leaned back on his elbows, his eyes on the chapel door. "I expect Tom's auntie told you what happened here a few years ago."

Emma nodded. "She said there'd been some trouble with the press after that rock singer drowned. Kate Cole seems to think it might happen again. Do you?"

"Miss Susannah's what they call a celebrity, isn't she?" Bantry retorted. "And what with that old business and all, I reckon the vultures'll take an interest, right enough." His kindly gray eyes turned to slate. "We're not about to go through that again."

"How can you stop it?"

"Our Kate'll stop it, all right," Bantry said grimly. "Pride of Penford Harbor, is our Kate. She's a solicitor, you know."

Emma looked away, to conceal her surprise. Housekeeper,

lawyer—Kate seemed to be yet another multitalented member of the Penford Hall staff. From what she'd said about managing the press conference in Plymouth, she seemed to be Grayson's public-relations officer as well. "How bad was it when Lex died?"

"Bad enough." Bantry leaned forward, his shoulders hunched, his elbows on his knees, toying with a decapitated dandelion. "Don't want you to get the wrong idea," he said slowly. "We're decent folk. We believe in a free press, same as other decent folk, but those fellers printed nothin' but lies. Village had just got back on its feet again, but them vultures tried to turn it inside out." He shook his head. "Caught 'em in the schoolyard, worryin' the children, for goodness' sake."

"But why were they so persistent?" Emma asked. "What were they after?"

"Proof," Bantry said, tossing the dandelion into the wheelbarrow. "The bastards were looking for proof that His Grace murdered that bloke."

"Nothin' like a good murder for sellin' papers."

Bantry's words returned to Emma as she sat at the drafting table. Several hours had passed since she'd returned to her room, but the bitterness in Bantry's voice remained fresh in her mind. Clearly, it had been a galling experience for him to see his fair-haired boy mauled by a sensation-seeking press. Emma thought she could understand the old man's outrage, and she felt sorry for Grayson as well— it couldn't be easy, having celebrities keel over on your doorstep once every five years. Yet she, too, was curious to know what had led Lex Rex to his watery grave.

Richard would have been able to quote chapter and verse to her from the press coverage in the States, but Emma doubted that Richard's new bride would appreciate the phone call. Emma couldn't bring herself to press Bantry for details, either.

Leaning back from the drafting table, Emma examined her sketches, feeling a rush of pleasure when she saw how well they'd turned out. More often than not, her preliminary scribbles consisted of ragged lines, symbolic circles, rows of *X*'s, and lots of small arrows. These were finished drawings. There was the lavender hedge, on either side of the chapel door, and there were the irises and poppies, the old Bourbon roses and the clouds of baby's breath, exactly as she'd envisioned them the day before. It had come so easily, too, as though another hand had been guiding hers. Emma smiled at the notion, put her pencil down, and stretched. Once she added a touch of color to the drawings, she'd present them to Bantry for inspection.

She'd show them to Peter and Nell, as well. She was surprised to realize how much she'd enjoyed the time she'd spent with Derek's children. There'd been that odd moment of near mutiny when Peter had objected to Bantry's stowing the tools in the chapel, but after that he'd been fine. Bantry might teasingly label him a workaholic, but Emma had never considered industriousness to be a fault.

In his own way, though, the boy was as disconcerting as his sister. If Nell was too direct, Peter was too wary. When he looked up at Emma with those huge dark eyes—so like his father's—there seemed to be things going on behind them he'd never let her see. And there'd been that unsettling bounce in his step as he'd come into the kitchen, after learning of Susannah's accident. . . .

Emma bent to tidy up the drafting table, since it was time to dress for supper. Children must be subject to mood swings, the same as adults, she thought. Maybe Peter hadn't liked Susannah. She might have hurt his feelings—she seemed adept at that—in which case her accident would have been good news as far as he was concerned. Emma just wished she knew for sure that he'd been on the cliff path that morning, as he'd claimed. She'd have to remember to ask Derek about it tomorrow.

Emma smiled as she glanced at the crumpled business card propped crookedly against the jeweled clock on the rosewood desk. Mattie had rescued it from the pocket of her denim skirt when she'd shown up a half hour earlier to hang the freshly laundered corduroy skirt in the wardrobe. Looking pale but composed, the girl had apologized briefly for "making a scene," then whisked Emma out of her gardening clothes and into the blue robe. She'd also delivered a hand-knit cardigan made of a heathery gray-blue angora wool—another present from Nanny Cole, whom Mattie described as a champion knitter.

Emma wondered briefly if Nanny Cole was under orders to supply all of the duke's guests with complete new wardrobes, then dismissed the thought with a laugh. She doubted that the blustery old woman took orders from anyone, including His Grace. If Nanny Cole had given up nannying for knitting and sewing, it had undoubtedly been her own decision. Emma had no idea why Nanny Cole would bestow such a gift on her, but she knew just what to do with the sweater. It would look very well with her charcoal-gray trousers tomorrow, when she kept her appointment with Derek.

Eleven

$\mathcal{E}$mma stepped onto the terrace the next day to find Derek standing motionless, staring at the castle ruins, his hands thrust in the
pockets of his faded jeans. He acknowledged her arrival with an ab-
sent nod. "Good news about Susannah," he announced. "Kate called
from Plymouth."

"I heard: unconscious but stable." Emma turned from closing the
French doors to see that Derek was already halfway across the lawn,
head down and striding at top speed toward the arched entryway in
the castle ruins.

A day ago Emma would have tripped over her own feet, trying to
catch up. Now she watched with quiet amusement as Derek came to
an abrupt halt, looked around in confusion, then turned back to her,
bewildered.

"Good morning, Derek." Emma descended from the terrace one
deliberate step at a time. "Did you sleep well? Isn't it a beautiful
morning? And, by the way, do you think you could slow down, so I
won't have to run to keep up with you?"

Derek took the rebuke gracefully. "Sorry. Hear the same complaint from Nell all the time." He swept an arm toward the arched
entryway. "Please, you set the pace."

Mollified, Emma crossed the lawn, and they entered the castle
ruins together. "What was it you wanted to show me?" she asked.

"This and that." Derek cast a glance over his shoulder. "Chapel
first, then the library. Hope you don't mind." He smiled nervously
when he saw Hallard seated on the wicker chair, tapping the keyboard of his laptop computer. "A pity Susannah hasn't regained consciousness, but at least she hasn't gone downhill."

Emma nodded. Mattie had come to share the news with her first
thing that morning. Derek had nothing new to add to Mattie's report,
and they walked down the grassy corridor in silence. Emma watched

with increasing perplexity as Derek's eyes darted from doorway to staircase, scanned the way ahead, and turned to look back the way they'd come, and when she realized that she was doing the same thing, she stopped and turned to peer at him. "Are you looking for something?"

Derek blinked down at her for a moment before replying, "Suppose I am, actually. That's why I wanted to speak with you. Need another outsider, someone who's not familiar with Penford Hall, to bounce some ideas off of. Thing is"—he glanced over his shoulder—"just as soon we weren't overheard."

Emma looked around uneasily. Lowering her voice, she asked, "Does this have anything to do with Susannah?"

Derek was silent for a moment. Then he shrugged. "It might."

Emma nodded and they walked on, neither speaking again until they were in the chapel, with the door closed. Emma stood quite still, transfixed by the window's radiant beauty, but Derek went right up to it, frowning.

"Fair warning," he said, stalking back to Emma's side. "Going to sound a bit daft, but bear with me. If you still think I'm off my nut by the time I've finished, we'll forget the whole thing." He looked down at her anxiously. "What d'you say?"

"Go ahead," said Emma. "I'm listening."

Derek turned and pointed at the window. "Exhibit number one. What do you make of her?"

"She's glorious," said Emma. "Is she a local saint?"

"Semimythic heroine would be more precise. Legend has it that she used that lantern to guide one of Grayson's ancestors past the Nether Shoals one stormy night. Stood on this very spot. Chapel was built in her honor, window created to record her brave deed."

Emma walked halfway down the center aisle, noticing things she'd overlooked during her first, brief visit. Bantry's gardening tools were there, arrayed neatly along the back wall. Six rows of plain wooden benches sat on either side of the chapel's main aisle. A few feet to the left of the window was a back door even lower than the one they'd just come through. Centered beneath the window was a small granite shelf—for posies, Emma thought, though the shelf was empty now.

But there were no tools, no scaffolding, nothing to indicate that any work was taking place.

"Isn't this the window you're restoring?" Emma asked.

"It was supposed to be," Derek replied, "but it's wrong, it's all wrong."

"How do you mean?" Emma turned to look at the window as Derek walked past her to stand before it.

"Her cloak, for one thing. What color would you say it is?"

"Black," Emma replied. "A sort of translucent, smoky black. Why?"

"According to the legend, the lady should be clad in purest white. Grayson claims that when he was a child the cloak was gray. His staff back him up. They all claim that the cloak, and only the cloak, has gradually changed from white to black. Now, I'm the first to admit that glass can change color, that it can cloud up or weather or get dirty." He looked at Emma expectantly.

"I'm with you," she said.

"None of those things have happened here. So, unless a chemical reaction has occurred that is entirely without precedent in the history of glassmaking, I've no way to account for the darkening—no proof, in fact, that it's even taken place. Do you follow?"

"Just talk, Derek," Emma said impatiently.

Derek flushed. "Sorry. Being pedantic. Trouble is, I've tried to explain it to Peter and he's refused to understand. Boy's taken a liking to the lady. Been after me to 'fix her cloak.' That's what Grayson wanted me to do, of course. He'd hoped I could change the color with a chemical treatment, which I can't, or simply replace the glass, which I'm extremely reluctant to do, now that I've had a chance to examine it firsthand."

"Why not?"

"I'm very good at my job, Emma, but whoever created that window was a master. Wouldn't dream of interfering with his work. Grayson's disappointed, naturally, but he sees my point and quite agrees."

"But Peter doesn't?"

"No. Don't know why. He's usually quite reasonable." Derek

ducked his head. "Don't know why I'm going on about my son at the moment, either, when I've so much else to tell you. Shall we continue on to my second exhibit?" Derek strode up the center aisle to open the back door, and Emma followed him out. Sunlight blinded her for a moment and she blinked rapidly, then gasped, pressing herself back against the chapel wall, panic-stricken.

She was standing on the edge of a cliff. Like the lady in the window, Emma could look straight down two hundred feet to the monstrous waves crashing on the rocks far below.

"I say . . ." Derek peered at her worriedly. "You don't suffer from vertigo, do you?"

For the first time, Emma became acutely aware of the thundering surf, a sound that had hitherto gone as unnoticed as the beating of her own heart. "It's a little late to be asking that question, isn't it?" she managed.

Derek seemed perplexed, a little hurt. "Wouldn't have let you stumble," he said. "That's why I came out first."

Emma tore her gaze from the crashing waves to glare at him, but he'd already turned away.

"Exhibit number two," he said, opening his arms to indicate the panorama of sea and sky. "What strikes you immediately about this setting?"

Now that she'd caught her breath, Emma had to admit that she wasn't actually teetering on the edge of the cliff. It was the openness of the spot that had startled her. No stunted trees or tangle of bushes blocked the sweeping view, and no rail or retaining wall warned of the two-hundred-foot drop to the sea. All that stood between her and the precipice were a few yards of tussocky ground.

She released her hold on the chapel and took a cautious half step forward. Ahead of her, the English Channel stretched blue to the horizon. To her left, the beacon flashed from its rocky promontory, and to her right, beyond the chapel, the cliffs curved abruptly inward. She suppressed a shudder as a gust of wind snatched at her hair.

"It's unprotected," she said, in answer to Derek's question. "No shelter from the wind. I wouldn't want to be out here during a storm."

"But Grayson claims that this window's been out here, in all kinds of weather, for hundreds of years. Now, look." Derek reached up to run his hand across the irregular surface of the window. "You see? No pits, no scratches—no sign of weathering whatsoever. Even the solder is intact."

Emma frowned and leaned back against the wall. "So Grayson's supposedly ancient window shows no signs of age?"

"Strange, isn't it?"

"As strange as calling Penford Hall a ruin."

Derek's face lit up. "Nell's right. You do catch on quickly. Can't wait to show you the house plans. Here, let's go to the library."

Putting a protective hand on Emma's arm, Derek walked with her around the outside of the chapel garden to the rocky meadow where the cliff path began. The scent of gorse blossom was heavy and sweet and the air was clear. Emma could see the nests of gulls and black-faced oystercatchers on the opposite cliffs and hear their constant cries echoing off the scarred rockface. Once they were on the path, Derek dropped his hand and they strolled side by side.

"According to Grayson," Derek said, "the original lantern, the actual, tin-shuttered candle lamp used by the lady in the legend, is supposed to be kept on display in the chapel. Legend has it that the ruddy thing lights itself once every hundred years. When it does, the duke of Penford is required to throw a sort of elaborate bean-feast. Supposed to take place this year, in fact. It's called the Fête, and it carries all sorts of historical weight with the villagers."

Emma recalled both the duke's request that she have the chapel garden ready by the first of August and the empty shelf below the lady window. "The Fête's coming up in August," she guessed, "but the lantern's missing, and Grayson can't hold one without the other."

Derek looked impressed. "Exactly right. Keep it to yourself, though, won't you? The staff know the lantern's gone, but the villagers don't and they'd be very upset."

Emma agreed, though she didn't really understand what all the fuss was about. "Why doesn't Grayson have a copy made?"

"I can tell you Grayson's reason. He spoke with such conviction that I can recall his words precisely." Derek turned to look intently at

Emma. "Grayson said, 'I don't think you understand, old son. I believe in the legend. When the day of the Fête arrives, I fully expect the lantern to shine.'"

Emma's eyebrows rose.

"Quite," said Derek. "He asked me here not only to restore a perfectly sound window, but, because of my expertise in rummaging around old buildings, to search Penford Hall for an antique, self-lighting lantern."

As they approached the hall, Emma wondered how to pose her next question. Grayson appeared to be disturbingly willing to believe in anything related to the family legend—an ancient window that seemed untouched by time, a cloak that had mysteriously changed color, a lantern that lit of its own accord. Emma had heard of eccentric Englishmen before, but . . . "So, you're worried about the duke's . . . um . . . sanity?" she asked hesitantly.

"Worse than that, I'm afraid," said Derek, but he would say nothing more until they'd made their way through a door in the east wing and down a series of deserted corridors to the dark-paneled library. It, too, was deserted, and Derek's voice seemed startlingly loud as he crossed the room to take a large black morocco portfolio from a bookstand near the gallery stairs. "Grayson gave me a detailed set of house plans," he explained, "so I could search the place from top to bottom."

"Has anything turned up?" Emma asked.

Derek laid the portfolio flat on the long marquetry table behind the couch, then gestured to the portrait over the mantelpiece. "The dowager duchess's emeralds," he answered. "But Nell and Bertie stumbled over those."

"Nell and Bertie found Grandmother's wedding jewels?" Emma asked doubtfully.

"Stumbled over them. They were underneath a floorboard in the nursery. Must've thought it was the one place the old duke wouldn't look."

"*Who* must've thought?" Emma asked, thoroughly confused, but Derek's long strides had already taken him into a shadowy recess in the corner, where he bent low to retrieve a second portfolio. Its faded black leather was crumbling, one corner was cracked and peeling, and the covers were held together by frayed ribbons.

"Misplaced two sheets from the plans Grayson gave me," Derek said, laying the second portfolio beside the first. "Embarrassing gaffe, for a supposed expert in old houses. Came down to see if I could root out another set on my own. Found this." He placed a hand on the second portfolio. "It's the kind of survey that's done when a chap's thinking of putting his place on the market."

Derek gently teased the ribbons apart and opened the second portfolio. Emma glanced at the date on the topmost sheet. These house plans had been made fifteen years ago, only ten years before the most recent set.

"Like you to compare the two," said Derek. "They're a bit technical, I'm afraid, but, well, do your best."

Emma smiled tolerantly as she paged through the detailed drawings. She'd installed her share of mainframe computer systems over the years, laid cable in air-conditioning ducts, and rewired entire offices. She doubted that Derek could teach her much about reading house plans.

"You see . . ." Derek's fingers began to trace lightly across a page, then stopped as he cocked an ear toward the ceiling. Slowly, he raised his eyes to the gallery. "Nell," he said, sounding mildly affronted, and Emma looked up to see a curly blond head and a fuzzy brown one peering through the gallery's wooden railing.

"What are you doing up there?" Derek demanded. "Where's Peter?"

"Bertie said Peter needs time to himself," Nell explained. "And we found a little door up here, so—"

"Please inform Bertie that Emma and I would like some time to *our*selves, as well," said Derek. "Go ask Peter to read you a story."

"But Bertie said—"

"One moment, please, Emma." Taking the stairs three at a time, Derek ran up to the gallery, where he bent to confer with his daughter.

Emma turned back to the house plans and paged through them slowly, stopped, then started again. "New wiring," she murmured.

"New plumbing . . ." Twenty years ago the rose suite hadn't even had a sink, let alone its own bathroom, and there'd been no fancy stove in the kitchen. She looked up as Derek returned, a bemused expression on his face.

"Nell gone?" she asked.

"Yes, but . . ." Derek rubbed the back of his neck. "My daughter informs me that it's nearly lunchtime." He reached down to toy with one of the frayed ribbons. "Have you any plans?"

Emma shrugged. "I'd intended to go down to the village to buy a few things this afternoon."

"All right." Derek took a deep breath, then jammed his hands into his pockets. "We'll go down together, then. They do a slap-up lunch at the Bright Lady—the village pub." He hesitated before adding apologetically, "Seems I've also agreed to have supper with my children in the nursery this evening. Don't know quite how it happened, but . . . well, rather awkward. Means you'll be dining alone."

"That's okay," said Emma. "I'm used to it."

"Shouldn't be," Derek snapped. He flushed, then jutted his chin toward the gallery. "That is to say, my daughter, Nell, wondered if you might join us for supper." A look of concern crossed his face. "You *are* eating, aren't you?"

Pulling in her stomach, Emma replied stiffly, "I'm not dieting, if that's what you mean."

"Thank God. After a week of Susannah and her food-fads, I'm ready to set light to every diet book on the market. Nothing wrong with a healthy appetite. Why, Mary could put away—" He faltered, then went on, haltingly. "My late wife enjoyed food. Don't know where she put it. She was small, like Peter. Same dark hair, too." He glanced at Emma, then quickly looked away. "She died just after Nell was born. Pneumonia."

Was that it? Emma wondered. Was that why he'd been so upset by the duke's graphic description of drowning? Emma knew there was no set timetable for grief, but five years seemed a long time for a mere anecdote to elicit such a strong reaction. Yet, looking at him now, hearing the pain in his voice, she knew it must be so. She felt a brief stab of envy—what must it be like to be missed so desperately?—

but recoiled from it. If Derek's wife had loved him, she would not have wanted him to mourn like this. "I'm very sorry," she said.

"Me, too." Derek busied himself with closing the portfolios. "Look, why don't we head down to the village now? I can explain the house plans to you on the way. Don't mind walking, do you? Nell said it wouldn't bother you."

"Did she?" Emma smiled. Clearly, she'd made more of an impression on Nell than she'd realized. "I suppose Bertie expressed an opinion of me, too?"

Some of the strain seemed to leave Derek's face as he gave Emma a sidelong look. "He did, in fact. Thinks you're quite splendid."

Emma had never received praise from a stuffed bear before, but as she watched Derek return the portfolios to their respective shelves, she felt irrationally pleased.

Twelve

The cliff path wound around the east wing of Penford Hall and skirted the edge of the walled woodland before beginning a gradual descent into the valley that held the village of Penford Harbor. The prickly gorse soon gave way to bracken; the windswept rocky meadow to the still, sun-dappled shelter of the trees.

Derek had pulled off his sweater and tied its sleeves around his waist. He wore a wrinkled blue chambray workshirt underneath, and as he rolled up his shirtsleeves, Emma noticed his sinewy forearms. She wondered fleetingly how such strong hands could perform such delicate tasks—uncovering a whitewashed fresco, repairing fragile stained glass—then realized that Derek's eyes were on her, and redirected her gaze.

"Don't suppose you were able to make heads or tails out of the house plans," Derek said.

"I managed to pick out a thing or two," Emma admitted, amused but slightly nettled by Derek's condescending tone. "The plumbing and wiring have been completely revamped. New access panels, stack vents, feeder cables, supply lines, a whole new distribution board. If the cutaways are any indication, some floors have been raised and leveled, and a new roof's been put on." She glanced slyly at Derek. "Have I left anything out?"

"Er," said Derek.

"If I really struggled, I'll bet I could even figure out why you showed the plans to me," Emma continued, enjoying his discomfiture. "Let's see, now. The older plans suggest that the hall was in pretty bad shape fifteen years ago. If the old duke had them made up in order to sell the place, the family's finances must have been shaky, too. Your aside about the duchess's emeralds seems a little ominous. Why would she hide them in the nursery unless she was afraid that her son might try to sell them? And if Grayson's father was down to selling his own mother's wedding jewels—" She stopped walking and turned to face Derek, who was staring at her in amazement. "How am I doing?"

"Um." Derek blinked. "You work with computers, don't you?"

Emma nodded. "Sometimes my firm installs them. In great big buildings. With reams of technical drawings."

"Ah." Derek scuffed at the ground with the toe of his workboot. "Didn't mean to sound patronizing. Most women—"

"You'd be surprised at what most women know," Emma said lightly. "At any rate, I *do* see what you're getting at. Penford Hall underwent a major renovation five years ago. It must have cost a fortune."

"Repairs on the roof alone would run upwards of a hundred thousand pounds," Derek confirmed.

"A hundred thousand . . ." Emma gulped. "Just for the roof? Where did Grayson get money like that?"

"Susannah asked me the same question," said Derek. "Seemed to think I'd know."

"You were friends," Emma reminded him.

"Haven't seen him for ten years," Derek retorted. "And I never visited the hall. When I managed to make that clear to Susannah, she began asking me about Lex Rex. Went on about it until I was ready to chuck her over the nearest wall." Derek frowned suddenly, as though a new thought had occurred to him. "She must've been looking for me yesterday morning, when she . . ." His voice trailed off.

"Fell?" Emma suggested.

"That's the problem, you see." Coming to a halt, he turned to regard Emma worriedly. "A wealthy rock star drowns nearby, and Grayson's suddenly wealthy enough to refurbish the hall. Susannah claims to see a connection . . . and suddenly she's not around to ask uncomfortable questions anymore."

"No." Emma shook her head. "Grayson couldn't . . . He wouldn't . . ." She bit her lip, then tried again. "What I mean is, Grayson's so . . ."

"Charming? Gracious? I quite agree. But he's also a bit of a madman, wouldn't you say? And he knows how to sail, Emma. He's grown up hearing tales of shipwrecks and piracy, and he told me he'd do anything to make sure the bloody lantern lit on schedule. And in order for that to happen, the duke of Penford must be in possession of Penford Hall."

Emma opened her mouth to protest, then closed it again. After all, Mattie had told her outright that Susannah had been an unpopular figure at Penford Hall. Mild-mannered Bantry had come close to spitting on the duke's cousin, Nanny Cole had complained of her snooping, and, however well Kate had tried to hide it, she'd been annoyed by Susannah's needling. And Grayson . . . What had he said about his cousin? *She was raised by wolves, you know.*

She gazed at Derek, shaken. "Do you know what you're suggesting?"

Sighing, Derek ran a hand through his curls. "I know, and I hope it turns out to be a load of rubbish. But what if it's not? What if Grayson was involved in Lex's death? What if he got his hands on Lex's money? What if Susannah's found a way to prove it?"

Emma felt a sudden chill. When Kate had called this morning, she'd mentioned bringing Susannah back to Penford Hall as soon as she was well enough to travel. If Derek was right, if Susannah had discovered something connecting Grayson to Lex Rex's death, the hall might not be the safest place for her to recuperate. "Tell me more about Lex Rex," she said.

They walked slowly. Derek conscientiously moderated his long stride, and Emma was in no hurry. The path would eventually take them to the car park, and from there they would enter the village by the main—indeed the only—street. Until then, Emma had a lot of catching up to do. She listened closely while Derek told her what he knew of Charles Alexander King, more commonly known to his legion of fans as Lex Rex.

"They met in Oxford," Derek began. "Grayson was attending lectures and Lex was holed up in a garage somewhere, working on that first, dreadful video."

Emma searched her memory. "The black-and-white one with all the scratches?"

Derek nodded. "*Eat Your Greens.* In seven earsplitting minutes, Lex managed to offend environmentalists, vegetarians, pacifists, and right-thinking people everywhere. Everyone else thought he was fantastic. Grayson must've thought so, too, though I'm hard-pressed to say what they had in common."

"It wasn't the music," Emma objected, recalling the fine precision of the duke's playing. "Perhaps he enjoyed the shock value. The old duke couldn't have approved of Lex."

Derek shrugged. "Whatever the case, the friendship didn't last. The old duke died and Grayson came back to Penford Hall, while Lex went on to fame and fortune. Five years later, I was reading about them in the papers."

"Wait," Emma broke in. "Didn't you meet Grayson at about the same time?"

"If you're wondering whether I met Lex as well, the answer is no. I should think it would be self-evident. I was a grown man, with a . . ." He faltered, recovered quickly, and went on. "With a wife and an infant son to look after. Hadn't any time to waste hanging about garages with the likes of Lex Rex."

A breeze rustled the leaves overhead, and a chaffinch streaked across the path. Emma watched Derek from the corner of her eye, saw his jaw muscles knot, his hands clench behind his back.

"Now, where was I?" he asked gruffly.

"Lex had gone on to fame and fortune."

"Right." Derek cleared his throat. "According to the newspaper accounts, Lex decided to pay his old friend a surprise visit. Treacherous things, country houses. Never know who's going to turn up."

"Sounds like the voice of experience," Emma said wryly. "Do you have a country house?"

"Family does. In Wiltshire. Comes to me when the old man pegs out."

"You don't seem pleased by the idea," Emma observed. "Don't you want the family mansion?"

"Too many strings attached." Derek's mouth quirked in an ironic smile. "My father disapproves of my profession. I'm the son of an earl with the soul of a bricklayer. The lord of the manor is not supposed to get his hands dirty."

"And a woman's place is in the home. I've been hearing that since

I was old enough to wear an apron. Ridiculous, isn't it?" Emma picked up a stick and knocked the head off of a stray dandelion. "Your father should meet my mother. The world seems to be full of disappointed parents."

"A good many disappointed children, as well, I'll wager." Derek's smile softened.

"Please," Emma said, "go on with the story. I'll try not to interrupt."

"Interrupt all you like," said Derek, with a sidelong glance. "I don't mind." His curls tossed in the breeze and the sunshine made his blue eyes sparkle. Emma rumbled with the stick, then tossed it hastily away.

"Lex decided to surprise Grayson . . ." she prompted.

Derek gazed at her a moment longer, then ducked his head and continued. "Surprise was on Lex, as it turned out, because Grayson wasn't at home. Papers made a lot of fuss about this particular point, until it came out that Grayson had been in France, negotiating the re-purchase of paintings his father had sold some years before. Grayson was understandably reluctant to advertise his father's penury."

"But if Grayson wasn't home . . ."

"His staff is awfully fond of him, don't you think? Terribly eager to please?"

"I suppose, but . . ." But it makes sense, Emma thought. It could have been a plot, with Grayson as the mastermind and the staff as co-conspirators. She thought back to her first evening at Penford Hall, to Grayson's soothing, seductive words at the dinner table. She'd joined his cause without a second thought. If he inspired such devotion in a total stranger, what kind of fierce loyalty might he inspire in his staff? "Go on," she said.

"Lex arrived, with his band in tow, and no Grayson to surprise. Fools got into his brandy, then decided to hoof it down to the Bright Lady."

"That's the pub in Penford Harbor?"

"Where we're heading now. The band downed a few pints, jumped aboard Grayson's yacht, and took it out into one of the worst gales Cornwall's seen in fifty years. None of them were sailors, and the yacht was in poor repair. Miracle they got the ruddy thing going at all. But no one tangles with the Nether Shoals and lives to tell about it."

"The ship was wrecked?" Emma asked.

"Smashed to matchsticks. The band . . ." Derek's lips tightened. "They searched, of course. Grayson came tearing back from his trip to mount his own search, as well. But the currents around the Nether Shoals are notoriously unpredictable, even in fair weather. In that storm . . ." Derek shook his head. "Could be as far away as Spain by now."

Emma drew her sweater more closely around her. "And the press gave Grayson a pretty hard time?"

"Had a field day," Derek said. "Cro-Magnon musician perishes on aristocrat's leaky yacht—it was tabloid fodder. Yet another scandal at Buck House took the pressure off, but not before some enterprising journalist discovered that Lex had been virtually penniless. There was no estate left, after all the bills had been paid."

Emma wasn't surprised. The scenario was a familiar one—too many rock musicians lived life at high speed, spending their money faster than they earned it. Emma frowned suddenly and came to an abrupt halt.

"Penniless?" she repeated. She batted at a fly that buzzed in her face. "Then what are we worrying about? If Lex was broke, why would Grayson . . ." She hesitated, then finished lamely, ". . . do what you think he might have done?"

"This is the tricky bit." Derek peered cautiously into the woods on either side of the path, before saying, very quietly, "Lex's books—his financial records—were a bit of a mess. That's what gave rise to speculation in the first place. No one was quite sure what had become of his money, you understand?"

Emma nodded.

"The tabloids lost interest, and so did I. But Susannah didn't." Derek glanced around again, then leaned closer to Emma. His voice sank to a whisper. "Apparently, she befriended a chap, a banker. Happens I know him. Very precise sort of fellow. Collects butterflies. Susannah asked him to look into things, and he came away saying that there was something odd about the way Lex's accounts were set up. Nothing he could point a finger at. Just gave him a queer feeling that things weren't quite pukka."

"But how could Grayson—"

"Fiddle the books? No idea. Curious, though."

Emma agreed. As they resumed walking, she murmured, "It's a lucky thing Susannah's friend never talked to the press."

"Winslow?" Derek snorted. "Safe as houses. We were at school together. Hasn't changed a bit. If it hasn't got wings and antennae, he can't be bothered with it."

"I suppose that's why she approached him. If Susannah had blackmail on her mind, she wouldn't want to broadcast what she'd learned," Emma mused. Question after question cartwheeled through her mind. Had Grayson lured Lex down to Penford Hall? Had the shipwreck been planned? Had the staff been involved? Emma knew enough about computer security at banks to know that no electronic records were completely safe from prying eyes. It wouldn't be easy to break into private financial files, but it could be done. All you'd need was a fairly sophisticated . . . *"Hallard,"* she breathed.

"Where?" Derek asked in alarm.

Emma shook her head. "No, Derek, I didn't mean that. I just thought of a way for Grayson to syphon off Lex's funds. What do you suppose Hallard's doing with that laptop computer?"

"Hallard?" Derek said doubtfully. "Seems a bit dotty to me."

"Hackers frequently are," Emma replied dryly.

"Hackers?"

"Creative computer programmers," Emma explained. "Sometimes called computer nerds. They've been known to break into systems just for the fun of it."

"Fascinating."

Emma nodded, but her mind was already on other things. "Were there any witnesses to the shipwreck?"

"Only a few," Derek replied. "That's another thing that has me puzzled. Five years ago, the village of Penford Harbor was virtually abandoned."

.   .   .

The abandoned village is thriving, Emma thought, looking around the pub.

The Bright Lady was a low, whitewashed stone building on the harborfront, tucked between a half-timbered inn and the narrow, two-story harbormaster's house, which now served as Dr. Singh's infirmary. The pub was warm and cozy, dimly lit by the sunlight falling through the bull's-eye windows in the front. Pewter tankards and lengths of fishing net hung from the raftered ceiling, a back corner was devoted to a well-used dartboard, and a time-worn but lovingly polished bar jutted out into the center of the room, dividing it in two. On one side of the bar, an aged spaniel slept before a crackling fire, and the red-haired chief constable, Tom Trevoy, sat at a bare wooden table, writing doggedly on a pad of yellow paper and nursing a pint of the local ale.

Emma was sitting on the other side of the bar, at one of a half-dozen tables draped with linen and set with silver. Her table was in the front, near the windows, and she had a clear view of the harbor. Derek was speaking with three elderly women at a table in the back, answering the question Emma had heard many times as she and Derek had strolled down from the car park to the harbor.

Would Susannah's "mishap" delay the Fête? Everyone they'd met—from Mrs. Shuttleworth, quietly tending the marigolds in front of her husband's church, to the irascible Jonah Pengully, at whose ramshackle general store Emma had purchased work gloves, a sunhat, and a pair of Wellington boots—had asked Derek the same thing. Faces had fallen when he'd declined to give a definite answer, but the villagers remained hopeful that word would come down from Penford Hall before nightfall.

Emma sipped her cider and watched out the window as three fishermen guided their boat into the harbor. She knew without looking that the boat would be in perfect condition, not a speck of paint chipped off of its sky-blue prow. She knew it because everything she'd seen so far in Penford Harbor had been perfect.

The church, with its ancient carvings and shining brasses; the tiny schoolhouse, with its computer terminals; the bakery, the butcher's shop, the boathouse—nothing was rundown or weather-beaten. The whitewashed cottages, roofed in blue slate or wheat-colored thatch, looked as though they'd been painted fresh that morning.

The air of well-being was more than skin-deep. According to Derek, the small fishing fleet provided the village and the hall with a great variety of seafood, and Mr. Carroway, the greengrocer, grew vegetables all year round in a solar-heated greenhouse behind his shop. An inland town supplied Mr. Minion, the butcher, with mutton and beef—it was his van that Gash had been repairing—but Herbert Munting, a middle-aged widower with a passion for poultry, provided him with chickens, geese, and other feathered delicacies from his multilevel henhouse. Mr. and Mrs. Tharby, the proud owners of the Bright Lady, made their own ale, pressed their own cider, and experimented with flavored liquors, but claimed that Crowley was the local authority on wine-making.

Penford Harbor's air of cheerful self-sufficiency should have been appealing, but Emma found it almost eerie. It was too polished, too pristine. Old Jonah Pengully, with his cluttered shop, moth-eaten gray pullover, and curmudgeonly manner, had come as a refreshing change of pace.

Emma turned away from the window as Derek took his seat, and nodded when the matronly Mrs. Tharby stopped at their table to assure them that their lunch would be right out. When she'd left, Emma murmured uncertainly, "Did we place an order?"

Derek smiled. "One doesn't order at the Bright Lady. One eats whatever Ernestine Potts decides to serve. She trained under Madama, so there's no need to worry. Matter of fact, I've promised to bring Nell a pot of Ernestine's jam."

"Strawberry jam?" Emma asked.

"Why, yes. How did you guess?"

Emma studied Derek closely, wondering how he could possibly be unaware of his daughter's fondness for strawberries. "She seems to eat a lot of them," she replied carefully.

"Is that unhealthy?" Derek asked, faintly alarmed. Emma reassured him as Mrs. Tharby returned with their food.

"Supreme of Cornish turbot," Mrs. Tharby informed them as she unloaded her tray. "Filled with a light scallop-and-grainy-mustard mousseline, and served on broad beans cooked French-style with a Chablis sauce. Ernestine's having fun today. Enjoy." She'd just turned away when the front door swung open.

"Hello, boys!" Mrs. Tharby called. "Your missus is expecting you for lunch, Ted."

Three fishermen had come into the pub, their rubber boots trailing water, their hands and faces reddened from the wind and sun. Emma recognized them as the three she'd seen sailing into the harbor moments before. The youngest appeared to be in his late twenties, the oldest somewhere in his thirties. Emma thought she detected a family resemblance in their upturned noses and dark, wavy hair, and a moment later, Derek confirmed it, introducing her to the Tregallis brothers: Ted, Jack, and James.

"Told Debbie I'd stop by here to drop off the papers," Ted replied to Mrs. Tharby as she headed for the kitchen. "How're things up at the hall, Tom?"

"Peaceful, so far," said the red-haired chief constable.

Ted placed a bundle of newspapers before Chief Constable Trevoy while Jack and James came over to shake hands with Derek. Their heavy wool sweaters reeked of sweat, diesel oil, and fish.

"Press conference went well," Ted called from the chief constable's table. "Seen the rags yet?"

Derek shook his head. "How bad is it?"

"See for yourself." Ted brought several of the papers over to Derek. The first contained a black-and-white photograph of a scantily clad Susannah cavorting beside the words:

ASHERS SMASHERS!

"Blast," Derek muttered. "Must've got the snap from Syd."

"Bastards probably nicked it off him," said Jack, wincing as Ted jabbed an elbow into his side and told him to mind his language.

"The other one's not so bad," said Chief Constable Trevoy, holding up a second newspaper. Its front page featured an unflattering photograph of Grayson surrounded by white-coated doctors, paired with a gorgeous shot of Susannah in a semitransparent gown, stretched full-length on her back on a rocky beach. The headline screamed:

FALLEN BEAUTY!

"Doubt Debbie'll let me keep 'em in the house," said Ted ruefully. "Not with Teddy around. My ten-year-old," he explained to Emma.

"We could keep 'em on the boat," Jack suggested, and was rewarded with a swift clout in the head from James, who asked, "This won't affect the Fête, will it, sir?"

With admirable patience, Derek confessed yet again that he really didn't know, and the Tregallis brothers trooped off to Ted and Debbie's house for their midday meal, while Chief Constable Trevoy scanned through the rest of the papers. Mrs. Tharby returned to the table shortly, with a fresh round of drinks. Before leaving them to enjoy their lunch, she put a hand on Emma's arm. "I just wanted to say what a pleasure it is to meet the garden lady. God bless you, dear. I've heard so much about you." The Penford Hall grapevine, it seemed, was linked directly to the village.

Thirteen

*E*mma leaned over the retaining wall of the gray granite quay to look down at the lapping waves, while Derek stood beside her, facing the village. In the harbor, a gull plummeted headfirst into a wave, then rose back into the air, wings straining, a sliver of silver in its beak. A cool breeze caressed Emma's face as she followed the gull's flight upward and along the edge of the enclosing cliffs.

It was like standing at the bottom of a canyon. The curving walls were neither as steep nor as barren as they'd appeared from above. The rockface was cross-hatched with cracks, and a scattering of twisted cedars, buckthorn bushes, and tufts of purple rock samphire clung to narrow ledges.

The beacon and the chapel stood like sentinels on either side of the narrow opening in the canyon wall, where the sea swept in. Emma could easily imagine Grayson's pirate ancestor hiding out in this sheltered cove, though he would have had to be a good seaman to maneuver his ship past the shoals. Emma's gaze came to rest on a spot just beyond the mouth of the cove, where the water swirled and eddied, and ruffling waves seemed to break on an unseen shore.

"The Nether Shoals," she murmured. She and Derek had retraced Lex's steps from the door of the Bright Lady to the very spot where the duke's yacht had once been docked. The cleats were still there, set firmly in the stone walkway, even though, as Susannah had taken pains to point out, the yacht had never been replaced.

But nearly everything else in Penford Harbor had been. Derek observed that the village had almost certainly undergone a renovation as extensive as the one that had taken place at Penford Hall. "I know how long it takes for rafters to settle, new thatch to turn from yellow to dusty brown," he'd told her. "It's not an exact science, but I'm willing to swear that most of these buildings were decaying ruins

in the not-too-distant past. Someone's done a great deal to lure people back here and make them want to stay."

Derek turned to her now, his shoulder brushing hers as he leaned
beside her on the wall. "Another odd thing about the Penford family
legend," he murmured. "In order for Grayson to bring it to fruition,
there must also be a village."

Emma shivered. "Let's go back to the hall," she said, glancing upward. The sky was clouding over and the waves were kicking up. "I
need to think, and it looks like another storm is moving in."

Derek telephoned from the Bright Lady, and Gash came to meet
them at the car park, then drove them the rest of the way up. The azaleas fluttered by, but Emma scarcely noticed them, and when the hall
came into view, she smiled ruefully. She was ashamed to admit it, but
the past two days had, without doubt, been the most interesting two
days in her whole life. And a part of her didn't want them to end.

> *Lady Nell, Master Peter, and Sir Bertram of Harris request the
> pleasure of your company at supper tonight in the nursery.*
> *At seven o'clock.*
> *Dad's coming, too.*

The last two lines had been added as a postscript, crowded in
below the tempera-paint scrolls and flowery flourishes that framed
the rest of the hand-printed text. Emma stood on the balcony and reread the invitation. It had been lying on the floor just inside her room
when she'd returned from Penford Harbor, as though someone had
slipped it under the door. She hadn't yet sent her reply.

Derek had given her so much to think about. She would have
liked to spend some time in the garden—she always thought more
clearly with a trowel in her hand—but the clouds had moved in and
the air was heavy with ozone. Suddenly, there was a patter of rain,
then a downpour, brief and powerful, followed by a steady, ground-
soaking shower.

It's a good thing Bantry stored the gardening tools in the chapel,
Emma thought, turning to go inside. Otherwise, they'd be—

Emma froze in the doorway, then turned slowly back to watch

the falling rain. It had rained the other night, as well, the night before she and Nell had found Susannah. There'd been a heavy mist that morning, too. Bantry had tied an oilcloth over the wheelbarrow to protect his tools from just such weather, as any good gardener would.

But the oilcloth had not been on the wheelbarrow that morning. When Emma had reached for it, she'd found it on the flagstone path. Yet the tools had been bone-dry when Bantry had taken them from the barrow that afternoon. Emma touched a hand to her glasses, then folded her arms, perplexed. Someone had removed the oilcloth from the wheelbarrow sometime after the rain had stopped and the mist had burned off. Someone had been in the garden on the morning of Susannah's accident.

But who? Emma couldn't imagine Susannah soiling her hands on the old oilcloth, and if Bantry had untied it he wouldn't have left it lying on the path.

Peter, perhaps? He'd spent the morning on the cliff path, very near the chapel garden. He might have slipped inside to take a peek at the tools. It was only natural for a little boy to be curious about such things.

Should she ask him about it tonight? Emma glanced down at the neatly printed invitation, and shook her head. No need to spoil the children's grand occasion. She would ask Bantry about the oilcloth in the morning.

A hail of raindrops gusted onto the balcony and Emma ducked into the bedroom. Wiping the rain from her face, she crossed to the rosewood desk to compose an acceptance, then rang for Mattie to deliver it.

The invitation suggested that supper in the nursery would be a formal affair, and Emma went to the wardrobe, wishing she'd brought something other than her trusty teal, only to find another dress hanging in its place. Emma's hand slid slowly down the door of the wardrobe, then rose to adjust her glasses. She could scarcely believe her eyes.

Silver-gray satin gleamed like liquid moonbeams in the lamplight. The dress was simply cut, with three-quarter-length sleeves, a close-fitting bodice, a modest décolletage, and a full skirt that would fall just below her knees. Emma reached out a tentative hand to touch the skirt and sighed as the lustrous fabric rustled beneath her fingertips.

"Excuse me, miss."

Emma jerked her hand back and turned to face Mattie, who was standing in the doorway of the dressing room.

"I wouldn't handle it, miss, not until you've had your bath." When Emma made no reply, the girl added uncertainly, "I did knock, miss, but you didn't seem to hear."

"That's all right," said Emma, coming out of her daze. "But this dress, Mattie. Did Nanny Cole . . . ?"

"Lady Nell and I thought you might be needing a few extra frocks, seeing as you'd brought so few of your own, and Nanny Cole agreed. I hope you don't mind."

"Mind?" Emma looked back at the dress and smiled dreamily. "No. I don't mind."

The nursery occupied several large rooms on the top floor of Penford Hall. Peter was waiting for Emma at the door to the central room, which he referred to as the day nursery. He escorted her to an armchair, brought her a glass of fizzy lemonade, then stood nervously adjusting his tie and tugging at his blazer.

"You look very distinguished tonight," said Emma. She leaned forward for a closer look at his tie. "Are you at Harrow this year?"

"No," Peter replied. "This is Grayson's old tie and his blazer, too. He lent them to me for the evening. Nanny Cole had to take up the sleeves." He pulled at a cuff. "Papa wanted me to go to Harrow. That's where he went. I wanted to go, too, but—" Peter bit his lip.

"But what?" Emma coaxed.

Peter lowered his eyes, then murmured confidentially, "It's a boarding school."

"I see," said Emma, though she did not see at all.

"Grayson's been teaching me cricket," Peter continued conversationally. He frowned and pursed his lips. "I think I'm beginning to see the point of it."

Emma sipped her lemonade, uncertain what to say. She wasn't used to children pondering the meaning of schoolyard games. She wondered briefly if cricket inspired such dubious devotion in all young boys, but before she could frame a tactful question, Peter excused himself and went to see what was keeping Nell.

The day nursery had soft rugs, soft chairs, and a hard horsehair sofa. A map of the world had been painted on one wall, and the others held framed pencil drawings of Penford Hall, the ruined castle, and the harbor. Emma suspected that the drawings were the fledgling efforts of a young Grayson.

An enormous black-and-white rocking horse sat near the windows, a butterfly net leaned in one corner, and low shelves ran right around the room. The shelves were filled with books and toys and mysterious, unmarked boxes that might have held puzzles or models or brigades of toy soldiers. The large table at the center of the room had been set for supper, and Crowley stood over a long row of chafing dishes, waiting to serve the meal.

It took Emma several minutes to realize that the toys had been arranged in alphabetical order, a few minutes longer to figure out that the fifth place at the table had been set for Bertie. She looked from the wooden abacus to the stuffed zebra, and back to the encyclopedias piled on the chair to give the small brown teddy needed height, and wondered if all children behaved this way.

Emma raised a hand self-consciously to her hair. Mattie had brushed it until it crackled, then let it fall around her shoulders like a cloud. Nanny Cole had sent up the sapphire pendant that now hung around Emma's neck, and the pair of satin pumps that graced her feet. Nanny Cole, Mattie had informed her, as she threaded a thin silver ribbon through Emma's hair, was a stickler for accessories.

Emma's hand dropped to her lap when Derek ambled in, wearing the same faded jeans and wrinkled workshirt he'd worn to Penford Harbor. He hadn't even bothered to comb his hair. At the sight of Emma, he stood stock-still, then spun on his heel and left the room.

Emma looked confusedly at Crowley, who responded with a silent shrug. The glass of lemonade had barely touched Emma's lips when the hall door banged open again and Nanny Cole barreled in, her twin set and tweed skirt still trailing bits of yarn and snippets of thread.

"Up you get," she commanded, and Emma jumped to her feet. "Let's have a look at you." Blushing furiously, Emma turned in a circle while Nanny Cole muttered, "Lady Nell was right. Color suits you." A needle-pricked finger jabbed in the direction of Emma's chair. "Sit," Nanny Cole barked. Raising her head, she bellowed, "Lady Nell! Front and center!"

Peter came out first. His eyes were bright with anticipation and a certain furtiveness, as though he knew a wonderful secret they were all about to share. He came to stand beside Emma, then fixed his gaze upon the open doorway and waited.

The lights dimmed suddenly, a match flared, and Emma heard the hiss of escaping gas. She looked over as Crowley held a match to a gleaming brass gaslight mounted on the wall above the chafing dishes. He replaced the frosted chimney before circumnavigating the room, lighting gaslights as he went. When he'd finished, the day nursery was flooded with a diffuse, golden light that made Emma's new dress shimmer.

On his way back to his post, Crowley paused at Emma's elbow. "Have no fear, Miss Porter," he murmured. "Lady Nell requested that we use the gaslights this evening, but they are merely a temporary arrangement."

"What the bloody hell else would they be?" thundered Nanny Cole, blazingly affronted. "Think we'd pipe *gas* to the *nursery?*" She would have gone on to greater heights of vituperation, but even Nanny Cole fell silent when Nell stepped into the room.

The little girl was wearing silk. Her gown was white and floor-length, high-waisted and puff-shouldered, with long, close-fitting sleeves. Lacy wrist-frills hid her dimpled hands, satin slippers peeped demurely past the seed pearls at her hem, and a diminutive tiara twinkled among her golden curls. Her small chocolate-brown escort wore a black top hat and a dashing black cape lined in red silk. Radiant in the gaslight's gentle glow, Nell regarded them serenely, a tiny, ethereal empress, a fairy queen of charm and dignity, holding court.

Nanny Cole caught herself in the midst of a curtsy, growled, "It'll do," and blustered from the room. Emma, who had risen at Nell's entrance, had to remind herself forcibly not to bend a knee when Nell offered her hand.

"Good evening, Emma." The little girl looked past Emma, and her composure cracked a bit. "Papa!" she exclaimed. *"Mais, que vous êtes beau!"*

"Speak English, if you please, Queen Eleanor." The good-natured remonstrance came over Emma's shoulder, and she turned to see Derek standing there, tall and broad-shouldered and flawlessly attired in white tie and tails, shoes polished, hair combed, and chin freshly shaved.

"That was fast," said Emma, trying not to stare.

"Had Hallard's help. Someone else's, too, I think." Derek looked suspiciously at his daughter. "I don't seem to recall packing this outfit."

Nell's innocent blue eyes widened. "I found it in the storeroom, back with Mum——"

"Why don't we all sit down?" Peter broke in. "Come on, Nell." He took his sister unceremoniously by the wrist and led her to the table.

Derek hesitated for a moment, then drew himself up to his full height, executed an elegant half bow, and offered his arm to Emma.

Nell proved to be a charming hostess, encouraging her father to tell of past adventures, which ranged from being chased by a disgruntled ewe through a hilly field in Yorkshire to finding himself at the business end of a broadsword wielded by a drunken caretaker who'd discovered him prying up floorboards in a summerhouse in Devon.

"Tell Emma what you did then," Nell coaxed.

"I know how much a broadsword weighs," Derek replied, with a self-effacing shrug. "It's no match for a crowbar."

Derek's anecdotes gradually gave way to another kind of conversation, in which his daughter took the lead. Derek listened avidly as Nell described her new play group, and seemed taken aback when she informed him that Peter had dropped out of the Boy Scouts. Slowly, it dawned on Emma that Nell was bringing her father up to date on happenings at home.

"Yorkshire, Devon—your job seems to involve a lot of travel,"

Emma observed, wondering how long it had been since Derek had really touched base with his children.

"It does," Derek agreed. "Didn't so much when Nell was little, but it's built up over the years."

"It can't be easy, with a family," Emma commented.

"Wasn't, at first, though having the workshop at home made it a bit easier. Had an au pair from Provence for a while—that's where Nell learnt her French. But now we have a marvelous housekeeper. Lives in. Treats Peter and Nell as though they were her own."

"She doesn't tell us stories," Nell pointed out. "Not like Aunt Dimity."

Emma put her fork down and looked questioningly at Derek. "That's the second time I've heard Nell mention that name. The duke said something about an Aunt Dimity, too. Who is she?"

"A kind woman we met while I was working on the church in Finch," Derek replied. "The Pyms introduced us to her."

"She lives in London, but she's bosom chums with Ruth and Louise," Nell informed her. "Aunt Dimity sent you here."

Derek smiled indulgently. "Forgive my daughter. She has an overactive imagination, though in this case she may be right. Dimity Westwood does good works through something called the Westwood Trust. Grayson's grandmother was on the board, as Grayson is now."

Emma nodded. "So Grayson spoke to Dimity, and Dimity spoke to the Pyms, and they—" She turned to Nell. "Perhaps you're right, Nell. Aunt Dimity may have had a hand in bringing me to Penford Hall."

"Of course she did," Nell said blithely.

"She tells fantastic stories," Peter put in. "Better than books."

"She looks after people," Nell said. She cast a sly glance at her father as she added, "And bears."

"Now, Nell, we've talked about Bertie before," Derek scolded gently. "It was splendid of Aunt Dimity to give him to you, but you know very well that she made him brand-new, just for you." Turning to Emma, he said, "Nell's convinced that Bertie was around when she was a baby, that he somehow disappeared, and that Aunt Dimity 're-turned' him to her. Don't know where she got the notion, but—"

"It's all right, Papa," Nell said forgivingly. "You just forgot, is all. Bertie says it's because you were so sad when Mama died."

Peter choked on a mouthful of lemonade, and Emma patted his back, feeling a jab of impatience as the now-familiar shadow settled over Derek's features. Surely the children were allowed to mention their own mother in his presence. Who else could they talk to about her? The housekeeper? The affairs of the Harris household were none of Emma's business, but she wasn't about to let Derek spoil the children's evening—or hers—with another wave of self-pity. Leaving Peter to Crowley's ministrations, she took the bull by the horns.

"Well," she said briskly, "I'm sure your father had a lot on his mind when your mother died, Nell, but that was a long time ago. You'd never forget Bertie now"—she kicked Derek under the table—"would you, Derek?"

Grunting, Derek shot her a look of pained surprise, but answered hastily, "No. Certainly not. How could I forget old Bertie?" Bending to rub his shin surreptitiously, he added, "Peter, what on earth are you doing?"

Peter had slipped away from the table. "I'm helping Mr. Crowley," the boy said, flushing.

"There's no need, Master Peter," the old man said. "I quite enjoy stacking crockery."

"Why don't you play with the Meccano set, Peter?" Nell suggested, with a sidelong look at Emma.

"Splendid idea," Derek said. Noting Emma's puzzled expression, he told her, "I believe they're called erector sets in the States. Bits of metal, pulleys, motors. It's quite good fun. Peter built a working drawbridge for a science fair last year. Had to go into the school to explain that engineering is, in fact, a science."

"But the table's full," Peter pointed out. "Where will I set it up?"

"Come on," said Emma, kicking off her shoes, "we'll set it up on the floor."

"On the floor?" Peter said doubtfully.

"Why not?" said Derek, loosening his tie.

The mechanical masterpiece they created that evening would have made Rube Goldberg proud. After a tentative start, Peter hunkered down beside Emma and Derek on the rug, his tongue between his teeth and his tie askew, totally absorbed. The three of them carried on long after Crowley had cleared the table, while Queen Eleanor sat sidesaddle on the rocking horse, holding Bertie in her arms, humming softly to herself, and smiling down on them.

Fourteen

Syd Bishop came back from Plymouth the following day, ostensibly to supervise the installation of a hospital bed and other medical equipment. In fact, it was Crowley who directed the workmen, and Mattie who took charge of Susannah's things, while the paunchy, balding agent sat in the library, a shaken man.

"She don't know me," he'd said, when Kate Cole had guided him into the dining room, where Emma, Derek, Peter, and Nell were just finishing a leisurely lunch. The children had greeted Mr. Bishop politely while Emma and Derek exchanged troubled glances. The man did not look well.

Kate looked even worse. "Susannah has regained consciousness," she told them. Her voice was rough-edged, her eyes were bruised with fatigue, and her dark hair was tangled. "She seems to have lost her memory"—Syd groaned and Kate tightened her hold on his arm—"but it may be only a temporary condition. Dr. Singh hopes she'll be able to travel soon." Kate leveled a meaningful stare at Derek as she added, "I think Mr. Bishop—Syd—could do with a stiff drink."

Derek rose from the table at once. "Peter, Nell—run along to Bantry and stay with him. I'll join you later." The children exited quietly through the French doors, while Derek moved to put a supporting arm around Syd's shoulders. "Buck up, old chap. Susannah must be a great deal better or there wouldn't be all this talk about releasing her from hospital. That's good news, wouldn't you say?" As he spoke, Derek steered Syd out of the room and down the hall toward the library.

Kate waited until they were out of sight, then walked shakily to the nearest chair and sat down, covering her face with her hands. Emma rose from her place to join Crowley, who was hovering over Kate, but Kate waved them both away. "Nothing wrong," she said weakly. "Stupid of me. Just tired."

Crowley folded his arms and looked down his long nose at Kate, "We've been missing our meals, haven't we, Miss Kate. We've been staying up until all hours." He clucked his tongue and stalked from the room in high dudgeon before Kate could say a word.

Emma gestured to the bowl of peaches, the silver coffee service. "Can I get you anything?" she asked.

"Crowley will see to it." Kate brushed a strand of hair back from her forehead and reached for a napkin.

"He's right, you know." Emma pulled a chair closer to Kate's and sat down. "You do look as though you've been burning the candle at both ends."

Kate leaned toward Emma, weaving slightly, punch-drunk with exhaustion. "Television, radio, newspapers, magazines—it takes some candle-burning to keep the lot of them away from the hall."

Emma nodded thoughtfully. "Yes, Bantry told me about the trouble Grayson had a few years ago. I suppose you've made a special study of trespassing laws?"

Kate responded with a short, humorless laugh. "Why bother when we've had so much practical experience?"

Emma looked at her uncertainly. "But Bantry told me you were a lawyer—a solicitor."

"Is that what Bantry told you?" Kate raised a hand to her cheek and chuckled softly. "The old dear must be protecting my reputation." Kate leaned back in her chair and sighed. "If I were as old as Crowley, or a man, it wouldn't pose such a problem, but a young woman sitting at the foot of Grayson's table without benefit of clergy . . . Can't blame Bantry, really. Sometimes I wonder what I'm doing here, too."

"Grayson seems to depend on you," Emma said.

"True," Kate agreed. "Especially now. It's a real mess this time."

"But you don't act as his solicitor?"

Kate sighed. "I'm just the girl from Penford Harbor, Grayson's childhood chum. Good old Kate, that's me." She closed her eyes. "Sorry, Emma. Good old Kate is feeling older than usual today."

"Don't worry—I know just how you feel." Emma raised a hand to straighten her glasses. "But if you're dissatisfied with the . . . the situation, why do you stay?"

Kate's eyes opened and she turned her head to stare at Emma for a moment before replying firmly, "Penford Hall is my home, too."

The two women sat in silence until Crowley returned, bearing a large bowl on a silver tray. The scent of chicken soup wafted across the room, reminding Emma of Herbert Munting and his multilevel henhouse in the village.

"Miss Kate," Crowley declared imperiously, "Madama has prepared this especially for you. You are not to leave the table until you've finished every drop." He placed the bowl before Kate and remained standing over her, as though he intended to keep track of each spoonful. "We wouldn't want your mother to see you like this, now, would we, Miss Kate?"

The wistful expression on Kate's face gave way to one of warm affection. She reached up and punched Crowley lightly on the arm. "Humbug," she said fondly. "Do you know how long it's been since you've threatened to turn me in to Mother?" She faced Emma. "He used to do it all the time when I was a little girl. Had me and Grayson trembling in our wellies till it dawned on us that he'd never really rat us out."

Unmoved, Crowley pointed sternly to the bowl. "The bouillon is cooling rapidly, Miss Kate."

"Will we see you at supper?" Emma asked.

" 'Fraid not. I only came back to make sure Syd got here in one piece. It's all been a bit much for him. Gash will drive me back to Plymouth this evening, and I'll stay there with Grayson to arrange for Susannah's return. Dr. Singh thinks we should be able to bring her back in three or four days."

Crowley opened the hall door. "I beg your pardon most sincerely, Miss Porter, but Miss Kate really must eat, then get some rest."

Kate smiled wryly and picked up her spoon. "If you'll excuse me, Emma, the warder here prohibits talk during mealtimes."

Good old Kate is growing restless, Emma thought as she headed for the library. Still, it was unlikely that she'd ever leave Penford Hall. She seemed to love the place as much as Grayson, and the staff treated her with a special tenderness. To Bantry, Kate was the pride of Penford Harbor, and she was clearly the apple of Crowley's eye.

Slowing her pace, Emma thought back to her conversation with Bantry early that morning. She'd found him in the kitchen garden, watering the vines on the birdcage arbor. When she'd asked if he knew what had happened to the oilcloth, he'd led her to a side room that served as his potting shed. It had been roofed over with tightly joined wooden boards and fitted out with a workbench, shelves, cupboards, a pegboard with hooks, and a standing pipe that supplied water from the hall.

Bantry had pulled the oilcloth from behind a coil of rope in one of the large cupboards. It had been washed and neatly folded, but Emma could see a ragged tear at one corner, where a grommet had been pulled out.

"Gash brought it back with him from Plymouth," Bantry told her, "after he dropped off Kate and His Grace. Have to remember to bring it down to Ted Tregallis for mending."

Emma fingered the frayed edges thoughtfully. "Did you tear it when you uncovered the wheelbarrow the other day?"

"What're you talkin' about, Miss Emma?" Bantry squinted at her, perplexed. "I never uncovered the barrow, and I'd've had a thing or two to say to anyone who did. Don't hold with leavin' things lyin' about for the damp to get at 'em." He put the oilcloth back in the cupboard and brushed his palms together. "Nope. Lads on the chopper must've torn it, when they was loadin' poor Miss Susannah aboard."

Or, thought Emma, turning into the long corridor near the library, someone yanked the oilcloth off of the barrow hard enough to tear it. She slowed her pace once more. Peter had discovered blood on the handle of the grub hoe, hadn't he? Emma came to a full stop as a moving image filled her mind.

In the clear light of morning, a faceless figure ripped the oilcloth from the barrow, seized the hoe, and swung the long handle at Susannah's head. Susannah crumpled soundlessly and tumbled down the stairs. Panicked, the attacker shoved the hoe back into the barrow and fled the garden, leaving Susannah for dead.

Could that person have been Kate? Kate seemed to share Grayson's fanatic loyalty to Penford Hall, and where there was fanaticism, there might be violence. Emma removed her glasses and pinched the bridge of her nose unhappily. She liked Kate. She admired the way Kate had kept her head when dealing with the emergency in the garden, and her temper when faced by Susannah's taunting. Still, Emma conceded reluctantly, Kate had a motive to silence Susannah. If the duke's cousin exposed a cover-up of Lex's murder, Kate Cole would lose everything she held dear.

As she approached the library, Emma felt a prick of anger toward Susannah for stirring things up, but it passed quickly. No one deserved a death sentence for asking uncomfortable questions. Emma reminded herself that she would do better to reserve her anger for the person who'd passed that sentence. Replacing her glasses, she opened the library door. Derek caught sight of her, got up from his chair, and crossed to meet her.

"Derek," she began, but he cut her off.

"Not now," he murmured. "Think you should hear what Syd has to say."

Syd was seated on the couch. His face was ashen and the whiskey glass trembled in his hand. A fire was burning in the hearth and he stared at it without blinking. He didn't seem to notice Emma's arrival or Derek's return. "Poor kid," he mumbled. "Poor kid."

Derek slid into his chair and waited for Emma to take the one beside him. He rested his hands on the arms of the chair, crossed his legs, then asked in a soft, level voice, "You've known Susannah for a very long time, haven't you, Syd?"

It was like watching a hypnotist at work. Syd, the compliant subject, sat motionless, speaking in a flat monotone, as though a tape recorder were unreeling somewhere inside of him. "My grandpa was a tailor, and my old man went a step up, into fashion. That's how I got my start, setting up my old man's London office. Small potatoes, nothing fancy, not like them big shots on Savile Row. Stupid bastards wouldn't take a look at Suzie."

"But you would," said Derek.

"You bet I would. Suzie's ma brought her to me when she was, let's see, now . . . fifteen? Luckiest day in my life. Never seen anything like her. A regular ice princess. There's a lotta guys'd give a kid like that all kinds of crap. Not me. Always looked out for her. Never let her take crap offa nobody."

"You worked very hard to get her started," prompted Derek.

"Not as hard as Suzie. Lotta kids know what they want. Not so many want to work to get it. Always been a hard worker, Suzie has." Syd paused to wet his lips, then went on in his low monotone. "She hadda be, after her old man blew his brains out."

Emma turned, wide-eyed, to Derek, who motioned her to silence, then resumed his gentle interrogation. "When did that happen, Syd?"

"Like I told you, Suzie was just a kid. Her old man got suckered into some cheesy investments and lost his shirt." Syd shrugged. "Who hasn't? There's worse things could happen to a person, am I right? This poor schmuck didn't think so. Checked into a hotel in Ipswich and put a gun in his mouth. Left Suzie's ma in hock up to her fanny. That's how come Suzie started working. That's how come she won't quit."

"Why should she quit, Syd?" Derek's voice suggested only mild curiosity, but his knuckles were white on the arms of his chair.

"Not so much work anymore. Not top dollar. Not for a while now. It's a short-term deal, am I right? Fashions change, models get old. One day you're it, the next day the phone stops ringing. Happens alla time. Truth is, Suzie's broke."

"But she was so successful," Derek protested.

"She hadda pay off her old man's debts. And support her old lady. And now she's buyin' stuff she can't afford. What else is new? It's hard to swallow, knowin' nobody wants you. Don't know how we're gonna handle the doctor bills."

"I've told you not to worry about that," Derek soothed. "I'm sure that Grayson will see to anything the National Health doesn't cover."

"Damn right he will. He owes it to her."

Derek leaned forward in his chair. "How do you mean, he owes it to her?"

Syd slowly turned to face Derek, like a teacher disappointed by an inattentive pupil. "I told you," he said wearily. "Grayson's father, he's the one gave the bad tip to Suzie's dad. He's the reason Suzie's dad killed himself." He reached out a shaking hand to pat Derek's knee. "Hey, it's history, am I right? Maybe it'll work out for the best. Could be the publicity's all Suzie needs to get back on top." The old man's eyes returned to the fire. "Once they fix her kisser . . ."

Derek went to sit beside Syd. He removed the whiskey glass from the older man's unresisting grasp and placed it on the end table. "Why don't you let Hallard take you upstairs for a nice lie-down?" he suggested. "It'll do you a world of good."

"Yeah. I could use some shut-eye. Gotta be fresh for Suzie." Sid looked down at his rumpled plaid jacket and touched a finger to his gaudy floral tie. "Lookit me. A regular fashion plate."

Emma gazed through her glass of whiskey at the fire. The flames blurred and flickered, but they seemed to give off little heat. Derek stood close to the fire, one arm resting on the mantelpiece, as though he, too, had felt the sudden chill.

"I wonder . . ." Emma murmured. "Grayson knew all along that he'd inherit Penford Hall and that he'd need a fortune to restore it. Do you think he befriended Lex—"

"In order to kill him and take his money?" Derek shook his head. "Doubtful. If Grayson could've predicted Lex's success, he could've made his fortune in the music industry."

"I suppose you're right," Emma conceded. "But he must have known about Lex's drinking habits. And everyone knew how wild he was. Richard once said that Lex would do anything on a dare. So, when opportunity knocked . . ."

". . . Grayson simply arranged for Lex to kill himself." Derek nodded. "Very convenient. Who's Richard?"

"An old friend," Emma said, too carelessly. "He was a big fan of Lex's."

"Poor chap. Tone-deaf?"

Emma suppressed an unseemly snort of laughter and ignored the question. "So what have we come up with? Grayson arranges Lex's death and embezzles his money—electronically. Susannah, looking for a way to avenge her father's suicide, roots out Winslow—your boyhood friend, the banker—and Winslow discovers something funny about Lex's books. Susannah comes to Penford Hall bent on blackmail—"

"To punish the House of Penford for her father's death," Derek put in.

"And she ends up with her head caved in."

"That seems to be the gist," said Derek.

Emma frowned. "But it's been five years since Lex died. Why did Susannah wait so long to make her move?"

"Had to woo a cooperative banker?" Derek suggested. "It'd take some time to sweep old Winslow off his feet." Sighing, he finished the last of his whiskey and set the glass on the mantelpiece. "What a tangled web we've woven, Emma. And not a single strand to show to the police."

"I'm not so sure about that." Emma tapped a finger against the side of her glass. "Susannah wouldn't have come to Penford Hall empty-handed, not with a score like that to settle. I think Winslow told her more than she let on. I'm willing to bet that she came here with some sort of hard evidence to flaunt in Grayson's face."

"A pity she can't tell us where to find it," Derek commented. "What do you make of Susannah's amnesia, by the way? Could she be faking it?"

"Possibly. The smartest thing she can do is pretend she's forgotten everything. She's at their mercy, after all." Emma swirled the whiskey in her glass. "I had an interesting conversation with Kate after you left. She's just as crazy about Penford Hall as Grayson is."

"Unfortunate choice of words," Derek said, "but I see your point. It would make sense for Susannah to approach Grayson through Kate. She does act as his lieutenant."

"I was thinking . . . Maybe Kate scheduled a meeting in the chapel garden to discuss Susannah's demands. And maybe the meeting got out of hand." Emma quickly recounted the scenario she'd envisioned: the confrontation in the garden, the angry exchange of words, the sudden grab for the hoe's long handle, the tearing of the oilcloth, the silent fall, the panicked escape. "Whoever tore the oilcloth from the wheelbarrow knows something about Susannah's accident," Emma concluded. "I'd hoped we might be able to dust the oilcloth for fingerprints or something. But when I checked with Bantry this morning, he'd already cleaned it."

Derek had strolled away from the fire and was standing very near Emma's chair. He looked down at her in silence for what seemed a long time, then nodded, as though confirming something. "You're very good at that, you know."

"At what?" Emma touched a hand to her glasses self-consciously.

"Thinking things through. Imagining what it must have been like. Not my strong point, imagination."

"It's not mine, either," Emma protested. "I just try to think logically."

"Nonsense," Derek chided gently. "You've a very creative mind. A logical one, as well, but what good is logic without intuition?" Shoving his hands into the pockets of his faded jeans, he turned to face the fire. "Why didn't you tell me about the oilcloth last night in the nursery?"

"Oh, I don't know." The firelight made Derek's blue eyes sparkle as brightly as they had the night before. "It just didn't seem to be the right time or place, I guess."

"Suppose not," Derek agreed. "Had a splendid evening, though." He glanced shyly at Emma. "You?"

Emma's energetic nod sent whiskey sloshing onto the Persian carpet. As Derek knelt to wipe it up, Emma shrank back in her chair, crimson with embarrassment.

"Meant to thank you for the swift kick, by the way," Derek said. "I was drifting, wasn't I. Nell's complained of it before, but I thought she was just . . . being Nell. Don't understand what she's getting at half the time. A kick on the shin, though. Hard to ignore." He sat back on his heels, and his gaze was level with Emma's. "Was I really that bad?"

Emma wanted to comfort him, but couldn't. From everything she'd seen and heard, Nell's complaints seemed sadly justified. Carefully placing her whiskey glass on the end table, she said, "You must miss your wife terribly."

Derek looked down at the damp handkerchief in his hands. "Sometimes—when I'm working—I forget."

"Is that why you work so much?" Emma asked, very gently.

Derek raised his eyes, perplexed. "Not at all. That's for the children. I want to give Peter and Nell everything Mary wanted them to have."

She would have wanted them to have more time with their father, Emma thought, but she said nothing. She had no right to tell Derek how to run his life.

"Well, anyway, thanks." Derek's gaze lingered on Emma for a moment, then he rose to his feet, stuffed the handkerchief into his back pocket, and returned to stand before the fire. "Funny, really," he said, folding his arms. "I like Grayson enormously and I don't care a fig for Susannah. Yet all I can think about is protecting her from him. It's because she's helpless, I suppose."

"As helpless as we are," murmured Emma. Clearing her throat, she added quickly, "I mean, there's not much we can do to protect her, is there?"

"Not unless we can talk with her, find out if she has anything we can show to the authorities." Derek turned to stare at the fire. "Kate said she was due back in three or four days? Not sure what we should do. Let me think about it."

"I will, too. In the garden." Emma got to her feet. "Derek," she said hesitantly, "if you're not doing anything else, I could—that is, Bantry and I could use some help out there."

"I know," said Derek, his eyes still on the fire. "Nell told me. Unfortunately, I'm still looking for Grayson's bloody lantern."

Fifteen

As it happened, a mild pulmonary infection kept Susannah in the hospital for ten days. During that time, her head injuries improved steadily and her memory began to return, though it was sketchy and incomplete. She recognized Grayson and called him by name, but Kate's existence seemed to have, literally, slipped her mind. Overall, however, she seemed to be well on the way to recovery. Kate called every day with a progress report, which Mattie cheerfully passed along to Emma every morning.

Kate's public-relations campaign and Newland's cordon of watchers seemed to be paying off. Reporters who showed up at the gates were politely informed that His Grace would answer questions or pose for pictures at his hotel in Plymouth. The few who sneaked in over the walls were escorted from the grounds before they'd gotten halfway through the woods.

Still others tried their luck in Penford Harbor, where they were met not by resentful silence but by an avalanche of monologues. The Tregallis brothers regaled them with fishing stories, Herbert Munting lectured them on chickens, and Jonah Pengully grumbled about everything under the sun—except the one thing the reporters wanted him to grumble about. Like the other villagers, Jonah refused to say a word about the duke.

"It was brilliant," Derek enthused when he returned from a foray into the village. "Like watching a football match. Every time Grayson's name came up, Jack tossed the story to James, who booted it to Ted, who slipped right back into some flummery about cod-fishing." The village team won the match hands down, routing the visitors without giving up a point. The newspaper coverage slowed to a back-page trickle.

Nanny Cole continued to supplement Emma's wardrobe with dresses in fine wool, velvet, and hand-printed silk, hand-knitted sweaters in slate blue and dusty rose, two more pairs of trousers, and a third gardening smock. By the end of the ten days, Emma felt as though she'd acquired a private couturière, and Mattie shared her delight, pointing out details of workmanship that Emma never would have noticed. Emma's sole attempt to express her gratitude in person was met with a gruff "Stop being a ninny and get *out* of my workroom." After that, Emma simply made sure that the workroom was graced with fresh flowers every day.

She and Bantry spent long afternoons in the library, making up plant lists and discussing what would go where in the chapel garden. Bantry would use only rough copies of Emma's sketches, insisting that the duke would want to frame the originals, and he agreed with Emma's strong intuition that everything planted in the chapel garden should come from the other gardens of Penford Hall. "The dowager duchess would've wanted it that way," he said approvingly. "And we've plenty of plants to choose from."

It was an understatement, as Emma soon learned. The garden rooms in the castle ruins were as varied and as well tended as any Emma had ever seen. The rock garden was a swirling pastel watercolor—sky-blue primroses and white candytuft, purple lobelia and rosy-pink soapwort. The candytuft and primroses, Emma thought, would look wonderful edging the flagstone walk and the reflecting pool.

Clouds of early blossoms graced the rose garden, and Bantry told her all about the ones not yet in bloom. Emma chose a fragrant nineteenth-century Bourbon rose—*Madame Isaac Pereire,* Bantry informed her—to frame the green door, and a hybrid tea rose to plant beside the wooden bench.

Emma was enchanted by the knot garden. The close-clipped, interlocking chains of low-growing hedges formed a charming double-knot pattern that enclosed a marvelous selection of herbs. There, she discovered the deep purple-blue lavender she would use on either side of the chapel door, along with red sage, bronze fennel, angelica, and golden balm. She found a treasure trove in the perennial border she'd seen the first time she'd entered the castle ruins. Transplanted clematis and delphiniums would soften the stark granite walls, and irises, peonies, lilies, columbines, and a host of other old-fashioned flowers would restore color, form, and texture to the raised beds.

"I'd like a pair of butterfly bushes to tuck into the corners, where the chapel wall meets the garden wall," Emma explained to Bantry, "and a different climbing rose in the center of each of the long walls. We'll plant tall perennials to fill the space between the roses and the corner ledges—lupines, hollyhocks, that sort of thing—with shorter ones in front. The bottom tier should have trailing plants spilling out onto the lawn. The rosy-pink soapwort would work, or the verbena. And we'll need something special to put on the corner ledges."

"We've some nice orchids in the hothouse," Bantry offered.

"Hothouse?" Emma echoed. She hadn't noticed one in the house plans Derek had shown her.

"His Grace put it in year afore last," Bantry explained. "Miss Kate's partial to orchids."

They spent the next day in Penford Hall's conservatory, a two-story glass-enclosed set of rooms tucked away in the west wing. One section was devoted to orchids, ferns, and waving palms, another to miniature fruit trees and topiary, and a third, Emma noted with some amusement, was the source of Nell's almost constant supply of strawberries. Between the conservatory and the garden rooms, she found everything she'd need.

"Don't mean to sound sour, Miss Emma," Bantry cautioned, "but the chapel garden won't be at its best in August."

"I know that, and you know that, but I'm afraid we'll have a hard time convincing Grayson," said Emma, with a sigh. "He told me not to worry about getting it perfect, but I don't think he understands just how imperfect it'll be."

"Aye." Bantry squinted into the distance. "Be patchy this year, a bit better next. Mebbe the year after that it'll begin to come into its own. A good garden takes time."

Bantry knew what he was talking about. He displayed an awesome knowledge of the plants under his care, and spoke of them with an air of affectionate familiarity. "This 'un's daft," he commented, pointing to an early-blooming scarlet rambler. "Thinks it's June already. Does it every year, like it can't wait to come out and say hello."

Bantry's organizational skills were equally impressive. He'd trained a small cadre of dedicated undergardeners to help him with the mammoth task of maintenance. One by one, Emma met them, sixteen villagers in all, from shy, eleven-year-old Daphne Minion, whose special love was the knot garden, to placid, eighty-six-year-old Bert Potts, who tended the pleached apple trees that bordered the great lawn.

When Emma complimented Bantry on his talent for managing people, he responded casually that his time at Wisley Gardens had served him well. That was how Emma learned that Bantry had spent ten years at the Royal Horticultural Society's 150-acre centerpiece. He'd shrugged off her breathless questions by saying that, all in all, he preferred Penford Hall, where he didn't have to put up with "them smelly tour buses."

That revelation led to several others. When Emma told Derek of Bantry's illustrious past, he reminded her of a conversation that had taken place in the library the night Emma had arrived. Under pressure from Susannah, he recalled, Kate had acknowledged that she and Nanny Cole had once lived in Bournemouth. Bantry, Kate, and Nanny Cole—three of Penford Hall's mainstays—had apparently been forced to leave the hall for greener pastures at some point in the distant past. Curious, Emma and Derek decided to see if the same held true for the rest of the staff.

Judicious questioning of Mattie revealed that Crowley had been living in a furnished bedsitter in Plymouth when Mattie was born. Hallard, Gash, and Newland, Derek learned, had each spent some years in London. With the sole exception of Madama Rulenska, it appeared that all of the servants had left Penford Hall at some point.

Clearly, Susannah's father hadn't been the only one to suffer from the old duke's reversal of fortune. As they sat together in the library four days after Syd's return, Derek theorized that Penford Hall had been all but deserted, much like the village.

"Grayson's father gave them all the sack," Derek concluded, "and

Grayson, when he was able, hired them back. Argues for a high degree of loyalty. A pity."

"We can't really trust anyone," Emma agreed sadly.

"We can, though," said Derek. He leaned forward. "Syd's an outsider, and he'd do anything to protect his Suzie. And it wouldn't seem strange for him to want to stay by her side." Derek sighed. "If only we could figure out a way to snap him out of his funk."

Emma nodded. Visibly aged, Syd had taken meals in his room since his return from Plymouth. According to Crowley, he simply sat and stared out of the window. Emma knew where she went when she was upset, but it was ridiculous to assume that the same thing would work for Syd. Or was it?

"Derek," she said slowly, "this is probably going to sound silly, but. . . what if I took Syd out to work in the garden with me?"

"Green-thumb therapy?" Derek mulled the idea over, then shrugged. "Why not? It'd get his mind off of things, get him moving again. Not at all silly."

"I'll ask him tomorrow morning." Emma looked at the fire, feeling satisfied.

Derek cleared his throat. "About the chapel garden," he began. "Sorry I haven't been out to lend a hand. Blasted lantern search is turning out to be more complicated than I'd expected. Place is honeycombed with tunnels."

"Sounds spooky."

Derek smiled. "Not really. Miss the sun, though. Seem to spend all of my time in the dark lately." He glanced at Emma, then looked down at the toes of his workboots. "Miss our little talks, too."

"Do you?" Emma said, taken by surprise. "So do I. I wish we didn't have to talk about such gruesome things, though."

"Know what you mean. Seems we've skipped over the civilized chitchat and gone straight to . . . well . . . murder, theft, attempted murder, and suicide. You know, I always thought detective work would be fascinating, and it is, but it's also a bit . . ."

"Disturbing?" Emma offered.

"Indeed." He bit his lip, then turned toward her. "Look, why don't we give ourselves an evening off? Just talk about . . . well, anything. I feel as though I hardly know you."

"There's not much to know," said Emma, with a shrug. "I was born and raised in Connecticut, but I've lived in the Boston area all of my adult life. I went to MIT and got a job right out of college. I'm still with the same firm, though I've moved up a few rungs on the corporate ladder. I love my work and, as you've probably noticed by now, I love gardening, too. And that's about it." Emma sighed. Her life sounded strangely barren, even to her own ears. "To tell you the truth, Penford Hall's the most exciting thing that's ever happened to me."

"For me, it was the birth of my children," said Derek. "Don't mean to be a bore, but Peter and Nell truly are the most wonderful son and daughter a man could ask for." He reached down to brush a fleck of dust from his left boot. "Have any? Children, I mean."

"No." Emma touched a finger to her glasses. "I never really wanted any."

"Never wanted children?" Derek murmured doubtfully. "I must say that I can't imagine what life would be like without Peter and Nell. But, of course, with your work and, er, being on your own, I suppose it's very sensible of you not to have any. That is, I mean, if you *are* on your own." He gave a nervous cough and looked toward the fire. "Don't mean to pry. It's just that Nell was wondering and, well, I told her that, naturally, there must be *someone* in your life. This Richard fellow . . . ?"

"Richard got married two months ago," Emma informed him.

"Married?" Derek swung sideways in his chair to face her, incredulous. "To someone *else?*"

Declarations of independence, statistics on divorce, and cogent arguments against outmoded social contracts darted through Emma's mind, but none of them seemed as important at that moment as the marvelous, miraculous fact that she was sitting down and empty-handed. She couldn't cover herself in mud or throw her silverware around the room or spill anything on the priceless carpet but tears, and for some reason she didn't feel at all like crying. Unaccountably tongue-tied, Emma bowed her head to hide her confusion and, with rapidly blurring vision, watched her glasses slide off the end of her nose.

Emma's hand shot out, but Derek's got there first. Arm length and perfect vision were on his side: the glasses landed squarely in his palm. He looked up and his fingers brushed the side of Emma's face as he reached for the left arm of the glasses, which was still hooked behind Emma's ear. As he removed it, Emma felt a tickling sensation and shivered, goosebumps running all up and down her arms.

"Looks like a screw's popped out," said Derek. "I'll have a look round." He got down on his hands and knees to examine the carpet minutely. A moment later, he sat back on his heels and held out his hand, triumphant. "Found it," he said. "I've very good eyes, you know."

"Oh, God," Emma breathed.

Derek's salt-and-pepper curls tumbled forward as he bent low over Emma's glasses, and his strong hands were as dextrous as a surgeon's as he put the tiny screw back into place and tightened it with his thumbnail.

He's a grieving widower, Emma reminded herself sternly. He's got a son and a daughter and a house near Oxford and he's English and he's completely and totally out of the question.

"Not only tone-deaf but a fool as well," Derek was saying. "Of course, who knows where I might've ended up if I hadn't met Mary? Matter of luck as much as anything. The right person. The right time and place."

Emma stared at him blindly and clenched her hands in her lap to keep them from reaching out to brush the curls back from his forehead. It's Penford Hall, she thought. It's the fire and the rain and the sense of isolation that stirs up this foolish feeling of us-against-the-world. It will pass, she told herself. She knew exactly what the future held in store. She'd planned it years ago.

"There." Derek polished the lenses with his shirttail, then bent forward to slip the glasses into place on Emma's face. He frowned suddenly. "Emma," he said, "are you crying?"

Emma brushed the tear away and got to her feet. "It's nothing. I'm just overtired. I've had a long day and there's a lot to do tomorrow. Think I'll turn in."

Derek said nothing, but Emma could feel his blue eyes on her until she closed the library door behind her.

Pleased by Emma's invitation, Syd was as pliant as a lamb. He leaned on her arm as he shuffled slowly down the stone steps in the chapel garden, where Bantry and the children were already hard at work.

"My old man was a businessman," Syd informed her, "and so was his old man. But both of 'em were farmers at heart, you get me? Country people. My grandpa, he grew tomatoes would make your mouth water. And my pop, he always kept a nice patch of pansies for my kid sister, Betty." Syd looked vaguely around at the half-stripped walls and the withered vegetation. "Whatsamatter here?" he asked. "You got a drought or something?"

Nell moved to Syd's side and placed a trowel in his hand. "Come and help me dig up dandelions, Mr. Bishop. Some of them are perfect beasts."

Syd turned the trowel in his hands, then reached out to pat Nell's head. "Sure, Princess, sure. You show me the dandelions, I'll dig 'em up for you."

Peter looked askance at Syd's freckled pate, left the garden, and returned a short time later with a shapeless, broad-brimmed straw hat that had been hanging on the pegboard in Bantry's potting shed. "Here," he said shyly, offering the hat. "It gets pretty sunny out here sometimes."

"Hey, Petey-boy, thanks a million. That's some chapeau." Syd admired the hat at arm's length, then plopped it on his head. "Need to take care of the old noodle, huh? That's real thoughtful of you. You gonna help us out with these here dandelions?"

Syd spent the rest of the morning pottering contentedly from dandelion to dandelion and chatting with the children, the straw hat pulled low on his forehead, his checked pants acquiring a patina of rich, dark soil. When lunchtime came around, he was reluctant to leave, and though he took a nap that afternoon, he was back in the garden the following morning, with a surer step and a clearer mind. The news of Susannah's extended stay at the hospital didn't seem to faze him, and by the next day, Emma was convinced that her green-thumb therapy was working.

She doubted that it would have been half as effective without the children's help. Peter had taken to gardening with a vengeance, and now spent most of his waking hours near the chapel. Nell's approach was more relaxed but no less productive. Her daisy chains decorated Syd's hat and the handles of the old wheelbarrow, and her posies brightened the shelves in the potting shed and the bedside table in the rose suite.

In the evenings, when the tools were put away and the sun was sinking low on the horizon, Nell entertained them all with stories of the bold Sir Bertram's amazing deeds. Emma found herself unexpectedly caught up in Bertie's battles with the evil Queen Beatrice, and Syd was vastly amused by the misadventures of the lazy buffoon, Higgins.

The only one who wasn't amused was Derek, and that was because he never showed his face in the garden. Nell seemed serenely unconcerned about her father's absence, but, though Peter said little, it was hard to ignore the way his head swung around every time the green door opened, and difficult to miss the disappointment in his eyes when Bantry or Syd Bishop came through it.

Emma told herself that it was just as well. She wasn't sure what was going on between them, but, whatever it was, she wanted to stop it before it got out of hand. It would be unfair to Peter and Nell for her and Derek to start something they couldn't finish. Children needed a future, and that was the one thing Emma couldn't possibly give them.

Sixteen

On the eighth evening of the long week following Susannah's accident, Emma dined alone. The candles were lit in the dining room, and Crowley saw her to her chair, but hers was the only place set at the table. Crowley informed her that the children had eaten supper in the nursery with Nanny Cole, and Syd Bishop had taken a light meal on a tray in his room, then gone directly to bed.

"He's not ill, Miss Porter," Crowley assured her, when she expressed mild concern. "Quite the contrary. He informed Hallard that he was retiring early because he intended to be, er, 'up and at 'em' at the break of dawn. Gardening seems to agree with him."

As for Derek, Crowley knew only that Mr. Harris had retired to his room late that afternoon, leaving strict instructions that he was not to be disturbed by the staff.

Emma told herself that she'd worn her newest Nanny Cole creation—a flowery William Morris print in bronze and gold and copper—to suit herself, not to please Derek. Still, she had to admit that, if she'd known that Crowley would be her sole companion in the dining room, she might not have anticipated supper quite so eagerly.

Emma ate quickly, then went up to her room to change into a skirt and blouse and pull on Nanny Cole's heathery angora sweater. She left her room for the library, stopping just long enough to knock on Derek's door, hoping that his instructions to the staff did not apply to her. Receiving no reply, she went on her way. She was usually in bed and asleep by ten o'clock, but she'd been meaning to read up on old Bourbon roses and tonight seemed the perfect opportunity. She peeked into a few other rooms on her way to the main staircase, then wandered into the billiards room, the music room, the drawing room, and various salons on the first floor before settling in the library with one eye on her book and the other on the tall case clock in the corner.

When the clock chimed ten, Emma decided that what she really needed was a breath of fresh air. Armed with a flashlight provided by Crowley, she made straight for the chapel. The moon had not yet risen, and stars blanketed the sky. The castle ruins were a maze of shadows, and she had to step carefully to avoid falling on her face. She wasn't hurrying, she was simply walking briskly, because it was a proven fact that exercise promoted sound sleep and she had every intention of sleeping soundly that night. When she pushed open the chapel's low rounded door, she saw immediately that Derek wasn't inside.

But his son was. Peter was wearing a blue melton jacket over striped pajamas, and warm woolen socks stuffed into brown leather slippers, and he carried a Day-Glo–orange emergency lantern, the kind Emma kept in the trunk of her car at home. He was halfway to the back door by the time Emma's flashlight picked him out, but when she spoke his name, he stopped.

"I'm sorry," said Emma. "I didn't mean to disturb you. I'll go away, if you like."

Peter glanced over his shoulder at her, then looked away again. He shrugged. "I don't mind if you stay."

Emma hesitated. She respected Peter's privacy, but she was curious to know what had lured him to the chapel in the dead of night. He hadn't struck her as the kind of boy who would get up to any mischief, but he was obviously AWOL from the nursery. What had compelled him to risk the wrath of Nanny Cole?

Emma walked slowly up the center aisle. "I'd rather not stay by myself," she said, sitting on the front bench. She was careful to speak softly. She didn't want Peter darting out the back door in the dark.

Peter turned the lantern on and placed it on the shelf below the lady window, then backed slowly to the bench and sat beside Emma, his hands jammed in his jacket pockets, his eyes never leaving the lady's face.

"She's beautiful, isn't she?" he murmured.

"Yes, she is." Even in the darkness, the window retained its power. The lantern picked out glimmerings of color and softened the fire in the lady's eyes. Her face hovered above them, serene as a full moon sailing across a midnight sky.

"Dad says that lots of people think Miss Ashley-Woods is beautiful," said Peter. "But I don't."

Emma kept her voice steady as she asked, "Why not?"

"She's all bones," Peter replied bluntly, "and she has mean eyes. She was bothering Dad all the time before you came. Keeping him from his job."

A job that was, for some reason, very important to the boy. A chill hand seemed to grip Emma's heart. Oh, no, she thought, could it be as simple and as terrible as this?

"Peter," she said, "is this where you were that morning, when Miss Ashley-Woods fell down the stairs?"

Peter's body tensed and for a moment Emma thought he might bolt. Instead, he gave a forlorn sigh and bowed his head, and the tension left his body as tears began, silently, steadily, falling bright as diamonds on his dark wool jacket.

"Nanny Cole told me to play outside," he said, "but—but I didn't want to. She's supposed to give me lessons and she wouldn't and I was—was angry."

"So you came out here instead?" Emma prompted gently.

"I'm not supposed to," the boy admitted. "Dad—Dad wants me to get fresh air and—and sunshine. But I like it here. The lady needs me." The boy sniffed, then scrubbed at his nose with the sleeve of his jacket.

"Needs you?" Emma asked.

"To tell her that everything will be all right." Peter put a fist to his forehead and uttered a strangled moan. "But I don't know . . . I don't know if it will be anymore. No one will listen to me."

Emma put an arm around the boy's shoulders, then tightened her hold as he turned to bury his face in the soft angora sweater. Awkwardly, tenderly, she smoothed his dark hair. "Did you hear anything while you were in here that morning?" she asked. She hated herself for pressing the point, but she had to hear Peter's reply.

Peter tilted his tear-streaked face up to her. "Not until the shouting started. Then I went out that way"—he pointed to the back door—"and round the outside to the cliff path. I—I didn't want Dad to know I'd been in here. I've never disobeyed him before."

Emma could well believe it. Peter was the most obedient child she'd ever met. "Did anyone see you go out onto the cliff path?" she asked softly.

Peter nodded. "Teddy Tregallis was down in the harbor, on the boat with his dad and his uncles. They all looked up and waved, so I waved back. He's a good chap, Teddy. He's going to be a fisherman when he grows up. He says he likes fishing more than school."

Emma looked down into the boy's luminous eyes and knew he was telling the truth. He wouldn't have admitted to witnesses, otherwise; it would be too easy for her to confirm his whereabouts with the Tregallises. Peter had disobeyed his father's orders and Nanny Cole's instructions, and he'd compounded his wrongdoing by lying about it afterward, but that was the worst of it, and Emma was weak with relief.

"I don't see any reason to tell your father where you were," she said. "I don't think anyone else has to know. Okay?"

The boy gulped and nodded, then lay his head against her, as though the confession had drained his last reserves of energy. Emma thought for a moment that he had fallen asleep, but then he spoke, in a voice so low that she scarcely caught the words.

"Dad says she's perfect and Grayson says her cloak should be gray. But they're both wrong." He sighed. "She should be wearing white."

"That's what the legend says," Emma agreed.

"It's nothing to do with the legend," Peter insisted. "I just know that's how she's supposed to be."

If Emma had had more experience with children, she might have tried to persuade him, for his own good, that his father knew best. But Peter spoke with such conviction that she was willing, for the moment, to try to see the lady as Peter saw her. Closing her eyes, Emma conjured up an image of the cloaked and hooded lady, clad in white.

Slowly, the picture took shape. Streaks of purple, violet, and aquamarine filled the stormy sky, the sea was a swirling mosaic of greens flecked with silvery froth, and the lantern's blaze split the darkness like a bolt of lightning. Now, Emma thought, what would it be like if the cloak and hood were . . .

The image came to her with startling clarity. The billowing black cloak became a pair of celestial wings, and the hood encircling the raven hair was transformed into a glowing nimbus. My god, Emma thought, it's an angel. There was no mistaking it, and she knew beyond all doubt who that dark-haired angel was in Peter's eyes.

"Can you see her, too?" Peter whispered.

Emma could only nod. How could anyone fail to see it? Derek must have known what the window would become once he changed the glass. Had it been too painful for him to face the image of his dead wife, here in this lonely place?

"Dad will listen to you," Peter said.

Emma knew what he was asking, but she had no desire to interfere in Derek's work and no right to intrude on his grief. She wanted to leave the chapel, to forget about the window, but the boy held her there, looking up at her with such hope and trust that she couldn't back away.

Again, she nodded. "I'll try," she promised. "It may not happen right away. It may not happen at all. But I'll try."

"It'll happen," Peter declared, adding more softly, "It has to."

Emma trembled inwardly. "It's getting late," she said. "I think I'll try to get some sleep. How about you?"

Peter stood and together they went back into the hall and up the main staircase to the nursery, where Nell was waiting for them, sitting on the rocking horse, with Bertie in her arms.

"Nanny Cole's snoring like a grampus," Nell informed them.

"You should be asleep, too," Peter scolded. He lifted Nell down from the rocking horse, buttoned the top button of her white robe, and checked to make sure she had slippers on.

"Bertie wasn't tired," Nell explained. "He wanted to hear a story." She turned to Emma, who was watching discreetly from the doorway. "Will you tell Bertie a story, Emma?"

The request took Emma off guard. "Well, I . . ." She glanced uncertainly at Peter, who was yawning hugely and rubbing his eyes. "Yes, all right, I'll tell you a story, Nell. Peter, you get straight into bed."

"Yes'm. But don't forget to put a glass of water next to Nell's bed. Bertie gets thirsty sometimes." Motioning for Emma to follow, he led the way past a kitchenette, a large bathroom, and a lavatory, stopping when they reached a pair of doors. Peter opened the door on the right, but turned back to shake a finger at his sister. "Only one story," he reminded her, then went inside and closed the door behind him.

Opening the other door, Emma peered into Nell's room, amazed by the trouble the duke had taken to ensure Queen Eleanor's comfort. A bedside lamp cast a soft glow on the child-sized canopied bed, the mirrored dressing table, the skirted chaise longue, and the wardrobe. Everything was white and gold, including the bear-sized rocking chair sitting beside the chaise.

While Nell hung her robe in the wardrobe and crawled into bed, Emma dutifully filled a glass with water in the kitchen. Glass in hand, Emma waited while the little girl fussed over Bertie, making sure that his fuzzy brown head was precisely centered on the pillow and tucking the covers under his chin.

"I hope Peter goes straight to bed," Emma said, moving to place the glass on the bedside table. "He's very tired tonight."

Nell settled back on her own pillow and regarded Emma with that strangely intimidating air of self-possession. "Peter's always tired," Nell said. "I told you that before."

"Did you? I must have forgotten."

"Don't forget," said Nell. She slid one arm out from under the covers and reached over to touch Bertie's ear. "That's why I told you. Somebody should know. Not just me."

"Know what?" said Emma.

"When Papa's away, Peter has to do everything."

Emma smiled. "Now, Nell, you know that isn't true. You have a very nice housekeeper, remember?"

"Mrs. Higgins is a boozer," Nell stated flatly.

Emma nearly laughed. "But in those stories you told us in the garden, Higgins was a clown."

Nell gazed at her levelly. "She's not funny, Emma." Rolling over on her side and curling her knees up to her chest, the child turned her back on Emma. "You can turn out the light now. I'm ready to go to sleep."

Emma was disconcerted. "What about Bertie's story?" she asked.

"Bertie's asleep, Emma. He doesn't need a story."

The frost in Nell's voice told Emma that she'd been rejected as well as dismissed. Unsettled, and sensing that she'd failed some obscure test, Emma stared helplessly at the back of Nell's head, then switched off the bedside lamp and left the nursery.

Back in her own room, she spent an hour on the balcony, trying to figure out what had just happened. Emma might not know the fine points of parenting, but she'd seen Derek go out of his way to dress up for Queen Eleanor, and he'd been equally willing to sprawl across the floor for Peter. A blind person could see that he adored his son and daughter. He'd never leave them alone with a . . . a boozer.

On the other hand, Derek didn't spend much time at home. He hadn't known about Nell's new play group or Peter leaving the Boy Scouts. And why had Peter quit the Scouts, anyway? He loved the outdoors and was always after Bantry to show him how to tie a new knot or identify an unfamiliar insect. It didn't make sense.

Emma turned. From the balcony she could see Derek's crumpled business card, still propped against the clock on the rosewood desk. Since Derek worked out of his home, the phone number on the card would allow her to speak directly to Mrs. Higgins. One telephone call would put her mind at rest about the housekeeper and spare her a potentially embarrassing conversation with Derek. Too bad it was so late.

Emma rubbed her forehead tiredly, remembering that another uncomfortable discussion with Derek was already in the offing. Why in the world had she promised Peter to talk to his father about fixing the window? Emma sighed, then went into the bedroom and turned off the lights. It wasn't fair. After years of doing everything she could to avoid having children of her own, she lay awake now, worried sick about someone else's.

Seventeen

"*I*t's none of my business," Emma muttered, stabbing the pitch-fork into the dirt. "Absolutely none." She yanked a mass of bindweed up by the roots and tossed it into the wheelbarrow. They'd finished clearing the south wall and another of the raised beds before lunch, and she was determined to make a start on the lawn before supper. She jabbed the fork back into the earth and leaned on the handle, wiping the sweat from her forehead and wishing she'd remembered to wear her sunhat. It was too hot to work without it. Not a breath of wind stirred in the chapel garden, and the sun beat down relentlessly from a cloudless blue sky.

"Hey, Emma, you tryin' to kill yourself?" Syd Bishop looked over at Peter and Nell, who were sitting like wilted flowers in the shade cast by the chapel's projecting wall. "You kids take a breather. Go ask Gash to squirt you with the hose, or see if Bantry'll let you play in the fountain. Go on. Outta here!"

They'd gotten word that morning. Grayson, Kate, and Dr. Singh would bring Susannah back to Penford Hall the following day. Excitement in the hall had risen to a feverish pitch as the staff threw itself into preparations for receiving their disabled guest and welcoming home their long-absent master.

Bantry was trimming the hedges at the front of the hall and freshening up the tulips in the beds around the fountain at the center of the circular drive. The drive itself looked like an eccentric used-car lot. Gash had emptied the garage and was busily washing Grayson's cars. Why he thought it necessary to wash all of them at once, Emma couldn't say, but the Rolls-Royce, MG, and Jaguar were in line with an ancient but meticulously maintained forest-green Landrover and a badly rusted orange Volkswagen bus. The last, Gash had informed her sadly, belonged to Derek. "Have to do something about it," he'd muttered, surveying the decrepit vehicle with a calculating eye.

Crowley was supervising a phalanx of villagers who were polishing, dusting, scrubbing, or sweeping every inch of the hall. Mattie was fussing endlessly about what linens would look best in Susannah's room, Hallard was pounding furiously at his keyboard, and Newland had his men on alert for last-minute gate-crashers, while Madama and three assistants were preparing a welcome-home supper with more courses than a college catalogue.

Derek hadn't surfaced all day, and Emma was well past being a little peeved.

"Emma, will you quit already? Whaddya tryin' to do, dig your way to China?" Syd removed the pitchfork from Emma's hands with unexpected strength. Raising a gloved hand to shade her eyes, Emma realized that the old man had never looked better. His face had the ruddy glow of good health, and his eyes were clear and alert. Perhaps too alert. Emma quickly averted her angry gaze.

Syd took off his straw hat and plopped it on Emma's head. "Get over there and sit your fanny down before you give yourself a stroke."

Red-faced and winded, Emma stalked over to the wooden bench, folded her arms, and sat. Her hair was sticking to her back, and her face was streaked with mud and sweat. "What are you doing?" she snapped, when Syd came up behind her.

"I'm tuckin' your friggin' wig up in your bonnet. You gotta nice head of hair, Emma, but a cape you don't need on a day like this. Sit still or I'll give you such a clout . . ." Syd twisted Emma's long tail of hair into a French knot and pushed it up into the oversized straw hat. With the hair off the back of her neck, the heat in the garden was almost bearable.

Syd sat down next to her. "You gonna tell me what's eatin' you or do I have to pry it outta you?"

Emma's lips tightened.

Syd leaned back on the bench, stretched his legs out in front of him, and crossed his ankles. He raised his face to the sun. "Okay, so I was a little rocky for a coupla days there. Seein' Suzie all banged up kinda took the wind outta my sails. But I'm okay now. This here chapel garden's like a tonic." He nudged Emma with his elbow. "You think I don't know what you done, bringin' me out here? You think I ain't grateful?"

"I'm not mad at you, Syd," Emma said stiffly.

"I know that, honey. But I gotta return the favor, you understand? Maybe I can help."

Emma took her work gloves off and placed them in her lap, then turned to face Syd. "Do you think Nell is a truthful child?"

Syd's eyes slid toward her. "Sure," he said. "She's a bright kid. She may embroider a little here, a little there, but she knows what's make-believe and what's not."

"Then what would you say if I told you that Nell implied that Derek leaves her and Peter alone for extended periods of time with no one but a drunk to look after them?"

"I'd say you should be discussing this with Derek," said Syd.

"How can I?"

Syd waved a hand in the air. "You go up to him, you say, 'Derek, got a minute?'—"

"No, Syd, that's not what I mean. I mean, in a larger, philosophical sense, what right do I have to interfere? Why should it matter to me what Derek does with his children? It's none of my business."

"Seems to me that, in a larger, philosophical sense, you're already makin' it your business. You get much sleep last night?"

"Not much." Facing forward, Emma ran her hand along the smooth, silvery arm of the wooden bench. Half-angry, half-embarrassed, she said, "I called there this morning."

"There where?"

Emma sighed. "I called the number on Derek's business card. And a woman answered. She was friendly, in a vague sort of way, but it . . . it did sound as if she'd been drinking. Oh, Syd, I could practically smell the liquor on her breath." Emma drummed her fingers on the arm of the bench. "She introduced herself as Mrs. Higgins."

"You don't say." Syd let out a low whistle, then laced his fingers together and cracked his knuckles. "I'll tell you one thing. If it is true, it ain't Derek's fault."

"How could it not be?" Emma demanded.

" 'Cause he loves those kids. He wouldn't leave 'em hangin' like that. Not on purpose." Syd shrugged. "You ever think maybe he don't know?"

Emma's fingers stopped drumming.

"I mean, the love goes two ways," Syd went on. "Those kids'd do just about anything for him, am I right? That Peter . . ." Syd shook his head. "Never seen a kid wound so tight. Now, there's one who don't tell the truth."

"What do you mean?" Emma asked.

Syd gave her a pitying look. "I raised three sons, Emma. I got five grandsons. You think I don't know when a little boy's telling a fib?" He rubbed the bridge of his nose. "Lies about funny stuff, too. Like, he was tellin' me about a football match at his school, right? And maybe he thinks he can fool me on account of I'm a Yank. But I been in this country twenty years, Emma. I know from football, and not just that the Brits don't call it soccer. And I'm tellin' you, if that kid ever saw a football match in his life, I'll eat that sweaty old hat. Why should he lie about something like that, huh? You tell me."

Nell's words seemed to ring in Emma's ears. *When Papa's away, Peter has to do everything.* Emma realized suddenly that, apart from that evening when they'd built their Rube Goldberg machine, she'd never seen Peter playing at anything. He was the first one in the garden every morning and he was usually the last to leave. Nanny Cole had scolded him for straightening up the nursery, and Bantry had sensed that something was amiss when he'd caught the boy tidying up the potting shed. Emma remembered Peter's vaguely puzzled attitude toward cricket and, with a sinking heart, began to understand why the boy had elected not to attend Harrow. A boarding school would have taken him away from home, where he was needed.

"But that's terrible," she said. "Why can't he just go to Derek and tell him the truth?"

Syd snorted. "You're makin' me lose patience with you, Emma. You think that kid don't know his father's heart is broke? You think he wants his pop to feel worse?"

Emma was appalled. "You think this has been going on since Derek lost his wife? But Peter was barely five years old and Nell was——"

"Nell was his baby sister, what needed looking after. I'll tell you something, Emma, and it ain't something I tell too many people. I lost my mother, God rest her soul, when I was eight years old. My sister, Betty, was only two. I know what this boy's feeling. What I didn't know was about the drunk. That changes things. You gotta tell Derek about the drunk."

"Can't you tell him?" Emma asked.

"You're the one got the invitation." When Emma looked at him blankly, Syd rolled his eyes. "Emma, what's a person gotta do to get through to you? What do you think, Nell don't know how to keep her mouth shut? You think she tells you about that hooch hound for nothing? You ever heard of a cry for help?" Syd pursed his lips, disgusted. "Oh, I forgot. It ain't none of your business."

Emma flinched.

"So, this is why you been so mad at the poor guy?" Syd asked.

"I am not mad at—" Emma cleared her throat. "I'm not mad at anyone."

"And I'm the queen of Romania." Syd shook his head reproachfully. "What do you think, I'm stupid? You been a pain in the butt ever since that dope did his vanishing act."

"Do you know where he is?" Emma asked, more quickly than she'd intended.

Syd examined his fingernails. "Madama says he's been eatin' in the kitchen at weird hours. Whatsamatta, he didn't tell you?"

Emma swallowed once, then looked down at the ground. "No. Why should he?"

"Because that's what people do when they care about each other," Syd answered simply. He gave Emma a sidelong look. "Am I right?"

Emma's glasses began to slide down her sweaty nose. She pushed them up again and sighed disconsolately. "I wouldn't know."

"You're learnin', though, huh?" Syd squeezed her arm sympathetically. "It ain't easy, bein' in love."

Emma's shoulders slumped. "Who said anything about being in love? And even if I were, that doesn't mean that I would expect Der—whoever I might be in love with to account to me for every minute of his time."

"You like bein' miserable?" Syd asked.

"No, I—"

"Then you gotta lay down some ground rules. Next time you see that dope, you smack him in the kisser and tell him, he ever pulls this kinda stunt on you again, you'll give it to him twice as bad."

"I don't have any right—"

"He gotta right to make you worry?"

"No, but—"

"You gotta be patient with him. But firm. Otherwise those kids're gonna grow up seein' you miserable and never seein' their pop at all."

"Syd . . ." Emma looked up at the sky. It was beginning to cloud over and she hoped for a good rain, to clear the heaviness from the air. "I appreciate your concern, but I must have given you the wrong impression. I have no intention of getting married, ever, much less to someone who already has two children."

"Two kids and a bear," Syd corrected. "You know, Emma, if you'd stop thinkin' so much, you'd save everyone a whole lotta heartburn. Listen to your Uncle Syd. You turn off that brain of yours and give your heart a chance. It won't steer you wrong. You got my guarantee on that."

Emma looked down at her work-roughened hands, then reached up to brush at a tendril of hair that had escaped from Syd's hat. "I think I'll go in and wash up," she said softly.

Syd reached over and tucked the loose tendril back into place. "Don't be too hard on the guy, Emma. He's out there strugglin', just like the rest of us."

A mountain of thunderclouds had moved in over the sea by the time Emma emerged from her dressing room, freshly bathed and wrapped in her terry-cloth robe. Not a drop of rain was falling, but the sky was an unbroken mass of angry gray clouds, and the temperature had dropped so dramatically that Emma was glad to come in from the balcony. Although it was nearly time for supper, she stretched out on the bed, exhausted. She'd scarcely slept the night before, and she'd been hard at work all day. She was much too tired to sort through her conversation with Syd, or to battle her way through Crowley's cleaning brigade to reach the dining room, and she wasn't really hungry anyway. All she wanted to do was rest her eyes.

Emma awoke with a start. She reached toward the bedside table to grope for her glasses before realizing that she hadn't taken them off. She was still wrapped in her robe. Peering at the jeweled clock on the rosewood desk, she saw that it was nearly midnight. Yawning, she looked around the room sleepily, wondering what had awakened her. Thunder, perhaps? She went to the balcony and saw that the storm had not yet broken, though the wind was blowing hard and lightning flashed far out at sea. Emma shuddered to think what the garden rooms would look like in the morning, then turned as she heard someone knocking at her door.

Wincing guiltily, Emma came in off the balcony. She shouldn't have left her lights on. It was probably Mattie, coming to ask if she needed anything. Summoning an apologetic smile, Emma went to open the door.

The hallway was empty. Emma squinted into the darkness beyond the pool of light falling from her room, but saw no one. Perplexed, she closed the door.

Again she heard a knocking sound. It seemed to be coming from her dressing room. The hairs on her arms prickled as she picked up Crowley's flashlight and hefted it. It was sturdy and she was fairly strong. Creeping quietly to the dressing room, she flung the door wide and leapt back, raising the flashlight above her head.

Nothing. Emma put her head inside the room, then uttered a startled yelp when a loud knock sounded right next to her. It seemed to be coming from her wardrobe. Cautiously, she opened the wardrobe door.

"Derek?" she called softly. "Is that you?"

A muffled voice came through the wardrobe's back panel. "Who else would it be? Glad to know I've got the right address, at least. Think you could let me in?"

"I don't know," said Emma. "You're in back of a wardrobe that must weigh at least a ton."

A muted groan came through the wall.

"Hang on," said Emma. "Let me take a look." She dumped her

clothes unceremoniously out of the wardrobe and onto the floor, then flicked on Crowley's flashlight and examined the back panel. "I don't see any hinges, but there's a row of pegs down the center of the panel. Maybe, if I . . ." She climbed into the wardrobe and, crouching, tugged at the top peg. It came away in her hand, and the others followed suit. Stepping back out of the wardrobe, she called, "Try sliding the right side of the panel sideways."

The panel rattled, creaked, and finally began to shift slowly, one half slipping neatly behind the other. Cool, musty air wafted out of the darkness; then Derek emerged, with a flashlight in one hand, dusty smudges on his face, and cobwebs in his hair.

Emma pulled her robe around her and schooled her face into a neutral expression. Derek took one look at her and began to apologize as though his life depended on it.

"Emma, I can't begin to tell you how sorry I am that I didn't let you know what I was up to. I should've come by sooner, and I meant to, but I've been rather on the go these past few days, and I simply lost track of the time, and I know it's a piss-poor excuse, so all I can say is that I hope you'll forgive me and I promise that it won't ever happen again." He paused to take a breath, sneezed three times in a row, wiped his nose on a dusty sleeve, sneezed once more, then peered down at her imploringly and added, "What d'you say?"

Emma was vaguely unsettled by the amount of pleasure Derek's heartfelt apology gave her. "I guess this means that I don't get to smack you in the kisser," she said, half to herself. Then, smiling: "It's okay, Derek. Now, go in the other room and wait there while I put on some clothes."

Emma changed quickly into her gray trousers and Nanny Cole's blue sweater, returned the rest of her clothes to the wardrobe, and joined Derek in the bedroom. He was perched on the arm of one of the overstuffed chairs, peering at a schematic drawing from the old portfolio.

"Told you the place was a honeycomb," he said. "Meant to take my time exploring it, but, circumstances being what they are, I pushed it a bit." He handed her the house plan. "An annotated version."

"Secret passages?" Emma asked, tracing a line of red ink with her finger.

"Most weren't included on the older set of house plans, none at all on the newer ones. Want to see what I've found?"

Emma didn't bother to answer. Instead, she turned off all the lights in her room, switched on her flashlight, and headed for the wardrobe, where she moved aside to let Derek take the lead. Once she'd closed the wardrobe door behind her, she pushed through the hanging dresses and stepped into the gaping hole, then waited while Derek slid the panel back into place. As the darkness enfolded them, Derek said, in a low, excited voice, "You're not going to believe this."

Eighteen

The flashlights danced an eerie pas de deux on the smooth stone walls, and the silence was absolute. No moaning wind disturbed the musty air, no lightning pierced the inky darkness. The coming storm might break and shake the rafters, but it would not touch the core of Penford Hall.

The massive building slumbered all around them, and the passage stretched before them endlessly. The floor was dry and level, the ceiling high enough for Emma to walk upright, though Derek crept, half-crouching, by her side. They scanned the way ahead, their shoulders touching, the thick stone walls absorbing every sound.

"I imagine the castle had a network of passages just like this one," Derek told her. "Grayson's predecessors probably used it to store their loot."

"But I thought the first duke gave up piracy," Emma objected.

"And what did he get in return? A title and a scrap of land unsuitable for farming. Old habits die hard, Emma, and food must be put on the table. I'll wager the old devil gave up piracy for smuggling and perhaps a spot of wrecking now and then."

In the past, small coastal towns had considered shipwrecks a boon to the local economy. For some, "wrecking" had become a way of life. Emma had read chilling tales of bonfires lit to lure ships to their doom, of sailors left to perish while their vessels were plundered. "The Nether Shoals would make it easy enough," she agreed, with a shudder.

"I'm all for carrying on family traditions," Derek commented dryly, "but there's such a thing as carrying them too far. Ah, here we are." He played the beam of his flashlight on a narrow opening to his right, where a spiral staircase wound away into the darkness. "Runs from the subcellars to the roof," he explained. "This passage and several others feed into it, and at least four rooms open off of it."

"Sounds like a main thoroughfare," said Emma.

"Hasn't been used for a long time, though. Took hours to get the hinges on all the doors oiled up and working properly." He jutted his chin upward. "Our first stop is up there." Emma started forward, but Derek put an arm out to block her way. "Not so fast. We'll have to kill the torches first."

"You want me to turn off my flashlight?" Emma peered uncertainly into the gloom.

"I'm afraid so. It's the only way we'll be able to see if light's leaking around the doors. If it is, we'll have to assume that someone's on the other side and pass them by."

"But what if someone's asleep inside one of those rooms?"

Derek shook his head. "No bedrooms lie off of this staircase. I've checked."

Emma watched unhappily as Derek turned off his flashlight and hooked it on his belt. She understood the need for caution, but she wasn't thrilled by the idea of groping her way up an unfamiliar staircase in utter darkness.

Derek seemed to read her mind. When she hesitated, he reached for her hand. "We'll take it slowly," he promised. "One step at a time." He tightened his grip. "I won't let you fall."

Smiling weakly, Emma thumbed the switch on her flashlight. Derek vanished, the walls seemed to close in around her, and she was acutely conscious of the great weight of stone hanging just above her head. Please, God, she prayed, as her heart began to race, please don't let my palms perspire.

Derek's disembodied voice was reassuring. "Remarkable, isn't it? Like being in a mine. I'm just glad there aren't any rats."

Emma's hands turned to ice. "You're sure about that?" she asked faintly.

"Quite sure." He tugged her gently forward. "Come on, now, slide your foot straight ahead. . . ."

Climbing the stairs wasn't so bad, once Emma got the hang of it, although it would have been easier if she hadn't been straining to hear the rustle of rodent feet. Her imagination populated the darkness with tiny glowing eyes and razor-sharp teeth, and though she tried to ignore the morbid fantasy, she couldn't quite shake the feeling of being watched.

Derek stopped and Emma squinted as his flashlight flared, illuminating a narrow landing and a sturdy wooden door. A heavy iron ring was bolted to the door, and Derek reached for it.

"We'll have to keep our voices down once I open the door," he warned, passing his flashlight to Emma. "This room's buried in the servants' wing." Gripping the iron ring with both hands, Derek planted his foot on the wall, and heaved. As the door swung silently toward them, Emma nearly screamed.

"*Rats,*" she hissed. Her heart began to thud and her knees turned to water and Derek's strong arms were all that kept her from fleeing headlong down the stairs.

"No, no, no," he whispered urgently, his breath warm on her face. "*Computers.*"

"Wh-what?" Emma slowly turned her head to peer again into the room. Raising a hand to straighten her glasses, she saw that the red and orange pinpricks punctuating the darkness weren't beady rodent eyes, but the telltale lights of a bank of electronic equipment. Beyond the thunder of her pounding heart, she heard the steady hum of computers at work, a sound she'd heard every day for the past twenty years. Limp with relief, she laid her cheek on Derek's chest and murmured, "Sorry."

"No need for that," Derek soothed, his hand floating lightly through her hair. "Be still a moment, get your bearings."

A strange, halting note in Derek's voice made Emma tremble. Raising her face to his, she saw him wince, and it was only then that she realized she'd jammed both his flashlight and hers directly into his rib cage.

"Oh, God, I'm sorry, Derek," she said, but though she tried to pull away, he only drew her nearer, and the kiss, when it came, was so sweet and so surprising that she forgot about the flashlights altogether.

Derek remembered, fortunately, and when at last they paused to take a breath, he caught both flashlights neatly before they clattered down the stairs. As Emma's senses swam back into focus, she murmured muzzily, "We shouldn't, Derek, we really shouldn't."

"Quite right," he breathed, burying his face in her hair. "Not here, at any rate. You'll break both our necks. What do you wash your hair in, Emma? Incense?" When Emma made no answer, he wrapped his arms around her and closed his eyes. "I know," he whispered. "Not the right time or place. May never be, for us. I never expected to find you, and I know you weren't looking for me."

"It could never work," said Emma.

Derek took a deep breath, then blew it out in a long sigh of resignation. He straightened, and looked down at Emma. "I know," he said softly. "It's just a dream."

"Just a dream," Emma murmured. She pulled away, touched a finger to her glasses, then turned unsteadily toward the colored lights. "Let's take a look."

The room they entered was unlike any Emma had seen in Penford Hall. Not a single painting hung on the stark white walls, no carpet covered the tiled floor, and although the furnishings were expensive and extremely well made, they weren't priceless antiques. As her flashlight glided over computers, printers, fax machines, photocopiers, and telephones, Emma felt as though she'd stepped into the nerve center of a modern office building.

"Oh my," she breathed, as the beam of her flashlight came to rest on a sleek black computer at the center of the room. She approached it slowly and rested one hand on the monitor, watching in awe as numbers, graphs, and complicated charts scrolled rapidly across the divided screen.

"What is it?" Derek whispered.

"A Series Ten," Emma replied. "I've read about it, but I've never gotten my hands on one before."

"Latest thing?" They stood a little ways apart, and carefully avoided each other's eyes. Emma's voice was too businesslike, Derek's too chipper, and they both spoke much too quickly.

Emma nodded. "It's based on a new, high-performance chip. Five times the speed, more capacity than you can imagine."

"What's it doing?"

"Monitoring ongoing transactions." Emma studied the screens. "Looks financial to me. Money transfers. Deutsche marks, pounds,

Swiss francs, yen." She frowned. "Wait a minute. There should be . . ." Shining her light around the room, Emma spotted a wall-mounted rack covered with wires. "I thought so. High-speed data lines. He'd need them to keep current with international markets." She bit her lip, perplexed, then gestured for Derek to return to the spiral staircase. When the door was safely shut, she asked, "Why would Grayson need that kind of setup? It's powerful enough to run a fair-sized corporation."

"Why don't you ask the machine?"

Emma shook her head. "Too risky. It'll report any interruptions in its automatic functions. And I think it's safe to assume that Grayson's done what he could to protect his data. We'd need a password, maybe even a series of passwords, to do anything at all."

Derek nodded thoughtfully. "Does this prove that Grayson could've fiddled Lex's accounts?"

"All it *proves* is that he knows a lot about computers. What it *suggests* is that, if Lex's accounts were kept electronically, Grayson could've made them dance. Oh, damn." Emma rattled her flashlight, which was beginning to fade. "Don't suppose you have an extra set of batteries?"

"Sorry." Derek switched off her flashlight and hung it on his belt. "Take mine. It's not much better, but it'll last long enough to get us where we're going. No need to turn it off. The next stop on our tour is a bedroom, but it is definitely unoccupied."

A dozen steps took them to another long, low corridor that led away from the silent heart of the hall to a second door, identical to the first. Again Derek braced himself to tug on the iron ring, and when the door swung open this time, Emma recoiled from the howl of the wind. It seemed deafening after the stillness of the staircase.

"Good Lord," said Derek. "Hope the Tregallis boys' boat is safely into port. Not a night to be out fishing."

"I hope Bantry's harvested the runner beans," said Emma. "That wind will strip the arbor bare." She peered into the room, but her view was blocked by some kind of heavy fabric. "A tapestry?" she asked. She lifted the edge of the cloth, then ducked under it. Closing the wooden door behind him, Derek ducked under the tapestry after her.

There was nothing stark or modern about this room. It was sumptuous, crammed with furniture that looked as though it had been there for a very long time. The canopied bed was hung with richly embroidered black satin curtains, and a pair of caryatids held up the marble mantelpiece. The painting on the ceiling featured a dozen languid, buxom beauties whose thin gowns left little to the imagination. They reclined on facing couches, waited on by plump cupids who flitted through a pristine blue sky.

A pair of gold brocade chairs faced the hearth, and four dainty green velvet chairs were grouped around a gaming table. A green velvet divan sat before the draped windows between a pair of ornately carved end tables, and there was a low, cushioned bench at the foot of the bed.

A dizzying array of objects crowded every table and shelf: vases, candlesticks, paperweights, porcelain figurines, lacquered boxes, photographs in silver frames. Paintings large and small covered the walls, each featuring a different garden scene. Emma turned eagerly to Derek, then lowered her eyes and tried to sound casual. "Is this Grandmother's room?"

Derek nodded. He crossed to open the drapes, then stood with his back toward Emma, as though mesmerized by the intermittent flashes of lightning. "I've exceeded my brief by coming here," he admitted. "Grayson asked me expressly to leave her room alone."

"Isn't it the most logical place to look for the lantern?" Emma asked.

"Grayson assures me that they've searched it thoroughly. It's clean, as far as the lantern is concerned." He glanced over his shoulder with an unexpected twinkle in his eye.

Emma was unable to suppress her excitement. "Come on, Derek, show me."

"Don't suppose I should take such pleasure in this," he said, crossing from the windows to stand before a lute-strumming marble angel perched upon a marble pedestal, "but it's really quite wonderful. Watch." He grasped the angel's head and tilted it forward, and the wall behind the pedestal swung away into darkness.

Emma was astonished. "How did you even know to try that?"

"I didn't. I was just poking around and bumped into it. Thought I'd broken the blasted thing. Want to take a look inside?"

Emma edged past the decapitated angel into a round room with seamless marble walls rising to a domed ceiling. The curving walls were inset with a series of arched niches, and each niche held a stringed musical instrument. An antique mandolin was nearest to her, its neck intricately inlaid with mother-of-pearl. Beside it was a lute, and next to that . . .

Emma stared, dumbfounded, as the beam of Derek's flashlight picked out a shiny black electric guitar inlaid with a silver lightning bolt, the trademark of Lex Rex.

"I don't believe it," she breathed, turning to face Derek, who had followed her into the room.

"Didn't think you would," said Derek proudly. "Doesn't really prove that Grayson murdered Lex, though."

An eerie peal of laughter cut through the moaning wind, and Emma gasped as a flash of lightning from the bedroom window limned a familiar figure in the doorway. Derek stiffened, then swung around as a voice sounded behind him.

"Don't be squeamish, dear boy," said the duke, stepping into the room. "Of course I murdered Lex Rex. And I know precisely what I'm going to do with both of you."

Nineteen

"*Y*ou're back early, Grayson." Derek took an unobstrusive backward step that placed him between Emma and the duke. "We didn't expect you until tomorrow."

"Disappointed?" Grayson asked.

"Not at all," Derek assured him. "Merely . . . surprised."

"I can see that," the duke commented dryly. "Had I known of your interest in antique musical instruments, I would have returned sooner."

Emma moved to Derek's side. She appreciated his chivalrous instincts, but it was maddening to stand behind him, unable to see the duke. If something dreadful was about to happen, she wasn't going to let Derek face it alone.

She was content to let him do the talking, though. So far, the two men were acting as though this were nothing more than a chance encounter at a somewhat unusual house party. Derek's sangfroid suggested that it was perfectly normal to be facing a murderous madman in a secret room, lit only by the dimming beam of a dying flashlight and the brief white fire of lightning.

"It's this ghastly weather that brought me home," the duke was saying. "It may clear up overnight, or it may settle in for a week. Since neither Kate nor I could countenance another week in Plymouth, home we came, jiggety-jig."

"Leaving Susannah behind you?" Derek asked.

"Indeed not." The duke turned his head, distracted by a loud thump and a few muttered words that came from the dowager's bedchamber. The keening wind made it impossible for Emma to identify the voices. She gripped Derek's arm involuntarily as the duke turned back to them, smiling.

"As I was saying," he continued, "Dr. Singh gave Susannah the all-clear, so we brought her with us, one big happy family. She's in her room now, with Mattie and Nurse Tharby." Grayson looked at Emma. "Nurse Tharby is Dr. Singh's assistant, though she'll be his equal once she's completed her studies. I believe you met her proud mother at the Bright Lady."

Emma nodded. She recalled Mrs. Tharby very well. She also recalled how loyal the villagers had been when facing the onslaught from the press. They wouldn't welcome anyone who threatened the generous lord of the manor. They might even see to it that Susannah took a sudden and entirely plausible turn for the worse. The same thought must have crossed Derek's mind, for his arm had turned to steel beneath the soft cotton of his blue workshirt.

"Like to see her," he said, with absolute composure. "Susannah, that is. Welcome her back. Let her know she's among friends."

"Not possible, old man." The duke raised his hands, palms out. "Nothing to do with me. Nurse's orders. If she declares that Syd and Mattie are to be Susannah's sole companions this evening, I'm afraid we must bow to her authority."

Derek relaxed a bit. "Syd's up there, is he?"

"Planning to camp there, by the looks of it. I say, Emma, it was awfully clever of you to put him to work in Grandmother's garden. Magical place, that garden. It's done him a world of good."

The duke turned his head again as a wavering glow began to penetrate the darkness in the dowager's bedroom. Fire? Emma thought. She cast an uneasy glance at the marble walls and tried very hard not to imagine what would happen if the duke barred the only exit after setting the well-oiled antique instruments ablaze.

"Please," said the duke, facing them once more, "won't you join me? It's frightfully uncivilized to stand chatting in doorways. And we have so much to talk about." As he turned on his heel and left the room, Derek looked down at Emma and smiled encouragingly. Emma couldn't quite return his smile, preoccupied as she was by thoughts of how thick the walls were in Penford Hall's hidden passages, and how easy it would be to seal someone—or a pair of someones—in an out-of-the-way dead end. She comforted herself with the knowledge that Derek was probably as good at demolition as he was at restoration.

With a bit of luck and the blade of his penknife, they'd be able to dig their way out. In a year or so.

Gathering her courage, Emma followed Derek through the doorway.

They reentered the dowager's bedchamber in time to see Crowley rise, red-faced, from the gold-veined marble hearth, where his exertions had produced a brightly burning fire. Emma saw at once that the divan had been moved to one side of the fireplace, a high-backed gold brocade armchair to the other, and the ornate end tables had been pushed together to form a coffee table.

Hallard stood nearby, illuminating Crowley's labors with a gold candelabra filled with flickering white candles. Kate was there, as well, in an oatmeal-colored fisherman's knit pullover and dark-brown trousers, standing with folded arms before the door-concealing tapestry. No one seemed surprised to see them.

As immaculate as ever, Grayson was dressed in fawn cavalry twills, a hacking jacket, an ivory shirt, and a silk tie. He nodded cordially to Crowley as he sank into the gold brocade chair and motioned Emma and Derek toward the divan.

Crowley tugged his waistcoat into place, straightened his black tie and upright collar, then gestured for Hallard to follow him through a pair of white-and-gold doors that led, apparently, to the hallway.

For a moment, the only sounds were the moaning wind, the snapping fire, and the distant rumble of thunder. Then another rumble sounded, just outside the bedroom doors.

"Watch where you're going, you nincompoop!"

"Sorry, Nanny, but your needles nearly caught me in the—"

Emma jumped as the bedroom door banged open and Nanny Cole swept in, magnificent in a red plaid robe and brown corduroy slippers, clutching a yarn-filled basket bristling with half a dozen lethal-looking knitting needles. Chief Constable Trevoy trailed after her, carrying a flashlight and keeping a close watch on the basket.

"You're a ninny, Tom Trevoy, and you always were," Nanny declared. "A poke in the goolies might stiffen your backbone, but I doubt it. Now, stop your whingeing and fetch me a chair!" She paused to glower at Derek and Emma, growling, "Nosey-parkers. Can't bear nosey-parkers." Peering around the shadowy room, she demanded, "Where's that blasted daughter of mine? Comes mincing in without so much as a by-your-leave. Ah! There you are!" She crossed over to Kate, while Chief Constable Trevoy hastened to move the other gold brocade chair close to the fire, then sat meekly on the low bench at the foot of the bed, stroking his red mustache.

"Kate, you look like death," Nanny Cole barked. "Off to bed with you, my girl, quickstep march!"

"I'd very much like Kate to stay," Grayson murmured.

Nanny Cole's lower lip protruded obstinately, but all she said was "Suit yourself. But don't blame me if the chit keels over. I've a good mind to dose the pair of you before the night is through."

The sound of footsteps in the hall announced the arrival of Gash, the chubby mechanic, and Newland, the taciturn gatekeeper. Newland went over to conduct a low-pitched conversation with Kate, then parked himself before the hall doors, rolling his long silver flashlight from hand to hand with the contained energy of an athlete. Emma's heart sank as she realized that, although the gatekeeper was in his midsixties, he was in remarkably fine physical condition.

Gash approached the duke. "Power plant's buggered," he reported. "We've got the backup generator for emergency systems and alarms, and we still have the telephone, but the rest'll have to wait till morning."

"I'm sure you've done your best," said the duke.

"Always do, Your Grace." Gash nodded to Derek and Emma, then took a seat beside Chief Constable Trevoy.

A moment later, Newland opened the doors for Crowley and Hallard. Each carried a large silver tray, which they placed on the tables at Emma's knee. Crowley's tray held an enormous silver teapot, nine cups and saucers, a silver creamer and sugar bowl, nine teaspoons, and a stack of small plates. Hallard's was freighted with four three-tiered pastry stands filled to overflowing with dainty, crustless sandwiches.

"About bloody time," grumbled Nanny Cole. "What's Madama sent up?"

Hallard pointed out paper-thin slices of lamb piled on nutty homemade bread, with a side dish of fresh mint sauce; morsels of lobster on toast rounds, topped with a dab of mayonnaise; triangles of white bread filled with translucent wafers of turbot; a round of cheddar cheese, a bunch of glistening grapes, and a bowl of peaches.

A flurry of activity ensued, as tea was poured and sandwiches were distributed. Although Emma had slept through supper, she had little appetite, and the rattle of her teacup on its saucer betrayed her nervousness. Were she and Derek about to be tried and convicted by the duke's kangaroo court? She stared gravely at her teacup, then frowned, vaguely puzzled. What kind of kangaroo court served *tea* to the accused? She raised her eyes to search the faces that surrounded her. How could she feel threatened by these people? They'd shown her nothing but kindness. Newland was an unknown quantity, of course, but apart from him—and Nanny Cole's knitting needles— did she really have anything to fear? Gradually, Emma's nervousness subsided, to be replaced by an intense curiosity. What was the duke up to?

"Where's Bantry?" Emma asked suddenly.

"With the children," Kate replied. She had pulled a chair over to sit slightly behind and to one side of the duke. "We didn't want them to be alone on a night like this."

The duke polished off his sixth sandwich while Emma was still toying with her first. He flicked the crumbs into the fire, put his dish on the tray, then leaned back in his chair to survey the group.

"I think that's all of us," he said. "Crowley, Hallard, do have a seat. You hover with great aplomb, dear chaps, but surely it's inadvisable after such a tiring day." When Crowley and Hallard had settled soundlessly at the gaming table, the duke went on. "Since this is the first chance I've had to see some of you since my return, let me start off by saying what a pleasure it is to find myself once more at home and in your company.

"I can't tell you how deeply I appreciate everything you've done in my absence. Newland's defense of the perimeter was nothing short of brilliant. Tom's orchestration of the villagers sent the invaders packing with all due speed, taking nothing with them but the somewhat dazed impression that Penford Harbor is inhabited exclusively by a bunch of daft wheezers." Gash clapped the chief constable on the shoulder and gave Newland a hearty thumbs-up. "Thanks to the rest of you, I never had a moment's worry about the smooth running of the household. As you can imagine, it made my task in Plymouth that much easier."

"How're we doin'?" Gash inquired.

The duke smiled. "You'll be pleased to know that the tabloids have deemed Penford Hall unworthy of their attention." He paused as a murmur of approval washed through the room. "And we owe that happy development to the untiring efforts of our dear old Kate."

Kate smiled shyly. "I seem to recall that you played a role as well, Grayson."

"Without your support, I'd've wilted," the duke declared. "Sorry, old thing, I'm afraid you must take full credit for a job well done."

"Here, here!" called Crowley, and Kate flushed as a ragged cheer went up.

"Your Grace." Chief Constable Trevoy raised his hand. "About Miss Ashley-Woods—"

"We'll get to that a bit later, if you please, Tom. At the moment we must attend to our honored guests." The duke crossed his legs and tilted his head to one side, regarding Derek quizzically. "I can understand your desire to view my grandmother's collection of instruments privately, Derek, but I must confess that I am somewhat disappointed in you."

"Not half as disappointed as I am in you, Grayson," Derek retorted mildly.

"You agreed to keep away from Grandmother's rooms, did you not?"

"The circumstances have changed."

"Have they?" The duke shook his head. "Your perception has, no doubt, but the circumstances are much the same as they've always been."

"They most certainly are not," Derek countered. "I haven't *always* known you to be a murderer, a thief, and a liar."

"Dear me . . ." The duke raised a hand to fan his face. "Such heated accusations. I've always admired your forthrightness, so I shan't complain now, but honestly, old man, you quite singe my eyebrows with the warmth of your convictions. I presume you will permit me to offer a word in my own defense?" When Derek nodded curtly, the duke leaned forward, his brown eyes flashing, all trace of good humor gone.

"Yes, I murdered Lex Rex, and I had every right to do so."

"Look here, Grayson," Derek began, but the duke would not be interrupted.

"As for being a thief, I deny that categorically. I only took what was mine, and even Milord will agree that hardly qualifies as theft. A liar, though . . ." Grayson sat back in his chair again and examined his fingernails. "There you have me, dear boy, for I am nothing if not a liar, and an unrepentant one at that." He raised his eyes to Derek's. "The very worst sort. But I feel compelled to tell the truth before you and Emma . . . depart. You are an old and trusted friend, Derek, and you, Emma, are my gardening angel. It grieves me to see the suspicion in your eyes. Before this night is through, I intend to put you both out of your misery. My friends . . ." He paused, and Emma stiffened as Derek's arm went around her shoulders. "May I present the late, and most assuredly unlamented, Lex Rex?"

Emma waited, then looked slowly around the room. There was Crowley, sitting quietly, his head tilted attentively toward the duke; Hallard, gazing absently into the middle distance; Nanny Cole, knitting a sweater in cobalt blue; Newland, keeping watch from the doorway; Kate, gazing gravely at Grayson; Tom Trevoy, stroking his mustache; Gash, leaning against the foot of the bed, his hands folded serenely across his round belly. Emma looked up at Derek, saw that his confusion mirrored her own, then turned back to the duke. "Excuse me?" she said.

Derek was more severe. "Don't like charades, Grayson," he said bluntly. "Never have. If you've got something to say for yourself you'd best come out with it."

The duke sighed. "That's what I thought you'd say. Well, all right then . . . Pour yourselves another cup of tea, everyone. This may some time."

Twenty

The rain came then, pounding down without preamble. It swept in from the sea and dashed against the bedroom windows, driven by gusts that would leave the rose bushes in tatters, flood the great lawn, and flatten every one of Madama's vegetables. Emma thought of the freshly turned topsoil in the chapel garden and wondered if it would all be washed away by morning.

Newland, monitoring the storm's progress through the earphone of a shortwave radio, confirmed that gale warnings had been sounded all up and down the coast and that residents had been advised to sit tight.

Chief Constable Trevoy placed a quick call to the village, where Mrs. Tharby cheerfully informed him that all was well, the boats were safe at harbor, and the only casualty so far had been Mr. Minion, the butcher, who'd slipped on a slick cobblestone and sprained his left wrist. Dr. Singh had seen to the injury and Mr. Minion had recovered sufficiently to hoist a few by candlelight at the Bright Lady.

Gash had long ago wired the hall's windows with sensors. If a pane was broken, the beeper in his pocket would sound and its digital readout would give him a rough idea of the window's location. The staff as a whole seemed remarkably nonchalant about the storm.

"We're part of the headland," Gash explained. "Whole bloody ⸏ock'd have to blow away afore any harm'd come to Penford Hall."

Hallard added wood to the fire, Crowley refilled cups, and Nanny ⸏ a few more sandwiches, while Derek fidgeted impatiently, ⸏eered worriedly at the driving rain. Very gradually, activ- ⸏ a deep stillness fell over the room. Tearing her gaze ⸏ Emma saw that everyone was seated, and that all ⸏rayson.

⸏he bedside table, staring down at a photo- Gently, he picked it up, dusted it lightly with his sleeve, and returned with it to his chair, where he sat gazing at it for a few more silent moments before handing it to Emma.

Emma looked down at a portrait of a British army officer. The background was smoky and indistinct, the uniform unrelieved by gleaming brass or bright ribbons. Slender and fine-featured, light-haired and sporting a pencil-thin mustache, the man bore a striking resemblance to the duke, save for the great sadness in his eyes. In his right hand he gripped a riding crop, but his left sleeve was folded back on itself and pinned at the shoulder.

"My father." The duke sat with his face turned toward the fire, and his animated hands lay becalmed on the arms of his chair. "The thirteenth duke of Penford was an unhappy man. I leave it to you to decide if it was due to his unfortunate place in the succession, but I'm rather more inclined to blame it on his unfortunate place in history.

"He lost his own father and all of his uncles in the Great War. He lost his first wife in a daylight raid on the Plymouth dockyards, his arm in the Ardennes, and his second wife, my mother, shortly after I was born." He glanced at Derek, then lowered his eyes. "To pneumonia. Not even a healthy son and heir could put paid to all of those losses, and he became something of a recluse."

Derek stirred restlessly. "Look, Grayson, I'm very sorry, but—"

"Patience, dear boy," said the duke.

Nanny Cole glared at Derek. "It's your fault we've been dragged out of our beds in the middle of the night, so you just keep still or I'll box your bloody ears."

Chastened, Derek fell silent.

"My father," the duke continued, "left much of my upbringing to my grandmother, who saw to it that I was educated at home by a governess who has since passed on. My grandmother was a wonderful woman in many ways, but she was . . . selectively attentive. If I was neatly dressed and well behaved, she would spend hours with me. When I was bad-tempered—"

"Never had a bad-tempered day in your life," Nanny Cole stat firmly, and the others murmured their agreement.

"Let us say, then, that I was, at times, overly energetic," the conceded.

"Bouncing off the walls, more like," muttered Gash.

"At such times," the duke continued doggedly, "which occurred far too often in my grandmother's estimation, I was banished from her presence."

"And dumped in our laps," huffed Nanny Cole.

"Not that we minded," Gash put in.

"Didn't say we *minded,* did I?" retorted Nanny Cole.

"As a result," Grayson went on, "I spent most of my formative years under the watchful eyes of Nanny Cole and the rest of the staff. I adored my grandmother, but these good people . . ." He let his gaze travel slowly around the room. "These good people, I loved."

"Mawkish nonsense," muttered Nanny Cole. "Get a grip, Grayson, or you'll have Kate blubbering."

"Mother," said an obviously exasperated Kate, "will you please allow Grayson to speak?"

"Never been able to stop him, have I?" Nanny Cole scowled at her daughter, but remained silent as Grayson continued.

"My father's decision to withdraw from the world had a catastrophic effect on both the hall and the village. New tax laws encouraged him to dabble in speculation, but he'd neither the skill nor the patience to succeed at that game. He was forced to sell our land in Kent and Somerset, and to dismiss the underservants, all of whom came from Penford Harbor. When they sought employment elsewhere, their houses were left vacant and the village began a slow and painful decline.

"As for the hall . . . Well, I'm sure you've heard the story many times before, Derek. Routine repairs were neglected, and the place ~an to fall apart. My father closed off room after room, until we ll living cheek by jowl in the central block."

~e a bad time," Gash murmured, and the others nodded

ow bad," Grayson commented. "The staff shielded hip and made it seem like jolly good fun to be hat. After my grandmother died, however, and began selling off the contents of

"Was he allowed to do that?" Emma asked, with a timid glance at Nanny Cole.

"He wasn't, actually," replied the duke. "The hall and all that it contained were entailed to me and should've been handed down intact. But with Grandmother gone, there was no one to stop him." The duke's gaze roved over the walls, taking in every painting, every priceless ornament, while his hands caressed the rich fabric on the arms of his chair, as though reassuring himself that it was real. "I'm so proud of Grandmother for hiding her emeralds," he said softly.

From the corner of her eye, Emma saw Nanny Cole raise her eyes to Kate, who looked quickly away.

"We think she must have done the same thing with the lantern," Grayson went on, "and for the same reason. Unfortunately, she neglected to inform anyone of the hiding place. By then, you see, there was hardly anyone left to tell." The duke folded his hands and tapped the tips of his thumbs together. "Imagine waking up each day to the loss of a beloved sister or brother, uncle or aunt, and you will begin to comprehend the distress I felt when my father began to dismiss the staff. Soon only Nanny Cole remained, and I refused to believe that Father would send her away. With Grandmother gone, Nanny Cole was the only mother I had."

"I was the only one left to make your blasted bed, you mean," Nanny Cole put in. Her knitting needles had stopped moving and she peered fondly at the duke. A faint pink flush rose in the old woman's cheeks as she sensed that the attention of the room was on her, and she pulled her needles back into action, growling, "You just get on with the story, my lad."

"Where was I? Ah, yes . . ." The duke sighed wearily. "Father then informed me that I was to be sent away to school. That was bad enough, but on the afternoon of the very same day, not a month after my grandmother's death, I saw her harp being loaded into a van and taken away. You must understand that the harp was her prize possession. Its removal forced me to face the awful fact that nothing and no one was safe.

"Father and I had a terrific set-to that evening, at the conclusion of which I ran away. I was a mere boy at the time—Peter's age—an weather was as rough as it is tonight, so I didn't run very far. I went to the lady chapel, in fact, to have a good, self-pitying weep. Much to my amazement, Aunt Dimity was there when I arrived—"

"Dimity Westwood?" Derek asked.

"There's only one Aunt Dimity," Grayson replied.

"But how did she know—" Emma left the sentence unfinished.

The duke smiled and shook his head. "I have no idea. She'd learned of Grandmother's death, of course—"

"And she may have heard rumors about the sale of the harp," Kate put in.

"Perhaps," said the duke. "But . . ." He shrugged. "Who knows?"

A tingle crept down Emma's back. Dimity Westwood was beginning to sound vaguely supernatural. She returned long-lost teddy bears to bereft little girls, and she just happened to appear out of nowhere to soothe tormented little boys. And the mysterious woman might have had a hand in bringing Emma to Penford Hall, as well. Emma glanced up at Derek's sapphire eyes and broad shoulders, wondering how far Aunt Dimity's powers extended, then shook her head and gave her full attention to the duke.

"Aunt Dimity listened to my woes," he was saying, "then told me, flat out, that I would think of a way to save the hall. I don't remember what happened next, but when I awoke the following morning, I felt as though I'd been reborn. I saw clearly that an enormous task lay ahead of me—but not an impossible one. That made all the difference."

As though galvanized by the memory, the duke pushed himself out of his chair and stood before the fire. Thrusting one hand into a trouser pocket and clutching a tweedy lapel with the other, he struck a professorial pose. "Now," he said, "if one asks an adult how to raise an enormous amount of capital in a relatively brief period of time, one will invariably reply . . . ?" He raised an eyebrow and stared at Emma.

"Money?" Emma ventured.

"A banker." The duke nodded his approval. "If, however, one puts the same question, one will receive two dozen different answers, each more outrageous than the last. I speak as an authority, having come up with a dozen dozen different schemes over the next few years, but dismissed them all as too time-consuming and/or dangerously illegal.

"Then, one night at school, Pogger Pratt-Evans was listening to some particularly noisome rock music. When I asked him to turn it down, Pogger replied with the immortal words . . ." The duke turned his face to the ceiling and enunciated each word carefully, as though he were reciting Shakespearean verse. "'Fat lot you know about music. These guys must be good—they've made millions.'"

The duke closed his eyes for a moment, as though savoring the words, then began to pace excitedly before the fire. "I couldn't sleep a wink that night, not with 'they've made millions' ringing in my ears, and by morning I had put together a plan—an outrageous, ridiculous, impossible plan, which I knew in the depths of my twelve-year-old heart would save the hall. In fact, I think it's fair to say that it was at that moment that Lex Rex was born."

Derek frowned. "Are you saying that *you're*—"

"I am not," the duke declared. He came to a halt squarely in front of the fire, his hands in his pockets, his hair a golden halo above his shadowed face, looking as though he'd never quite left his twelve-year-old self behind. "I'm saying only that an idea was born." He spread his arms wide. "It was this distinguished collection of geniuses who nurtured that idea until it became the loathsome creature we know as Lex Rex."

"You mean, you're all—?" Emma touched a hand to her glasses and looked from one wrinkled face to another. "You're *all* Lex Rex?"

"Our star pupil triumphs again," proclaimed the duke. He gave them no time to digest this startling news, turning quickly to ask Kate to go on with the story.

Kate Cole cleared her throat. "As you know, Mother and I had moved to Bournemouth after the old duke gave Mother the—after Mother left Penford Hall."

"Broke her heart to leave," said Nanny Cole, eyeing her daughter with unexpected gentleness. "But we couldn't go back to the village. Bloody place was deserted. No school, no children to play with . . ."

"So we went to Bournemouth, where Mother worked as a seamstress."

"Kate was never happy there," Nanny Cole went on. "Only time she perked up was when she got Grayson's letters. So, when she came to me with his crack-brained scheme, I thought, Bugger it, I'll jolly them along. Anything to get Kate up and punching again." Nanny Cole sighed and looked down at her cobalt-blue yarn. "Hated to see her in such a funk."

"Mother was wonderful," said Kate. "She drew all sorts of costumes and I sent the drawings on to Grayson. We wrote to each other three or four times a week. His plan didn't sound preposterous to me."

Nanny Cole snorted. "None of Grayson's plans ever sounded preposterous to you, my girl." She glanced at Crowley with a devilish grin. "Remember the two of 'em tunneling under the arbor, looking for pirate gold?"

"I do indeed, Nanny," Crowley replied. "Quite a time we had, pulling them out. I believe it was Miss Kate who christened Lex Rex. Isn't that right, Nanny?"

"Very true," Nanny Cole replied. "Lex from Alexander—one of Grayson's other names—and Rex . . . Well, she wanted her duke to have a promotion, didn't she?"

"I thought it sounded well together," Kate explained, coloring. "At any rate," she hurried on, "it seemed to me that the most important part of the plan was that it be carried out in secret."

The duke nodded eagerly. "Quite right. If I didn't want to spend the rest of my life as Lex Rex—and I most certainly did not—we would require the help of people whose loyalty and discretion would be absolute."

Kate smiled. "Grayson had kept in touch with everyone, not just *f but the remaining villagers, as well, those who'd refused to ~nford Harbor. We selected a core group and, with Moth-
~n to visit them, one by one, to sound them out."

~ was quite astonishing," said the duke. "Within the
~e staff working together to breathe life into Lex
~ed to do something with pop music, but I
~he one who figured that out."
bsently at the duke.

"I was just telling Derek and Emma that you invented Lex Rex," said the duke.

"Yes, yes." Hallard blinked owlishly. "Just created a character, really."

"Hallard," the duke informed Emma, "is also known as Hal Arden."

"The writer?" Emma gaped at the bespectacled old man. "Spy novels?"

"My publisher prefers to call them espionage thrillers, but never mind," said Hallard. "Don't hold much with labels."

"But I've read everything you've ever written!" Emma exclaimed.

"He'll autograph a complete set for you, won't you, old man?" The duke beamed at Hallard. "Our writer-in-residence was instrumental in putting together Lex's biography."

"Just listened to His Grace and Miss Kate, really," said Hallard. "Bit of a poser, really, making a character who was literally three-dimensional. But I liked the challenge."

"And rose to it," declared the duke. "Hallard was the one who discovered that ownership of England's great estates falls into five basic categories: surviving families, few and far between; foreigners who wish they were English; corporations, which use the houses as retreats for harried executives; the National Trust, which turns them into museums—"

"And pop stars," Hallard concluded. "Interesting subject, really, and His Grace made the research that much easier. It was like having an agent in place, really, with him spying on kids like Pogger and telling me what they fancied." Hallard leaned forward, rubbing his palms together as he warmed to his subject. "Lex Rex couldn't be a pretty-face pop phenomenon, y'see, because we couldn't have people concentrating on His Grace's face. We didn't want a band with too much staying power, either. A medium-sized hit twice a year for five years would do us nicely. I figured that, if *Time* magazine called Lex the next Beatles within the first two years of our run, we'd done the job."

"Their predictions inevitably fade," explained the duke. He smiled slyly and scratched the end of his nose. "Hallard wrote the lyrics for Lex's songs, as well. 'Kiss My Tongue' was, in my opinion, one of his noblest efforts."

"I don't know," Kate teased. "I've always been fond of the ecological motif of 'Slug Soup.' And let's not forget 'Chafe Me, Baby,' and—"

"That'll be quite enough out of the pair of you," Nanny Cole scolded. "Hallard may have written tripe, but *you,* Grayson, wrote the putrid music."

"I did," Grayson admitted sheepishly.

"But you're a talented musician," Emma exclaimed. "How could you bring yourself to—"

"Create such cacophony? I was following Hallard's script. Everything about Lex had to be off-putting, to keep people at bay. And there Nanny Cole came into her own."

Nanny Cole eyed him suspiciously, then turned to Derek and Emma. "I designed Lex's costumes and makeup," she said. "I created his bloody-awful image. Had to turn Grayson into a raving lunatic. Not as much of a stretch as he'd like to think."

"Nanny's costumes were brilliant," Grayson said. "She has the soul of a poet and it embarrasses her terribly. Hence the bluff exterior."

"I'll buff your posterior if you don't stop," Nanny Cole growled, and Derek flinched as she grabbed him by the wrist. "Keep still," she ordered as she held the sleeve of the nearly finished sweater up to Derek's arm. "Good Lord," she muttered, dropping the arm. "Built like a bloody great ape."

Grayson snorted. "Nanny shaved my head and painted it red for the cover of the first album. I promise you, not even Grandmother would've recognized me once Nanny had finished with her paint pots. I scarcely recognized myself."

"Surely you made some personal appearances," Derek said, rubbing his wrist.

"Very few," said Kate. "Lex refused to attend ceremonies of any kind and he was never seen in public without his makeup. It was perfectly in keeping with the character we'd established."

"The press posed some danger," Grayson went on, "but Hallard solved that as well. Whenever they showed up, Lex would scratch himself rudely and spout all those words one mustn't say on the telly, at decibel levels impossible for microphones to miss. And we had Newland here, to look after security."

Newland nodded but, unlike the rest of the staff, made no effort to explain his role. An uneasy silence enveloped the room, and everyone turned to Kate gratefully when she broke it.

"And then there were the videos," she said.

"A godsend." Grayson clapped Derek on the shoulder. "Remember the chaps I ran around with in Oxford?"

Derek nodded.

"One of them is a well-known rock singer now. I won't mention his name, as he's made an assiduous effort to deny his bourgeois past, but he's the one who put me on to rock videos. That's how we were able to get in at the right time."

Kate's eyes were dancing. "Lex Rex became the first pop star to take full advantage of the video boom. And we filmed them right here, in Gash's studio."

Gash twiddled his thumbs. "Jury-rigged from start to finish. Had no idea what I was doing, but that didn't bother His Grace. Had no capital, neither, so I had to make do. Cleared out one of the subcellars, soundproofed it as best I could. Bought secondhand stage lights and cheap video equipment and off we went."

Emma rolled her eyes, recalling the praise Richard had heaped on Lex Rex's "rough-edged authenticity." She wondered what he would say if she told him that the qualities he most admired were due solely to inexperience, ineptitude, and a tight budget.

The duke flopped into his chair and crossed his legs. "As it turned out, we had eight years in which to plan the whole thing, down to the smallest detail. I was twenty years old when my father died."

"Grayson came down from university to follow in his father's reclusive footsteps and disappear from public view," Kate went on.

"When I reappeared, I did so as Lex Rex," said the duke. "After eight years of intensive study, I was able to give rock-music fans exactly what they wanted. Then, of course, I gave them more of the same."

"Look at any best-seller list," Hallard murmured thoughtfully, "and you'll know where that idea came from."

"But . . ." Emma scratched her head. "But what about the Series Ten?"

"The what?" said Hallard.

"Hallard simply uses the computers," the duke put in. "We leave the rest to Crowley."

"Crowley?" Derek and Emma chorused.

From his place near the gaming table, Crowley smiled his polite, distant smile, tugged at his stiff cuffs, and folded his hands in his lap. "After leaving the old duke's employ," he began, "I moved to Plymouth, to be near my only daughter." He looked down at the floor for a moment, then shook his head. "What the others have failed to tell you is that it is not a simple matter for a person of mature years to find employment. Nanny Cole had her flair with the needle; Gash, his mechanical skills; Hallard, his God-given gift with words; and Newland . . ." He squinted at the tight-lipped security man. "Well, I'm not at all sure what Newland got up to, but I do know that his talents are in demand in many places.

"But what did I have to offer?" Crowley sighed. "Thirty years of loyal service counts for very little in the modern world, it seems. You can imagine my relief when I eventually won a post at a bank, entering check numbers on a computer. It was a very low-level position and tedious to the extreme. Sheer boredom led me to read up on computers and to explore my little machine's capabilities."

"Crowley was to the keyboard born," the duke declared. "He took to programming like a duck to water, and he's a dab hand at code-cracking, too. He's had the best trackers after him, and they've yet to find a single broken blade of grass. Only one came within shouting distance, but he backed off."

"Tut, tut," Crowley murmured, accepting the tribute with a self-effacing wave of the hand.

"He salted records with facts about Lex's alleged background," said Kate, "and he managed every pound of Lex's income."

"He managed to make it disappear," the duke put in. "Crowley tied Lex's money-trail in so many knots that it would have taken a magician to unravel it. He made it appear as though Lex had frittered away his fortune on playthings." The duke clucked his tongue. "Just another self-indulgent pop star."

Emma pictured Crowley's storklike figure hunched over the keyboard of a computer late at night, after the bank had closed, sailing freely through the electronic networks, and she was filled with awe. It wasn't every day that she got to meet a natural-born hacker who'd discovered computers at such an advanced age.

Derek rubbed his jaw. "I don't know, Grayson. This doesn't sound like you. I find it difficult to believe that you could be quite so cynical."

"Of course I was cynical, dear chap," the duke acknowledged easily. "But you must admit that it was a healthy sort of cynicism. Lex Rex did not wish to be loved—he wished only to be paid. It kept his ego in check, kept his mind focused—it kept him from drink, drugs, and all the other slings and arrows that had slain so many before him. He never promoted such things, either. My alter ego's only sins were poor taste and a severely limited vocabulary—"

"Which you enjoyed to the hilt," Nanny Cole reminded him.

"Well . . . yes," the duke admitted, with a shame-faced grin. "It was rather . . . liberating." He tugged on an earlobe, then settled back in his chair, businesslike once more. "At the end of the second year, we'd earned enough to replace the roof and begin restoring the hall's interior. In four more years, we'd amassed a fortune, which Crowley invested with good results. Computers were not the only thing he studied at the bank."

Derek nodded. "Then you decided that it was time for Lex's abrupt departure from the world of rock music."

"Poor old Lex," the duke agreed, with mock sadness. "He never was much of a sailor, was he, Tom?"

"No, indeed, Your Grace." The chief constable chuckled. "It were the Tregallis boys that fixed that up. Born fishermen, they are, and want nothin' more'n to carry on as their father had done. The Tharbys at the Bright Lady felt the same way, and so did old Jonah Pengully and my mother. So we worked it all out with Hallard and watched the weather maps, waitin' for a storm. When it looked as if a likely one was brewin', His Grace hightailed it for France—"

"I was traveling a great deal by then," the duke added, "recovering my family's scattered treasures."

"Me and the boys went aboard His Grace's yacht," the chief constable continued, "and had a fine old time, smashing it to bits. Ted and Jack steered it onto the shoals, and James picked them up in a dinghy."

"Only expert sailors could've managed that trick," Derek commented. He looked thoughtfully at the fire, then frowned. "But why go to all that trouble? Wouldn't it have been safer to stage his death somewhere else, to make it a bit less spectacular?"

Kate shook her head. "Lex's death would've attracted attention no matter where it took place," she said flatly. "This way, we could control the situation and make the best use of the resources we had at hand."

"Taciturn Cornish villagers make very credible eyewitnesses, really," Hallard explained. "Lots of practice at it, I suppose, with all the smuggling that used to go on."

"But what about the press?" Derek asked.

"A temporary nuisance," Grayson said dismissively.

"Still," Derek persisted, "you were taking an awfully big risk, weren't you? How many people were involved? Fourteen? Fifteen? And now you'll have to add me and Emma to the list. I've no doubt that Newland knows his stuff, but how can you be sure there'll be no leaks?"

"We can't," the duke replied simply. "Look, Derek, I may very well be the dunderhead Nanny considers me to be, but Hallard isn't."

Hallard was cleaning his glasses with his handkerchief. "Just have a devious mind, really. I knew the truth would come out eventually. It's human nature to want to share a secret." He carefully replaced his glasses, then folded his handkerchief and returned it to his pocket. "So I prepared a story line for every situation we're likely to face."

The duke smiled indulgently at Hallard. "It's no use grilling him on what those story lines may be. He's got them hidden away on

Crowley's blasted Series Ten, with instructions on how to get at them, should we ever need to. But he hates discussing his work. Won't even let me read his book flaps."

"Pesky things always give the plot away," Hallard put in.

"All we know for certain," said the duke, "is that Hallard's come up with a number of likely and unlikely scenarios for us to follow. Based on his past performance, I have every confidence that, whatever happens, the outcome will be satisfactory for all concerned."

Emma sipped tea that had long since grown cold, then put her cup and saucer on the tray. "There's one more question I'd like to ask, if I may," she said. "The answer may seem obvious to you, but . . . Well, it sounds so complicated, and it took so long to plan. I'm just wondering why you were all so willing to help out."

Uncertain looks were exchanged, throats were cleared, fingernails were examined, and feet were shuffled. Finally, Gash proposed an answer.

"It was fun," he said. "Whether Lex Rex panned out or not, we had a good time working on him. When you get down to it, fixing flats in the local garage can be pretty bloody boring."

Now Crowley spoke up. "Self-interest played a role, as well. There was always the outside chance that His Grace's scheme would succeed, that we would achieve our individual goals. All I wanted was to return to my place at Penford Hall. Newland wanted a quiet patch of woods to prowl, Gash dreamt of a first-rate garage, and Hallard wanted privacy and time to write."

"It's the same in the village," said the chief constable. "As I said before—"

"*Balls!*" roared Nanny Cole, rattling her knitting needles. "Sod that nonsense, Tom Trevoy, and the same goes for you, Ephraim Crowley. Fun and self-interest—what a load of rubbish." She sniffed derisively. "You know as well as I do why we listened to His Grace, and why we went ahead when common sense told us we hadn't a chance in hell of succeeding. It was *him*." She looked proudly at the duke. "He's a proper little wizard, is our Grayson, and always has been. He can charm water from a rock. He can twist a stiff-necked old biddy like me around his little finger."

"Now, Nanny . . ." Grayson murmured.

"Don't you 'Now, Nanny' me, you cheeky blighter. They all know what I'm talking about. They know how you make folks believe that everything's possible, that dreams were *meant* to come true. If you'd told us we could fly to the moon, we'd've tried to build a bloody rocket." She glared fiercely around the room. "And I dare any of you to deny it."

No one took up the challenge. Derek ran a hand through his curls, then shook his head, bemused. "Fascinating," he murmured. "Truly fascinating. And, in all that time, no one ever suspected the truth?"

The duke didn't answer at first. A faint smile played about his lips as he rose and stood staring silently into the fire. Finally, he spoke. "In all those years, only one person saw through my ruse, and that was because I wanted her to. When the *Great God of Thunder* album went platinum, the fourteenth duke of Penford received a request for a rather hefty donation to a certain children's fund in the City. I can recall the accompanying note word for word. It said: 'Perhaps you can see your way clear to making other children's dreams come true.' It was signed by Aunt Dimity."

Twenty-one

Outside the warm cocoon of the dowager's bedchamber the storm raged on. Thunder cracked and rolled, lightning slashed the roiling sky, and driving rain battered the windows and walls, the roofs and towers, the balconies, turrets, and terraces of Penford Hall.

Crowley and Hallard had cleared away the tea things, replacing them with a decanter of port and nine delicately etched wineglasses. The decanter was passed from hand to hand, the aromatic wine glinting ruby-red in the firelight.

What an amazing story, Emma thought. It was the most amazing— No. The most amazing story was that she had been permitted to sit there and listen to such an amazing story. Sipping the sweet wine, she contemplated the still figure of the duke. She knew that she was in the presence of a remarkable man, a man who inspired such devotion that those who knew him best had given years of their lives to ensure that his dream would come true.

Nanny Cole's offhand comment about building a rocket to the moon was more apt than the old woman probably realized. The world of rock music must have been as alien to these elderly people as the red dust of Mars, yet they had mapped the terrain and exploited it as fearlessly as any team of space explorers.

While clearing away the tea trays, Crowley had described Lex Rex as a limited partnership in which all members of the core group, staff and villager alike, held equal shares. Thanks to Crowley's impeccable management, each person in that room was independently wealthy. All of them could have left the hall behind to build their own castles, but they stayed on, because Penford Hall was their home, and the world beyond its walls offered nothing they didn't already have.

"Grayson," Derek said gruffly, "owe you an apology, old man. Shouldn't have doubted you. Sorry I did."

"Me, too," Emma added. "I should have trusted the Pym sisters.

They told me you couldn't be guilty of any serious wrongdoing, and they were right."

"Were they?" the duke mused. He turned his glass slowly in his hands. "I'm not so sure. One person, at least, appears to have suffered greatly as a result of my scheming. We mustn't forget about Susannah."

"What do you mean?" Derek said sharply.

"Can't you guess?" the duke asked in return.

Derek's eyes narrowed and he glanced down at Emma, who nodded for him to go on. Looking back to the duke, Derek said, "Susannah told me she had reason to believe you'd had a hand in Lex's death." He hesitated. "Do you know about her father?"

"Syd told me, on the way to the hospital," Grayson answered. "Until that moment, I had no idea that such a tragedy had occurred. When I think of her poor mother coming here, asking for help, and being turned away . . ." Grayson bowed his head. "No wonder Susannah felt unable to approach me directly. But we'll discuss this matter later. Please, continue."

Derek explained the way in which Susannah's accident had triggered doubts in his own mind about the circumstances surrounding Lex's death. He described the reasons he'd enlisted Emma's aid, and the gradual evolution of their suspicions. "But none of it matters now, does it?" he asked. "If you were prepared to deal with the consequences of exposure, then none of you would've had a motive to harm Susannah. Her fall must have been an unhappy accident."

"Unhappy, to be sure," said the duke gravely, "but not, I fear, an accident. Tom?"

The red-haired chief constable nodded grimly. "Knew there was some funny business going on the minute I heard about her shoes. Kate told me they was all clean and shiny, like she'd just polished 'em up that morning."

Emma could picture Susannah's high-heeled shoe poking out from beneath the oilcloth; the broken heel had gleamed in the morning sun, but it hadn't registered until now. "It had rained the night before," she said slowly. "If she'd walked to the chapel garden in those shoes, they would have been muddy."

"And they wasn't even wet," the chief constable declared. "But I didn't hear about it until two days later. The evidence was gone by then, and the crime scene was contaminated, as they say, so I thought I'd just ask around, quietlike, before reportin' to my superiors. Asked Newland to give me a hand." He stared down into his wineglass. "Between us, we've been able to account for everyone in the hall and the village. We've come up with a lead, but . . ." His voice trailed off and he looked to the duke for support.

The duke cleared his throat, then ran a finger around the inside of his shirt collar. He favored Derek with a troubled, almost apologetic smile, then hunched forward and said, in a confidential murmur, "You see, old man, we know that Susannah was pestering you a great deal. As you observed earlier, it's difficult to keep secrets in a place like this."

Derek blinked in surprise. "Grayson, if you're accusing me—"

"I'm not. Madama has confirmed that you were breakfasting with Bantry in the kitchen." The duke wet his lips. "Fact is, old man, I'm accusing your son."

"Peter?" Derek stared at the duke in astonishment.

The duke sighed regretfully. "Wanted to discuss this with you privately, but . . . The truth of the matter is that Peter was seen going into the garden early that morning."

"By whom?" Derek demanded.

"Bantry. He didn't think anything of it until Tom and Newland had struck everyone else off the list. It was only then that he recalled Peter's repeated expressions of concern about Susannah interfering with your work. Viewed in that light, the boy's presence in the garden on that particular morning suggested the possibility . . ." The duke averted his gaze. "I'm sure you understand what I'm getting at."

"Yes," Derek murmured, setting his wineglass on the tray. "Yes, I quite see."

"No," Emma broke in. "You don't see at all. None of you do." She reached for Derek's hand and hoped that Peter would forgive her. "Peter did go into the garden that morning, but he didn't spend any time there. He was in the chapel until the shouting started; then he slipped out through the back door and went around the outside to the cliff path. You can check with the Tregallis brothers. They saw him go out there." She pulled Derek around to face her. "He didn't want to get into trouble for hanging around the chapel. That's why he told you he was—"

"Shouting?" Newland spoke from the doorway, then came to stand over Emma. "Did you say that the boy heard shouting?"

"Well . . . yes," Emma replied, unnerved by the man's hawkish gaze. "That's what he told me."

"First I've heard of any shouting," Newland growled. He surveyed the other faces in the room. "Any of you lot forget to tell me about shouting?"

As murmurs of denial sounded all around her, Emma tried to recall whether she or Nell had cried out upon finding Susannah. She was sure they hadn't. She clearly remembered being impressed by Nell's calmness and amazed by her own, but, before she could open her mouth to reply, she felt a tremor pass through Derek's body.

"My God," he murmured, half to himself. "If none of you were shouting, then Peter must have heard someone else." His head snapped up. "I breakfasted alone that morning. Bantry only stopped by for a cup of coffee." He grabbed Emma's arm and pulled her to her feet. "Come on. We've got to get up to the nursery."

As they darted into the darkened hallway, Emma's mind raced. She refused to believe that Bantry would harm Peter, but he might have lashed out at Susannah. She remembered that first afternoon in the garden, when he'd spoken so harshly against anything that threatened to disrupt the peace of Penford Hall. He'd known where the grub hoe was and he had the strength to wield it. He'd cleaned the oilcloth, as well, and stowed it safely in his cupboard. And now it looked as though he'd tried to cast suspicion on Peter, the one person who might identify his voice and place him in the garden with Susannah at the crucial time.

Footsteps pounded behind them and flashlights glinted maniacally from the rippled panes of leaded glass that lined the long, arcaded corridor. The main staircase loomed ahead and Derek leapt for it, nearly colliding with Bantry, who was hastening downstairs.

Derek seized the old man's shoulders, shouting, "Where's my

son? What have you done with my boy?" until Newland got to him and wrestled him away.

Bantry took a faltering step backward, then sat abruptly on the stairs, squinting dazedly as half a dozen flashlights focused on his nut-brown face. When he had elbowed his way to Bantry's side, the duke bent down to ask calmly if Master Peter were still in the nursery.

The old man shook his head. "No, Your Grace," he said earnestly. "I were just comin' down to tell you. The boy's gone. Don't know how he slipped by me, but he's not in his bed nor anywhere else up there." He gripped Grayson's arm urgently and jutted his grizzled chin toward the windows. "He's taken his jacket and a torch, Your Grace. Lady Nell thinks he's out there in that storm."

Without a second thought, Emma headed down the stairs.

"Where are you going?" Derek cried.

"To the chapel," she replied, over her shoulder. "Don't you see? He's gone to check the window."

Derek shook off Newland's hold and plunged down the stairs after Emma, while Grayson hung back, issuing rapid orders to his troops. The last thing Emma heard before reaching the entrance hall and turning for the dining room was Nanny Cole calling out to Kate to phone for Dr. Singh.

"Should've brought the flashlight," Derek muttered as they groped their way through the darkened dining room.

"I don't think it'd be much use out there," Emma said. The wind buffeted the French doors, and rain gusted in sheets against the panes. "I won't be much use, either," she added, raising a hand to her glasses. "I won't be able to see a thing."

"We'll be even, then," Derek said wryly. He reached for the door handles and, when Emma nodded, he flung the doors wide.

Emma gasped as the cold rain hit her, and she was soaked to the skin before reaching the terrace steps. Tucking her chin to her chest, she fought her way across the lawn, blinded by the driving downpour and slipping on the sodden grass until they reached the relative sanctuary of the ruins, where the wind's roar became a moaning chorus as it swirled and eddied through empty hearths and gaping doorways.

Trailing fingers along the rain-slicked walls, Emma sprinted down the grassy corridor until she reached the banquet room, where the constant strobe of lightning showed a scene of utter chaos. Stakes and leaves and flattened stalks littered the graveled path, and vines streamed from the arbor's dome like pennants in the wind. Derek tried to rush ahead, tripped, and sprawled, but Emma hauled him to his feet, and together they staggered forward to the far end of the room and the corridor beyond.

They left the green door banging on its hinges as they stumbled down the chapel garden's stairs. Waterfalls spilled from the raised beds' low retaining walls, and the flagstone path was a mire of clinging mud. Emma longed to reach the stillness of the chapel, to slam the door on the storm and catch her breath, but although Derek strained against it, the chapel door refused to budge. Teeth chattering, Emma darted forward to add her weight to Derek's, and the door slowly gave way, moving inward inch by inch, until the gap was wide enough for them to slip inside.

Emma paused to wipe her glasses, then gazed about in stark confusion. Peter's orange emergency lantern lay on its side on the granite shelf, pointing toward the back door. The back door had been left wide open, and the force of the wind that ripped through the doorway had shoved the benches askew and held the front door shut against them. The old wheelbarrow had been wedged into the gaping doorway, and a rope stretched tautly from its wooden handles into the seething darkness.

"What the—" Derek turned to Emma, but she was already tugging on the rounded door, held fast once more by the roaring wind.

"Don't touch the barrow until we've had a look outside!" she shouted. "We don't know what that rope is holding!"

Derek seized a pitchfork and used it to lever the front door open. It banged shut again behind them as they raced up the stairs and out of the chapel garden. Together they ran along the garden wall, but when they swerved into the rocky meadow, the wind slammed into Emma and drove her to her knees.

"Go!" she screamed when Derek stopped to pull her up, and he barreled ahead, while she groped blindly for the wall on hands and knees, searingly aware of the long fall that lay only a few yards away.

The knuckles of her flailing left hand scraped rough stone and she struggled to her feet. Hugging the stone wall, she stumbled forward until she reached the corner, rounded it, and saw the faint pool of light outside the chapel's rear wall, where the rope stretched, glistening, over the edge of the cliff and straight down into the devouring darkness. Derek was almost there, the rope was almost in his hand, when Peter's lantern faded and winked out.

"No!" Derek's anguished cry rang out above the roaring wind, and Emma froze, paralyzed by fear. Then, through her rain-blurred glasses, Emma saw the air begin to shimmer.

The glow was all around them. It came from nowhere and from everywhere and grew brighter by the minute, until the rain glittered bright as diamonds, bright as Peter's tears, streaking downward like a million falling stars. Emma saw her bloodied knuckles, saw the blades of stunted grass, saw each rock and leaf and puddle as clearly as though it were midday.

Derek saw the rope. He lunged for it, and Emma leapt to help him as he dug his heels into the rocky ground, hauling fiercely, hand over hand, his muscles straining against his rain-drenched shirt. The rope bit into Emma's palms and fell in coils behind her, but she looked only at the point where it slithered slowly over the cliff's edge.

All at once, a hand came into view, white-knuckled, clinging to the rope. Then Peter's face appeared, and as his shoulders rose into the light, Emma saw that he was tied fast to the limp and pallid form of Mattie.

Derek eased them onto solid ground, then nicked his penknife open and cut the rope. As the light began to fade, he hugged his son, kicked the wheelbarrow aside, and shoved the boy toward Emma, who swept him into the safety of the chapel, where she held him at arm's length, scarcely believing that he was alive and in one piece.

Peter wobbled slightly on his feet, blinked dazedly, then stiffened. His mouth fell open and he tried to raise his arm to point, but his eyes rolled back in his head and he tumbled, fainting, into Emma's arms. Emma glanced over her shoulder as Derek stumbled in, carrying Mattie, and in the last fluorescence of the fading light, she thought she saw the lady in the window, clad in white.

Twenty-two

The moment Derek closed the back door, Grayson, Gash, and Newland came barreling into the chapel. They'd been struggling with the front door for some time, their efforts hampered by flapping slickers and the blankets they were carrying.

"Dear old Kate," Grayson said, draping a blanket across Emma's shoulders. "Jolly brilliant of her to think of the flares, what?"

Shivering, Emma pulled the blanket tightly around her. She'd tried to get a clearer look at the window, but the lights, and everyone's attention, were focused on Mattie, who lay on the rear bench, unconscious. "Grayson—" Emma murmured.

"Hush." Grayson squeezed her shoulder and turned to watch Newland, who was crouching beside Mattie, checking her pulse. "Not a word, my dear, not until we've got you all back in the hall." Newland looked up and Grayson nodded. "Right, then. Everyone ready? Off we go."

Derek cradled Peter in his arms, Gash and Newland carried a blanket-wrapped Mattie between them, and Grayson put an unexpectedly strong arm around Emma's waist as they left the chapel to face the storm once more. Emma felt lightheaded, and she moved through the mud and the pelting rain on legs that had turned to rubber. The castle ruins closed around her, then fell away, and the light in the dining-room windows hovered like a dream on a distant horizon.

Kate and Hallard were there, bearing ornate candelabras, since the electricity was still off, and they led the motley parade to the library, where Dr. Singh was waiting. Chilled to the bone, Emma told Grayson to go ahead with the others, then made her solitary way up the darkened staircase and through the silent corridors to her room, oddly comforted by her ability to find her way without a light to guide her.

The rose suite was warm and dry and quiet. Emma let the rain-soaked blanket slide from her shoulders, dried her glasses on the quilted coverlet, then knelt on the hearth and fumbled with numb fingers to start a fire. She gave up, finally, pulled the coverlet from the bed, and huddled beneath it, too exhausted to move. She wasn't sure how much time had passed before she was aroused from her stupor by the sound of a voice from the hallway.

"Emma, honey. It's me, Syd. You think maybe you could get the door?"

Syd Bishop's candles were balanced on a round tray. "Room service," he announced, placing the tray on the low table between the pair of overstuffed armchairs. "Hot coffee, and a bowl of chicken soup. I'd go straight to hell if I was to say it's as good as my grandma's, God rest her soul, but I'm tellin' ya, Madama musta stole her recipe." He filled a cup with steaming coffee and handed it to Emma, wincing when he saw her bloodied knuckles. "Ouch. Caught yourself pretty good there, huh? And what are you doin', sittin' here all this time in wet clothes? C'mon. Let's get you changed before you catch pneumonia."

Syd's years behind the scenes at fashion shows had not been wasted. He knew how women's clothing worked and was disarmingly matter-of-fact about nudity. He stripped off Emma's dripping clothes and tucked her into her blue robe, wrapped a towel around her head, and sat her in an armchair without spilling a drop of her coffee or bringing the faintest blush to her cheek.

The coffee had revived her and the scent of chicken soup proved irresistible. While Syd bent to start a fire, Emma emptied the bowl, then sat back, wishing there was more. Her hand was sore and her knees were beginning to ache, and she knew she'd be stiff later on, but at that moment, with a bowl of warm soup inside her and a second cup of coffee to sip, a soft chair to sink into and a fire beginning to crackle at her feet, she felt as though she'd washed ashore in paradise.

"Is Peter all right?" she asked, as Syd settled into the other chair.

"Petey-boy? He's gonna be just fine after he gets a little shut-eye. I'm tellin' you, Emma, I'm so proud of that kid, I could bust." He turned to pour a cup of coffee for himself. "He saved Mattie's life, you know."

"No, Syd," said Emma. "I don't know. What was she doing out there?"

"Tryin' to off herself." Syd nodded, picked up his cup and saucer, leaned back in his chair. "Crowley found a note."

"Oh, no," Emma whispered.

"Yeah, I know. Terrible thing. Terrible. Such a young girl. She's gonna be okay, though. Busted her arm and banged herself up pretty good, but the doc, he says she'll be fine."

"But *why?*"

"Didn't know how to explain things to Crowley. Didn't want her old grandpa to be ashamed of her." Syd paused to drink from his cup, then looked toward Emma. "She's the one what clobbered Suzie."

"Mattie?"

"That's what the note was about. There was pages and pages of it and, I'm tellin' ya, it was a real eye-opener." Syd put his cup on the tray, folded his hands across his stomach, and sighed. "Mattie had her heart set on goin' into the industry," he began. "She was crazy about Suzie, real thrilled about meetin' a pro. So, when Suzie told her to come to the chapel garden that morning, and to keep everything hush-hush so Nanny Cole's nose wouldn't be put outta joint . . ."

. . . *I couldn't say no, Granddad.* Mattie paused to listen for a moment, then smiled. It was much too late for anyone to be knocking on her door. It was only the wind that had disturbed her, rising to a keening wail outside the window of her room. Such a nice room. She'd cleaned it from top to bottom after supper, and put her things neatly on the dresser, where Granddad could find them and send them home to Mum afterward. Now all that remained was the note. Mattie chewed thoughtfully on the end of her pen, then bent to her task once more.

I put all my sketches together and packed my blue bag with the dress Nanny helped me make—the crêpe de chine, with all the tucks. Nanny says it's my best one yet, but I wanted a professional opinion, so I just had to show it to Ashers. And then I thought about accessories. You know how strict Nanny is about them, but I didn't think my dress needed too much fuss and feathers, as Nanny calls it. The right pair of shoes would be enough. Mattie raised her pen from the paper and looked toward the windows again. The wind was blowing harder than ever, and that was good. It would make everything easier.

"She snuck the shoes outta Suzie's room," Syd explained, shaking his head. "Poor kid thought it'd be real impressive to show her dress with Suzie's shoes."

I put the shoes in the bag with the dress, Mattie wrote, *and told Nanny I was going down to help Madama. Then I told Madama I was going up to help Nanny. Then I came out to the garden, where Ashers was waiting. I know you don't like Ashers, but she was wonderful, at first. She said I had a real eye for detail and she told me she could put me in touch with all the right people. Can you imagine? I thought I'd died and gone to heaven.* Mattie reread the last sentence, then scratched it out.

I was very happy, she wrote instead, *until Ashers started asking those questions. You know, the ones she was asking Mr. Harris, about that grotty band that stole His Grace's boat. I told her I didn't know anything about it, but she said that you did, and told me to ask you.*

I couldn't do that. I tried to be nice about it, but Ashers kept after me, just the same way she kept after Mr. Harris. She got really mean, Granddad. She started shouting at me. She called you a thief. She said she'd have you put in prison if I didn't help her. Mattie's hand began to tremble and she reached for her cup of cocoa to steady her nerves. This was the hard part.

"Things kinda got outta hand," Syd went on. "One minute Suzie's standin' at the top of the stairs, laughin' at the kid, and, the next thing Mattie knows, she's got the grub hoe in her hands and Suzie's out cold on the ground."

I didn't mean to hurt her. Mattie underlined the words. *I just wanted her to stop saying all those awful things about you. And then she was lying there, not moving, and I knew I'd done a dreadful thing. Not just dreadful for me, but for everyone.*

You never talk about it, Granddad, and neither does Nanny Cole, but Mrs. Tharby at the Bright Lady told me how bad it was after that rock singer drowned, and I knew this would be even worse. I didn't mind going to jail, but His Grace might have to close up the hall if the newspaper people started coming round again, and I couldn't let that happen. You've been so happy here.

So I tried to make it look like an accident. You can probably guess how. I broke one of Ashers's high-heeled shoes, and took off the flats she was wearing. I put the high heels on Ashers and hid her flats in my bag. I put the flats back in her room the next day. Mattie put down her pen, and reread what she'd written, then turned to stare at her reflection in the window. It had begun to rain.

"All the time Suzie was in Plymouth, it was grindin' away at Mattie," Syd said. "And when they brought Suzie back to the hall, she kinda cracked. Said it'd all come out once Suzie got her memory back, so she might as well save everyone the trouble of a trial. And she hadda tell her grandpa the truth, so he could tell the police so nobody else would get blamed for it. Also so he'd know how sorry she was for what she done and not be too mad at her for . . . for not sayin' goodbye." Syd sighed again and shook his head, adding softly, "Kids."

That one word summed up Emma's complex feelings. She should have known something was bothering Mattie the moment the poor child fainted in the entrance hall. "Do you think they'd let me see her?" Emma asked.

"Nah," said Syd. "She's out cold, and so's Crowley. Nurse Tharby thought he was havin' a cardiac when he came staggering into Suzie's room with all them scribbly pages. Poor guy." Syd leaned over and punched Emma in the shoulder. "But I'm tellin' you what I told him. You got nothin' to blame yourself for. Mattie put on a helluva good act and it ain't your fault you couldn't see through it."

"Thanks, Syd, but . . ." Emma set her coffee cup on the tray and turned to face Syd. "I should have paid attention, at least. I treated Mattie as though she were invisible."

"That's 'cause she was makin' herself invisible. You gotta believe that, Emma. Hey, look, things worked out okay, didn't they? Thanks to you and Derek and Petey-boy, Mattie's got a long life ahead of her, plenty of time to get over all of this garbage. Things could be worse, am I right?"

Emma smiled wanly. "When you're right, you're right, Syd." She leaned toward him. "Do you know the rest of it? How Peter ended up saving her?"

"Not for sure, but I can make a good guess. Let's see, now." Syd squinted into the middle distance. "Mattie's gonna toss herself off the cliffs, right? But maybe she changes her mind at the last minute. And then she slips—you know better 'n me how slick it is out there—and she goes over accidental-like. And she ends up on one of them little ledges, holdin' on to one of them tough old bushes."

Emma nodded. "Then Peter goes out to the chapel to check on the window. . . ."

"And he hears somethin' funny out back," Syd went on. "And when he figgers out what's wrong, he goes and grabs some rope from Bantry's shed—"

Emma interrupted. "Why didn't he come back to the hall for help?"

Syd shrugged. "Hey, Mattie's out there hangin' in the breeze. Maybe he figgered he didn't have time to spare. So Petey drops the rope to Mattie, but she can't use it on account of her busted flipper. So he goes down to help her—"

"And then *he* can't get back up," Emma broke in. "So he ties himself to Mattie, and stays to ride out the storm with her." She slumped back in her chair, one hand on her heart. "My God . . ."

"Yeah." Syd's voice was filled with satisfaction. "You ask me, Petey-boy deserves a medal." He let the silence linger for a moment, then gave Emma a sly, sidelong look. "You didn't do so bad yourself. You and Derek, you made a pretty good team, huh?"

Emma looked at the fire, embarrassed. "Yes, well, that was . . . automatic. The only thing I could think about was that, if anything happened to Peter, I'd . . . I'd . . ." Emma shook her head and looked at her hands. "He's such a good kid."

"Nell ain't so bad, neither, once you get used to her."

"Afterward," Emma went on, slowly raising her gaze to the fire again, "when I had Peter safe with me in the chapel, just for a split second, I thought I saw . . ." Emma held back. She could tell the truth to Syd without mentioning the window. It might be better to say nothing of that until she'd seen it in the clear light of day.

"I saw something that made me realize how unfair I've been to Derek," she continued. "I can't begin to understand what he went through after his wife died. I'm sure he's done his best to look after Peter and Nell since then, and I know that, once I've told him about the problem with Mrs. Higgins, he'll straighten it out right away."

"That's real big of you, Emma," Syd commented dryly.

Emma glanced at Syd's impassive face, then looked quickly back to the fire. "I realized something else, too," she said, in a voice so low that Syd had to lean forward to hear it. "Derek's already lost his wife, and tonight he nearly lost his son. I . . . I don't want him to lose anyone else."

"Interesting," Syd murmured, nodding judiciously. "Excuse me, but is it old-fashioned of me to want to hear a little mention of love in there somewhere?"

"Well, of course I love him, Syd." Emma toyed with the belt on her robe. "I fell in love with him the minute I laid eyes on him. Isn't it ridiculous? And I just know he's going to ask me to marry him," she added worriedly. "That's the kind of man he is."

"I should hope so," Syd stated firmly. He wrinkled his nose suddenly. "Is that the problem? What've you got against marriage?"

"I'm not sure anymore," Emma said, with a helpless shrug. "I mean, it's not as though I've tried it. Maybe it just frightens me because everyone says it's so unhappy."

"Of course it's unhappy!" Syd shouted. Lunging to the edge of his chair, he turned to Emma, exasperated. "And it's boring and crazy and funny and sad and everything else you can think of, and then some. 'Cause that's what marriage is. It's life times two, the most complicated equation there is. You can spend a whole lifetime workin' on that one, Emma." Syd eased himself back into his chair and refolded his hands across his stomach. He stared silently at the fire for a moment, then leaned toward Emma and said quietly, still looking at the fire, "You know, Emma, those people who think you gotta be happy all the time"—he dismissed them with a wave of his hand—

"they're kids. They shouldn't be messin' with marriage, which is for grown-ups. But you, Emma. You ain't no kid."

A slow smile returned to Emma's lips. "No, Syd, I'm not." She ducked her head sheepishly. "But what if he doesn't ask me?"

"Oh, I got a feeling he'll be reminded."

Emma turned to Syd, alarmed. "Syd, you *wouldn't*—"

"Not me," said Syd. "I won't say a word." He reached over to fill his coffee cup again. "Y'know, Emma, honey, when I left the library, Derek and Grayson were having a little drink. They didn't look like they was goin' anywhere."

"Really?" Emma pulled the towel from her head and ran her fingers through her damp hair. "After everything he's been through tonight, he should be in bed." She stood up. "I think I'll go downstairs and . . . and make sure Grayson doesn't keep him up too late."

"Yeah, that duke, he's a real chatterbox," said Syd, putting the pot down. "You sure you ain't too tired?"

"Isn't it amazing? I thought I'd be exhausted, but I feel wide awake. It must be the coffee."

"Must be." Syd sipped from his cup, but refrained from further comment.

Emma left the room without a candle, but again she found her way easily in the dark. She had no idea what time it was, but she suspected that most of the hall's inhabitants were in bed and asleep. She met no one on her way down the stairs and saw no lights until she opened the library door.

The library was flooded with light. Dozens of candles, in candlestick holders of every conceivable size and shape, stood flickering from every available surface. Grayson and Kate were seated side by side on the couch, and Derek faced them from his accustomed chair near the fire. His curls were almost dry, and he'd changed into fresh jeans and a cobalt-blue cableknit sweater. Grayson had changed, too, into another well-cut tweed jacket, another immaculate shirt and silk tie.

Derek looked up as the door opened, and Kate and Grayson turned to look as well, and Emma suddenly remembered that she was wearing nothing but her robe and slippers. But it didn't matter. Nothing mattered but the glorious fact that Derek was still awake.

"Emma?" Derek rose from his chair. "Shouldn't you be in bed?"

"I was about to ask you the same thing." Emma crossed over to stand before him, unable to decide whether the sweater or Derek's eyes were a deeper blue. "How's Peter?"

"Sound asleep," Derek assured her. "He was a bit delirious, but Dr. Singh says there's no sign of any head injury, so we think it must be due to shock."

"Delirious?" Emma asked.

"Babbling about the window changing color," said Derek. "Not surprising, really. D'you know you were right? The young fool went out in that godawful storm just to make sure his precious window was intact."

"Fool?" Emma echoed, a hint of heat in her voice.

"I say, Derek, old man," murmured the duke.

"One moment, Grayson." Derek looked down at Emma, perplexed. "Yes. Fool. What would you call a ten-year-old boy who risks his life to look at a bloody window?"

Emma's foot began to tap. This wasn't the conversation she'd had in mind. "I'd call him a very worried little boy," she replied evenly.

"Worried?" Derek laughed. "I'd say he's verging on delusional. Let's face it, Emma. Those were hurricane-force winds out there, and Peter's not exactly a tower of strength."

"And I suppose you are?" Emma folded her arms.

"Er, Emma?" Kate's soft voice held a touch of concern.

"In a minute, Kate." Emma adjusted her glasses, then squared her shoulders. "Are you aware of the fact that that puny son of yours saved Mattie's life tonight?"

"He's lucky he didn't get her killed," Derek retorted.

"Lucky?" Emma's voice cracked. "How about courageous and heroic and brave? How about magnificent? Frankly, I think Peter's luck ran out when he got you for a father."

"What do you mean by that?" Derek sputtered.

"I mean that, if you can look at what he did tonight and see nothing but foolishness and luck, then you don't deserve your son. For your information, the window *has* changed."

"*What?*" chorused Grayson and Kate.

"Now *you're* sounding delusional," scoffed Derek.

"If anyone's delusional, it's *you*," Emma shot back. The discussion was spinning out of control, but she couldn't turn back now. "You're the one who thinks that everything at home is fine and dandy."

"I don't see how my home situation—"

"Do you have any idea what Peter's gone through while you've been feeling sorry for yourself? When's the last time he brought a friend home from school?" Emma demanded. "Why did he drop out of the Boy Scouts?"

Derek stepped back, self-righteous and thoroughly confused. "Peter's very conscientious about his studies. Why, Mrs. Higgins says—"

"Mrs. Higgins?" Emma squeaked. "Have you smelled Mrs. Higgins's breath lately? I imagine the only work she does is propping her feet on the coffee table when Peter's vacuuming the carpet."

"Hoovering the carpet? What on earth are you talking about? You can't possibly know what Peter does when he's at home."

"Give me Mrs. Higgins's job description and I'll tell you exactly what he does. You ask Nell. Better yet, pay Mrs. Higgins a surprise visit, or just give her a call. I did, and it was very enlightening."

Derek was aghast. "You've been spying on me?"

"I've been paying attention to your children, which is a hell of a lot more than I can say for you."

Derek drew himself up and looked down at Emma from a great height. "For someone who never wanted children of her own, you seem to be taking an inordinate amount of interest in mine."

"Someone has to!" Emma snapped. "And if I were around, someone would. But there's no danger of that. I wouldn't marry you if you were the last man on earth." Emma fell back a step, remembering a moment too late that she hadn't yet been asked.

Derek's recall was unfortunately precise. "Who said anything about getting married? One kiss and you've already got us racing up the aisle? You *must* be desperate."

"A woman would have to be desperate to even consider marrying you!" Emma roared.

"Emma, Derek, please." Grayson's voice was calm and conciliatory as he came to stand between them. "You've both been through a dreadful experience. I'm sure that everything will look quite differ-ent after a good night's rest. Kate, old thing, why don't you take Emma upstairs and—" He stopped short as Emma turned the full force of her wrath in his direction.

"If you call Kate 'old thing' one more time, I'm . . . I'm going to smack you in the kisser. Why don't you put that poor woman out of her misery?"

"Emma," Kate muttered urgently, reaching over to touch Emma's arm.

"You stay out of this," Emma barked, pulling her arm out of reach. Glaring at Grayson, she went on, "Can't you see that she's in love with you? And she *wants* to get married, though I can't for the life of me understand why. So let's get down to business. Grayson, are you going to marry Kate or not?"

Grayson touched his tie nervously and lowered his eyes. "Forgive me, Kate. I'd hoped to make this announcement at a more suitable time and place, but since Emma's being so . . . so refreshingly direct—"

"Just answer the question," Emma commanded.

"Yes, Grayson," added Kate, rising to stand behind Emma, "just answer the question."

"Of course I intend to marry you, Kate," Grayson said, with as much dignity as he could muster. "I've intended to marry you all along. But I couldn't!"

"Why not?" Kate and Emma said together.

"It wouldn't have been proper," Grayson replied, as though the answer were self-evident. "I didn't have Grandmother's ring."

While Kate sank back onto the couch, open-mouthed, Emma gaped at the duke, too stunned for words. Next she did something she'd never done before and would probably never do again. She seized the duke by the knot of his silk tie and jerked him toward her, thundering, "Do you think Kate cares about *jewelry?*" Then she pushed the duke aside and stalked toward the door. *"Men!"* she roared, before gathering up the skirts of her blue robe and marching from the room, slamming the door behind her for good measure.

Twenty-three

When Emma awoke, it was late afternoon, the sun was streaming through the balcony door, and Nell was sitting cross-legged on the end of her bed. She was watching Emma's face intently, and when Emma's eyes opened, she clambered across the bed to sit companionably near Emma's pillows.

"Your bath is ready," she said.

Emma blinked sleepily, not quite sure whether she was awake or only dreaming. The friendly little girl in the rumpled blue jeans and kelly-green sweater, who was toying with the laces on her scuffed sneakers and whose curls were as tousled as Derek's, bore little resemblance to the picture-perfect and coolly self-possessed Lady Nell she'd come to know. Emma's eyes widened as the dream child leaned over to pat her shoulder with a very real hand.

"Don't worry, Emma," Nell said consolingly. "Everyone won't be mad at you forever."

Emma's only response was a prolonged and pathetic groan.

"That was a good scold you gave Papa last night." Nell's voice was filled with admiration and an unaccustomed earnestness. "I never heard anyone scold him like that before."

Emma peeked over the edge of the bedclothes, horrified. "You weren't there, were you?"

" 'Course I was," said Nell. "Up in the gallery."

"You should've been in the nursery," Emma reminded her.

"Bertie wanted to know what was going on. You can see everything from the gallery. I watched Dr. Singh fix Mattie's arm. He's a good doctor." She pointed to Emma's bruised knuckles. "You should let him fix your hand."

I should donate my body to science, Emma thought miserably. A twinge shot through both shoulders as she reached for her glasses, and there was a distinct tenderness where her knees met the bedclothes through her flannel nightgown. Her palms were sore and her knuckles throbbed, but those aches and pains were minor compared with the pangs of conscience that assailed her. How could she have let herself go like that? Why had she said all those dreadful things? Kate would probably strangle her, the duke would banish her, and Derek would never speak to her again. She put her glasses on and lay back on her pillows, wondering what on earth had come over her.

Whatever it was, it seemed to be affecting Nell, as well. The ethereal princess who'd carried herself with such dignity and grace was now bouncing on the bed and looking as though she were bursting with news. More extraordinary still, her bear was nowhere in sight.

"Where's Bertie?" Emma asked.

"Keeping Peter company," Nell replied. "Dr. Singh says he's supposed to stay in bed all day. Do you want to have your bath now?"

"I don't know, Nell." Emma sighed. "I may just stay in bed for the next few weeks."

Nell giggled. "That's what Bantry said when he saw the garden."

Emma braced herself for more unpleasant news. "How bad is it?"

"It's a bloody mess," Nell replied cheerfully. "But Bantry said he'd still rather be out there than in the bloody hall with a bunch of bloody lunatics. Oh, Emma, it's been *such* an exciting morning."

"I'll bet it has," Emma said weakly. She looked toward the balcony door, then propped herself on her elbows, knowing that she had to get up. She couldn't leave Bantry to clean up the garden rooms by himself. "You can tell me all about it while I'm having my bath."

Emma watched in amazement as Queen Eleanor scrambled to the floor and scampered toward the bathroom, shoelaces flying, tossing a stream of gleeful, breathless chatter over her shoulder.

Groaning, Emma swung her legs over the side of the bed and hobbled toward the bathroom, feeling as old as the Pym sisters but not half as spry. Nell was waiting for her in the dressing room, and when she opened the bathroom door, billows of steam emerged, redolent with the heavy scent of camellias.

"Use a little bath oil?" Emma asked, wiping the steam from her glasses.

Nell nodded proudly. "Smells pretty, doesn't it?"

As the clouds of steam dissipated, Emma saw a stupendous mountain range of bubbles covering the tub. One majestic peak had made its way over the lip of the mahogany surround and was cascading slowly to the floor. Emma put a towel on the sudsy puddle, then reached into the tub to feel the water. It was still blessedly hot.

With a fine sense of decorum, Nell had remained in the dressing room, leaving Emma to face the laborious task of pulling her nightgown over her head, wrapping her hair in a towel, and easing herself gingerly through the bubbles and into the water. The heat was so deliciously soothing that Emma could almost imagine getting dressed and facing the consequences of her intemperate behavior. But not just yet. Not until she had a better idea of just what she was about to face. Settling back against the terry-cloth pillow, she called to Nell.

Nell entered the bathroom carrying Emma's blue bathrobe in both arms. She heaped the robe on the marble bench across from the tub, then climbed up to sit beside it, her sneakers dangling well above the floor. "Do you feel better now?"

"I'm beginning to," Emma replied. "Thank you, Nell. A long soak in a hot bath is just what I needed."

"Grayson, too. But just his head. That's what Kate told him, anyway."

Emma thought that one through, then blanched. "You mean, Kate told Grayson to go soak his head?"

"Uh-huh. At breakfast. She said he needed to get his pri-pritor—"

"Priorities?" Emma suggested.

Nell nodded. "She said he had to get those straight. And then Nanny Cole tried to talk and Kate told her to shut up."

"She *didn't*," Emma gasped.

"She *did*. I heard her. Nanny Cole looked very surprised. And then Kate threw her napkin on the floor and stomped out of the dining room."

Emma closed her eyes and slid slowly down the back of the tub until the water was lapping her lower lip.

"And then Papa said what did Grayson expect and Grayson said why didn't Papa ring up Mrs. Higgins and Papa said why didn't he mind his own business"—Nell took a quick breath before racing on—"and Grayson said children were everybody's business and Papa said he was a fine one to talk and why didn't he get some of his own and then *Syd* told them both to pipe down and stop acting like a pair of palookas."

"Oh, God . . . "Emma moaned, covering her face with her hands.

"It was *wonderful*." Nell kicked her legs back and forth, wriggling with delight. " 'Specially Kate. She shouts almost as good as you do."

"Now, Nell, there's nothing good about shouting," Emma protested feebly. "It's never good to lose your temper. I feel terrible about shouting at your father. I said all sorts of things I shouldn't have said."

Nell nodded sympathetically. "Papa says I do that all the time."

"Well, sometimes you can hurt people by doing that. I'm sure I hurt your father." Emma wiped bubbles from her chin. "I'm going to have to apologize to him."

"You can't," said Nell. "He's gone."

"Gone?" Emma asked. "Gone where?"

"I don't know. He stomped out of the dining room, just like Kate. But he didn't throw his napkin."

"That's good," Emma said hopefully.

"He threw his *whole plate!*" Nell's peal of laughter rang with such unabashed joy that Emma couldn't help smiling, though she was ashamed of herself for doing so. "That's when Bantry stomped out to the bloody ruins and Nanny stomped up to her bloody workroom and Grayson stomped off to the bloody library. Syd and I helped Hallard clean up Papa's eggs," she added virtuously.

Emma sobered as the mention of Syd Bishop reminded her of Susannah, and of Mattie. Pushing herself up and moving the bubbles aside so that she could see Nell more clearly, she asked, "Did anyone mention how Mattie's doing?"

Nell's swinging legs slowed, then stopped. "Mattie's sleeping," she said briefly. "Dr. Singh gave her some pills. Crowley's sitting on a chair next to her bed. He's been there all day. And Syd's . . ." Nell scratched her nose. "Syd's with Susannah, but she's awake. I heard them talking. Syd said . . ." Frowning, Nell scratched her nose again, then fell silent.

Wordlessly, Emma reached for a towel and wrapped it around her as she rose from the tub. Stepping quickly to the bench, she pulled on her blue robe, then sat beside Nell, looking down on her tousled curls. Nell's head was bowed and her hands twisted restlessly in her lap, as though seeking the kind of comfort only Bertie could provide.

In her own way Nell was as tough and brave as Peter, Emma conceded, but she wasn't Lady Nell or Queen Eleanor or a wise old woman in disguise. She was just a little girl who'd been working hard to make sense of the world on her own, and who'd learned enough to realize that she couldn't do it anymore. Nell had come to Emma, finally, to help her make sense of the world.

"What did Syd say?" Emma asked, putting her arm around Nell's shoulders.

Nell's troubled eyes scanned the sink, the mirror, the ceiling, and the towel rack, finally coming to rest on Emma's knees. "Syd said that Mattie . . . hit Susannah." She began to rock, very slightly, back and forth. "Was Syd telling the truth?"

"Yes," said Emma. "Syd was telling the truth."

"Oh." The rocking stopped for a moment, then resumed. "Was Mattie angry?"

Emma rocked with the child. "Mattie was afraid and confused. She didn't mean to hurt Susannah. And she's sorry that she did."

"Is she very sorry?" Nell asked.

"She's very, *very* sorry," Emma confirmed.

The little girl stopped rocking, snuggled up to Emma for a moment, then sat back and released a rushing sigh. "Poor Mattie," she said. "Poor Susannah."

Yes, Emma thought, poor Mattie, and poor Susannah. The best they could hope for was that Syd would be able to convince Susannah that Mattie had suffered enough already.

Nell had clambered off the bench and was kneeling at the side of the tub, carefully molding a mound of suds into a rounded dome. Emma went to kneel beside her.

"I know about the window," Nell said suddenly.

Emma kept her eyes on the little girl's busy hands, feeling preternaturally alert to Nell's every word. "What do you know about the window?" she asked.

"I know that it's changed," Nell replied. "I went to see it today, for Peter. It's white, like an angel. Peter says it's Mummy."

Emma watched as Nell teased her dome of bubbles into a taller, narrower shape that bore a faint resemblance to the silhouette of the lady in the window. "Do you believe what Peter says?"

Nell stared at the glistening, quivering pillar of fragrant bubbles. "I don't remember Mummy," she said softly, "but I think angels are in heaven." She blew on the sudsy sculpture, and bubbles swirled into the air. "Could she be in two places, do you think?"

Emma shrugged. "I don't see why not. What do you think?"

"I think Mummy can be wherever she wants to be," Nell concluded firmly, as though the subject had been settled to her satisfaction. She rested her chin on her hands and said slyly, "I know something else about the window, Emma."

Emma was so relieved to see a mischievous glimmer return to Nell's eyes that she was willing to play along. Leaning her own chin on her hands, she asked brightly, "What's that, Nell?"

"I know what made it change."

"Do you?" Emma asked, trying to sound enormously intrigued.

"Uh-huh." Nell nodded vigorously. "It was the light."

Emma sat back on her heels and stared at the child, disconcerted. "The light?"

"The really bright light that lit up the rain last night. That's what made the window change."

Emma frowned slightly. "Are you talking about the flares Kate shot off?"

Nell snickered. "Kate said Grayson was a twit and she didn't know anything about any ratty old flares. It's not flares, Emma."

Emma's heart began to beat double-time. "But you saw what made the light? You saw where the light came from?"

"You can see everything from the gallery," Nell reminded her.

"Can you show me where the light came from?" Emma asked.

" 'Course I can."

Emma nodded. It was ridiculous to let herself get so excited. Nell had probably been working on a story all morning and was about to try it out. Except that all of Nell's stories so far had been true. Emma pulled the towel from her head and let her hair fall loose. Ignoring mild protests from her back and shoulders—the hot bath really had worked wonders—Emma scooped Nell up from the floor and carried her across the bedroom and out onto the balcony.

"Okay, now, Nell," said Emma, swinging the child onto her hip, "show me where the light came from."

Nell slowly raised a dimpled finger until she was pointing directly at the elaborate wrought-iron finial on the top of the birdcage arbor. Emma's jaw dropped.

"Emma?" Nell asked, fluffing Emma's hair.

"What is it, sweetheart?" Emma asked distractedly.

"What's a palooka?"

Emma looked at the child's face, only inches from her own, then planted a kiss on Nell's cheek and put her on the ground. "I'll explain while I get dressed," she promised, taking the little girl's outstretched hand and leading her back into the bedroom.

Twenty-four

Grayson was trudging stolidly up the main staircase when Nell and Emma came hurrying down it. He stood to one side, eyeing Emma warily until he caught sight of her left hand, which Nell had insisted on bandaging from wrist to fingertip with what seemed like several yards of white gauze and an equal amount of medical tape acquired, according to Nell, from the stores of the ever-helpful Nurse Tharby.

"Good Lord, Emma," Grayson exclaimed. "I'd no idea you'd injured yourself."

"Just a scratch," Emma said. She flexed her hand to prove it, then tucked it out of sight in the front pocket of her violet-patterned gardening smock. Looking down at the toes of her Wellington boots, she began, awkwardly, "Er, Grayson——"

"I'll meet you in the banquet hall," Nell said abruptly. She looked from Emma's face to Grayson's, then turned and ran back up the stairs.

When Nell's footsteps had faded into the distance, Emma tried again. "Grayson—about last night. I can't tell you how sorry I am. My behavior was inexcusable and I apologize."

"Oh, I don't know. . . ." Grayson leaned back against the banister and sighed. "Had it coming, I suppose."

"That may be true," Emma said, "but it shouldn't have come from me."

The duke smiled wryly. "I've gotten plenty of it from Kate since then. Kate and everyone else. Even Crowley, preoccupied as he is, found time to sniff disapprovingly in my direction when I stopped by to look in on Mattie. But, then, Kate always was his great favorite."

"How's Mattie doing?" Emma asked.

Grayson's smile faded and his brown eyes clouded over. "Time will tell," he replied gravely. "Dr. Singh believes that she'll recover from her physical injuries readily enough, but as for the rest . . ."

Grayson sank down onto the stairs, as though too burdened by misery to consider finding a more comfortable spot. "It's my fault, of course. I can't help thinking that, had I been more welcoming to Susannah—"

"Hold on a minute, Grayson." The birdcage arbor would have to wait. Emma looked down at the duke's slumping shoulders and remembered the way he'd showered the staff with praise for creating Lex Rex, shrugging off his own contributions. The duke's generous nature seemed reserved for others; he kept all the blame for himself.

"Before you start the mea culpas, may I remind you of a few things?" Emma sat beside Grayson on the steps, rested her hands on the padded knees of her gardening trousers, and regarded the duke with sympathetic eyes. "I don't mean to speak ill of the . . . ill, but Susannah did show up here without an invitation. She used a very tenuous family connection to move herself and her manager into your home for an unspecified amount of time. While she was here, she hounded Derek and insulted your staff. She was rude, overbearing, and malicious, and her sole purpose in coming here was to ruin you because of something your father did. I'm not saying that Susannah deserved to be hit in the head with a grub hoe, but . . ." Emma put her hand on the duke's shoulder. "Under the circumstances, I'd say that you were more than gracious to your cousin."

Grayson rested his chin on his fist. "Perhaps you're right," he said reluctantly. "Still, I can't help feeling that, if I hadn't placed so much importance on preserving Penford Hall, Mattie might not have gone to such drastic lengths to protect it."

"Mattie wasn't thinking about the hall," Emma said. "She was trying to protect her grandfather. Besides, if she'd gone to Crowley in the first place instead of going off half-cocked, none of this would have happened."

"True," the duke admitted grudgingly. "Crowley would've given her whatever story Hallard's concocted about Lex Rex's death, and Susannah would've had to lump it. She might even have been persuaded to go away."

"But Mattie took matters into her own hands, and that's not your fault."

The duke squinted at Emma suspiciously. "If I didn't know you better, my dear, I'd say that you were doing your level best to cheer me up."

"I wish I could," Emma admitted. "If Susannah decides to press charges——"

Grayson bowed his head. "Susannah must do as she sees fit, of course, but I hope she'll be lenient. Syd's been in with her since——" He broke off, looking up in consternation as an uproar sounded from the second floor.

"Unhand me, you lout!" thundered Nanny Cole. "I can find my way to Susannah's room without any help from you."

"Sure you can, Mrs. Cole." Syd's voice drifted down to them, pitched to a placating murmur. "But you know how it is—a gentleman always wants to lend a hand to a fine lady such as yourself."

"A *gentleman* wouldn't be seen dead in those bloody awful trousers," Nanny Cole responded tartly.

"Funny you should mention my ensemble . . . Excuse me a minute, will you, Mrs. Cole?" Syd's face appeared over the railing of the second-floor landing. "Emma, sweetheart, how's it goin'? Nell said I'd find you here. Hey, Duke! You still willin' to foot the bills?"

"Absolutely," the duke replied.

"Catch you later." Syd winked before disappearing from view. A moment later, his conversation with Nanny Cole resumed. "Like I was saying, Mrs. Cole, I got a little proposition for you. Strictly business, you understand."

"What the bloody hell else would it be, you appalling tick?" Nanny Cole grumbled, and then a door closed, cutting off the rest of her words.

The duke continued to stare upward for a moment, a thoughtful expression on his face. "Well, well, well," he murmured. "I do believe that Syd's hit upon a possible solution. Susannah's always placed great importance on her career."

"Nanny Cole and Susannah?" Emma turned the idea over in her mind.

"Mmm . . ." Grayson tapped a finger against his lips. "An exclusive new line of women's clothing? A boutique, perhaps?"

"It might work," Emma said doubtfully, "as long as Syd's around to keep the peace."

"There is that," Grayson conceded. He ran a hand through his silky blond hair, then leaned back on his elbows. "Ah, well. We must simply put our faith in Syd and hope for the best." He eyed the upstairs landing speculatively. "Wonder if he'd consent to act as my go-between. Kate's locked herself in the south tower and won't have anything to do with me. Hasn't happened since we were children."

"You're not children anymore," Emma reminded him. She got to her feet and pulled the duke up with her. Brushing her hands lightly across the shoulders of his tweed jacket, and straightening his tie, she went on, "I've heard that you can charm water from a rock, Grayson. So I want you to go up to the south tower and persuade Kate to come with you to the banquet hall in the castle ruins."

"You want us to come to the kitchen garden?" the duke asked.

"In fifteen minutes." Emma started down the stairs, but turned back to ask, "Do you know where Gash is?"

"Finishing his repairs on the power plant. Hallard will call him for you, though. He's in the library, sorting out the candles." The duke bit his lower lip, bemused. "You're being very mysterious, Emma."

"Fifteen minutes," Emma repeated. "Good luck."

"I'll need it," Grayson muttered, turning to fly up the stairs.

Though Gash had reported that Mr. Harris had driven off in his battered orange van early that morning, Hallard was unable to inform Emma of Derek's immediate whereabouts. Stifling her disappointment, Emma gave instructions to Hallard to pass along to Gash, then invited the bespectacled footman to join her in the banquet hall. "Bring your laptop," she added. "You may be able to use this in your next thriller."

The weather had been the last thing on Emma's mind when she'd carried Nell out onto the balcony, so she was faintly shocked when she stepped onto the terrace. The sky was a flawless arc of blue, the air was sweet, and a gentle breeze ruffled the grass on the great lawn. Had it not been for the apple trees, now stripped of leaf and blossom and trailing broken branches, she would have been hard-pressed to prove that a raging storm had indeed passed this way. But the apple trees were only a hint of what she would find within the castle ruins.

The storm had ravaged the garden rooms. As Emma surveyed the wreckage, she tried to remind herself that no one had died, but gratitude wasn't easy. The perennial border was a tattered, ragged mess, the rock garden was more rock than garden, and there was not a single bud or blossom left on any of the rose bushes. By the time she reached the banquet hall, Emma was almost numb.

Bantry crouched ankle-deep in mud, plucking green tomatoes from a tangle of battered plants. He'd cleared most of the debris from the graveled path, pulled the broken vines from the towering arbor, and filled the wheelbarrow with salvaged vegetables. When he caught sight of Emma standing dazedly in the doorway, he held out a tomato, calling cheerfully, "Looks like we're in for a spate of Madama's chutney!"

Emma raised a hand to her mouth and shook her head forlornly.

"What've you done to your hand, Miss Emma?" Bantry asked, his brow furrowing.

"Nothing really. Nell was practicing her nursing skills." Emma waggled her gauze-wrapped fingers to reassure him, then folded her arms. The kitchen garden looked as though it had been trampled by a herd of cattle, but there were a few green sprouts here and there.

"Don't you fret, Miss Emma." Bantry tossed the tomato into the wheelbarrow, put his hands on his hips, and surveyed the scene without flinching. "It's a right old mess and no mistake, but we'll sort it out soon enough. That's the way it is with gardens. Never the same two days in a row."

The old man's optimism began to revive Emma, and Hallard's arrival reminded her that she'd come here with a mission. Raising her eyes to the top of the arbor, she asked Bantry if he knew how the finial was attached to the dome.

Bantry squinted upward, scratching his head. "Well, now, Miss Emma, I were just up there this mornin', cuttin' back the runner beans. Seems to me there's a big old bolt holdin' that fancy bit in place."

Gash walked in while Bantry was speaking, and when Emma had relieved him of the toolbox and oilcan she'd asked him to bring, she sent him to help Bantry fetch a ladder from the potting shed. She tucked the oilcan into the pocket of her smock and squatted down to rummage through the toolbox for a hammer and a long-handled monkey wrench. She was slipping the tools into her pocket when she heard Peter call out.

The boy seemed to have grown two inches overnight. He was tearing along the grassy corridor, bright-eyed, undaunted by last night's ordeal. Nell trotted in his wake, carrying Bertie and regarding her big brother with such pride that Emma bit back a reminder about Dr. Singh's orders and flung her arms wide.

Peter ran to her. "Did you see her, Emma?" he asked, breathless with excitement. "Did you see the window?"

"I saw it last night," Emma assured him. "I'm so happy for you, Peter. And you should be very proud of yourself."

Peter dug the toe of his boot into the gravel, blushing shyly. He hesitated, then looked up at Emma, as though seeking reassurance. "Everything'll be all right now, won't it?"

"Yes," Emma declared, going down on her padded knees, to envelop him in a bear hug. "Everything will be fine."

The boy hugged her back, wriggled out of her arms, and went squelching through the mud, calling for Bantry, while Nell remained high and dry on the gravel path, staring thoughtfully at the arbor.

"Don't worry, Emma," she said finally. "Bertie says that, if Grandmother could do it, so can you."

Emma looked at her, perplexed. "How did Bertie know——" She broke off as she caught sight of the next trio of arrivals.

Kate Cole had been lured down from the south tower, but Emma suspected that Syd rather than Grayson had persuaded her to unlock the door. The redoubtable business manager had placed himself between an icy Kate and an increasingly frustrated Grayson.

"Please tell His Royal Highness that I'm here at Emma's request and that I have no intention of remaining in his company for one minute longer than is absolutely necessary."

"Kate says——" Syd began.

"Confound it, Kate," the duke grumbled. "I've said I was sorry. I don't know what more——"

"Sorry!" Kate snapped. "Please inform Lord High-and-Mighty that he doesn't know the meaning of the word."

"Kate says——"

"Blast, blast, blast," Grayson muttered.

Gash, Bantry, and Peter had returned with the ladder, and Emma directed them to lean it against the arbor. A car door slammed in the distance, and she wondered fleetingly if Newland had gotten word that something odd was going on and driven up from the gatehouse to investigate. Then she focused her attention on making sure the ladder was planted securely on the graveled path. The top rung reached only to the bottom of the dome, but the decorative metalwork would provide plenty of hand- and footholds. As she helped the men maneuver the ladder into place, the three-way conversation continued behind them.

". . . and you can inform His Gracelessness that I wouldn't touch that ring to save my life."

"Kate wants me to tell you——"

"It wasn't just the ring," Grayson expostulated. "Don't you understand, Kate? I couldn't ask you to marry me until the hall was put to rights. How could I ask you to share my life when I had so little to offer?"

"Please tell——"

"Enough already!" Syd held up his hand to silence Kate, then turned to the duke. "You're a swell guy, Duke, but if I was thirty years younger, I'd poke you in the nose. What do you mean, you had nothing to offer? You think this beautiful lady gives a good goddamn about a ring or a fancy-schmantzy house? You hadda heart to give her, you doofus! You had hopes and dreams, am I right?"

"That's all very pretty, Syd, and I appreciate your concern, but one can't live on——" The duke stopped short. His gaze wavered for a second, then seemed to focus on thin air. "Good Lord," he said, half to himself. "Whatever would Aunt Dimity say if she heard me spouting such nonsense?" He blinked dazedly, and his hand drifted to the knot in his tie. "You're quite right, Syd. I've been so wrapped up in details that I seem to have forgotten the point of it all. I, of all people, should have known that one *can* live on dreams. Oh, Kate . . . I am so dreadfully sorry." He bowed his head, and Syd edged out of the way as Kate slowly unfolded her arms and put a tentative hand on Grayson's shoulder.

"Emma!" Syd hollered, coming to stand with the others at the foot of the ladder. "You tryin' to break your neck?"

Emma had reached the top rung and was stepping onto the narrow wrought-iron ledge at the base of the dome. "I'm fine, Syd," she called down. "Don't worry."

"What, me worry?" Syd replied.

"Have a care, now, Miss Emma," Bantry said. "Them boots of yours is pretty slick, remember."

"Do be careful, Miss Emma," Hallard urged.

"I would've gone up for you, Miss Emma," Gash added.

The mutterings of concern increased until Nell stunned everyone to silence by shouting: "Pipe down, you palookas!"

Emma smiled gratefully at the little girl, and continued her climb. The view from the top of the arbor's dome was spectacular. Sitting with her feet braced in the twining wrought iron, Emma could see the chapel, the beacon, and the sprawling mass of Penford Hall. She saw that old Bert Potts had come up from the village to repair the damage done to his beloved apple trees. And she saw, much to her surprise, an exquisitely coiffed and elegantly robed Susannah sitting in a wheelchair on the terrace, with Nurse Tharby looking on while Nanny Cole waved sheets of sketching paper and spoke emphatically. Emma grinned, then bent to examine the foot-high, dome-shaped finial.

Odd pieces of pewter-colored tin and four slender panes of glass had been cleverly hidden inside the finial, attached to the wrought iron by thin strands of dark wire that had been virtually invisible from the ground. Elated, Emma fitted the wrench to the black bolt and tightened its grip. It took a few taps with the hammer to loosen the bolt, but the oil helped, and soon Emma was able to reach in and unscrew the bolt by hand.

After tossing the tools, the oilcan, and the bolt down to Gash, Emma pulled the finial into her lap, and looked up in triumph, but nearly lost her balance as she saw Derek step out onto the terrace. He glanced in her direction, froze, then ducked his head and turned to go back into the hall.

"Wait!" Emma yelled. She pointed to the finial in her lap. *"I've found the lantern!"*

Derek swung around, open-mouthed, and ran down the steps. Inside the banquet hall, pandemonium erupted. The air rang with cries of amazed delight as Bantry scrambled up the ladder to take the heavy finial from Emma and pass it carefully to Gash, who carried it to the ground and placed it on the top step of the birdcage arbor, shouting for Hallard to bring his toolbox. Peter hopped from one foot to another, explaining the significance of Emma's discovery to a bewildered Syd, and Kate left Grayson's side to help hold the ladder as Bantry and Emma descended. A cheer went up as Emma's feet touched the ground, and many hands reached out to shake hers. Emma quickly pointed out that it was Nell who had first located the source of the miraculous light, and Nell was equally quick to give full credit to Bertie.

"I fell asleep," she explained, "but Bertie woke me up when he saw—Papa!" Nell cried, spying her father standing in the doorway. As she ran to greet him, Peter broke off his conversation with Syd and bounded down the gravel path to throw his arms around his father's waist. Derek looked down at his children, swallowed hard, then knelt and pulled them to him, hugging them so fiercely that Nell was forced to caution him against squashing Bertie. Emma watched Derek's gray head bend urgently over the dark one and the light; then she turned away, unwilling to intrude.

The excited babble of voices had faded. There was a clatter and a clank as Gash pushed the pieces of the dismantled finial aside, and the others fell back a step as he lifted the reassembled tin lantern by its wire handle and placed it squarely on the top step of the arbor.

"That about does it," he said, wiping his hands on a bit of rag. He tossed his tools into the toolbox and closed the lid, got to his feet, and stepped away from the lantern. Wordlessly, he turned to face the duke.

Grayson stood where Kate had left him, a few yards away on the graveled path. He seemed fragile and terribly alone, unaware of the eager faces that had turned in his direction or of the quiet shuffling of feet as they moved aside to open a path between him and the lantern. The fine lines around his brown eyes had deepened, and his face had grown so pale it seemed almost translucent. Smoothing a lock of blond hair back from his forehead, he drew himself up, then stepped slowly forward, moving as if in a dream. Kate walked beside him, and together they sank onto the step beside the lantern.

"Kate," Grayson whispered, in a voice filled with wonder. "It's all come true. All of it." The duke raised a trembling hand to his forehead and closed his eyes.

"Of course it has," Kate murmured. "A brave lad saved a life last night and the lady held her lantern high to help him. Of course she did. We always knew she would. It's in the blood, my love. Like you, the lady lets us see a world lit by the light of dreams. Come, now. Up on your feet. We've the Fête to prepare for, and a wedding to plan, and—Lady Nell? What are you doing?"

Nell and Peter had joined the group clustered at the base of the birdcage arbor, and Nell had crept forward until she was within arm's reach of the lantern. The duke's eyes opened and he watched, transfixed, as Queen Eleanor favored him with a regal nod.

"Sir Bertram says it's time to bring the lantern to the lady," she informed him gently, and lifted the tin lantern by its wire handle. She turned a dignified shoulder on the group and picked her way daintily up the path, heading for the chapel.

A bemused look crept over Grayson's face as he got to his feet and offered his hand to Kate. Arm in arm they led the others in a silent procession, with Peter proudly taking up the rear. When they had all disappeared from view, Emma turned to Derek.

He was still waiting at the edge of the banquet hall, like an outcast. His eyes were red-rimmed with fatigue, his chin rough with stubble. His hands were thrust deep into the pockets of the jeans he'd worn the night before, and the same blue sweater was flecked with lint and rumpled, as though it had been slept in.

"I've been home," he said. "Had a chat with Mrs. Higgins. Had a look round her room. What used to be her room." He paused to rub his tired eyes. "I've spoken with the children. We'll talk again, of course, but they . . . they seem remarkably willing to let bygones be bygones." His weary sigh seemed to come from somewhere near his soul. "You're quite right, Emma. I don't deserve them."

"Derek . . ." Emma walked slowly toward him. "I shouldn't have spoken like that to you. I meant to tell you about Mrs. Higgins, but not that way."

"Perhaps it was the only way," said Derek. "Don't think I'd've listened to anyone else."

"But I had no right to say it to you. Do you hear me? No right at all. Before you and Peter and Nell came into my life, I had no idea what it would be like to lose someone I loved. I didn't shed a tear when Richard left, but I swear, Derek, if I lost you I . . . I don't know what I'd do."

"It couldn't be worse than what I've done," said Derek.

"What have you done?" Emma demanded. She stood before him, now, peering up into his guilt-shadowed eyes. "You worked hard, you hired an apparently responsible caretaker, and you raised two children to be strong and clever enough to fool you. Two children who were willing to do whatever it took to give their father time to heal. I think you should be proud of those kids and proud of yourself for raising them. And I think—" Emma's voice broke and she looked down at the muddy toes of her Wellington boots. "I think you must be pretty sick and tired of hearing what I think."

Derek pulled his hands from his pockets and reached for Emma's. "I wouldn't say that," he murmured. "Quite the contrary. In fact—" Derek looked down in horror. "Emma, darling, what have you done to your hand? My God, is it broken? Has Dr. Singh seen it? Are you in any pain? Oh, my dear—"

"It's nothing, Derek." Emma unceremoniously ripped the bandage from her hand and tossed it into the mud at the side of the path. "See? Just a few scrapes and bruises where I hit the wall. Nell's the one who wrapped it up like that. She insisted on making sure that it was well protected."

Derek subjected Emma's hand to a close examination before tucking it into the crook of his elbow. "Left hand, eh? I think I know exactly how Nell feels." He closed his hand gently over Emma's bruised knuckles and began strolling toward the chapel. "You know, Emma, there's something I've been meaning to discuss with you."

Emma stepped carefully around and over the few straggling bits of debris that still littered the path. "What's that, Derek?"

"Shall we move to Boston or shall you move to Oxford?"

A sudden dip in the gravel threatened, but Emma sidestepped it neatly. "Well . . ." she said thoughtfully, "I'd like to have the wedding here—"

"You wouldn't mind a wedding, then?" Derek stopped and turned to face her.

Emma looked up into his blue eyes. "Syd tells me you're not the kind of man to offer anything but marriage."

"But is it what *you* want?" Derek insisted.

"After the wedding," Emma repeated firmly, walking on, "I thought we might all move to a third place."

Derek caught up with her, his eyes shining. "A novel solution. Have a particular spot in mind?"

"As a matter of fact, I do." Emma leaned in to Derek as he swung his arm up and put it snugly around her shoulders. "I've never been there, but I did promise to visit. . . ."

Epilogue

"Derek, you darling man," drawled Susannah, "if you don't disarm that son of yours before the show begins, I'm really going to become quite cross."

"Quite right," Nanny Cole chimed in. "Boy's become a menace to society. Jonah's fault, of course. Don't know what he was thinking, handing out water pistols to all the little beasts on the day of the Fête. I've a good mind to boycott his bloody shop."

Having delivered their demands, the oddly matched delegation strode away across the great lawn, Susannah floating as gracefully as ever and Nanny Cole marching with her familiar bulldog gait. Derek watched them go, then popped another strawberry into Emma's mouth.

"I know exactly what old Jonah was thinking," he murmured lazily.

Emma hid her smile behind the broad brim of her sunhat and hoped that her fiancé would keep his voice down. She wanted no more confrontations with Nanny Cole. She'd been up at dawn to put the finishing touches on the chapel garden, and now, in the long afternoon of this lovely high-summer day, she felt positively sybaritic. The ribbon on her sunhat matched the pale-blue frock Mattie had hemmed the night before, and the sapphire on her finger was as blue as Derek's eyes. She reclined against a pile of soft cushions on a cashmere blanket in the shade of a beach umbrella, with her fingers twined in Derek's salt-and-pepper curls, a dish of strawberries close at hand and a half-empty bottle of Dom Pérignon settling into a silver bucket filled with rapidly melting ice.

Derek lay on his back, with his head in Emma's lap, concealing with consummate skill any urgency he might feel about ridding society of the menace his son had become. "He hit Mrs. Shuttleworth square in the shoulder as she was doling out the punch," he commented, selecting a strawberry for himself. "Splendid shot."

Emma was fairly certain that Derek shouldn't be taking quite so much pleasure in Peter's assault on the rector's wife, but she let it pass. Peter had spent the summer discovering the joys of mischief, and if she'd been his age, with a water pistol in hand and a ruined castle to defend, she'd have matched him shot for shot.

"Emma, my dear!" Grayson came bounding across the lawn to fling himself down on the blanket, slightly out of breath and looking very boyish in his white flannels and open-necked white linen shin. He reached for the bottle of champagne and held it to his forehead. "Just ran the gauntlet in the ruins. I say, Derek, did you know that Peter scored a direct hit on Newland? He'll be having a go at Nanny Cole next."

"He's already had a go at the rector's wife," Derek said complacently.

"You'd be well advised to take him in hand before the show starts," Grayson warned. "Mrs. Shuttleworth may be saintlike in her patience with young hooligans, but Nanny Cole is rather more inclined to box their ears." Grayson set the champagne bottle back in the bucket, then turned to Emma. "My dear, the chapel garden has everyone agog. As for myself— Derek, do be a good chap and close your eyes. I am about to express my gratitude to your bride-to-be in a most unseemly fashion." Leaning over, he kissed Emma tenderly on the cheek, and remained there for a moment, his face close to hers. "You'll think I've gone completely round the bend, but I could almost see Grandmother sitting there beside the reflecting pool, surrounded by the roses. I really am most awfully grateful." He gazed at her a moment longer, then sat back and wrapped his arms around his knees. "Oh dear," he murmured. "Nanny's going after Debbie."

Emma had already spotted Nanny Cole scolding a red-faced and exceptionally pretty Debbie Tregallis, wife of Ted, the fisherman.

"What the hell are you doing out here?" Nanny Cole demanded. "You and that dratted son of yours should be in the dining room, getting changed."

"I'm sorry, Nanny Cole," Mrs. Tregallis said meekly, "but I can't find Teddy anywhere."

"Shall I tell Debbie that her bloodthirsty little son is happily slaying all comers in the rock garden?" Grayson said from the corner of his mouth. "Ah. Not necessary. Nanny Cole has enlisted another eager volunteer to appear with Debbie in the fashion show. Poor Billy."

Nanny Cole had collared Billy Minion and hauled him over for a quick inspection. She fished a red water pistol from the pocket of his shorts, held him at arm's length, then thrust him toward Mrs. Tregallis, with an abrupt "This one'll do."

The mutinous slouch in Billy's shoulders did not bode well for the fashion show, but Mrs. Tregallis hustled the boy off to the dining room, whispering urgently in his ear. Emma thought it highly probable that she was threatening to turn him back over to Nanny Cole if he put a foot wrong.

Grayson tossed a strawberry up into the air and caught it in his mouth. "I think——" He paused to wipe the juice from his lips with the back of his hand. "I think the Fête's going rather well, don't you?"

"It's going splendidly. The good people of Penford Harbor have every reason to be happy with their duke," Derek assured him. Emma agreed. A day that had begun with the rector's benediction, and continued with jugglers, magicians, and frenzied preparations for the fashion show on the terrace, would conclude that evening with a piano concert under the stars. Grayson had locked himself in the music room for days on end to practice a piece he'd composed for the occasion. Emma had listened at the door, entranced by the music's evocative beauty, and she'd threatened to wring Derek's neck when he'd suggested that they request a chorus of "Kiss My Tongue."

While Grayson had labored at his piano, the villagers had been hard at work, too, transforming the grounds of Penford Hall into something midway between a county fair and a traveling circus, in which they would be both performers and audience. The green-and-white-striped marquee stretching the length of the eastern wall sheltered trestle tables laden with food, and the air was filled with a hubbub of contented voices, the tinkle of music from the diminutive carousel, and the occasional squawk of a bystander caught in the crossfire within the castle walls.

A determined Daphne Minion had mounted a fierce defense of her knot garden, but Bantry had long ago abandoned the rest of the garden rooms and found solace at the Tharbys' table, hoisting pints with Gash and Newland and hooting with laughter at Chief Constable Tom Trevoy's repeated attempts to master the trampoline.

Nearer the hall, a black-gowned Madama, wooden spoon in hand, silently supervised the endless stream of dishes passing between the kitchens and the striped marquee, while Ernestine Potts handed bowls of cinnamon ice cream to James and Jack Tregallis, and Mr. Carroway cut another wedge of carrot cake for Ted, father of the errant Teddy.

At the far end of the tent. Dr. Singh, Nurse Tharby, and the rector were participating in a wine-tasting presided over by Crowley, who glanced up from his sommelier's cup and his array of dusty bottles long enough to smile at Mattie as she bustled over to Susannah, a bundle of pale-peach chiffon folded over an arm that had long since healed.

"There's something else you should be proud of," said Emma, nudging the duke.

"Nothing to do with me," said the duke. "The knock on the head brought Susannah to her senses, not I. My cousin made amends with Mattie all on her own."

"But you were there, weren't you?" Derek pressed.

"Merely as an observer," said the duke. "I was as surprised as anyone when she confessed to Mattie that her amnesia had been an act, and absolutely floored when she admitted that perhaps she'd pushed the girl into taking a swing at her. Actually begged Mattie's pardon." The duke gazed at his cousin with admiration. "Good of her to take Mattie under her wing."

Emma smiled. As usual, Grayson refused to give himself the credit he deserved, but she knew that his efforts to heal Susannah's wounds had included many small gestures and at least one magnificent one. He'd set aside a suite of rooms for Susannah's exclusive use, so that she might always consider Penford Hall her home. The duke would have given over his own rooms or his grandmother's without demur, but in the end Susannah had surprised them all by selecting a much humbler suite, because of its proximity to Nanny Cole's workroom.

Their partnership had flourished beyond anyone's wildest expectations. Susannah recognized Nanny Cole's genius with the needle, and Nanny respected Susannah's hard-won business acumen. The two abrasive women understood each other very well, and both were committed to teaching Mattie all they knew.

"Oh, how simply scrumptious, Mattie!" Susannah held the peach chiffon out to the light. "You're quite right. We must get Mrs. Tharby out of the mauve at once. Well done."

Grayson's eyebrows rose. "Mrs. Tharby, in chiffon?"

"The mind boggles," Derek murmured.

"Oh, I don't know. . . ." Emma pictured the matronly barmaid dressed in a classic Nanny Cole creation, and found it pleasing. Syd kept saying that Nanny Cole's designs would revolutionize women's fashion, and although Emma suspected hyperbole, she hoped he would be proved right. "That's what I love about those clothes. They're meant for real women, not—"

"Flat-chested chits?" Derek suggested.

"With no discernible hips," Grayson added. He watched as Kate came out onto the terrace, radiant in green linen, a rich, dark shade that complimented the square-cut emerald she now wore on her left hand. "Don't know about you, old man, but I'm rather keen on hips."

"Couldn't agree with you more," said Derek, nestling his head deeper into Emma's lap. "And if someone in the family must be flat-chested, I'd just as soon it were me."

Grayson leapt to his feet to escort Kate back to the blanket, stopping on the way to have a word with Ben Potts and Jonah Pengully, who were seated on campstools facing the entrance to the castle ruins, enjoying the element of havoc Jonah's water pistols had added to the festivities. Jonah's largesse had given him immunity, but anyone else entering the ruins did so at his own risk.

It was a risk people were willing to take. Throughout the day, in ones and twos and small family groups, the villagers had passed through the ruins on their way to admire Emma's handiwork and to pay their respects to the village lass. The lantern had not brightened on the day of the Fête, but no one complained. They'd seen the light split the darkness high above the village on that stormy night in May, and heard of Peter's brave deed. Each felt honored to have witnessed the unfolding of a new chapter in the legend.

The storm had been a setback for Emma's work on the chapel garden. Bantry's contacts in the horticultural community had ensured a supply of shrubs, cuttings, and seedlings from other gardens, but he and his crew had had their hands full replanting the garden rooms, and Syd had been preoccupied with Susannah, so Emma had been left to soldier on alone.

Freed from the lantern search, Derek had helped as much as he could, shoveling the wet soil back into the raised beds and rolling the freshly sodded lawn, but Emma had planted every seed and cutting with her own hands. It had been backbreaking work, and the results were far from perfect. The verbena didn't trail all the way to the ground, and the roses didn't cover the walls. The candytuft was patchy at the edge of the flagstone path, and it would be another year at least before the lavender hedges came into their own. Emma had to admit that her moment of greatest satisfaction had occurred that very morning, when she'd gone out at dawn to plant a cutting that had come from a most unexpected source.

Emma raised her eyes to look toward Nell's table, but her attention was diverted by still another unexpected sight. "I don't believe it," she murmured. Looking down at Derek's sleeping face, she added, "If you want to see Madama talking, you'd better wake up fast."

"Hmmm?" Derek murmured drowsily. Emma watched his blue eyes open and slowly focus. He smiled up at her, turned his head, and squinted at the marquee. "Sorry, love. Don't quite get the joke."

Emma looked again and saw that Madama was alone once more, slicing a loaf of bread in silence. "But she was there a minute ago, Derek, a white-haired woman, with a huge handbag. Madama was talking to her a mile a minute." Emma shrugged. "Go back to sleep. It's not important. The only reason I mentioned it was because it's the first time I've ever seen Madama talk. Do you know, I'm not even sure what language she speaks?"

"Nor is Grayson," Derek observed. "Madama came over as a war refugee, but Grayson's father was never able to ascertain her country of origin. Grayson claims that she must be from Mount Olympus, since she cooks meals fit for the gods." Derek propped himself up on one elbow, displaying more energy than he'd shown for the last half hour. "Did you say that the woman was carrying a handbag?"

Emma nodded. "A big one. A sort of carpetbag, I think."

"Fascinating. Sounds almost like . . . No." Frowning, Derek shook his head, then stretched out again. "Hardly likely. She rarely leaves London."

A familiar peal of laughter drew Emma's gaze back to the table where Nell sat, resplendent in white georgette, playing hostess to the three guests who had arrived the night before.

"Dearest Nell, that was really . . ."

". . . most amusing, but is Bertie quite sure that the vicar wanted . . ."

". . . a strawberry in his punch?"

"I'm sorry, Vicar," said Nell, contritely. "Bertie's been a terrible palooka lately. I'll get you a fresh glass."

Derek propped himself up on his elbows again, chuckling. "The vicar's going to regret driving the Pyms here after your children are through with him."

"*My* children?" Emma exclaimed.

"I accept no responsibility for their abominable behavior," Derek declared. "Before they met you, they were perfect angels."

Emma caught sight of Peter speaking earnestly with Mrs. Shuttleworth and watched as Nell carried the vicar's brimming glass of punch through the throng without spilling a drop. "They still are, aren't they?"

"Spoken with the sickening conviction of a besotted stepmother-to-be. I rest my case." Pulling himself into a sitting position, Derek reached for his flute of champagne and raised it to Emma in a silent toast, then leaned back against the cushions. "You seemed quite pleased by the thingummy the Pyms brought with them. Couldn't believe you were out there this morning, sticking it into the ground."

"Thingummy?" Emma rolled her eyes. "Derek, that's not a thingummy. It's a tree peony. And it's not just any tree peony, but a cutting from the Pyms' own tree peony, which they grew from a cutting the dowager gave them years ago."

"I see," said Derek, watching Emma's face carefully.

"Ruth says it has amber blossoms," Emma went on. "The flowers can get to be a foot in diameter, and the whole plant can grow as high as seven feet tall. It's going to look wonderful against the north wall."

"Sounds impressive," Derek commented.

"It will be, but it's not just that, Derek." Emma looked eagerly into his blue eyes. "I wanted so badly to have all the plants in the chapel garden come from Penford Hall. I didn't think it would be possible, not after the storm wiped out the garden rooms and I had to use the plants Bantry's friends sent. But the Pyms made it possible, at least in a small way. I've finally planted something in the chapel garden that really belongs there. I can't tell you how good that makes me feel."

Derek set his glass aside and reached for Emma's hand. "I do understand what you mean, love, and I'm very happy for you. Worried, too, of course."

Emma knew what was coming. The Pyms had brought Derek a copy of the Cotswold *Standard,* the nearest thing Finch had to a local newspaper, commenting in stereo that, since they'd received the delightful wedding invitation, they'd thought that Derek might be contemplating making a few other changes in his life. The advertisement describing the fourteenth-century manor house ("with outbuildings and courtyard") had been circled in violet ink. It was a stone's throw away from Finch and had apparently been on the market for some time. Derek had been fretting about it all day.

"I'm sure it'll be fine," Emma said, anticipating the change of subject.

"Doubt it," said Derek. "At that price, it's probably the local white elephant. Are you sure you understand what that means?"

"I think so," Emma replied serenely.

"I'm not talking about unpleasant wallpaper in the breakfast nook, Emma. It's likely to be in very poor repair indeed. I've seen this sort of place before. No indoor plumbing, no roof to speak of . . ." He glanced at her slyly. "I shouldn't be at all surprised if it has rats."

"We'll get a cat," said Emma. "Maybe two. I like cats."

"Yes, but, Emma, my dearest dear, it'll take me at least a year or two to make the place habitable. Until then you'll be camping out."

"Sounds perfect. Until Peter's finished making up for lost time, it might be better to live in a place that's already a mess."

"But what about Nell? Can't see her and Bertie huddling around a campstove."

Emma removed her sunhat and shook her hair down her back. "Nell will build castles wherever she lives," she said. "I think she'll enjoy helping you build a real one. And the Pyms will be on hand to pamper her."

Derek's eyes crossed suddenly and he flinched as a jet of water passed within inches of his nose. He scrambled to his feet with a roar and the marauders scattered, squealing with delight, save for one scamp, for whom Peter had expressed great admiration, who let rip a parting shot that hit Derek full in the face. Swiping a hand across his dripping chin, Derek flopped sullenly on the blanket and muttered that perhaps the manor house was worth looking into after all.

"A spot of rough living'll do the boy a world of good," he declared. He dried his face with the napkin Emma offered, then cast it aside and grew serious once more. "But what about you, Emma? If I'm spending all my time working on the house, I won't be bringing home many pay slips."

Emma picked up the discarded napkin and dabbed a few remaining droplets from Derek's forehead. "Not a problem," she said firmly. "I love my work and I, too, am very good at what I do. I'm sure I'll be able to find a job in London that I can commute to. I may even set up my own consulting business. I have no qualms about supporting the family until you've finished with the house."

Derek sighed. "Won't leave you much time for a garden," he said ruefully. "The Pyms' tree peony may be the last thing you plant for quite a while."

"I'll have the rest of my life for a garden," said Emma. "And you'll have some time at home with Peter and Nell. It'll give you a chance to get to know each other again."

"If I survive," Derek muttered. He sighed deeply. "You're a stubborn woman, Emma Porter."

"Wait until you see my plans for my home office," said Emma.

"I'll build you the office of your dreams," Derek murmured, and, twining his hand through Emma's hair, he leaned over to nuzzle her neck.

"Now, there's a sight that does an old heart good."

Derek swung around and Emma blinked at the glowing face and startling figure of Syd Bishop. It was the first glimpse she'd had of him all day, and she scarcely recognized him. He wore a relaxed, cream-colored three-piece suit, a shirt the color of weak tea, a silk tie in a deeper brown shot through with streaks of bronze, and, to top it off, a white Panama hat, tilted at a dignified angle above a beaming face. The duke and Kate slowly walked up on either side of him, their faces slack with astonishment.

Syd's smile faltered and he raised his hands with a questioning shrug. Pinching the lapel of his jacket, he asked, "What about it? Mrs. Cole's decided that I need a new look." He lifted his hat and held it rakishly above his head. "So, what do you think? Is it me or is it me?"

Five hundred years of breeding came to their rescue. "My dear fellow," the duke said gracefully, "if Nanny Cole says it's you, who are we to argue?"

Syd replaced his hat and glanced with pleasure at the subdued gold cufflinks on his sleeves. "I gotta admit, it makes me feel kinda young again." His eyes met Emma's as he added, "Not as young as some I could mention."

"Yes, Derek," remonstrated the duke. "What the devil do you think you're up to, disporting yourself so wantonly in front of the children?"

"The children are already used to it, Grayson," Kate informed him.

"We've gotten their permission," Emma added with mock solemnity.

"As a matter of fact," Derek said airily, "I was trying to dissuade my intended from embarking on a very risky venture."

"Anything I can do to help?" Grayson offered.

Derek eyed him warily. "Thanks, old man, but you're the last person I'd come to for help on this particular matter."

"Still worrying about the manor house?" Kate asked, sitting down beside Derek. "I don't know why it bothers you so. Emma's perfectly capable of paying the butcher's bills while you toil away in the drains."

"Spoken like a true duchess," Grayson declared.

Syd clapped him on the shoulder. "This's gotta be a big weight off your back, Duke. Petey tells me you don't got to worry about the Fête for another hundred years."

"I rather doubt that I shall be the one doing the worrying by then, but I take your point." Grayson smiled shyly. "It is a bit of a relief. Funny thing, though. I've spent my whole life preparing for this day, and now that it's here, all I can think about is the wedding."

"You keep thinkin' about the wedding, Duke," Syd advised. "Keep lookin' ahead. You gotta make sure there's a little duke to pass the whole shebang on to, am I right?" Emma tried not to smile as Syd pulled a pocket watch from his cream-colored waistcoat. "Listen, kids, I'd love to hang around, but the show's gonna roll in five minutes and Mrs. Cole'll blow a gasket if I'm not there on time. You comin', Kate?"

Kate sprang to her feet and took Syd's proffered arm. "I wouldn't miss it for the world. Have you seen Debbie Tregallis?" she asked as they turned to walk away. "Doesn't she look beautiful in blue?"

Syd paused to look over his shoulder at Emma. "Not half so beautiful as some I could mention. Catch you later, sweetheart."

"Catch you later, Syd." Blushing, Emma looked out over the lawn. People were streaming out of the castle ruins and away from the shelter of the marquee to cluster at the foot of the terrace steps. Grayson stood with his hands in his pockets, surveying the scene, and nodding warmly to the Pyms, who returned his nod, smiling their identical smiles.

"Terribly good of Ruth and Louise to join the fun," he commented. "Terribly good of everyone to pitch in the way they have."

"Well, I've been useless to you, Grayson," said Derek. "Didn't fix the window or find the lantern."

"Ah, but you found something much more important," Grayson pointed out, "and your children took care of the rest. It's quite fitting. Penford Hall has always owed a great deal to its children."

"Will you be sorry when the Fête is over?" Emma asked.

"I will, as a matter of fact. It's been such a splendid day." Grayson stiffened suddenly. "Good Lord," he said, "is that Teddy Tregallis? Oy! Teddy! Over here, old man!"

Emma looked over to see a tow-headed boy around Peter's age standing in the entrance to the castle ruins, his water pistol hanging limply from one hand as he looked back over his shoulder, grinning broadly. At the duke's shout, he came running, but the smile never left his face.

When the boy had scrambled to a halt at Grayson's side, Grayson put an arm around him and squatted down conspiratorially. "I say, Teddy, old man, it's no good making a target of yourself. Martyrdom's all well and good, in its place, but if you're determined not to be dragooned into service by Nanny Cole, then you mustn't stand around in plain view. Take it from one who knows."

"Yes, sir," said Teddy. "I mean, no, sir."

"Never mind," said the duke, mussing the boy's hair. "They'd probably reject you anyway, in your current damaged state. How'd you bung up the knee?"

The boy bent forward slightly to stare at the neatly taped square of white gauze that covered his kneecap. "Fell down in the ruins, sir, tryin' to hide out in the chapel." The boy looked over his shoulder. "A lady in the chapel fixed it for me. She was awfully nice, sir. Told me about the lady and the lantern."

Grayson's hand slid from the boy's head to touch his own knee as he, too, looked toward the castle entrance. "Did she?" he asked.

"Yes, sir," said Teddy. "Never heard it told like that afore. Said it 'minded her of you and Miss Kate, sir, you bein' the duke's son and Miss Kate the village lass."

"Is that so?" Grayson and the small boy slowly faced one another. "And how did the story make you feel?"

"Can't hardly say, sir."

"A bit dizzy?" the duke suggested. "But in a nice sort of way?"

The boy nodded. "That's it, sir."

The duke blinked rapidly, then pointed down at the cashmere blanket. "You stay here until the coast is clear," he said. He waited until Teddy had seated himself cross-legged on the blanket, then stood, staring once more at the castle entrance.

"You're being very mysterious, Grayson," Emma chided.

Derek's eyes narrowed as Grayson began to walk away. "What's up, old man?"

The duke paused. "Emma, Derek, dearest friends, if you'll excuse me, I—I believe there's someone waiting for me in the chapel." Looking every bit as dazed as Teddy Tregallis, the duke performed a courteous half bow, then turned and broke into a run.

Nell's Strawberry Tarts

Preheat oven to 375° F.

Pastry shells
Makes 8 tarts
8 3 1/2-inch tart tins, greased
3 1/2-inch fluted pastry cutter
3/4 cup flour
pinch of salt
1/4 cup superfine sugar
4 tablespoons butter
2 egg yolks

Filling
1 medium egg
2 tablespoons sugar
2 tablespoons flour
2/3 cup cold milk
2/3 cup heavy cream
1 pound strawberries
4 tablespoons seedless strawberry jelly
1/4 cup water
1 tablespoon shredded coconut

Pastry Shells
Sift flour and salt onto work surface. Make a well in the center; add sugar, butter, and egg yolks; work them together until all the flour is worked in. Add a few drops of water if necessary to bind the mixture. Knead until smooth, then wrap in foil and refrigerate for one hour.

Roll out on lightly floured surface. Use pastry cutter to cut out eight circles. Arrange these in the pastry tins. Bake for 20 minutes at 375°, until pale gold. Turn out to cool.

Filling

Cream egg and sugar, add flour, and stir to a paste with a few drops of the cold milk. Warm the rest of the milk, then slowly stir it into the egg mixture. Slowly heat mixture until it boils, then cook it for a few more minutes. Remove from heat; allow to cool. Whip the cream until stiff, then beat it into the cooled mixture. Spoon a generous portion of cream mixture into each of the pastry shells.

In the center of each tart, plant a whole hulled strawberry, point upward. Hull and halve the rest of the strawberries and arrange the halves around the whole strawberry to cover the rest of the filling. Heat the jelly with the water and use it to paint the strawberries, then sprinkle with coconut.